Woman Master

WOMAN MASTER

MEHRNAZ STARS

Cutting
Edge
Press

A Cutting Edge Press Paperback Original

Published in 2013 by Cutting Edge Press

www.CuttingEdgePress.co.uk

Printed and bound in Great Britain by CPI Group (UK) Ltd, Croydon, CR0 4YY

PB ISBN: 978-1-908122-28-5
E-PUB ISBN: 978-1-908122-27-8

To my grandmother, Esmat,
who taught me how to love.

To David, Sean and Layla,
the three loves of my life.

MY SPECIAL THANKS TO

Peter and Rosie Buckman
Martin Hay
Madjid Mirmotahari
Corinne Souza
and to Gharib and Maheen, my parents.

Hannah had not left her room for two days. She couldn't bring herself to see anybody. All she could think of was her man. He was gone, and her happiness had left with him. She was afraid to step into the world and face the void that his loss had forced upon her. Thirty-four years of sharing her body, her soul, her dreams and all of her thoughts. Her marriage had become a religion that held her hand and led her through life.

It was late April and the early morning breeze was dancing with the blossoms on the cherry tree near her window. It reminded her of the cosy feeling she used to get sitting with her back against the cherry tree in the garden of the house she grew up in. With the sun on her shoulders she had no notion of time and could have sat there forever.

Her grandmother's voice echoed in her head. "They told the lazy girl 'Why don't you go and sit in the shade', and she said, 'Why bother? The shade will eventually come to me'. Come on, *aziz-jan*, enough lazing about. I need a hand in the kitchen."

Hannah sighed deeply. If only her grandmother were here now to comfort her. "Don't cloud your mind, *aziz-jan*," she would say. "Everything is going to be fine. I promise." Her words were always so soothing, as if the words themselves had the power to make everything better.

Grandma Pari had always been in Hannah's life. She never tired of hearing her grandma's stories; her ups and downs, successes and humiliations. Hannah had never heard of anybody with such a diversity of life experiences, such tenacity and willpower to carry on.

And that made Hannah feel blessed...

CHAPTER

1

Tajel-Molouk, who was called Pari as of an early age, was brought up in a wealthy feudal family that owned four villages. Her blond hair, which was unusual for that part of the country, her bold and forward ways, and her physical strength, which she used to keep men at bay, had made her the black sheep of the family. Her smooth pinkish-white skin and her big hazel eyes were the envy of many women, and if it weren't for her nose, which she herself bemoaned as being oversized, she would have considered herself a beautiful woman.

Pari had met the love of her life when she was nineteen. Eleven years older, Yousef was a stocky man with a full head of brown hair. He always sported a nicely-trimmed moustache and he was meticulous about what he wore. He had his own charming ways of flattering a woman all the way to heaven. The more she saw him, the more she craved his companionship. Yousef had a village of his own with more than seventy peasants working for him. He was a master, an Arbab. Yousef was known to be a hospitable, extravagant man, never cheap. What did he care? Life was for enjoying and having fun in the company of friends, or at least people he called friends.

His only flaw was that he was already married to someone else.

But that was no hindrance to Pari. As far as she was concerned, it was no crime marrying up to four women, simultaneously, and no matter what anybody said about the moral repercussions, she was ready to become wife number two. She was aware of her own charisma and sense of leadership and knew that before long she would be the only mistress of the house.

Pari did not have any enmity towards Yousef's first wife, but she would claim her right to marry whomever she chose, without the interference of her parents or any matchmakers. Of course, no matter how righteous she felt, getting married to an already married man did not go down well with her father. Had Pari been a widow or a divorcée, becoming a second, third, or even a fourth wife would have

11

been acceptable, but attractive, nineteen-year-old virgins from good families did not have to settle for second-best.

Pari's father, with her older brother his constant accomplice, had taken every opportunity to denigrate Yousef's character.

For a while Pari endured this cruelty, but their words only served to harden her heart towards them and to drive her into Yousef's arms. Finally she decided: she would do the forbidden thing, the revolutionary thing; something that a decent girl from a good family would never dream of. She would run away with Yousef.

Had her mother not been taken from Pari three years before, perhaps she might have softened her father's heart? But no person on earth could have changed Pari's mind on this matter, not even her beloved mother.

She would wed the man she loved, and that was that.

On a cool spring night in late March 1935, as the rest of the household slept, Pari put on her polka-dot scarf, packed a single bag and left with Yousef. They headed towards a friend's house in Tehran. Everything was arranged, even the forged letter of permission Pari needed from her father to make the marriage official.

The next day without wasting any time they went to the registry office and she tied the knot with the man she had fallen in love with. It was all done and no one could stop her any more. She was sure that her father's wrath would not be everlasting; she just had to lie low for a while and let him blow his fury and disapproval until he ran out of steam. After all, she had shattered his dream of marrying off an obedient daughter to the man he deemed right. There would be no wedding feast, no guests, no chance for him to bask in the status gained when a good family makes a good match for a good daughter to a good man. But all Pari could think about was her wedding night and her new life with her new husband.

That night, she nestled in the arms of the man of her dreams. Her wish had come true. She was about to lose her virginity to the man she had chosen for herself, without anybody's interference, refutation or consent. There was no haggling or bargaining over the dowry, no hard feelings caused by forgetting to invite the third cousin of her auntie and no squabbles about the number of guests at the wedding ceremony. It was all about her and the person she was going to share the rest of her life with. She could look straight into his eyes without embarrassment or shame and invite him to make love to her for the first time. Her innocence, her eagerness, her fear of becoming a woman were as seductive as a man could wish for. The next morning, Pari saw the blood spot she had heard about on the bed sheet and felt proud of being a woman.

After one month of marriage a relative of Pari's came to Tehran with news that her father had calmed down and was willing to put his anger behind him. She did not believe her father would ever fully accept Yousef but a détente would suffice; now she could claim her place in her new home, in the fertile land of Varamin. She did not need her father's acceptance but the appearance of such would smooth the way into her new household.

Yousef had left the day-to-day running of the village to his chamberlain, Ali, a well-read and pleasant man in his mid-thirties. Ali knew everything there was to know about wheat and sheep farming. He and his brother had once owned a tract of land in the eastern part of the country. The land had been passed down through generations until Ali's brother gambled it away in a single game of backgammon. Ali started out west in the hope of finding a new life. For three years he travelled from village to village, taking work where he could find it, taking kindness where it was offered. But always he moved on. He knew he would never again own land but the belief that there was a place for him somewhere, a home, a lesser destiny, gave him strength and fed his spirit.

Ali lived with a pain that no place, no man nor woman, could assuage. It was a part of him, etched into the lines in his face and telling in his brooding eyes. Losing his birthright, his precious land, might have driven him to despair had not a loss a thousand times darker not already done so. All that was truly precious to him lived now only in his heart.

Ali had stepped into Yousef's village five years before and his heart had spoken to him. He knew he belonged there. What had been survival for so long might be a life again, in this place.

And so it was.

On the day of their return, Ali had arranged a feast for the newly-weds. Everybody, from the stable boy to Pari's father, was invited. Six women cooked from sunrise to sunset to prepare a seemingly endless supply of the highest-quality rice, the most tender lamb, and great silver platters of *zulbia-bamieh* that mesmerized the children and cheered even the sourest of guests. Thin-waisted glasses of finest brewed tea were filled and re-filled all night long. The smooth, vibrating sound of the flute and the rhythmic harmony of the tonbak lured many into dancing. Pari welcomed her father to her new home and was thankful that he was willing to make up with Yousef. As far as she was concerned, all was well.

Early next morning Pari stepped into the kitchen to supervise the preparation of breakfast for the household and there she encountered Noor, Yousef's first wife, for the first time. She had just arrived from her uncle's house forty-eight miles away and was taking a sip from the newly-brewed Gilan tea. Pari gave her a friendly smile and greeted her with a warm welcome. She felt no animosity towards the woman; if anything, Pari was the one claiming a share of her life.

Noor had been Yousef's wife for six years. As his second cousin, she was married off to him with the intention of living a comfortable life in safe hands. Although the premature wrinkles on her forehead and the unwanted fat on her face and body made her look older than twenty-eight, the sweetness in her wide brown eyes, flattered by long black lashes, lifted her into prettiness. Noor was calm and peaceful by nature and though she was not thrilled by the arrival of this new woman, deep inside she had known for a good while that her husband's affection towards her had been subdued. He wanted children, carriers of his name and heritage, and she couldn't make his wish come true. She was barren. She had known that sooner or later her quiet life was going to be rattled and she was ready to embrace the inevitable with dignity and grace. So, in response to Pari's greeting, she delivered a pale smile and said, "Has Banoo shown you around the house?"

"More or less," Pari replied. "I have not been introduced to everybody yet, but Ali is going to see to that." She walked towards Noor with her head held high, looked straight into her brown eyes and said, "How do you like chicken skewers for lunch, that's what I was planning to cook today." Noor wondered at the confidence of this woman standing so victoriously in front of her, and nodded.

Banoo spread the hand-made cloth on the floor of the big living room and set the cutlery and crockery with the help of the two young girls who worked in the kitchen. Ali, Banoo and six of the higher-ranked workers dined with the master and mistress of the house every day. Pari's entrance silenced the busy hubbub (this was the first time she had eaten with the household; yet another of the many tests she would face) until Yousef, always the diplomat, gestured to the diners to be seated. The heavy air broke and the noise of spoons bashing plates and workers chatting about the minutiae of their daily chores filled the room again. Great trays of chicken skewers and rice cooked with lima beans and dill were passed around. The speed with which the workers unconsciously piled food onto their plates contrasted with a sudden hesitancy when it was time to eat. What would it taste like? After all, who could blame them? Surely, with her privileged background, she had never raised a finger in the kitchen?

Their fears were soon dispelled.

She took delight (but tried not to show it) as the first few nervous nibbles turned quickly into whole-hearted acceptance. This woman could certainly cook. The tender chicken, garnished with saffron, melted in their mouths and the rice, fluffy with each grain perfectly separated, offered an aroma straight from heaven.

It was a success. Throughout lunch she made an effort to join in, to show no sign of self-consciousness. She agreed with both sides in every discussion. She laughed at even the slightest sign of humour. She listened, with interest, to every view and every whim.

When it was time to get back to work everybody thanked and complimented her, with exaggerated emphasis, so that she would really know that they meant it.

That afternoon, Pari went to the kitchen to make a pot of tea and chat with Banoo. The water in the samovar was already boiling. She put some Gilan tea in the big teapot, poured some water in, and let it brew on the samovar. Ali arrived after a few minutes.

"You came just at the right time," Pari said, "tea is almost ready." Banoo took three teacups with thin waists out of a wooden cabinet and placed them on china saucers then started pouring while peeping from the corner of her eye at the faces of these two customers anxiously waiting for their afternoon dose of tea. Pari lit a hand-rolled cigarette. It wasn't really customary for women to smoke. Pari had picked up the habit, rolling and lighting cigarettes for her father. And, oblivious to his negative remarks about her taking up smoking, she had grown to like the taste and smell of it. Yousef already knew about it and it didn't bother him in the least. He was a smoker himself. But the sight of a woman, and so young, puffing happily away caused Banoo to pour tea until the cups, the saucers, and half of the table were overflowing.

Ali popped a sugar cube into his mouth and took a sip of tea while absently staring at Pari's cigarette smoke. He was impressed by Pari; she was full of surprises. Ali had seen enough in his life to know that she was no ordinary housewife, and that made him feel good. Yousef's lax attitude and his chronic quest for entertainment and fun meant Ali had had to handle every detail of running the village and its affairs by himself. But now he could use the wits and solid determination of this woman and perhaps spread some of the workload.

Pari rolled a couple of cigarettes and offered one to Ali. She kept hers for later and instead refilled the teacups.

"So, how is the business doing?" she asked.

"It has been going along well," Ali replied. "The favourable spring weather will help us harvest a bigger amount this year, the whole herd survived the winter weather and with the ten extra camels bought last year we can transport more supplies to Tehran. This year is going to be very lucrative." Ali decided to seize the opportunity to throw in a few compliments. He took a puff from his cigarette and said, "Looks like your arrival has brought Arbab good luck."

Banoo overheard. She didn't favour his flattery. She gave him a look that told him it was time for him to get back to work.

Starting the next day Pari, the Zan-Arbab, took it upon herself to go and check on the farm workers and the shepherds regularly to make them realize that from now on she would be involved in the day-to-day running of the village. She also visited their families from time to time to establish good relationships and to find out about their needs. That was a wise policy. It wasn't long before quarrelling couples would go to her and seek advice. Women with sick children would ask her for the appropriate medicine, and in-laws-to-be would implore her for her participation and help throughout wedding preparations.

Pari's relationship with Noor was as good as might be expected under the circumstances. Noor considered herself a "retired" wife. All she wanted was a continuation of her comfortable lifestyle. She was not pugnacious by nature and showed no enmity towards Pari. That her husband still kept his respect and kindness for her was sufficient. The two wives had even started to enjoy afternoon sessions of tea and gossip. In Noor's eyes, Pari was a good companion, someone fun to be around. In her presence, Noor became a giggling, playful girl again; indulging in emotions long buried by the sorrow of childlessness.

Pari, the Zan-Arbab, the woman-master, had become the true custodian of the village.

With the coming of the summer heat, camel drivers were getting ready to transport shipments of melons to Tehran. The sweetness of Varamin's honey melons, water melons and cantaloupes was famous throughout the province. Pari had arranged for the dispatch of a good supply of those melons as a summer gift to her relatives in Tehran.

The vegetables in her personal garden were almost ripe. The smell of courgette and aubergine fried with garlic and spices turned the head of anybody who was passing by the kitchen. Fresh, crunchy cucumbers were an essential ingredient of the most sought-after lunch during the hot summer days in Varamin: yogurt diluted with water and ice, mixed with diced cucumber, raisins and mint, served with freshly baked bread. And the dairy products, all made by Pari's hand, were scrumptious enough to raise healthy appetites to insatiable levels at the breakfast gathering. Such simple delights, and the peaceful atmosphere of the country life, attracted her relatives from Tehran.

Pari's cousin Zeeba appeared at her doorstep one early morning in July, before the sun grew too hot for travelling. She carried some small luggage in one hand, and her little one-year-old daughter, Malous, was cradled in the other. Her pale, yellowish complexion, that she religiously hid beneath a daily coating of blusher, was naturally reddened by her journey. Zeeba was a year younger than Pari and physically a lot weaker, though she could wear anything she pleased, with no unsightly bulges. She was tall and slim with small, firm breasts that complemented the light summer dress she wore beneath the austere silhouette of her chador.

Two years before, Zeeba had met a young army lieutenant, Amir, at a relative's house. He was a distant cousin who'd taken a few days leave to visit his family. Zeeba immediately took a fancy to his mannered style of talking. He had an impressive knowledge of literature and art, and the charming way he had of looking straight into her eyes when he talked sealed the deal for her. She was not shy by any means. In fact, her mother had admonished her more than once for not properly covering her hair.

Zeeba made arrangements to meet Amir the next day. She wore the flowery silk dress she had made herself. It was meticulously sewn; she was a perfectionist when it came to handicrafts. A little saddened that she had to hide her beautiful dress and her shapely figure beneath the chador, she put her big scarf on and told her mother she was visiting friends.

They met in a crowded bazaar to avoid scrutiny or suspicion. Amir tried to impress her by bragging of his skills in painting and calligraphy. He even promised to draw a portrait of Zeeba one day.

She was taken by his flattery.

It wasn't long before Amir took his parents to Zeeba's house to ask for her hand in marriage. The wedding preparations went smoothly; there were no objections to this matrimony. Thereafter, Zeeba started her married life at her new abode with Amir's family.

"It's been almost a year. I'm so glad you're here," Pari said, hugging her tightly. Pari took Malous in her arms and directed them towards the kitchen. She prepared breakfast, and as much as Zeeba did not care to eat that early in the morning, the smell of fried eggs and freshly baked bread and Gilan tea were too tempting to ignore.

Pari put Malous on her lap, slid her fingers through her pitch-black hair and started talking to her in a little voice. She fed her with small pieces of bread dipped in enriched milk. Although busy handling the child, she couldn't miss the pallor on Zeeba's face.

"So, how is Amir? Is he going to join us *very* soon?" Pari asked.

Zeeba rolled her eyes. "I hope not. I am here to be rid of him and his whole family."

Pari was perplexed. "I'm sure things aren't that bad? You two can sort it out?"

"There is nothing left to sort out. I am sick and tired of his stinginess, his complete lack of concern for me and his daughter, and his unbearable selfishness. All I have become to him is an official figure he can introduce to people as his wife. He spends all his free time with his friends, hunting and fishing. And even when he is at home, he makes himself busy with his paintings.

"Do you want to hear what he said to me the other week? He said he cares more about his stupid German Shepherd than he does about me. And please don't get me started on his family. The extent of his father's tightness is something you would believe only if you saw it with your own eyes." Zeeba snapped her fingers together as if the image might appear in front of them. Her eyes widened. Pari's mouth widened. "At lunch, he rations everybody's meal and whatever you get on your plate is your lot." She looked down at an imaginary plate with sorrow in her eyes, then she opened her hands and sighed so deeply Pari became worried she might forget to breathe in. "Anyway, there is no way I would go back to that hell. My brother has already talked to him and is arranging for my divorce. He even gave Amir a hard punch in the nose…which I have to admit made me so pleased."

Zeeba clutched her cup of tea, contemplating her life in silence, brooding over her early days with Amir. She couldn't distinguish any more whether it was his impeccably-cut uniform that took her fancy or Amir himself. She liked men in uniform; it made a difference. She was ashamed of herself. She had no reason to marry this waste-of-bread in the first place. She fell for his clothes? His looks? It was true, she thought, it was lust that pushed her towards Amir, and now she was paying for it.

Pari felt sorry for her cousin. She had pleasant childhood memories of Zeeba and over time they had forged strong bonds of affection. Zeeba was the most selfish person she had ever met. But she was such fun. Pari wished things had gone better for her friend. She took Zeeba and Malous for a stroll in the nearby field. There were plane trees and poplars to provide shelter from the hot summer sun. Zeeba wetted Malous's feet in the cold stream to cool her down.

"I'm thinking about going back to study to get my high-school diploma," said Zeeba. "I could become a teacher and earn my own money. I can see that my mother's not exactly ecstatic about having to support me and *his* daughter now."

"*His* daughter?" Pari repeated. "She's as much your daughter as she is his. How could you talk so callously about her?"

It seemed to Pari it was a game of pick-and-choose for Zeeba. Whenever she felt jolly and cheerful, Malous was her daughter.

"She's got Amir's eyes. When I look at her, I remember my mistake."

Her words sent a shiver down Pari's spine. This was too much. So she quickly hid her own thoughts from herself. Zeeba had been badly mistreated. She was not thinking straight. In a few months she'd come to her senses, even feel guilty about what she said today.

That night they joined the circle of villagers around the fire and immersed themselves in the warm tones of Ali's voice over the husky accompaniment of a dozen hubble-bubbles, as he told of his journey from the east side of the country.

Zeeba nestled her head on Pari's shoulder. She felt so cosy. She didn't want tomorrow to arrive.

The next morning, Pari overslept. She struggled with a strange dream. She dreamt that a powerful force had jammed her eyelids shut. It seemed that each time she was on the verge of waking, of opening her eyes, the force would push her back down into the abyss. She finally woke with a dizzy head and a thumping heart. Still half-asleep, she got up and stumbled her way to the kitchen. When she got there she rubbed her eyes hard. The blackness gave way to watery outlines that gave way to the vision of a middle-aged woman drinking a cup of tea.

It was Auntie Goli; second cousin of Zeeba's mother, but everybody in the family called her auntie. Heir to a childless marriage, after her husband's death, she had an adopted home at everybody's house, staying for two months here, three months there. If she didn't like the atmosphere of the house she would move out in a couple of weeks. The truth was no one minded her staying over for months. Auntie Goli had a very pleasant, sociable character and up to now, nobody had managed to escape the pain of belly-laughing at her jokes. And if she wasn't telling jokes, she would play tonbak and sing. She was known as the *sugar* of every gathering.

Auntie Goli's arrival was welcomed all round, especially by Zeeba, who thought that the cheerfulness of this guest would make her grief go away, even if for a short while. After breakfast, Noor announced her plan of taking a day trip to the holy city of Ghom for a pilgrimage and made it clear that she didn't mind having some companions. They all accepted the offer, even Zeeba, who had never displayed any tendencies towards religion. To her, it was a day out.

By the time they got to Ghom, the summer heat had worn them out. They decided to find a tea house to get some rest and quench their thirst. Auntie Goli started moaning about the heat with a loud voice in the hope of getting faster service. It was well-planned. Enough curious heads turned towards their table to warn the tea-house owner that the only way to shut this woman up was by putting her in front of others waiting to be served. They ordered a big jar of cherry sherbet, and asked the waiter to bring four loaves of Barbari bread with white cheese and a selection of fresh herbs: basil, mint and chives, to go with it.

Auntie Goli's booming voice, her expressive eyebrows that couched her words in a kind of delightful deceit, and her playful manner, attracted the attention of a Mullah, who was at least fifteen years younger than her. She had pushed him towards the sin of staring at a woman stranger. The poor man was trapped; all he wanted was a break between his classes in philosophy and interpretation of the Hadith. Instead, he was being lured closer and closer to the devil's gates by the temptations of this seductive creature.

By the time they paid for their meal and got ready to leave, the poor Mullah was drowning in a sea of forbidden thoughts and imaginings, barely keeping his head above the surface.

When the four women left the tea house, he started following them, simultaneously drawn to this unlikely siren, and battling with his own hormonal imperative. Finally, the devil inside him drove him to speed up to Auntie Goli and whisper into her ear, "I want to get inside your pants."

Without a single trace of emotion, Auntie Goli answered, "I will fart so bad that you'll choke inside them." The words hit the Mullah like a hammer. In an instant he was released from his sexual trance, entirely defeated and embarrassed. He was off in less than a second.

The rest of the day went by peacefully. Zeeba decided to sit outside in the shade of a plane tree near the pond the Mullahs used to wash before prayer, while the others visited the tomb of the holy lady: one of the close relatives and a disciple of Mohammed the Prophet. Zeeba thought herself beyond any religious beliefs and despised the fear it engendered. She wasn't one for abiding by a list of taboos. Zeeba wanted to be free.

No trip to Ghom was complete without a visit to the bazaar to buy some of its famous sweet, sohan: a scrumptious combination of honey and pistachio. Pari also bought a small silk carpet that she couldn't resist. It was thin enough to fold and carry. They left the city soon after nightfall.

It was supposed to be a short visit but Auntie Goli decided to spend at least three weeks at Pari's place. She was having a whale of a time, and the endless supply of summer honey melon and cantaloupe, her favourites, was a further encouragement. Besides, at Pari's house she didn't have to lift a finger. Pari wouldn't have it.

Auntie Goli had brought some news for Zeeba regarding her divorce. She didn't want to ruin the joy of her arrival by ranting about such matters. Zeeba's mother had told her that Zeeba's husband had agreed to give custody of Malous to Zeeba if she agreed to forego alimony or child support. Zeeba's brother, Mehdi, was more than happy with the arrangement, as he had promised to provide for his niece. His import-export business with Russia was extremely lucrative and he loved Malous like she was his own.

Zeeba was happy. She wanted rid of him. She had followed her temptations, but she was only human and had a right to make mistakes. As far as Zeeba was concerned, all her worries were over; what mattered now was she could get on with her life and not look back.

Auntie Goli was having a verbal wrestling match with Ali at the breakfast gathering when a woman villager, Karim's wife, stumbled into the room howling in excruciating pain. Her eyes were swollen and crimson with infection. She hadn't the courage to go and see a doctor (a different species to her) in Tehran. To her, Pari was the nurse, the doctor and the hospital.

"Zan-Arbab. Please. Two or three drops of that solution you poured into my eyes last time? I didn't get a wink of sleep last night.

My eyes are burning like somebody lit a fire inside them."

"Take a seat, I'll be right back with the medicine."

The magical medicine was an off-the-shelf eye solution that Pari had brought back from a trip to Tehran. Every time she went to the city to visit relatives, she loaded her bag with painkillers, medicines, bandages, ointments, and any interesting syrups or herbal remedies she could find. The problem now was that she had already used the whole bottle of eye solution on the poor woman's eyes.

She couldn't let the peasant woman down. She paced up and down, then sat and rocked to and fro. The peasant woman sat in patient silence, waiting for her cure. The villagers had already elevated Pari to the station of village healer, and even without her bag of medicines, she knew she had to fulfil their expectations. It was her duty to heal this woman. Pari glanced idly at a cut of meat she had placed in a large bowl of lime juice and herbs to marinade. She thought at first about slapping the meat onto the woman's eye, the way she had done whenever the men in the village took to blackening each other's eyes. Then she remembered how they would cure meat with salt to prevent it from decaying. *If the salt subdued the decay, then why not this infection?* Tons of salt. They used tons of salt every year. And the meat was always fine. She took a glass and half-filled it with tepid water. She stirred a full teaspoon of salt into it until there was no trace visible to the naked eye, and then she poured the concoction in the eye-drop bottle. The medicine was ready. And it was the doctor's secret to keep.

Auntie Goli and Ali winced as Pari opened the pus-infested eyes of Karim's wife and dripped a drop of her kitchen-made medicine into each of them. The poor soul gritted her teeth and pounded her legs with her fists. It wasn't the first time that Karim's wife had felt the magical solution from far-off Tehran drop into her eyes and then slowly start to burn. Burning was good. Burning meant the medicine was working.

Karim's wife let out a scream to wake the dead, jumped up and ran around the room like a headless chicken.

"Get it out! Get it out!" she cried. Every cell in her body was on fire, being consumed by Pari's wicked remedy. "My eyes! My eyes!"

"What did you give her, Pari? What have you done?" The panic in Auntie Goli's voice was tangible.

Pari froze.

"Water! Get some water," Auntie Goli cried. "Let's wash her eyes before she goes blind." Ali ran outside to fetch water.

"God, help me! What went wrong with your medicine, Zan-Arbab?" Karim's wife moaned. She swayed this way then that, helplessly stupefied by the burning salt.

"Ali will be here in a moment. Let's wash your eyes and get that filthy medicine out of them." Auntie Goli tried to calm her.

Karim's wife was having none of it; who knew what else they might have in store? She saw a light and ran towards it; the door, *it must be the door*, to get the hell out of this torture chamber.

"Ach, aahy, aahy…" There was a dull thud, then another, as she careened into the kitchen door then dropped like a sack of rice. Semiconscious, but determined to make her escape, Karim's wife tried to drag herself up. Dizzy from the burning and now, the blow to her head, she staggered her way out of the kitchen.

"What now?" asked Ali, holding a jar of water.

Auntie Goli pursed her lips to quell a nervous giggle.

"Well, that's very nice of you. First she blinds her, then you laugh at her," said Ali, shaking his head. "Let's pray to God that she's still got her sight."

The next day, before the breakfast gathering, Karim's wife entered the kitchen. She pounced on Pari and showered her hands with kisses. Pari had to stop her when it looked like she was going to kiss her feet. "What's going on?" she asked, perplexed. "You must have mistaken me for a holy person."

"You may as well be a holy person. The medicine you poured into my eyes yesterday put me out of my agony. I slept like a baby last night. I don't know how to thank you, Zan-Arbab."

"Okay, okay. It's all right. I'm happy you feel better. You'd better get back to your chores, your husband must be waiting for you."

After breakfast, Ali marched towards the samovar with the excuse of having another cup of tea, so that he could have a chat with Pari.

"That wasn't the usual eye-drop you gave her yesterday, was it now?" Ali whispered.

"No. It wasn't," said Pari, with a smirk.

"So, for the love of God, what did you pour into the poor woman's eyes?"

"What do you think? It's not like I was planning on blinding her. It was salt."

Ali was baffled and a little irritated by Pari's confidence.

"You don't get it. Do you? It was a fluke that you happened to use the right amount of salt in that solution. You could have blinded her. For God's sake, from now on, instead of playing doctor, use your influence to make them go and see a proper one."

Pari ignored him. She couldn't be bothered to prolong the argument. The end result was favourable and that was all that mattered.

Zeeba was leaning on a Mokhateh, a big, colourful cushion, on the living-room floor watching Malous play, when Pari entered with a tray of tea for four.

"Where are Auntie Goli and Noor?"

"They left ten minutes ago to go to the public baths. Auntie Goli wasn't sure if she could borrow your pumice, but she took it anyway."

"Well, I hope you fancy a fresh cup of tea."

Pari noticed her cousin's deep stare while she was pouring.

"You've built quite a kingdom for yourself here. People seem to trust whatever you do or say as if it were a verse from the Quran."

"I guess I have charisma," Pari snapped, the way she always did whenever she detected sarcasm. "They've made the right decision to confide in me. I always look out for them and try to help every one of them to the best of my abilities."

Zeeba wasn't the kind to hear the last word and sit back. She was brought up by a mother who used to punish people around her for giving in to failure, for being clumsy or acting timidly.

"What do these poor ignorant peasants know? They would trust in the devil himself if he appeared in the shape of a Zan-Arbab today." She turned her face away, as if to say she'd won the argument. Pari sniffed (her habit when she found something unsatisfactory). She'd let the tension between them abate, for now.

That night, after dinner, Auntie Goli declared that her short visit was very close to an end and that she was leaving in two days. She picked up the tonbak and started singing and jiggling her eyebrows. When she left a place, she left no trace of resentment or bitterness. Everybody joined in; they clapped and sang along. Zeeba whispered to Pari that she was heading for Tehran with Auntie Goli. She knew that sooner or later she had to go back and face the music. And she was certain that sooner was better.

4

Pari had been married to Yousef for a year and hadn't regretted a day of it. So far, she had seen nothing but kindness and respect from her husband. His lucrative business had provided her with an extravagant lifestyle and her own determination had won the obedience and respect of the villagers. At the age of twenty she had everything; life was as good as it gets.

One afternoon she was cracking almonds in the company of Banoo when she heard Yousef laughing loudly as he greeted some guests. She looked through the window but couldn't recognize any of the seven people that her husband was ushering in. As they entered the sitting room Pari greeted them. She went into the kitchen with Banoo to make fresh tea and prepare a tray of pastries. Yousef followed her to explain that these were good friends of his, passing through with their wives, and that it was important to him that they were properly looked after.

She started serving the men without even glancing at their faces. Since puberty she had developed a habit of not looking men in the eye. It used to make her self-conscious and uneasy. She placed tea and pastries in front of the women with a jolly, welcoming smile.

Yousef took his guests out to the garden to smoke a hubble-bubble and left the sitting room to the women. During her conversation Pari found out that three of them were wives of Hashem Khan and one of them had recently been married to Hashem Khan's brother, Kazem. The third man was his brother-in-law. Hashem Khan was an important and influential figure in his tribe and his fortune matched his social status. As his wives took their scarves off Pari saw the evidence of the man's wealth. Each woman was draped in solid gold: twenty-two-karat thick bangles, wide necklaces and long hanging earrings. Their thick, braided hair was down to their bottoms and their plumpness betrayed Hashem Khan's taste in women. His youngest wife, Firouzeh, an eighteen-year-old brunette with pinkish cheeks and big hazel eyes, was close to labour.

"You look like you're in your last month, if I'm not mistaken." Pari smiled to impart her best wishes.

"It should be any day now," she replied, almost out of breath.

"Don't you think you should be at home with a midwife handy instead of travelling?"

"I'll go where my husband goes." Then she pointed at Khanoom, the first wife, and said, "Khanoom will help me deliver the baby. She has done this many times before." There was not a trace of fear or panic in her voice. She sounded as if she was going to ride a horse for the first time and her trainer was standing right next to her handling the harness. Firouzeh was a tribal woman and, like any tribal woman, she had an upbringing that emphasized mental and physical strength, leaving no room for delicacy.

Pari lit a cigarette. She had noticed that her daily diversion of smoking a few here and there was turning into an addiction, but it didn't bother her; she had access to an ample supply of tobacco to satisfy her habit.

All her guests rejected her offer of a smoke and instead drank more tea. Khanoom evaluated Pari with a single look. She had everything a worthy woman should have: a strong, reliable body with enough beef on it, pinkish glowing cheeks that heralded health and diligence, and swiftness in her movements that ruled out laziness.

"So, when are we going to have the honour of holding your first child?" Khanoom said with a pride that might have been reserved for her own daughter.

"Whenever God grants us one," Pari replied with a hint of shyness. She assured herself that it was still not too late; she had heard of women who hadn't got pregnant even during the first three or four years of marriage. She was a healthy young woman; as far as she could remember she had hardly caught a cold. Pari was certain that one day, very soon, she was going to make Yousef a proud father.

After performing the evening prayer, Pari marched to the kitchen to organize dinner. She gave the instructions for preparing the aubergine and courgette stew to Banoo and took the responsibility of making the rice herself. Then she went to the arbour to let Yousef know about the dinner plans.

As she made her way there she was struck by a strange smell; almost like burning rubber, but somehow different, sweet. The aroma almost overwhelmed her by the time she reached the arbour.

Yousef and his guests were sitting around a brazier with glowing charcoals passing a long-stemmed pipe from hand to mouth. The billowing smoke, which had already fogged a good part of their consciousness, stung Pari's lungs. Pari didn't know the smell, but she knew what it was: it was opium. They were smoking opium, the entertainment of the rich; finely produced in Isfahan, city of art and culture.

Pari couldn't make up her mind how to react. She was not offended or angry. After all, opium wasn't *harom*, a forbidden thing in her religion. It wasn't something one should feel guilty about; it wasn't alcohol. But then again, she didn't want her husband to make a habit of it. She had heard enough stories about people who had lost their wealth and families by choosing to laze about the opium brazier all day.

She stared at Yousef, the way he handled the pipe, the way he inhaled just the right amount; he was not a first-time smoker. In a way, that comforted her. Surely Yousef only smoked occasionally with his friends for entertainment? He hadn't developed a habit? They had been married for a year and this was the first time she had seen him next to an opium pipe. There was no sensible reason to fret over it.

Pari didn't waste her time declaring the dinner plans to the soporific assemblage. She informed Banoo that they would set the dinner for the five of them, leaving the men's share of the meal to be served later, when their heads had cleared and appetites returned.

On the third day of their stay, before the first ray of sunlight invites the morning prayer, Pari woke up to a blood-curdling scream. She leapt out of bed. By the time she got to Firouzeh's room, the other three women were already busy. Khanoom manoeuvred Firouzeh onto an oversized clay tray, telling her again and again to "push", as if keeping time to some inaudible song. The poor girl's face was purple from the pain of the contractions and the pressure of forcing the baby out.

"Stop pushing!" cried Khanoom, abruptly. "The baby hasn't turned around. It wants to come out feet first. Someone get me a bottle of oil, olive oil." Khanoom washed her hands and greased them with the oil. She shoved her hand inside the mother, as if she were in the fields delivering a calf. She tried to turn the baby and she shouted "Push! Push!" at the top of her lungs. If Firouzeh had heard her it would have been a miracle; the girl's mouth was hanging wide open. Her vocal cords had given out. She was close to unconsciousness.

With her last ounce of strength Firouzeh popped the baby out and, after hearing the child's first cry, she passed out. Khanoom held the baby up. "It's a boy!" She cut the umbilical cord, wrapped the baby in a clean sheet and gave him to Mona, the second wife of Hashem Khan, to be taken care of. Then, before Firouzeh regained consciousness, she expertly stitched her maternal battle wounds. Khanoom's stoic expression belied the pride welling deep within her.

It was a happy day for everybody. Hashem Khan was holding his son in his arms with a solid smile. Pari was relieved that she didn't end up witnessing the demise of her guest or her baby. She was so perplexed by the whole operation, and the gore of it, that she couldn't stop feeling dizzy all day. The miracle of birth entangled with the strange combination of agony, blood and ecstasy was too much to absorb in one go.

The next morning Pari went to visit Firouzeh to find out how well she was recovering. The new mother was lying on her mattress breastfeeding her son. She had a trace of pink on her cheeks and the life that had almost left her eyes the day before was back in full force. The sheer joy on her face would make any female envious of becoming a mother; she was a complete woman.

An hour later, Mona entered the room with a bowl in her hand. She showed it to Khanoom to get her approval. "This is fine. This is the right amount for now." Khanoom noticed Pari's baffled look and explained, "You lose a lot of blood and energy when you give birth and drinking this bowl of cow's fat is the best way to compensate for it. She should drink it for three or four days in a row."

Pari was so appalled by the thought of drinking animal fat that all she could bring herself to do was nod a sign of approval. She didn't want to risk opening her mouth in case she blurted out something that would offend her guests.

Repulsive or not, their treatment worked and Firouzeh was back on her feet after six days, looking healthy and shiny, ready to go back home with the rest of her family.

It was Pari's second winter in her own home and away from her father's house. The shepherds had started bringing the sheep back to ensure they wouldn't get caught in the heavy snows of Varamin.

Winter was a quiet time, spent mostly indoors. Banoo equipped the living room with the family korsi: a wide, almost square, short-legged table with a charcoal brazier underneath. First, she laid a rug, specially woven in a reciprocal weft-weave, on the korsi then she draped a large quilt over it; big enough for family and guests to snuggle under. She placed a plain tablecloth then a samovar on the quilt, to make sure that tea was in plentiful supply and trips to a cold kitchen were unnecessary, then she arranged a circle of velvet cushions around the edge of the quilt.

The first snowflakes came in late December, putting a playful smile on the children's faces and giving adults something to chatter about during the afternoon tea. It was heavy enough to coat the entire land, yet not too severe to impede the return of the remaining herd. Yousef had seized this opportunity to go to Tehran to meet a few business associates for a few days and had left the affairs of the village to Pari and Ali, his chamberlain.

Pari felt bored and suffocated inside the house. After lunch, she grabbed her cigarettes and matches and asked Banoo if she wanted to go for a walk. What Banoo wanted was a cosy nap with her feet tucked up under the korsi. She wouldn't dream of swapping that feeling of comfort for Rezah Shah's throne itself and so she declined Pari's offer. Ali suggested that Pari should go on horseback, just to be on the safe side, but she ignored him.

The flat landscape of Varamin was a vast blanket of snow with the occasional tree dotted here and there. Pari passed by a handful of noisy children busily building an arsenal of snowballs for the battles to come.

She had put far behind her the stables and the last of the

villagers' homes before she realized that maybe she had come a bit too far. Save a few crows on a bare tree there was no soul around. She became fearful, but knew she still had just time enough to get back before nightfall.

The tea drinking after lunch suddenly caught up with her. She simply had to pee, right there and then. She took advantage of a nearby tree; a little extra privacy amid the frozen solitude. She lit a cigarette and settled down to answer nature's call. When she had done her business and smoked her cigarette and was ready to head back, she heard something move in the snow behind her. She whipped round. Two glazing blue eyes shone back at her out of a crouching silhouette. She stopped breathing. A deathly chill enveloped her. *Wolves hunt in packs.* The thought almost sent her into unconsciousness.

She had no weapon; a good Varamin girl would never carry weapons. A villager, a man, might carry a staff or a knife. There wasn't a stone, not a stick, not even a blade of grass she could use to defend herself against this hungry creature. Wolves are not stupid. It wouldn't take long before it knew that Pari was easy prey. Maybe if she stayed still, unmoving, like a statue, it wouldn't attack? If she held her breath for long enough, maybe someone would come? The beast snorted, its breathing became heavier, constant, a rhythm that betrayed concentration. Twilight was becoming night. No one would come.

She was going to die.

Eventually, it would realize that she posed no threat. There would be no savage lunge, no gnashing teeth searching for the throat of a reluctant victim. Better to conserve precious energy. It would simply come over and eat her.

The light was fading fast.

Fire!

Wolves were afraid of fire. She had fire. She had her trusty matches. She would frighten it away with fire. She tried to slide her hand into her pocket to find the fire that would save her. Her eyes were fixed on the spot where she knew the wolf waited. Her hands were so cold, like great slabs of dead meat. She felt around for the opening of her pocket. She couldn't find it. Her pocket seemed to have disappeared with the arrival of the wolf. The beast crept closer.

Just a few cautious inches; better to make sure than allow the meal to escape, or worse, to fight back. It paused as she rustled around in her big coat pocket for the fire that would send this demon away. The tiny movements of her fingers scratching against the matchbox in her pocket were amplified by the barren terrain and the peril before her. Her sense of hearing had become as sharp as her fingers were dulled. The box of matches clattered around like a basket of firewood being emptied onto a stone floor.

She had no choice now, but to take out a match and light it. It was simple. She'd done it fifty times a day for a year without thinking; a reflex action so familiar she'd never even noticed it. Now she had to concentrate so hard, to focus all of her energies, to make her fingers remember the simple choreography of retrieving some matches from her pocket. She'd wait until the wolf ran, then she'd climb the tree under which she'd peed an eternity before, in another happy life when peeing under a tree seemed dangerous. *It will be enough. It will be enough*, she repeated like a prayer as she fought to prepare the match with hands that would hardly do her bidding. In a moment this beast would be gone. She'd be up a tree. Then she'd wait.

She drew the match across the rough sandpaper of the matchbox. The match head ripped into life. The sulphur smoke at once stung her eyes and mingled with the breath of the beast. It looked like a dragon ready to breathe fire. It sat no more than four feet from her. It blinked. She held out the fire with a hand that seemed disconnected from her body, as if someone else were holding the match, someone come to deliver her to safety. *The beast would run. The beast would run.*

The beast didn't run. It cocked its head sideways like an old sheepdog wondering what its master was about. The match burned into her fingers. She felt no pain. As the flame died, the beast growled. It was dark. It was a black, moonless night. She might have been blind. But she wasn't deaf. The wolf was moving. She fumbled with another match. She struck it. Again the beast cocked its head then lowered itself onto its haunches and showed its teeth. It licked its lips in anticipation of an easy feed.

She knew she was going to die.

She struck another match; she wanted to look her slayer in the eye. The wolf inched closer. There was a hissing sound. The wolf yelped. Its paws seemed to disappear into the ground in front of it. A thick yellow liquid dripped from its eye. Another hiss. The wolf tried to extricate itself from the hole it was sinking into. Spots of the liquid appeared on the wolf's head, and around its mouth. It frantically dragged itself out of the hole and cowered backwards. Pari was enveloped in the most foul odour that at once revealed her unlikely saviour. As the wolf rubbed its face this way and that in the snow, a skunk scurried out of the hole and immediately lifted its hind quarters into the air and walked towards the already defeated wolf, all the time clicking its teeth and hissing. The wolf ran. The skunk gave Pari a look and hurried back into its burrow.

She was saved.

They ran from the house as if it were on fire. Pari had plumped herself down on a kitchen chair. In a few moments the gift her odorous saviour had bestowed declared itself in every room. Pari didn't notice and wouldn't have cared if she had. It was Banoo who first summoned the courage to come back into the house, pinching her nose defensively, to find out what on earth was going on. The rest of the household shuffled around outside, hugging themselves tightly (no one had dared to waste a second to fetch a coat) and exchanging second-hand explanations through chattering teeth.

Pari's bedraggled clothes, and a smell you could almost touch, concentrated Banoo's efforts on the more immediate problems. She'd leave the questions for later, when she could breathe.

"We can't take you to the Khasineh for this." Banoo used her free hand to clumsily fill a basket with tomatoes, making sure not to loosen the grip on her nose with the other. "They'd have to demolish the public baths if we took you down there." She ferreted around for the box of baking soda she knew she'd put somewhere. "You'll need more than soap and water for this."

She spent the next hour scrubbing Pari down with her magical mixture of tomato juice and baking soda; a long hour for the rest of the household, who had been instructed to burn Pari's clothes before they were banished to the front garden where they all but froze to death. By the time Banoo gave the all clear nobody seemed to mind inhaling the last few wisps of the smell that still decorated most of the house. They ran into the kitchen and jostled for position around the fire.

It had gone nine when Pari opened her eyes; too late for her normal routine, she performed a belated morning prayer. On her way to the kitchen she overheard the subdued whispers of a conversation intended to be hidden. Pari's headache told her not to engage in the conversation. After throwing a dim "good morning" to Banoo and Ali, which startled them into silence, she poured a cup of tea, sat on a stool and pulled a face so sour as to drive Ali out of the door.

"I didn't wake you up for the morning prayer. I thought after your fright, you could use some rest."

"Well, the rest didn't do me any good. My head is splitting. Do we have any of those painkillers left?"

Banoo went to the pantry and came back with a few pills. "These?" She offered them with a shaky hand.

Pari took them with a sip of tea. Without so much as a look, she asked Banoo to think of something for lunch and shuffled back to her room.

Around twelve-thirty Banoo announced lunchtime by dropping a plate on her way to the living room. Pari got up and prepared the korsi for lunch.

Banoo set down a great bowl of rich soup decorated with dried mint and saffron. It wasn't long before the soup's aroma attracted hungry workers.

"Well done, Banoo, this is just what the doctor ordered. Nice hot soup to fend off the winter cold," Ali said jovially, through a mouthful of bread.

Pari was hungry. The soup was good. She asked for more. Banoo accidentally flipped the ladle over, spilling soup all over the korsi.

"What is wrong with you today?" snapped Pari. "You've been acting like a dimwit all day."

Ali threw her a look.

Banoo was shaken but determined. This was too much. She drew herself up until her back was bolt straight then she allowed the silence to prepare a space where her voice might be heard. "Zan-Arbab, don't take that tone with me. I am the daughter of an Arbab myself and if it wasn't because of my father's…" She fought for the right word, "misfortune, I wouldn't be here serving you, being talked to like I am nobody. Don't you tempt fate, Zan-Arbab." She wagged an accusing finger. "You never know what's around the corner. You never know if my misfortune ever befalls you and one day you end up serving other people." Her manner was so heartfelt, she might have been casting a spell. She liked Pari, but had no tolerance for lack of respect, especially in front of other people. To Banoo, such behaviour only served one purpose: to belittle.

Returning to her duties Banoo left to fetch a cloth to clean up the mess.

Pari felt the familiar taste of guilt in her mouth. She'd hurt an old woman who had shown her nothing but kindness. She had thoughtlessly succumbed to her greatest failing: a lack of self-control; the urge to lash out when irritated, a blemish, a weakness that betrayed her as callous and unfeeling.

In penitence, Pari took the cloth from Banoo's hand and smiled. "It's all right. I'll take care of it. It's no excuse, I know, but my headache is almost unbearable. I think it got the better of me."

Banoo let her take the cloth, but her eyes granted no forgiveness.

The coming of March saw a flurry of activity in the village. New Year, Norouz, was only three weeks away with all of the preparations in front of them.

It was the custom to clean every window, door and floor, to dust every corner of the house and to wash each curtain and chandelier to welcome the spring. Fathers bought new clothes for their children to wear during the New Year ceremony. The women joyfully, but with serious intent, competed to create the most sophisticated sweets and delicate pastries to decorate their Norouz tables.

Norouz would bring many visitors; some might stay for days. Pari had ordered a supply of pastries, mixed nuts and fruits to be delivered from Tehran. The break from the winter cold allowed her to pack the korsi away and have the carpets washed and aired, with the best woollen rugs laid out strategically for visitors' feet, and the finest silk carpets hung in the public rooms for visitors' eyes.

She was combing her hair when Yousef entered the room.

"I have to go visit a friend near Tehran. I'll be back in two days."

"What friend?"

"Hedayat Volla."

"Why now, before Norouz?"

"He needs my help. He's too embarrassed to come here and show his face. He needs money."

"Well, he's certainly come to the right person. Anyway, why would Hedayat Volla need your money? He's a wealthy man."

"He was a wealthy man up until a week ago. He needs to borrow money to pay for the New Year's ceremony just the same as every year."

Pari was baffled.

"Gambling. Until last week, almost every bet he made was a winner. Then he gets involved in a game with a merchant from Tehran. This man turns out to be much more skilled than him. Of course, the idiot had the choice to pack it in and call it a day. But no, his arrogance got the better of him. So he raises his stake again and again until he's put his whole fortune on the table. The merchant wiped him out in a single hand. So, he gambles again. But this time, he's got no money so he gambles his daughter. He lost his daughter."

"Oh my God, he made a whore out of his own daughter."

"Well, the merchant was honourable enough to make it clear that he was going to marry her off to his son with a proper wedding ceremony."

"And you're going to help out this low-life?"

"Believe me when I say that the disgrace he's caused is going to haunt him for the rest of his life."

Pari knew that there was no point trying to dissuade him. He'd made up his mind. He was going to help that worthless creature.

She carried on brushing her hair.

After he packed his bag, he made to kiss her goodbye. She turned her face away.

The unending preparations made the gatherings around the fire at night, smoking and chatting, all the more welcome. Pari joined them from time to time, to listen to their stories and adventures.

That night Sardar, the head shepherd, had brought his favourite camel with him. He lit his pipe and passed it around. The sweet aroma woke the camel and in a second its head appeared among the circle of smokers. It snorted and spat.

No one gave the camel a second look.

Pari was puzzled and amused. "What is wrong with that camel?"

Ali explained, "Sardar and his camel are both opium addicts. That's why he's always walking next to Sardar, to get his dose. If he doesn't get his fix, he goes into a filthy mood and Sardar can't handle him."

Ali was the most popular storyteller among them. He had travelled widely, had seen various places, people from different areas with different cultures. But mostly people listened because Ali had a beautiful, soothing, almost melodious speaking voice.

He stared at the fire, head bowed, and with a sad expression in his eyes.

"I was eleven or twelve years old when what I am about to tell you happened, but I have borne its scar all my life. It was late April, springtime. My friends and I used to play near a lake that was a haven to various birds: geese, ducks, cranes, sparrows…We had noticed that a lot of them had laid eggs and were protecting them until they hatched. One of my friends came up with a 'dazzling' idea, as he put it. He suggested that we do an experiment. We should choose two different kinds of birds and switch their eggs and wait and see what happens when they hatch. At the time, it didn't sound like there was any harm in it—not that we really cared one way or another, we were a bunch of kids after excitement and adventure. So, the genius who came up with the idea switched two crane eggs for two goose eggs. We went to that lake every day to check if the time had come. One day, as we were approaching our nest, we heard a loud commotion with cranes jumping up and down, flapping their wings, feathers flying. Three of them were poking the head and body of the mother bird with their beaks. That was her punishment for being unfaithful to her mate. They had already killed the two tiny geese that had disgraced their tribe. The poor mother bird was lying there, bloody and still. The three cranes made sure she was dead before they left."

Ali's eyes were watering, his voice wavering. He was on the verge of tears.

More than his story, Ali's reaction touched the gathering. A cloud of silence descended. Ali's story was more than they had bargained for.

Sardar's camel rattled about. He needed more opium.

6

Almost two years had passed since Pari had seen Zeeba. With her husband off visiting his gambling friend she decided it was a good time to go see her cousin in Tehran before the Norouz celebrations. Pari had heard that Zeeba's divorce had come through without difficulty. Divorce was the domain of men. No matter how badly a man treated his wife, no matter the circumstances or the rights and the wrongs of things, divorces could only be granted by the husband—wives were at their mercy. Zeeba had traded dowry rights for her freedom. This was the way it was for most women. Before any marriage, the parents would agree on a dowry: a sum of money that the husband-to-be had to promise in return for the hand of the bride. In the event of divorce, this dowry was supposed to be given over, by the husband, to the wife. In principle, it was a pre-nuptial agreement for the total amount of alimony. In practice, whatever the amount of the dowry, it was seldom paid; it would be traded away for either the right to divorce, or in payment for custody of the children. In Zeeba's case, it was she who requested a divorce, and she also demanded custody of their daughter. The rest was open and shut; she would never see a penny of the not insubstantial amount her father had negotiated before her marriage.

Zeeba had always wanted to be a teacher; a solid income stream, painless working hours, three months' summer vacation and, although she'd never admit it, she was attracted to the idea of reminding people of all the effort expended on their children.

Three weeks after gaining her high-school diploma Zeeba found herself in front of a class teaching home economics.

Pari left early in the morning for Tehran. She needed the services of one of the villagers to help carry her bags and the many gifts she had prepared for her relatives. The journey was difficult; she had to perch herself atop a rather cantankerous mule to get to the bus station.

Halfway there, the mule skinner stuffed a precious sugar cube into the animal and its mood melted into a détente that lasted, mercifully, until she stepped off and onto the bus. The roads were rough, and even though it was spring, and the worst of the weather had long given up its assault on the route from the village to the city, still her hands became sore and calloused from gripping onto the seat in front of her. She afforded herself the luxury of a taxi from the bus station to Zeeba's house, and made the driver curse with her punctilious instructions on handling her belongings.

It was Friday – holy day – everybody was relaxing at home. She entered the front yard and found Malous playing on her own near the small pond. Pari ruffled her curly black hair and kissed both her cheeks. Malous welcomed her with a giggle. Pari instructed the taxi driver to take the gifts to the kitchen and marched towards the living room. Zeeba had just spread a length of cotton fabric on the living-room floor for a dress design she had improvised the day before. Zeeba's mother, Shamsi, was supervising her daughter's work.

"What a wonderful surprise." Zeeba sprang towards her cousin with such enthusiasm Pari had to weave to one side to avoid the scissors Zeeba had forgotten were still in her hand.

"It's been such a long time. I missed you. A teacher. I'm so proud."

"Home economics."

"You've done well."

"You just earned a dress. I'll have it ready before you leave."

Zeeba's two brothers, Mehdi and Haady, and Mehdi's wife joined them for lunch. She was two months pregnant and rather tetchy at the sight of food. Mehdi had become the head of the family after the death of their father. He was a handsome man with kind, warm eyes that exuded comfort and hinted of hidden depth. No one in that house loved him the way Malous loved him. She always sat on his lap during lunch and dinner and savoured every morsel of food fed her by his hand. He was about to become a father himself, although his love for Malous would not be usurped; she would remain always the equal in his affections of any child born of his own seed. Haady, the second brother and a year younger than Zeeba, was a loud, brash, seemingly over-confident giant of a man who would take on the whole world, save for his mother, whom he feared. Zeeba had always felt protective towards him; he was her little brother. In every other walk of life he was as successful as he chose, but in the company of his mother he was a shambles, a stuttering fool.

"How is Arbab Yousef? I haven't heard from him in ages." Mehdi spooned some rice into Malous.

"He's fine. He sends his regards. He'll be in Tehran in a month on business. I'll make sure that he comes to see you," Pari replied.

Haady tried to join the conversation. "Three weeks ago Auntie G… G… Goli came for a visit. She wouldn't stop talking about your chamberlain. Quite clever I take it? She mentioned that he's from th…the east country."

"Here we go again. 'He's from the the the the the east country.' Can't you try a little harder? My side of the family never had any speech defects. It's your father's side. God bless his soul." Shamsi spooned some stew onto her plate. The clinking of silver against china reverberated through a cavernous silence that seemed larger than the room, larger than the house, now populated by one middle-aged woman munching obliviously among a collection of lifelike statues.

Pari winced. The silence expanded. Zeeba's mind raced. Mentally running a finger down a list of possibilities that might erase Shamsi's brutal small talk she lunged into a sentence, any sentence.

"I had such a wonderful time in Varamin with you and Auntie Goli. I must visit again. Soon."

Zeeba kicked herself for being unprepared. These words, these attacks, laced with poison that only a certain kind of mother could deliver, were a daily fixture. The family hardly even noticed when there was no one outside the household to bear witness. But Pari's presence had illuminated Shamsi's cruel routine.

Pari remembered now, suddenly, as if the memories had been locked away behind a strong door that Shamsi's words had shattered. She remembered Zeeba's expression, as a child, when Pari's mother would rain kisses upon her. She remembered how she longed to share her own mother's love with Zeeba, to pass it on as if love were as common as water and she could quench the great thirst she sensed in Zeeba. Indeed, Shamsi was barren of love.

Haady left to be with friends and get away for the rest of the day. Shamsi went to her room to nap, as if nothing had happened. Mehdi and his wife retired to their quarters and took Malous with them so that Pari and Zeeba could have some time to themselves.

Zeeba tried to raise herself above the gloom that Shamsi had planted by remarking on another side to Haady's character. "Haady writes poetry. His poems are enchanting. He's very fond of literature and philosophy. His room is packed with books."

"I'm sure he'll end up with an important career. I wouldn't take your mother's remarks seriously."

Pari didn't want to dishearten her cousin by admitting that Shamsi wasn't what you would wish for as a mother. She knew that hearing the truth is not always the best remedy; there are times when you should allow people their misconceptions; allow them to simply be.

The week in Tehran passed quickly. She was enjoying time spent with her cousin. Zeeba persuaded Pari to illicitly visit a photographer with her. Decent women did not have pictures of their uncovered hair taken in the sole company of a male photographer. Although not a civil crime, it might as well have been. Shamsi would have seized the right to administer a severe tongue-lashing if she had known. But the secret was safe; their sense of adventure satiated, and their reputations intact.

Zeeba's family enjoyed a comfortable life; Mehdi's business was thriving. He did the bulk of his trade with Russia and had cultivated contacts and Russian friends who could bring little personal luxuries and items of scarcity.

Malous's birthday was approaching and Mehdi had ordered an exquisite Russian doll through one of his associates. It was expensive – an exceptional toy, not the traditional peasant doll that contained dolls within dolls – but he imagined the expression on his niece's face and couldn't resist it. Besides, he wasn't sure that his niece would be getting anything fancy (or anything at all) from her mother or grandmother on her birthday.

Mehdi didn't judge them for that. They were old-fashioned; children should be seen and not heard. It was as if they didn't ascribe sentience to children simply because they were young. They believed they could talk about anything in front of children or even "talk behind their backs" in front of their faces and the children would be none the wiser. Mehdi didn't want to think about why his mother looked at life the way she did. Having been brought up in that house, he had seen enough to know that her bitterness towards God's creatures had no age limits; she always had an excuse, an explanation for her complete disregard of other people's feelings, no matter what age they were. All he could think of was that she was still his mother and under no circumstances could he bring himself to deny her respect.

Two days before Malous's birthday the doll arrived. It was so exotic; even Mehdi's wife couldn't take her eyes off it. He didn't show it to anybody else and kept quiet about it. On the evening of his niece's birthday, after coming home from work, he rushed to his room to get the present then he charged into the living room. They were busy with dinner preparations. Malous was sitting on the floor playing with an old toy. As soon as she lifted her head and spotted her uncle, her whole face brightened. He was the messenger of all the good in the world.

Mehdi knelt next to her, kissed her head and gave her the birthday present that was wrapped in fancy paper. It took some effort to open the present with her small hands. Her smile was so great, as if it were bursting out of the seams of her face. She had never seen anything as beautiful in her short life. The doll was almost the same height as her; it was a friend, a playmate. She was speechless. She jumped at him, tied her small arms around his neck and went on a kissing rampage. She didn't need anyone else in life when she could have him.

"This is Hannah," he said.

On the eighteenth day of Pari's stay, as Mehdi was leaving for the north of the country, the household was cheered by the arrival of Auntie Goli. She had come for a one-day visit, bringing news about the daughter of Shamsi's second cousin.

"Meena gave birth to a daughter thirteen days ago. This is the first grandchild of Akbar Khan. You should see how elated and proud he looks. He has arranged for a feast to celebrate his granddaughter's birth. It's in three days. Sixty people have been invited for lunch including you, Zeeba and her brothers. They knew I was coming here today, so they asked me to pass on the invitation."

Shamsi muttered, "We have to think of a proper gift. I can't arrive with only a bunch of flowers in my hand. Akbar Khan is too important." Then she addressed Zeeba. "Today, you're going to the bazaar. I want you to buy some high-quality fabric and some fancy ribbons to go with it. We should start on the baby's clothes and accessories as of tomorrow. But I still have to think of a substantial present to take along with the baby's clothes."

Pari decided to go fabric shopping with Zeeba, but Auntie Goli pulled her aside to ask for a favour.

"You know how much I enjoy your cooking. Will you be an angel and cook the lunch today... for Auntie Goli's sake?" she added with a wink.

Pari couldn't bring herself to say no, so she stayed to arrange for the lunch and Auntie Goli accompanied Zeeba to the bazaar instead. After the lunch preparations, Pari took a break to sit in the garden and smoke a cigarette. She stared at Malous playing with her new Russian friend, her precious birthday gift, serving imaginary tea and holding polite conversation.

Pari yearned for the day that she would become a mother; she would give all her love on a silver platter to her child. She envisaged the future, building scenarios in her head about what she would and wouldn't do if she ever had a daughter like Malous. Her train of thought was disrupted with Shamsi calling her: "You'd better check on your stew. Seems like it needs more water."

Shamsi was watering her roses and precious geraniums. Malous was too lost in her own world to take notice of her, or anybody else for that matter, but her singular attention to her imaginary tea party piqued Shamsi's curiosity. For the first time, she looked at the doll with a critical eye. Indeed it was exquisite; something that could never be found in the main bazaar in Tehran. That sparked an idea in her mind; a clever idea, the way she saw it.

She strolled towards Malous. She smiled. She knelt beside the little girl. She stroked her hair. She smiled some more but Malous didn't notice. She sat. Malous smiled. Shamsi stroked the doll's head then gradually eased the doll out of Malous's arms.

"She needs to take a nap."

Malous acquiesced. Perhaps her precious friend was tired?

"If you make her play all day long she will get ugly and dirty and won't look nice any more."

Malous seemed perplexed but the welfare of her new best friend was paramount.

"I'll put her straight to bed."

Malous watched, expressionless, as Shamsi took her friend into the house and to bed. She pulled at a few blades of grass and wished that her new friend wasn't tired, and that she could play all day.

Zeeba and Auntie Goli managed to get back in time for lunch. Zeeba took the fabrics she'd bought to Shamsi to see if they would pass her critical eye or if she'd have to take them back. She noticed that Shamsi seemed elated.

"You look happy! Did you come up with an idea for the gift?" Zeeba asked, wondering what her mother had up her sleeve this time.

"As a matter of fact I did. We can take the Russian doll for Meena's baby. I can assure you that no one will arrive with a present as fancy as that."

"But what about Malous? She loves that doll."

"I'm sure she'll survive. It's not the end of the world. You can buy her another doll from the bazaar."

Zeeba didn't put up much of a fight. After all, like her mother said, there was no shortage of dolls around and Malous could always have another; maybe not as eye-catching as the Russian one, but it would still be a toy for her to play with.

On the day of the party, after ironing the baby clothes that Zeeba had made, Pari went to the living room to find out if her cousin needed help to wrap the presents. Zeeba was wrapping Malous's doll.

"What are you doing? Isn't that Malous's birthday present? The one Mehdi bought her?"

"Yes, it *was*. And now it's going to be a birthday present for Meena's baby."

"But, how could you separate her from that doll? You know how much she loves it."

"It's not the end of the world. She'll get over it. I'll buy her another." Zeeba was not even aware she was parroting her mother, in both words and deed.

Pari's heart sank. There was no point arguing with Zeeba over the doll; she had made up her mind or rather, as far as she was concerned, there was nothing to make her mind up about. Pari left her to get on with her wrapping.

As much as she tried not to judge, there were times she couldn't help feeling that Zeeba didn't deserve to be a mother; that she wasn't capable of experiencing unconditional love.

Pari decided to go home the next morning. She couldn't bear to stand bereft of comfort while little Malous's heart broke. If she stayed to offer succour she would surely ignite the wrath of not one, but two generations of maternal intransigence, neither of which would hear any charge against them. Her interference would simply confuse and upset Malous. Better the child suffer an unavoidable loss than learn why she had to suffer at all.

Pari's third spring at her own home was as pleasant as the previous ones, save for the increasing frequency and intensity of her headaches, which would put her out of commission for hours at a time. The winter had been merciful, the harvest plentiful. Pari made plans to expand her own garden.

An extra joy was the announcement of the engagement of her brother to a distant relative. Both sides had agreed to a wedding ceremony in early summer. Pari was pleased they had designated a hand in the preparations to her; she wanted to see her brother settled and it comforted her to know that he would live at her father's house with his wife.

During the third week of the new year, Ali delivered a message from Eshrat, one of the women villagers, to Pari. She asked if Zan-Arbab could spare an hour to go visit her. Eshrat was an old woman who lived with her son (or, to be more accurate, her stepson). She had outlived her husband and his second wife. Her son had a lame leg, but was fit enough to work in the stable and provide for his mother.

Pari packed a basket of cheese and eggs and yogurt, and a bag of rice, to take to Eshrat's house as a gesture of the new-year's spirit.

When Pari arrived Eshrat was in her sickbed. Her face was as pale as a ghost, her eyes sunken, almost deprived of life. Eshrat's son tenderly placed another pillow under her head then left the two women.

"It's very nice of you to come and see me right away."

"Do you want me to get you anything? A glass of water, a cup of tea, or...?"

Eshrat grabbed Pari's hand and squeezed it tightly.

"No, Zan-Arbab, I just want you to sit here and listen to me." She fumbled with a handkerchief. "My son took me to Tehran to see a doctor two months ago. Remember, you paid for it." She wiped her eyes and sighed deeply. "They told me the disease has spread all over my body and my time has come. I'm not afraid of dying, what I am worried about is the burden I'll be taking with me."

Eshrat's mouth quivered. Pari rushed to fetch a glass of water. She lifted her head to help her drink.

"Are you sure you don't want to rest instead of talking to me?"

"I'll be resting for eternity very soon. I have to talk to you."

She took another sip of water.

"I know you're a spiritual woman. You obey the Holy Book and the ways of the Prophet. I know I can confide in you. Talking to the local Mullah makes me edgy and uncomfortable.

"Many years ago, in my early years of marriage to Agha, God blesses his soul, I fell pregnant. We were so happy to become parents and we were looking forward to the baby's birth, but something went wrong; I had a miscarriage. Thereafter I was never able to bear a child.

"Agha took another wife two years after that. I hated it; if I could have given him a child, he wouldn't have brought another woman into our house and I wouldn't have become an appendage to his life. The second wife gave birth to a son in the first year of their marriage. Agha was ecstatic; he couldn't contain himself. It was unbearable to watch them."

Eshrat looked straight at Pari, the pain etched in her face.

"But if it weren't for this baby, they would be as miserable as I was and she would be no better than me.

"I pretended to love the baby and helped to care for him. Meanwhile, I found a woman who was an expert in herbs and potions. I asked her for a poison to drain the life out of someone little by little."

The wave of compassion that had enveloped Pari at Eshrat's sad memories disintegrated into a sickening apprehension. What was Eshrat telling her?

"Every time I fed the baby, I put a drop of poison in his milk. He got sicker and sicker day by day, until he finally gave up his battle and died after three weeks. Agha and his wife were devastated and no one could tell them what went wrong. Me, on the other hand, I was content to see my plan succeed and to make my substitute sink as low as I had."

She delivered her tale matter-of-factly, as if reporting a successful recipe. Pari sat, open-mouthed, unable to fully comprehend what the old woman was saying but unwilling to stop her; to interject might end the story prematurely. But the old woman, without a trace of self-consciousness, continued her gruesome history.

"Unfortunately, she didn't stop there. She was determined to get pregnant again and give him the child he craved. After eight months, she declared that another baby was on the way. The labour passed with no difficulties and there they were with a healthy boy again.

"As a matter of fact, it was less nerve-racking for me when it came to poisoning the second child. My plan had succeeded before, so I applied it again. The second child didn't even last three weeks. He perished after sixteen days.

"I had engineered the most effective way to repel my husband from her. They were miserable and that made me cheerful."

Pari's throat was as dry as the desert. This old woman, fending off the angel of death with the last morsel of energy left in her, was a cold-blooded killer. A child murderer.

Pari grabbed the water jug on the bedside table, poured herself a glass of water and retreated from the old woman.

Eshrat didn't notice. She was so engrossed in her story: her confession. "His second wife, although she was a good number of years younger than me, she wasn't as stupid as I imagined her to be. After the death of the second baby, she grew colder towards me. She had sensed something but she was wise enough to keep it to herself. To tell her husband that I killed their children? No. Too far-fetched; he would never believe it, would he?"

"It took her a year to overcome her grief and there she was; pregnant again. I was exasperated. It was becoming a career. But if she wanted a war I'd give her one. I would never give up. I would crush her. I'd crush her and I'd crush her children. I would never give up.

"For the third time, she delivered a healthy baby boy. But this time she resorted to any excuse to keep me away from the baby. My previously successful plan was doomed but I wouldn't be denied. Their joy sickened me. She had become the saviour of my husband's hopes.

"With her diligence and constant care the boy made it to his third birthday. There were times when he would go his own way when his mother got too busy to watch him. I finally saw my chance.

He was on the porch by himself. I looked around and couldn't see anyone nearby. With one stroke, I pushed him down the stairs. I thought he was dead but after a pause he started howling with pain. His leg was turned around at the knee. The damage was severe enough to leave him lame for the rest of his life. No one ever suspected me.

"A year and a half later my husband's second wife contracted a disease that ended her life in a few months. He took it hard; three deaths, one after the other. He looked to me for succour and begged me to rear his son as my own. It was perfect; I was a mother."

Eshrat's voice became thin, her chiselled features seemed to soften. Tears welled in eyes that a moment before had burned with horror. She blew her nose and tucked the handkerchief up her sleeve.

"I looked after his son and cared for him as best I could. I grew to love him like he was my own. My husband passed away twenty-one years later and ever since his death my son and I have been inseparable."

Eshrat's face had become a picture of remorse. She looked at Pari, searching for any trace of compassion or absolution. She wanted Pari to mediate between her and God.

"Zan-Arbab, I want you to promise me that when I'm gone, you'll take my son under your wing. Find him a good wife; he needs a family of his own. He shouldn't stay lonely."

Pari couldn't speak. She nodded.

"Do you think God would ever forgive me for what I've done?"

Eshrat was ravenous for redemption, but there could be none. Pari would watch over the woman's son but she could offer no dispensation.

"I don't know, Eshrat. I don't know."

One week later Eshrat passed away. Ali brought word to Pari that Eshrat's son had a request; he wanted Pari to take part in the burial ceremony.

Pari accepted. On the day of the funeral two women villagers helped to wash Eshrat and wrap her in a shroud, then her son came and took the body to the grave he had dug himself. Pari had never taken part in a funeral but she knew what to do: She climbed down into the grave, sat next to the corpse and read prayers to make it less frightening for the soul of the dead to pass to the other world. Pari remembered the desperation of Eshrat, hoping for any chance of absolution.

She whispered a special prayer for her forgiveness.

Pari had never seen such a beautiful meadow. The scent of fresh grass was soothing. She couldn't see any boundaries, it looked like a green ocean, extending to eternity. She strolled hand in hand with Yousef in the benign sunshine until they reached a tree heavy with ripe green apples. Yousef picked one. He took a bite. Pari made to pick one for herself but with every attempt to get closer, the apple got further away. She turned to ask for Yousef's help but he wasn't there any more. She tried again and again to no avail. Why wouldn't the apple stay still? The frustration was overwhelming. She reached then she lunged then she jumped. She turned her back then swung around fast, to try to fool the tree, but the apple moved too quickly. She breathed deeply; a strange sound, it was Ali's dog, his bark calling her to the land of the living.

She was awake now. Her mouth was dry, her heart thumping. Yousef had already left their bed to start his day. Pari splashed cold water on her face to wash away the dream.

In the kitchen her breakfast was waiting but Pari needed a smoke first thing in the morning. Banoo sat next to her and nibbled at a crust.

"What do you know about dreams?" Pari asked, then she inhaled deeply on her cigarette.

"Well, I know the meaning of some signs and objects but to be on the safe side I usually refer to my book."

"What book?"

"Years ago my mother gave me this old book that cites the interpretations of experts in this matter. I have used it a lot in my life."

"Could I borrow it? It's just that I had this dream and I really don't feel up to talking about it. I'd rather find its meaning in your book."

Banoo fetched the book from her room and handed it to Pari.

"Zan-Arbab, bear in mind that these interpretations are not written in stone. Two people could have the same dream but under different circumstances their dreams could have different meanings."

"I'll keep that in mind."

She took the book to her room, lit another cigarette and searched for the word "apple". It read: "The meaning of apple in your dream hinges on its colour. Seeing a green apple in your dream and taking a bite denotes having a child."

The whole dream passed through Pari's mind: Yousef took a bite but she couldn't reach the apple, no matter how much she tried. As much as she wanted to be sanguine about it, Pari couldn't fool herself; she couldn't deny that after five years of marriage and five years of trying to become a mother, she was still childless. It seemed to her that there was no other meaning to this dream; she was barren.

Pari couldn't make out why such a destiny was imposed on her. Was this her punishment for taking over Noor's life? Or was it due to some terrible deed that she had committed in the past but had no memory of?

She didn't tell anybody about the details of her dream. That night, after Yousef fell asleep, she prayed to God to grant her a miracle, to give her the ability to bear a child. Her mind was too occupied to let her sleep; she was assailed by disturbing thoughts, about the future, her childless future, the loneliness of old age; no children to care for her, no grandchildren to seek comfort in her.

She finally got up and walked towards the window. She needed fresh air. All was still but for the vague outline of Ali's dog marching up and down the garden with a purpose that seemed out of place with the calm around him. Her mother's words of gentle wisdom found her: "If it's meant to be, it will be. No point sulking. May as well get on with your life."

The full moon was dazzling, its stunning beauty, its power, made her feel at one with the universe and all of its beings. She was a tiny part of this chaos, of this order, of this world and that meant that she wasn't alone. If being barren was what God had destined for her, she would surrender to it. But she would stay proud. She vowed that she would never allow herself to feel any less of a woman.

Pari stayed up until dawn prayers. She had no desire to go back to bed. The early morning breeze touched her skin. The clean air filling her lungs seemed to energize her. Who knew what the future would bring? But she was certain of something; she would always fight her own battles and never feel sorry for herself.

There were so many chores to be done. Three large pitchers were waiting in the corner of the kitchen to be filled with butter and yogurt. It wasn't an easy job by any means but if Pari delegated the task she would only have herself to blame if the butter was sour or the yogurt too thin.

She bade two strong villagers carry pots of milk to the kitchen and place them on her stove. With so much milk to be boiled, it was going to be a while before she needed their help again for draining, stirring and transferring the half-finished products into other pots. She knew that her whole day was going to be taken up by this chore.

After checking the boiling milk, Pari lit a cigarette and initiated a chat with Banoo.

"Is it this week that Noor's going to visit her parents or next week?"

"She told me she was planning on a trip by the end of this week."

"I guess I'd have to wait till she comes back. I wanted to ask her to go shopping with me. I'd like to buy some silk fabric for a new dress. I could use her opinion, she's got good taste."

"Zan-Arbab, I have an idea that we've got a good candidate for marrying off to Eshrat's son. Asghar's daughter has just turned seventeen. She's not half-bad looking and she's more than capable of running a household. What do you think?"

Her question was met with silence. Banoo wondered if she had said anything inappropriate; she studied Pari's face for signs of trouble. The flaming red sheen that seemed to materialize instantly on Pari's face gave Banoo cause for fright. But surely Pari's expression was too acute to be triggered by such an innocent remark?

"What's wrong, Zan-Arbab? What happened to you? You're scaring me."

It was a few minutes before Pari managed to gather herself: "Splitting headache. It hit me so fast, as if I were hit by an axe. It's been getting worse but never as bad as this."

"I'll get you some painkillers."

Pari swallowed four and staggered towards her room. She lay down and closed her eyes. Her head was like a ton of bricks on her shoulders. She was scared to open her eyes in case the room was still spinning.

It took a good three hours before she felt some slight relief. She asked Banoo to carry on in the kitchen without her. Everybody knew how strong she was but that pain had really taken it out of her. She was completely drained.

After two days, she headed for Tehran to see a doctor. The journey was a burden but this wasn't any ordinary pain to be ignored. Bad news or not, she had to know what was happening to her. She didn't want to hide from the truth.

The doctor offered a mixture of bad and good news. She didn't have a terminal disease but she was suffering from a combination of extremely high blood pressure and migraine, neither of which were curable. She could see her future; a futile battle against pain.

Months passed. Her suffering ranged from severe to bearable, but its constant presence was changing her behaviour. She was easily irritated and quick to snap at anyone within range. There were times that she would lock herself in her room, disappearing for two or three days at a time. Her problem had become a problem for the whole village. Everybody was trying to find at least a temporary cure to calm this flaming volcano. Pari's agony left her open to any and all suggestions. Anything with the slightest hope for relief was pounced upon as a potential miracle cure.

"Zan-Arbab, may I come in?" Ali asked after knocking at her door with some hesitation.

"What do you want, Ali? I can't even open my eyes."

"One of the women villagers is here. She says she has a cure from an old man who treats people with herbal remedies he concocts himself."

"Why not? Let her in."

The woman tip-toed towards Pari with some caution and more than a little curiosity. Her steps were so light; as if she were walking on eggshells.

"Zan-Arbab, I've brought you medicine. The old man told me it will definitely work."

Pari examined the concoction. It had a strange colour and a foul smell.

"What is this? It looks disgusting."

"Well, he told me it's a mixture of bull's droppings, chamomile and two other herbs I hadn't heard of…but, everybody goes to him. He knows his stuff."

Pari wished she had never asked about the ingredients. She felt so angry at her own desperation. Pain had sunk her to a level that she would even consider drinking bull's excrement. But perhaps anything was better than being condemned to this torturous prison of agony without relief? She shut her eyes and tried to divert her mind. A few sips were all she could handle. She turned her back towards Ali and the woman villager to persuade them to leave.

Later that night Banoo took a tray of food to her. Looking at her face, muscles taut, the smallest veins fracturing on her cheeks to leave her skin mottled and unattractive, her eyes red, almost bereft of life, Banoo knew Pari was still suffering deeply.

"Banoo, take the food tray back. I can't eat right now. Go and find Ali and ask him to come and see me."

Ali appeared ten minutes later, curious to find out whether the medicine had had any effect.

"Did it work at all?" he asked anxiously.

"No. Not that it's any surprise." She sighed. "Ali, I'm desperate. Get me some opium."

Ali didn't budge. Motionless, he didn't even blink, he stared straight at her. His silence was quite self-explanatory.

"I know what you're thinking. I have no choice. I have to get some relief or I'll end up in bedlam."

"God help you, Zan-Arbab. You're playing with fire."

A short while later, Ali came back with a pipe and Yousef's brazier filled with hot coals. He placed some opium and a burning coal in the pipe and hesitantly handed it to Pari. She took the pipe and paused. She knew this was as big a mistake as Eve eating the forbidden apple, but she felt helpless, without any choice. She had made up her mind. She had chosen to trade her determination, her self-control and her pride with opium in return for peace and release.

"This is your first time; you'd better take it easy. Don't take very deep puffs." Ali had given up on the idea of talking Pari out of enslaving herself to this demon.

Pari inhaled and waited. The contracted muscles, the convoluted nerves behind her eyes started to unravel. The agony washed away. A tranquillity enveloped her. She could enjoy being alive again. For the first time in months, she fell asleep feeling soporific, cosy, at peace.

The next day Pari announced her comeback by leaving her room and taking part in the everyday affairs of the village. Yousef was too pleased to see his wife up and active again to question the source of her rejuvenation. He had witnessed her agony and desperation and he would not take the high moral ground on the consequences of her remedy. Pari took to sleeping in a small spare room; she felt uncomfortable taking her medicine in front of Yousef, or anyone else, for that matter.

She took the pipe every time the monstrous pain rose. She had become quite adept in eliminating it; she knew all the ins and outs she had to know about her medicine.

Five more months passed. Time wasn't an issue to Pari any more; she had no notion of it. Her propensity to stay in her room and evade participation in handling her responsibilities in the village was quite clear. There wasn't much talk about "Zan-Arbab" among villagers the way there used to be.

Banoo placed a teacup and a container filled with sugar cubes on a tray and walked slowly, almost reluctantly, towards Pari's room. She opened the door and snuck her head in. Pari was lying on the floor facing the wall, her opium paraphernalia next to her. She was in a stupor and most probably she wouldn't notice her tea tray. Banoo felt irritated and she was fed up with Pari. If she couldn't be bothered to turn and drink her tea before it got cold, then so be it.

She stood by the door and looked at the shell of this woman stretched on the floor. Who was she? Whatever happened to the pleasant, sociable, strong-willed woman she shared her days with? Banoo became overwhelmed with this veritable conundrum of emotions, her anger blunted only by loneliness and a deep sense of betrayal.

"Zan-Arbab. Zan-Arbab. I've brought you tea."

The words made Pari open her eyes slightly. Squinting as if the sun were blinding her.

"Tea. Tea."

Banoo's words swirled around Pari like chirping birds, far off, echoing. "I'm so thirsty."

"Thirsty? For what?" Banoo folded her arms.

Pari sat up, or tried to. It was as if the simple act of lifting one's head required all the strength in the world.

"What is it that you thirst for, Zan-Arbab? Mmm?

Pari lifted the teacup. It swayed this way and that before she managed to manoeuvre it to her mouth, then she slurped at it.

"Do you have a headache, Zan-Arbab?"

Pari looked up at Banoo quizzically.

"No you don't. You haven't had a headache all week, have you? And you had no headache the week before that."

Banoo wiped her tears away and left.

Pari turned towards the door and found the room empty. She sat on her mattress. She sipped the tea and wondered why Banoo had cried. Now she was remembering the recent past as if it were ancient history, something that might even have happened to someone else. When she started her medication regime she had been careful to ration the opium. Just a tiny crumb when the pain became unbearable. Then she had increased the dose, just a little, when the headaches were so bad they almost blinded her.

But now she was remembering. She remembered how if she took a good dose at the onset of the headache, rather than wait until it was raging within her skull, she could avoid the pain completely. A few hours in bed and she was fine; dazed but fine. Then she remembered how it had occurred to her that if she had a busy day ahead of her she could take just a few crumbs, to get her through the day without worrying whether she might be hit by the sledgehammer of pain that the migraines brought.

It was fair to say that she hadn't volunteered to become opium-dependent, she hadn't started smoking it for pleasure and she didn't plan a long-term relationship with it. *What difference do any of these justifications make?* she thought. In the end, it was her and only her who chose comfort in this demon, and it was only her who could break the chain and rescue her dignity, rediscover her soul. There was no room for inadequacy or self-pity in her life. She was better than that.

She would have to end this addiction. She knew it. All her life she had despised people wrapped up in themselves and now she was one of them. She would end it today.

She filled her pipe and lifted it to her mouth. Yes, this would be the last day.

Then she caught herself in the mirror. She was thin and gaunt, the skin around her dull eyes was slack and grey; flakes of skin mottled her complexion.

She remembered how the few crumbs became a few more. A sleeping draught at the end of the day, then a few more instead of morning prayer.

Instead of morning prayer? Instead of morning prayer?

The woman with the pipe in the mirror would end it today, then tomorrow, then it would end her.

She put the pipe down, lit a cigarette and drank the rest of the tea that Banoo had brought for her. She covered the opium tray with a scarf and pushed it away.

Banoo went after the two girls who helped out in the kitchen. There were shallots and garlic cloves to be peeled and prepared for the pickle jars. Pari had already got a head start but extra hands were always welcome (if she wanted to finish that day).

"We'll have a simple lunch today. That way we'll be able to get rid of this mess in the kitchen before nightfall."

Banoo nodded happily. She was glad to have her companion back to full strength. Of course, there were times that Pari's migraines or high blood pressure would put her in a foul mood but even then they managed to get along.

Yousef entered the kitchen, searching for some bread and cheese to quieten a noisy belly.

"You stayed in Tehran for a long time, all right. Anything interesting that maybe I could see next time I go to Tehran with you?" He had taken too long in the city (or at least Pari believed he had taken too long) and she couldn't hold the question in any longer (nor could she hide the sarcasm in her tone).

"It was important to meet some merchants…I had to wait for two days on them arriving."

As he was leaving the kitchen, Noor got hold of him and asked if she could have a chat in private. Banoo raised an eyebrow and whispered to Pari, "Nothing worth talking about has happened…so far as I know."

Pari was more than aware of Banoo's need to find out about everybody's affairs in that village. "I'm sure we'll know all about it very soon." Her thirst for this particular piece of knowledge outmatched even Banoo's curiosity.

Half an hour before lunch, Pari took a break from the pickle preparation and marched towards her room for a lie-down. She was feeling well that day and didn't want to push her luck. She knew if she drove herself too hard she might summon a migraine.

Five minutes later, Yousef joined her in the room. He looked as if he'd been trying to solve a puzzle. He didn't look too pleased either.

"Is everything under control? Ali has been handling the affairs diligently?"

"Yes. I had a chat with Ali and everything's fine."

"Well, you don't look exactly happy. Did Noor say something?"

"She wants a divorce."

"She's always looked content to me. And besides, we get along very well."

"I know. She had no complaints and she wasn't in a foul mood when she broke the news to me."

"So, how come all of a sudden this decision?"

"She says that she'd feel more at ease and comfortable if she stayed with her parents. Apparently, her father's illness is getting worse and she wants to be near him. She says now that you're here she doesn't have to worry about me being lonely either. She feels more useful back at her parents'."

"It's a shame. I'll miss her. She is a decent human being."

"She's made up her mind. She's leaving in two days."

Late afternoon that day, as Pari had started to fill the pickle jars with peeled onions and garlic cloves, she heard some giggling outside the kitchen. Seconds later, Auntie Goli entered with a small bag and a big smile.

"Your chamberlain Ali has got a good sense of humour. I do enjoy chatting with him. Say, dear, do you have any henna handy? I'm going to take a bath first thing tomorrow morning before anybody else gets to use up the bath water."

"As a matter of fact I have a full bag, which is just as well. I can see your grey roots. And yes, you can take my pumice with you."

Auntie Goli's visit was too cheerful an event to let go to waste, and Pari wanted to spend some time with Noor before she left. She wanted to reassure herself that Noor was leaving with a good memory of her. So, after Auntie Goli's two-hour bath, she suggested that the three of them should take a trip to the holy city of Mashhad in the east of Iran.

Noor hesitated at first since she wasn't sure about a ten-day trip, but she came around when she considered that perhaps Pari needed her blessing in some way. After all, she was Yousef's first wife and she was leaving. Pari would be on her own from now on and maybe she wanted to make sure there was peace between them?

There was no problem convincing Auntie Goli to take the trip; she was always ready for adventure.

They packed their bags, took orders for saffron, carnelian rings and pendants, prayer stones and mats, and finally got on their way to the east country; they also took with them the prayers of the well-wishers in the village. Pari's wish, to spend time with Noor before she left the village, had been granted.

It took three days to get there. They stopped in several towns and villages on the way to rest and to make the trip more enjoyable. When they reached Mashhad they were famished and headed straight for the nearest restaurant. After eating, Pari enquired of the restaurant owner about a good place to stay; somewhere clean and reliable and close to the pilgrim area.

After settling down in the house recommended by the restaurateur, they decided to go for a walk, and maybe some window shopping; Pari had never visited Mashhad before.

The soothing sound of Azan, the call to prayer, filled the air, sweetly beseeching the faithful to gather for evening worship. A particular bonus offered by holy places such as Mashhad was that the quality of the Azan singers was unrivalled; it might have been the voice of an angel calling the pilgrims to prayer.

The three travellers followed the obedient crowd to the mosque adjacent to the sanctuary to perform their daily praise to God.

Pari stood with the other women in the great cavernous mosque, ready to start the evening prayer. The beauty of the architecture (ethereal, almost not of this world, so delicate the masonry, so unlikely the building's confident thrust to the heavens) and the sophistication of the patterns on the tiles adorning the walls and ceilings (like mathematical equations transformed into pictographs) diverted her concentration. She had to repeat each sentence in the prayer two or three times before she got it right. She felt ashamed at her lack of piety but she couldn't help herself.

The next morning after breakfast they made for the sanctuary. They passed the vast ponds where people wash before prayer. They passed the hopeful, the desperate, tethered to the building; pilgrims who had made the journey in search of the miraculous, a cure for cancer, regained sight, perhaps to walk again? They had literally tied themselves to the building. Pari wondered whether the rope around their ankles was a challenge to God that they wouldn't leave until he helped or perhaps they wanted to paint their wretchedness into the holy place, to embarrass the Almighty into action? But she knew that she was no different, just more fortunate, she needed miracles too, tiny miracles compared to healing a broken spine or pouring light into dead eyes but she needed miracles nonetheless and in this life there was no greater miracle than a child. For a moment she saw herself tying her own ankle in rough hessian and explaining to her friends, her fellow travellers, that she had to join the forlorn group and tether herself until God ploughed the possibility of life into her fallow womb.

The three women walked into the main building. The walls were lined with desperate souls begging the spirit of the saint in the sanctuary to intermediate between them and God, to convince the Almighty to answer their prayers.

The heart of the building was a rather small, enclosed room with shining golden grid walls adding material meaning to the grave of the holy man buried in the centre of it. The golden grid was for more than show though. A stranger might have thought that such opulence was purely for this world and of this world, but the pilgrims believed that the grid itself was magical, that it could resonate with prayer, amplifying the heartfelt desires of the faithful; that God himself could hear a prayer rise above the rest, that perhaps they really could, in this place, have a miracle made to order. But to get God's full attention believers had to grab the grid with all of their strength and silently scream their desires. The corridor leading to the room was overcrowded well beyond any reasonable point of sanity. Their wondrous stroll through the sanctuary was becoming more uncomfortable with every inch towards the golden room; it was starting to feel like they'd been shunted into a cattle truck.

A wave of panic swept simultaneously over Pari, Noor and

Auntie Goli and with it they were physically washed away in different directions. Pari was so tightly wedged into the crowd trying to reach the holy grid that her feet left the floor; she entered the room without setting foot in it. There was no mercy. She gasped for air. The place was a battlefield. She had so looked forward to becoming a part of a collective soul seeking purity through prayer and meditation. But instead, her disgust was boiling, turning into rage; she wanted out of that room.

She could take no more. She could throw bales of hay over the heads of three men. She could lift and carry a full churn of milk all day long if she had a mind to. She would not be crushed by an unthinking mob. She coiled herself tightly then burst out, twisting her body and thrusting her arms until she had carved a space around her wide enough that her feet descended to the floor. But the mob was ferocious, and as she tried to take a tiny step towards an exit they folded in on her, a heaving wall of oblivious humanity now denying her the slightest movement of any limb. She was embalmed. Mummified. Inert.

It was the worst, most frightening moment of her life; or at least she thought so. In a moment her predicament would seem like a stroll on a fresh spring day. When it happened, a thousand thoughts thundered into her mind. She remembered now; she remembered the old women in the village talking about this, when she was a child, she hadn't understood; they were laughing about it.

At first it was her breast. As if he was trying to rip it from her body someone grabbed at it violently, brutally, painfully. She could hardly find the space to lower her chin to see it, but it was there, disembodied, a hand, its back covered in hair, its fingers short, stubby; fingernails dirty, grabbing, throbbing.

Something pinched her thigh. A hand. Another hand. The same man? She couldn't see it in the faces around her. When a face came into view it was suffering as she was, in a kind of hell; not the heaven they had sought. It slid up her thigh, but not her naked skin, her garment offering some kind of barrier.

It reached the top of her thigh. Surely not? Surely this would end? The crowd clear? Her attacker take fright? She'd be free. Or he'd stop. This was enough. This was what he came for; no more than this?

A last gasp of air fired out of her as something tried, with the force of anonymous desperation, to work its way into her. This could not be? She was being sodomized by the invisible hand of an invisible monster in the holiest place in the land, where the eighth successor of the Prophet lies, where she came with her good friends to make peace and say goodbyes.

It must have seemed to the seething crowd outside the holy room that the Prophet's successor himself had risen from the grave. It wasn't the high-pitched wail of the bereaved, or the screech of a woman in fear. It was throaty, it started almost as a growl, it rose quickly in force but not pitch. It reverberated around the little room, as if gathering strength before gushing forth through the door. The vice she was in gave an inch; enough. She might have been a warrior flailing her arms to beat her enemies.

In a moment it was over.

The hand disappeared. She stopped screaming. She didn't look round. What if she saw him? What if she saw two men? Or three?

What would haunt her the most?

She did not look round, but the people that had all but crushed her peeled away until she could walk, almost unhindered, out of the room and through the corridor.

She sat on the floor of the great hall. She couldn't see any sign of Noor or Auntie Goli.

After a few minutes, she gathered herself and went to the yard for some fresh air. She took deep breaths to cool her fury and quieten her beating heart.

Her legs gave way.

Pari sat against a fence that was granted shade by a nearby sycamore. She was empty; no memories, no emotions or thoughts, no sense of place. Children running about, people passing with tearful eyes; some glanced at Pari. They thought she looked ill.

Two women stood in front of her and carried on a conversation. Pari could see their lips move, she could hear their voices but they might have been a thousand miles away.

"So, what do you think? Do you want to go now or wait a bit longer?" Auntie Goli yelled like she was talking to a deaf person.

She got no response.

Noor sat next to Pari and rubbed her shoulder. "What's wrong, Pari? Do you feel sick?"

Pari burst into tears. She cried the same way a child would cry when she'd been forgotten by her parents and left behind: with all the anger, fear and self-pity in the world.

"Now she's scaring me," said Auntie Goli. "For the love of God, child, what is wrong with you?"

"I want to go back to the guest house and rest for a while. Then…we could go out for lunch," Pari said softly.

She sat on the edge of her bed and lit a cigarette. Noor gave her a glass of cooling water then pressed a hand to Pari's forehead to see if she was running a fever.

"It doesn't seem to me like you're running a high temperature, but I could call a doctor if you feel ill."

"No. I'm going to be fine. There is no need for a doctor."

Pari told them about her ordeal in the core of the sanctuary and how lucky she was to get away. "I'm not going back to that room again. Tomorrow I'll go with you as far as the great hall and do my prayers in there. Please, no more talk of this. Ever."

Noor's first instinct was to try to comfort her, but comforting her would be to speak to her ordeal. The minutiae of normality was the only cure she could think of. "After we got separated, Auntie Goli and I were pushed past the core of the sanctuary and we didn't even get a chance to stay for five minutes."

Auntie Goli followed Noor's lead. "I don't have the energy to fight people off. Tomorrow we'll all stay in the great hall and perform our midday prayer there. After that, we could go to the bazaar and see to the list of orders we've been given."

That night, Pari stayed up to read some verses from the Holy Book. Her body was exhausted but her mind was calm. She didn't feel agitated or uneasy any more. She was enjoying the magnificent full moon and the soothing breeze sneaking in through the half-opened window. Pari thanked God for giving her the strength to overcome her opium habit and allowing her to cope with a chronic, untreatable illness. She promised God that no matter how many ups and downs she encountered, she would always be faithful to her beliefs and would never take God's most precious gift of life for granted.

Before the dawn, a commotion from the direction of the sanctuary rattled her light sleep. There was screaming, crying, and words of praise shouted at the tops of voices. Pari couldn't make out whether something good or tragic had happened. She shut the window so that Noor and Auntie Goli wouldn't wake up, tip-toed down the stairs and out of the main door.

She saw the shadow of the landlady in the yard.

"I'm sorry. Did the noise disturb you too?" the landlady asked.

"Not at all. I heard the commotion and thought I'd go downstairs to see what's happening."

"Maybe we could go to the sanctuary together and find out."

Pari and the landlady shut the main door quietly and walked towards the sanctuary's yard to quench their curiosity. People had gathered around a blind teenage girl whose parents had brought her in hopes of a miracle. The girl was in shock and the noisy crowd that encircled her was ecstatic. She was trembling and crying in her mother's arms. Her curious eyes examined everything and everybody caught in the first blush of the rising sun. With new life in eyes she would soon know were brown, she savoured the miracle of first sight; hoarding as much as she could in case it was taken away from her again.

Pari was uplifted; to witness such a cessation of misery erased her experience in the shrine and replaced it with an ecstasy that burned so strong it was contagious.

When Noor and Auntie Goli met Pari for breakfast she soon turned their glum expressions into joyous smiles. They had been worried that her time in the shrine might cling to her like a bad odour but God had shown himself, as much to Pari as the girl given the gift of sight.

Auntie Goli decided that this was all part of God's plan, and that it was a sign that they must do some more shopping before heading home. Their laughter rang out across the streets and in the many shops and cafés they visited that day.

10

For some months now Yousef's trips to Tehran had become more lengthy, and more frequent. But there was no use in pursuing the subject. When pressed he'd say he'd been meeting new business associates and had to spend more time in Tehran to get new deals.

With the way Yousef was living his life, Pari would have been surprised if he was working hard to get new deals. He evaded any problems regarding the business and had adopted an easy-going attitude of 'things will sort themselves out'. His absence had meant more work and responsibility for his wife and Ali. But still, there were no major difficulties; everything was under control.

Pari had become accustomed to handling her high blood pressure and her migraine attacks. She had even taken her doctor's advice about her diet, to an extent, and had cut back on her daily intake of six raw egg yolks to a mere two. Standing in for Yousef, the Arbab, and her extensive knowledge of farming (that she had learned from Ali these last few years) had gained Pari more influence and awe among the villagers than ever. There was no peasant in that village who wouldn't take the word of Zan-Arbab as seriously as they would take a verse in the Holy Book.

In the frequent absence of her husband, Banoo and Ali had become her constant afternoon tea companions. She loved spending her afternoons chatting and exchanging mundane stories of everyday life in the village. Smoking her cigarette, sipping her tea and enjoying the company of two friendly, candid people gave her much comfort.

One afternoon, as she was rolling her cigarette, a villager walked in wanting to talk to her.

"Zan-Arbab, I just came back from Tehran. There is something I must tell you."

"I'm all ears," Pari said, without lifting her head.

"Maybe we should talk in private?"

"I'm fine with Banoo and Ali here. Pour a cup of tea for yourself

73

and tell me all about it."

She lit her cigarette and lifted her head. She looked at him. He didn't exactly seem happy. He frowned, pondering where to start.

"I went to Tehran to visit a friend. He's been sick for a month. I thought if I wandered in the bazaar for a while, I'd find a nice gift for him. I was looking at some carpets when I saw Arbab Yousef with a very young woman coming out of a shop. I followed them until they reached a small house. Arbab Yousef opened the door with his own key and he and the woman entered the house together. As I was pondering whether to knock at the door or not, the woman from next door came towards me and asked if I was about to visit the residents of that house. I nodded. She handed me a bowl of soup and said it was for the new neighbours. I found out through her that Arbab had moved into that house with his wife three months ago."

The villager swallowed then carried on. "Of course, I was shocked but I tried not to show it. I took the bowl of soup from her and waited till she got back into her house. I put the bowl behind Arbab's door and disappeared as fast as I could."

The heavy, dark silence made the villager nervous. He sprung from his cushion, put his shoes on and excused himself. Pari hardly noticed his sudden disappearance.

Images, thoughts, emotions cut through her mind. At first she was hurt; betrayed. He didn't have the guts to tell her that he was about to take a third wife. He did it behind her back; without acknowledging her, without a grain of respect for all the years they'd been together. But then, she could hear her own voice mocking her: *He married you while he was already married to Noor. Did you really think he would change his way of life, his character, because you're so special? Are you that naïve? You failed him the same way Noor did. You can't bear him a child. He needs to plant roots before he leaves this earth. He needs to leave behind a sign of his existence, his manhood, his pride.*

Pari was thankful that Banoo and Ali kept quiet and didn't bother her with small talk about how everything was going to be fine. The afternoon gathering was over and everyone got back to their chores. Pari was certainly not looking forward to all the troubles this new situation was about to impose upon her. But she would not be beaten; she was going to sit it out and take whatever came without burdening herself with spurious plans.

Two days later Yousef came back from his trip to Tehran. After talking with Ali about the village affairs in his absence, he strolled towards the garden to see his wife. Pari was busy rearranging some of her geraniums.

"They look so healthy and beautiful," Yousef declared enthusiastically.

"Who is she?"

Yousef didn't hesitate. "She's the niece of one of my business associates."

"I hear she's quite young. How old is she?"

"She's sixteen."

"The younger the better, I guess. She'll last you for quite a while I expect."

"Her age was no matter of importance to me."

She dropped her trowel. "So, what was *the matter of importance* to you?"

"I'm not getting any younger and I still don't have any children. This business associate is the custodian of his niece. She was of marrying age. He knows me and is aware of my financial situation. He thought his niece would be safe with me."

"What a thoughtful man," she sneered. "He must have been quite desperate to marry her off."

Yousef took offence. She was making fun of him.

"She's six months pregnant," he said proudly. And he wanted to hurt her.

It felt like someone was crushing her heart so tightly it would surely stop beating.

Yousef suddenly sensed the gravity of his actions. He sensed her pain. He felt ashamed.

"Pari, I'm sorry. I didn't mean to hurt you."

She didn't reply. She carried on digging her little trowel into the soil. She tried to pretend she didn't care but inside she was dying.

"I'm going to the stable. I'll see you at lunchtime."

She was shivering. Her fury was going to cost two days of agonizing headaches.

But she was not going to hide away and play the victim.

Some days of silence followed; it gave them time to think. Two lives in two separate places was not for Yousef. He needed to re-establish himself in Varamin, his home. He didn't want to be a stranger; he enjoyed the respect, the comfort he was accorded in his village.

While Pari was smoking her last cigarette before going to bed, Yousef approached her. "I was thinking it would be a good idea if Pouran and the baby come and live here with us."

"So, Pouran is her name?"

"No need for sarcasm. Could we have a proper conversation?" He tried not to pick a fight. "You're my wife. I love you and despite what you think I do respect you. I don't want to squabble."

Pari put her cigarette out. "No squabbles. When will they be here?"

He was thankful that she had acquiesced. He felt guilt for keeping his second wife in the dark but it was his right to take another wife. He was only doing what any man in his position would do.

Pari had three whole months to get used to the idea of sharing her house with her husband's new wife and their new baby. Banoo and Ali declared their loyalty, but she made it clear that she wanted no trouble. There would be no recriminations, no bitterness.

Perhaps her penchant for accepting destiny had prepared her for such events? All through her life she had never complained and she wasn't about to start now. Her philosophy was straight and simple: *Something that has happened has happened. You can't turn the clock back. Just accept it and get on with it.*

It was November when Pari heard the news. Pouran had given birth to a baby girl; Yousef was beside himself with joy. He named her Aban, November, for the month of her birth. He came back from Tehran four days after the baby's arrival and announced that Pouran wouldn't be moving in for another month; she wanted to rest.

Pari thought she had made herself impervious to jealousy but looking now at the sheer delight in Yousef's eyes was breaking her heart.

The moment of meeting her husband's sixteen-year-old wife and his new baby arrived on a cloudy morning in mid-December. Pouran was petite with round hazel-green eyes and plump cheeks. She had thin, straggly hair but its healthy sheen trumped its sparsity. It was hard to evaluate her character from her appearance. An expressionless, teenage face almost matching the innocence radiating from the adorable baby in her arms made it hard to separate them into two individual beings. Innocence in the arms of an innocent.

Yousef left his two wives in the living room to give them time to get to know each other. He made sure Banoo joined them, just in case. There was an uncomfortable silence until Pari broke the ice. "Your room is ready whenever you feel like resting. One of the villagers made a crib for the baby as a welcome gesture. I hope you like it."

"Thank you. To be honest I would like to rest for a while after feeding Aban."

"Banoo will take you to your room and later on if you feel like it, she'll show you around."

Pouran took out her breast and put it in the baby's mouth. This was too awkward for Banoo. She knew the girl was oblivious but giving milk in front a childless first wife was just too much. She used the excuse of checking on the stew and escaped to the kitchen. Pari lit a cigarette and took up the conversation where she left off. "Do you have any brothers and sisters in Tehran?"

"Two brothers, both younger than me. My father died five years ago and my uncle has been our custodian ever since. I can't complain about him. He's been nice to my mother and us."

"Your mother must be missing you."

"She'll visit," Pouran said, solidly.

Pari sensed Pouran's seeming timidity was already fading. A nudge was all she needed to feel at home.

As the weeks passed Pouran showed no signs of homesickness. She seemed more relaxed every day. Pari's behaviour towards her was quite civil, although she refused to drop her guard. Already Pouran had proven that she was like any teenager; her tantrums were reason enough for Ali and Banoo to deny her the proper respect accorded a Zan-Arbab.

That winter turned out to be colder than usual, forcing the

household to spend more time in the living room around the korsi. Zeeba had placed an order for two high-quality woollen shawls to be knitted for Pari, and had asked a relative of hers to deliver them.

The arrival of Malak, the relative entrusted to deliver the shawls, was a surprise to Pari. She hadn't seen her since she divorced that awful husband of hers. Everyone thought she was wasted on him. And in that there was no wonder; Malak's smooth bone structure, and her long, black eyelashes that framed light-brown eyes juxtaposed to his raw, thorny features made them stand out incongruously; an odd couple. Of course, she had married for money but his miserly ways ensured she headed straight for the divorce court.

Pari ushered her and her six-year-old daughter, Sara, into the living room. Yousef was already settled in his usual spot at the korsi, enjoying warm tea and a plain cigarette. He straightened himself to welcome the woman. He had seen her before (in one of the lunches Pari's father had arranged), and didn't need to be introduced; she was too beautiful to easily slip one's mind.

She took the shawls out of her bag and handed them to Pari. They talked about the skill, the craft displayed in the shawls, the colours, the yarn, the length and breadth of the things until even the craftswoman herself might have thought the subject exhausted. The little girl's boredom overcame her bashfulness and she started a conversation with Yousef. The more she talked the more she felt excited and at home.

Maybe he was imagining things but Yousef could swear the woman was glancing at him; he was flattered.

As Pari was serving mixed nuts and citrus fruit, he cut in to chat to Malak. He didn't talk about anything in particular; it was an excuse to flirt. He had no idea what he was saying; he was simply entranced.

The little girl was becoming noisier and wilder, sneaking in and out under the korsi, playing with her imaginary friend.

"Can I join your game?" she begged Yousef, anxiously.

"What game, dear? Nobody's playing here."

"The game you and Maman are playing with your feet under the korsi."

Malak's face reddened. She pulled her daughter's arm and sat her down.

"Stop making up stories and stop bothering the gentleman."

"But, I'm bored. I want to play your game."

She shoved some pieces of orange in the child's mouth to shut her up. And to make sure her daughter got the message, she pinched her leg, sharply.

Pari looked at Yousef who pretended to be oblivious to this whole situation. She decided to go along with it. She didn't want to send their guest away with enmity. Pari had heard about her skills as a seductress and now she was getting a demonstration.

After that day, Pari chose to leave the subject dormant. Confronting Yousef would have only caused a messy quarrel and she wasn't up to it. The truth was that she wasn't up to it because she didn't care as much as she used to. She hadn't completely lost her affection for her husband, but she had lost the passion that might spawn jealousy. Pari didn't regret marrying Yousef; she only needed to look around to realize that she could have done much worse; there was no shortage of abusive, bad-tempered men. She didn't even have to look far. Her second cousin had married a handsome man, with prospects, but when the marriage went sour he refused to give her a divorce. He meant to keep her in a prison of a marriage for life. It was the same for many women. Always at the behest of their men; even when the husband became the enemy they had to curry favour to manufacture a painless escape.

Pari hadn't gone blind. She could see that Yousef wasn't a spiteful man. She knew he wasn't the type to go out of his way to hurt her. Even his latest bald move of marrying a sixteen-year-old wasn't planned to hurt her; his biological clock was ticking unstoppably. She knew that the respect and care he'd shown from the beginning of their marriage was still there. But despite being aware of all this, Pari was unable to rekindle her passion for Yousef; the same passion that drove a decent girl to run away with the love of her life.

Yousef's reasons for his third marriage seemed logical enough that while Pari had tasted the bitterness of betrayal, she would not choke upon it. But she would have been lying to herself if she had denied that a part of her heart, the young, hopeful girl within her, had died.

11

Pouran's daughter, Aban, was three months old already. She was growing week-by-week. Pari found her presence…agreeable. She wondered whether she was becoming accustomed to having her around, or was it more? When the baby smiled at her she wanted to scoop her up and cover her in kisses. But while she tried not to avoid baby Aban, she knew she had to remain, at least a little, aloof.

The biting chill in the air made it seem unlikely that Norouz and the first day of spring were only four weeks away. A living room with the family korsi at its warm epicentre was still a popular haven from a bitter February.

So many of the household crammed themselves around the korsi that the window had to be opened to let the cold air chase the stale air into the garden. Pari didn't like the draught and took her mortar and pestle to the kitchen to crush saffron.

Thirty minutes of making fine saffron powder was enough to invite the urge for a cigarette. She made for the living room to fetch her cigarettes, which she had left on the korsi. The room was empty now but for little Aban who was lying on a blanket laid on the carpet with the lower part of her tiny body exposed to the draught pushing its way through the gaping slit of the window.

Pari was furious.

She hurried to fetch the woollen shawl that Zeeba had sent and she wrapped Aban tightly. The baby's feet and her belly were like ice, but she wasn't crying. "She must feel numb," Pari said to herself, "that's why she's so quiet."

Pari cradled the baby in her arms and rubbed her legs to bring some warmth back. Aban laughed. Pari fondled and fluffed her hair and then she kissed her forehead. The baby clutched Pari's index finger and cooed. Pari was overwhelmed with the joy of it. As the baby's tiny feet kicked in the air, she could feel them kick in her womb.

It didn't matter that Aban wasn't delivered from her womb; she could still be a mother to her. And if anything, the baby would be much safer in her *experienced* hands than in the hands of a feckless teenager.

Pouran walked into the living room carrying a clean nappy.

"I went to get this but I got caught up in a stupid conversation with one of the girls who works in the kitchen," she said as she reached for Aban.

Pari snapped. "The baby was freezing. Lucky I walked in and wrapped her in this shawl."

"I hadn't planned to be long. Otherwise I would have covered her with something first."

"It doesn't matter how long you thought you were going to be. It doesn't change the fact that you don't leave a fragile baby exposed to this cold." Pari cradled Aban.

Pouran didn't like Pari's tone, and she certainly didn't have to put up with it, she was a Zan-Arbab too. "Who do you think you are? Talking to me like this? Yes, I can see you're a lot older than me…and you could be my mother, but you're not. And Aban is not your child. So, from now on, mind your own business."

Pari was twenty-five years old. Hard work and harsh weather had aged her, sure enough, but Pouran was trying to hurt her. Pari paid no notice. "No, she's not my child. But I'm not going to stand back and let you endanger her health."

"I left her here for *two minutes* to get a clean nappy."

"Look, there's no shame in making mistakes as long as you learn from them. But it seems that you argue against anything that makes sense just for the sake of it. I'm telling you this because with the way you're looking after this baby, she won't last till her first birthday."

"And this from a woman who's raised a house full of children of her own?"

Yousef interrupted before Pari got a chance to answer. He had heard enough in the corridor and he wasn't pleased. He wasn't pleased at all.

"That's enough, Pouran," he yelled.

"Why are you shouting at me? She started it."

"I'm shouting at you because apparently no one has taught you respect. Why don't you take Aban to the bedroom and change her nappy?"

Pouran was fuming. She pulled the baby from Pari's arms and stomped out.

"I'm sorry. She's just young."

"I never thought I would be so insulted in my own house."

"I never meant for this to happen. You know I care for you deeply."

"So you keep saying. But I still have to put up with her."

"I'll talk to her."

Pari lit a cigarette and looked the other way. She knew Yousef didn't like this any more than she did. She was sure he would keep his promise and have a serious chat with Pouran. But she also knew the days of trouble with Pouran were not over.

The thought of holding Aban in her arms calmed her. Pari was determined to take care of the child and watch out for her. This baby could be her only source of comfort in a world of compromise.

12

Pari wanted to be with Aban and Pouran was young; too young to raise a child. She couldn't help herself; more and more she left Aban with Pari while she did whatever it was that children with children do. Pouran was too headstrong to believe that Pari, Aban's stepmother, could take her place in Aban's affections.

Aban became accustomed to the woman she would never call 'Mother'. As time passed the bond between Pari and Aban strengthened. 'Auntie Pari', as she called her, had become a haven for Aban; she was a companion to share good times with and a shelter from trouble. There was nothing that Auntie Pari couldn't accomplish or fix; she'd whisper magic words to the corn grains and they would turn into popcorn. She made the most scrumptious pastries in the world. She had an endless list of stories to tell and if something unpleasant happened, Auntie Pari always knew best; she could soothe any pain, wash away any sadness.

Despite Pouran's jealousy, Aban sneaked most nights to Pari's bedroom to sleep next to her. Yousef didn't just tolerate this usurping of Pouran's motherly duties, he encouraged it; although he would never admit it, he believed Pari to be a better mother to his child than Pouran. The house was peaceful and that was enough for him.

Yousef's joy was indescribable when Pouran announced she was carrying his second child. This was all he ever wanted; a proper family in a house full of children. Children were proof of his manhood. Proof that he had lived; made a mark in the world.

Pari held no enmity towards the news of a second child. Any resentment she might have felt in the past had long been banished by the love of Aban.

A difficult pregnancy diluted Pouran's bitterness towards Pari and her daughter's relationship. At least Aban was safe and loved in Pari's care while Pouran could avail herself of any amount of time to relax and enjoy some peace before the baby arrived.

Pouran may have been harbouring a lessening of distaste for her *havoo*, wife of her husband, but Pari was more concerned with a listlessness that seemed to have assailed Aban and as her mother's pregnancy progressed she became weaker. She wouldn't eat. She lay around all day when she should have been charging about the house, laughing and playing like any normal three-year-old. She slept in the daytime; something she hadn't done since she was a baby.

"Aban hasn't felt well for the past two weeks. She's nauseous and won't eat," Pari said to Yousef as she was preparing a snack in hopes that Aban might eat something.

"Most probably it's just the summer heat."

"I hope you're right. Ali's going to Tehran the day after tomorrow. Aban and I will go with him to visit a doctor, just to be on the safe side."

The next day Aban was burning with fever, her face and eyes a sickening yellowish pallor. Pari recognized jaundice. She rushed to the kitchen to fill a bucket with cool water, then she took Aban's tiny feet and plunged them into it. She soaked a thin cloth and dabbed her cheeks. There was nothing else she could do. She felt helpless.

That same morning, Ali took it upon himself to bring a doctor from Tehran. By the time they got back to the village it was early afternoon. The doctor verified Pari's diagnosis, but there was no medicine to cure jaundice. He recommended the prevalent treatment of the day: Aban was to swallow whole a special type of tiny raw fish.

Pari's concern for Aban had overcome the fatigue caused by long vigils at her bedside. It broke her heart to see the child's delicate little body possessed by this demon of a disease, shivering while sweating, and so pale; as if life itself was deserting her. She was fading away right in front of her eyes. Pari had heard of children who had perished from this illness and the thought of losing Aban was almost too much to bear.

Twelve days passed with no sign of improvement. Twelve days without proper nourishment, the illness eating into her; it was too much, the kitchen servants could be heard weeping; they had given up hope. But Pari would have none of it; she was hanging onto Aban as if the little girl were the last branch of a broken tree Pari had latched onto in a flood. There was no room for surrender. Pouran spent most of the time in tears. The pain was almost too much for her.

Pari prayed to God every day that Aban might live. On the twelfth night, she stayed at Aban's bedside till dawn, citing every special prayer she knew. She implored the spirit of the Prophet and his disciples to deliver her desperate demand to the Almighty. She begged God not to take her Aban, her hope, away from her.

At sunrise exhaustion got the better of Pari and she fell asleep; then she dreamt. She saw a female stranger entering the room. A shiver ran down Pari's spine, but there was no foreboding, no sense of evil; it was a power, a pure power that seemed to burn through Pari's body like the morning sun after a cold night. When the woman moved towards her, she was mesmerized.

"I've come to let you know that your prayers have been answered. There is relief," the woman said with a voice like music.

Pari couldn't move but she could feel the tension leaving her body. She opened her eyes and looked around to make sure of her whereabouts. She held the back of her hand to Aban's forehead. The fever was gone. And her face, it looked so peaceful and calm. The illness had been defeated and Pari knew that recovery was on its way. Her joy, her delicate flower, had survived. She was going to live.

Yousef's second child was born on a sunny day in July. He had become father to a baby boy, Hameed. The baby's resemblance to Pouran showed itself more and more every day. He had warm, hazel-green eyes; a frequent smile accentuated his plump pink cheeks, and a fluff of wispy hair stood shock-straight on top of his little head, giving him an aura of perpetual surprise.

Yousef couldn't help but be proud that he had fathered a son. As much as he loved his daughter, his son would carry his name forward through time.

Pari loved the boy from his first breath but her affection for Aban was deep and strong; nothing could compare with the bond they had forged between them. She was the true mother to neither but she felt the true mother of Aban.

Now that Pouran had borne a son she became less territorial of her daughter's affections, even to the extent that she appreciated Pari's willingness to spend more time with Aban. Perhaps this was the way it ought to be in a house with two wives and two children? Either way, it offered Pouran more time to be with the baby, more time to work at her place with Yousef, and more time for herself.

Strangely, fatherhood had an almost tranquillizing effect on Yousef. In some men that might have been a good thing but Yousef was never one to get overwrought about anything. He was becoming more languid every day. With a new child to rear, a household to feed and indeed a whole village to support most men in his position might have redoubled their efforts but Yousef's behaviour was heading in the opposite direction. Instead of supervising his workers or handling his financial affairs he was, more and more, retreating into the house, when he was home, as if he were the one who had carried the child to term and now needed time to recuperate; his manner was just so kind and welcoming that nobody had the heart to confront him. The major part of Yousef's time was spent with friends or doing business, although nobody ever found out what that business might be. His absences were frequent and lengthy, a state of affairs that seemed to suit both Pouran and Pari.

Ali was left to take care of things. Ali worked hard. He saw to every detail and the villagers afforded him the respect normally reserved for an Arbab but it was too much. He needed Yousef to help but didn't have the stature to tell him as much.

13

The following five years seemed to pass as one. Pari's life was not exactly the idyll that she had once imagined her future would be but the harvests were satisfactory; leaner than they might have been but sufficient to feed everyone and to fund the next planting, and there was still room for some small joys that offset her recurring headaches. Yousef treated her always with respect and the villagers looked up to her as their Zan-Arbab.

Pouran was happy for Pari to be a second mother to Aban. Pari taught the little girl to read and write; she had no desire to leave such an important task to the schoolteachers. She taught her the ways of the kitchen. Preparing meals was a time for fun as much as work.

Things were as good as God would have them. She had no room for complaint.

It was almost the end of May. The farm workers had sown wheat and barley some months before and everybody was anxiously waiting for the harvest. Ali was busy organizing the workers and arranging the preparations for the harvest. He hadn't even the time to appear at the lunch gathering. Mostly, hunger would finally drive him into the kitchen two or three hours after everybody else had eaten. He'd throw the food into himself so fast sometimes he'd half-choke on the great lumps that would stick in his gullet.

"Is this the food you've put aside for Ali?" Pari asked Banoo while pouring herself a glass of sherbet.

"Yes. I suspect he'll show up very soon. Poor thing has been running around like a headless chicken lately."

"He's got his Arbab to thank for that," Pari said sarcastically. "Banoo, there isn't enough meat in his stew. Make sure you add some."

Ali arrived with a sweaty face and two dark bags under his eyes. He took his felt hat off and wiped his forehead with his wrinkled handkerchief. While waiting for his food to be warmed up, he lit a cigarette and drank the sherbet that Pari put in front of him.

"We live in the same place and I hardly get to see you," Pari said with the intention of acknowledging Ali's efforts.

"Well, someone has to take care of the affairs. It's not like I've got much choice in the matter. God forbid if Arbab gives me a hand."

"Every year I speak to him about this and every year he plays deaf. I'll try to be of more assistance. I'll make time for it," Pari answered apologetically. "So, how do you think the harvest will fare?"

"I'm hoping for it to be as unharmed as possible, but I wouldn't hold my breath. The grain crops of the neighbouring village have been infested by Hessian flies. Unfortunately, we haven't been immune but I'm hoping that the blight isn't widespread and that we've enough time to salvage most of the crop. If the larvae are still moving we have a chance, but if they're deep..."

"Does Arbab Yousef know this?"

"I went to talk to him about it. I think he had gone to visit a friend."

"Take me to the field."

"No. Stay. We won't know for a few days. It may be fine."

Pari knew she had been neglecting her affairs. The pain and emptiness thrust upon her by Yousef had been soothed and filled by Aban. Now the world, her actual life, the life where she was responsible for a whole village, not simply surrogate mother to its second-youngest member, again was calling to her. She would enjoy what time she had left. She would free herself from worry for just a little longer.

Three days later Ali came looking for Pari. He found her in the living room braiding Aban's hair. The expression on his face was like death. "Zan-Arbab, I need you to come with me."

"What's wrong, Ali? You look too upset."

"Just come with me. I have to show you something."

They walked fast. Before she knew it they had reached the wheat fields. There was a hissing sound all around them. The crop field was a brownish-grey sea with waves moving slowly across it from one side to the other. An army of Hessian flies had confiscated the whole crop and there wasn't anything anyone could do to rescue even a single ear of wheat. Pari picked up a stem. There was no trace of life left in it; it was dried out and dark.

Her heart sank. The lump in her throat was choking her, but she didn't want to release it in front of Ali. All that sweat and hard work had disappeared in one day. Their main source of income had vanished right in front of their eyes. It was like watching a sinking ship.

Pari asked one of the stable boys to ride to the village twelve miles away and get Arbab Yousef. She was fuming. A drum started to pound in her head. Her blood pressure was sure to exact revenge before the day was done.

"He's always meandering about looking for fun. He's never there when you need him," Pari yelled.

Ali knew better than to open his mouth; in case he said the wrong thing. Her anger gave him a fright. *You could stab her with a long knife and you wouldn't see a drop of blood; it's congealed inside her,* he thought to himself.

Pari stormed back to the house and into the living room and lit a cigarette. Pouran was feeding her son.

"Are you okay? You look like you're ready to have a heart attack," Pouran murmured tactlessly.

Pari wasn't in the mood to have a civilized chat with Pouran. She was certain that at that moment any conversation with her would end up in a row, so she kept quiet and carried on smoking.

Yousef arrived around noon. He was uneasy. He knew that Pari would never send after him unless there was something serious involved.

"I got on my horse as soon as I heard you'd sent for me."

"The crop is gone. Hessian flies."

Yousef took his hat off and quietly sat next to the doorframe. He looked lost.

"Did you enjoy yourself today then? You and your friend have some nice opium? You reek of it."

Yousef gave her an angry look and rolled his eyes towards the window. He knew what was coming and was in no mood for it.

"I don't even know why you call yourself an Arbab. You're a guest

91

here. You come and go whenever you feel like it. God forbid if you show any responsibility for running this place."

Pari had a full armament of sarcasm to direct towards Yousef. Her fury had energized her.

"It's not the end of the world. I'm sure the next harvest will be fine," Pouran interrupted Pari with a smirk.

"You didn't know the difference between shit and shoe-polish when you arrived here. So keep quiet!"

Yousef jumped in. "That's enough! This row is over! I mean it." He took a deep breath, lit a hand-rolled cigarette and said to Pari, "I'll sort it out. I'll ask one of my friends for a loan. We can replenish the seeds for the next harvest with that loan. We've still got the income from the sheep business."

Pari sniffed, like she always did when she was irritated. The atmosphere was too heavy for her. She needed some fresh air with her cigarette. Banoo joined her in the garden, offered her a glass of cherry sherbet and said: "Zan-Arbab, why don't you go and visit Zeeba for a few days? Let things cool down. Take Aban with you. I'm sure she'd love a trip."

"Running away every time you have a problem isn't going to make it disappear."

"I know. It's just that you need a break from this place; from Pouran, from Arbab and from those Hessian flies."

"I have to go to my father. I have to ask him for money."

Pari's brother answered the door. He was happy to see her but her plight was written in her expression.

"You look troubled, little sister."

She looked at him and she wanted to hug him. She felt thrown back in time. It seemed a hundred years since she'd left. It was more than a fleeting remembrance of a past life. For a moment she turned into that young girl. How easy her life had been here. Perhaps the premature death of her beloved mother had blinded her to her blessings? But no, it was only a moment, and it passed when she remembered why she was here.

"I have come for help," she said.

Those were also her first words to her father.

She explained the situation. She did not speak of her husband, only of their plight.

"Divorce him. Be rid of him. He's not worth it." Her father said it with a wave of his hand, as if dislodging one of the Hessian flies he had just heard were destroying the crops of Pari's village.

"I won't." She looked to her brother. He sat motionless, head bowed.

"Come here and live with me and your brother and his wife. You'll live well. You're not old. Maybe we can find you a husband?" He rapped a cigarette packet on the back of his hand, put the packet to his lips and slid out a cigarette with his teeth. He struck a match and lit the cigarette deliberately, the way one lights a pipe or an expensive cigar.

"You have four villages and one son. Your daughter is entitled to one third of your fortune."

"I have a fortune now, do I?" He turned to his son. "I'm a rich man." He kept his back to Pari, as if he were really addressing his son. "Divorce him. You'll have your inheritance after I pass from this world."

"We need only enough to get us through the year. Give me that and you," she stretched her neck towards her brother, "can have the rest."

"Divorce him. We all knew it would come to this. If your mother were alive..."

"Thank God she's not alive to see her husband play games with his own flesh and blood. And to watch her precious firstborn son abandon his sister. The kindness I once saw in you I know now was only a reflection of my mother's kindness."

Her father put the cigarette in his mouth and pursed his lips until the end glowed red and long then he took a great draught of air.

"I can give you what you ask." The smoke billowed from him. He breathed in and out. Smoke streamed from his nose and from his mouth as he spoke. "But you will no longer be my daughter. I cannot condone..."

Pari stood up. Her brother winced.

"I am no longer your daughter no more or less than I ever was. All we have is the truth. And the truth is that I will never set foot in this house again. Nor will I ever speak of either of you with the fondness I have carried with me until this moment."

Pari left as she had arrived. Almost penniless. The thought that she might have returned there, left her village, the people, her life, to take solace in her father's house was absurd. But her inheritance had gone. She knew that her father, and her brother, would believe she had made a decision, but that decision had already been made by the both of them. Her father would have withheld the proper third of his estate from her but given enough for a single harvest, with conditions attached?

No. Any money from her father in this spirit would be tainted, it would bring more pain than relief.

On Pari's return she discovered Yousef had managed to find the money he had promised her. He had procured a loan.

Putting the anguish of losing the harvest to the Hessian flies behind them, they sunk the money, and all of their hopes, into the autumn sowing for harvesting in late spring. They would sell some sheep to get them through the winter.

The spring yield was bountiful. The harvest had offered some respite but one good year was not enough. Pari hadn't seen any major change in Yousef's lax attitude and it frightened her. She knew better than to sit back and imagine that everything would be fine in the future because they had survived a single year of hardship. She believed that in the journey of life when people keep on striving and pushing forward, forces of nature join hands to help them move on. But the opposite was also true; without effort there could be no unseen help. Pari feared that Yousef's children were not in for a comfortable or prosperous upbringing and her heart went out to them. She even felt sorry for Pouran; poor thing, she was the picture of naivety but she didn't deserve the future Yousef was sowing; she had her youth but what of her destiny?

The biting chill that started in early November was the dark harbinger of a harsh winter. Korsis were already set up and the odour of mothballs floated through the house from winter wardrobes prematurely unpacked. Women villagers had filled the ears of their children with horrifying stories about wolf attacks to keep them indoors. There was no doubt that a harsh winter brings more wolves.

Sardar, the head shepherd, and his helpers weren't back yet. They had taken the flock through the usual route as they did every year. Sardar was no spring chicken. He had done this job for years and knew how to plan their journey so that they could avoid the heavy snows.

"I hope Sardar is on his way back," Pari said as she puffed on a hubble-bubble.

"I wouldn't worry about it. It's still not time for the worst of the winter snows," Yousef replied.

"From your mouth to God's ear."

"It's not my fault that you're always wound up. This is the way you deal with the world. You always have to be worried, in order not to be worried."

"Oh well, I didn't know I was conversing with a philosopher! If only your acts were as swift as your wisdom!" Pari sniffed and carried on smoking.

Yousef cut the conversation short. Pari's sarcasm was getting old. Also, he was well-acquainted with her mannerisms. When there was sniffing about, he'd better make himself scarce.

In three days the village was covered by the first snow of that year. It had started in the early morning and there was no end to it. During the next two days, howling winds joined the heavy snow to make matters worse. The last time the village had seen such a severe and early winter was more than twenty-five years ago. No one could get in or out. They were prisoners of nature.

It wasn't a mystery to Pari (or anyone else for that matter) that a good number of their sheep must have perished. Only a miracle could have turned the gloomy verdict of nature.

Sardar and his helpers arrived, exhausted and frostbitten. Pari had never seen their head shepherd so sullen. He stood at the entrance of the living room without removing his shoes; a silent declaration that he didn't want to socialize. He took his hat off and rolled it nervously, to give himself a few moments to gain control over his emotions.

"I brought the ears of the dead."

He handed over a filthy sack to Yousef. "There are five hundred pairs of ears in that pouch."

"Which leaves only one hundred sheep alive?" Ali said in a panic.

"A few of them don't look so healthy," Sardar added. "We were caught off guard. I have never seen such a severe storm. I did all I could."

Pari felt sorry for him. He was so desperate to prove that this disaster wasn't his fault.

"Come in and warm yourself by the korsi. You look like a ghost."

"I'm sure you did all you could under the circumstances," Yousef said, looking straight at his face.

Their understanding made Sardar even more emotional and left him with two watery eyes. But he wasn't about to let it out (especially in front of a woman). He wiped his eyes swiftly and lit a cigarette.

14

There's a Persian expression which says, "when misery strikes, expect more". Pari could tell that their fortunes had turned for the worse. She was wise enough to know that sooner or later they would have to pay for laxity and lack of diligence. They had sown the seeds of misfortune and all the forces in nature seemed to be lending a hand against them.

Everyone in the household could see that a streak of bad luck had gripped the Arbabs. The Hessian flies that wrecked the crop and thrust them into debt, then the winter of the following year that had decimated the flocks hung heavy in their hearts and stirred fears for the future. With the approach of summer nerves were frayed and opinions as to why their fortunes had turned were rife. "She's a bad omen. Ever since Pouran walked into this house, everything that could go wrong went wrong. She's got a heavy step," Banoo said while throwing slices of carrot into the chicken soup boiling on the stove.

"I don't know if it's her heavy step, but we've certainly had a bad run recently," Pari replied.

"Trust me. I know about these things. Some women are just bad luck," Banoo added. "I knew of a woman when I was a young girl. She married four times. Every man she got married to died of illness or accident. She brought misery to every one of them. No wonder she had to spend her old age as a lonely soul. No man dared go near her."

"Well, if you're right, then I guess we have to expect more trouble," Pari said.

Banoo and Pari could hear footsteps approaching the kitchen. They could tell who it was from the way Ali had of shuffling his feet (when he wasn't in a rush). He saluted both women and took off his felt hat.

"I could smell the chicken soup. I thought I could have some before leaving for Tehran."

"Who are you going to visit over there?" Pari asked.

"One of Arbab's friends. I'm supposed to ask him for a loan."

"How come he's not doing it himself?"

"He's going to the village by the river to see another friend of his and ask him for a loan too."

Pari sighed. This nightmare was never-ending. *It's funny how you take everything for granted, how it never crosses your mind that your nice cosy world could change forever,* she thought to herself.

By the time the locusts came, it seemed almost inevitable, as if fear itself had conjured the great black, shifting cloud that blocked the sun and stole all of their fortunes in a single day. Pari saw them and prayed to God to let the wind carry them past the fields. But despite the efforts of Ali and the farm workers, the money they had borrowed to produce the harvest was lost inside the belly of a million insects. The hunger of nature had no mercy for anybody; poor or rich, decent or vulgar, desperate or thriving, everyone was equal in its brutal eyes.

"Listen to the little bastards munching on the harvest," Pari said, caught in a trance.

"It makes you feel so despondent. It's like watching your family being slaughtered by a bunch of thugs. There's nothing you can do to stop them," Ali said through clenched teeth.

"We've taken too many blows one after the other. I doubt if we can handle any more." Pari's fear turned to panic. She looked to Yousef but his expression needed no words.

"We can't handle any more. I've got debts to pay and no one will lend me any more money," Yousef said.

"Are you saying what I think you're saying?"

"I have to sell the village."

"Maybe there are still people who would give you a loan?" Pari's voice trembled. "What about Volla? Hedayat Volla? You lent him money."

"He paid me already. Do you think I would give up if I thought I could soften a friend for a loan?"

"Friend?" Pari felt like she might explode. A hundred thoughts, a thousand emotions chased each other inside her. Everything she had worked for, everything she had fought for, was gone.

Ali looked pale. He was already dreading the difficulties of getting to know a new Arbab; the pain of adapting to every whim, every mood. Just as he had begun to imagine a quiet, peaceful retirement for himself next to people he could easily call "family". The hand of destiny had shredded the texture of his dreams. He had experienced the bitter taste of desperation in his life before. He had experienced the crushing weight of helplessness, the misery of having no control over his life, of living at the mercy of the emotions of other people when his brother lost their land and, God knows, that wasn't what he had in mind for his old age. He was aware that after the departure of Yousef and his family he would be back to square one in the village. Land was all he had known ever since his childhood, but he had no incentive left in him to start a new dance to a new tune at this point in his life. The only way out was to take his meagre savings to Tehran and invest them in his cousin's grocery shop. He could stay at his cousin's house. Who knows? Maybe his cousin's wife could find a nice, obedient woman for him and he wouldn't even have to spend his old age as lonely as an owl?

On his way to the stable, Ali took a turn to the left and followed the narrow path towards the nearby stream. He was feeling sorry for himself. *How many blows do you have to take in a lifetime?* He remembered the first time he laid eyes on the woman of his dreams. He was delivering a message from his father to one of his friends and as he was passing by the pond, the most beautiful face in the world captured his eyes. She had just washed some herbs and was about to put them in a sieve when she noticed the stranger staring at her. Ali was mesmerized. She was stunning. On his way back all he could think of was asking his parents to arrange for a khastegari, a meeting between the two families, in which they would ask for her hand in marriage to their son.

That she accepted him and they married was beyond his wildest dreams.

How could he forget his golden years with Gohar? The excitement they both felt when she told him she was pregnant. Their little daughter; so pretty like a doll with a smile to open the gates of heaven. His adorable girl was the talk of the whole village.

That was it, wasn't it? he thought to himself. *They coveted my family, my happiness. No sir, I wasn't allowed to have it all so young. It wasn't fair to those who had suffered painful loss in their lives. They had to talk about my good luck with bitterness on and on and on...until they got what they wished for.*

The stream of tears lost its way in Ali's beard. *There's no torment as harsh as outliving your child.* The excruciating memory of holding his daughter's limp body drove a knife into his stomach. *Why did we have to take a day trip to those mountains? Why did I let her near the river?*

For years after, Ali would catch himself extending his arms to grab his daughter; reliving the day of her death. Gohar didn't have the mental strength Ali possessed. Her spirit was broken. She sank more and more every day into an abyss of sorrow. Gohar had turned into a bag of bones, with no will or hope to carry on, and she finally gave in.

On the tenth day of her illness, Ali woke up next to the cold body of his sweetheart. He wailed like a beaten dog, pounded his fists on his thighs as hard as he could, put his head on her chest and begged her in desperation to come back and not to leave him alone in this world.

How he survived the agonizing loss of the two most important beings in his life was still a mystery to him.

But he did carry on. He took their memories everywhere he went and savoured each minute of those memories every time he felt gloomy and needed to be consoled. All throughout his youth and his middle age, Ali had failed to restore peace in his soul. As hard as loneliness squeezed him, he couldn't bring himself to replace Gohar with another wife. He still went to bed with Gohar every night and woke up next to her face every morning.

After years of wandering, settling at Yousef's village and being accepted as a part of the family had smoothed the harsh edges of his soul. Ali had begun to let himself go, to look for entertainment and fun, to feel high-spirited; he had begun to want another woman, someone to love, again.

Life carries on the way it always has and I will move on with it; the way I always have, Ali said to himself.

15

Selling his lands was like selling his children. It was tearing Yousef to pieces. It was too late to blame himself for being a careless guardian; useless to brood over a list of "should haves" and "shouldn't haves" and he was too hopeless to redeem a lost cause.

He had let something so close, so precious, slip through his fingers: the land of his fathers. He knew its texture, its being, its smell, the way a mother's senses are filled with the smell of her newborn baby.

And to Pari losing the village was losing everything. Stripped of her status as a Zan-Arbab she would be forced to live in suffocating accommodations with Pouran's tantrums, and with her husband a constant reminder of her ruin.

The village and its conditions were attractive enough for people with means to revive it and turn it back into a lucrative business. The problem was that they had a good notion of Yousef's desperation and hence a great opportunity for a markdown. Much as Yousef wanted to fight back and get a fair deal, he was a beggar and in no position to choose. He held out for a better price for some months but his predicament was no secret; the buyers simply waited and offered even less in the end.

"The money will change hands next Tuesday. The papers are supposed to be ready by then," Yousef said listlessly to Ali.

"I'll stay till Sunday, in case you need any help around here. I've already given my cousin some money for a share in his grocery shop. He's quite happy about me getting involved in his business. It takes some of the workload off his shoulders. For all these years he's been in business, he never trusted anyone to be his partner and that's why he's been working like a mule. Running the store three days a week will give me something to do as well. Not too busy to break my back, not too idle to feel jaded. And I'm taking Banoo."

"You are a good man, Ali. What about Sardar?"

"Sardar will stay. The new owners will need a head shepherd. And where would his precious camel get its opium in Tehran?"

Yousef raised a smile, but his mind was wandering somewhere else; he had a lot to worry about. Yousef had large debts to clear, after which he would be left with just enough to manage a frugal life for him and his family in Tehran.

"I guess the positive side of living in Tehran will be my children's education. They can easily go to school until they get their diploma. Here, they would have only been kept on for five years," Yousef said, latching onto any excuse to make this move a more bearable event. He offered an Oshno cigarette to Ali. They puffed their dreams and thoughts up into the air in search of consolation.

"Pari hasn't talked to me ever since I made the deal. That's not her style, as you've noticed. I have a really bad feeling about it. It's the calm before the storm. The usual Pari would have eaten my brain by now with a list of amendments to the deal, but she hasn't made a peep."

"She knows there's no point arguing over spilt water. What do you expect? She built her whole life around this village and now it's gone. But the Zan-Arbab I've known for all these years is as strong and solid as steel. She'll get through this pain. She'll carry on. I have to admit I'm proud to have known a woman like her," Ali said.

"I'm sending my wives and children to Tehran in two days. I'll move some of the furniture then. I'd appreciate it if you could help with the moving."

"No need to worry, Arbab. I'm on top of it. I'll make sure they won't have any problems."

Ali was planning to make the moving day as painless as possible for the family. He knew from experience that the way to keep any commotion to a minimum was to consult Pari and find out how she would like to arrange for the move. As far as he was concerned, she was still the Zan-Arbab and in charge of any planning. Pouran and the children were obedient soldiers who would tag along. He sought out Pari in the living room.

Pari had just finished her afternoon prayer and was about to light a cigarette.

"Oh, just in time for a smoke!" Pari said, offering him an Oshno cigarette. Ali had just finished one but he didn't rebuff her offer; smoking with her might smooth the edges a little.

"Arbab asked me to help out with the move. He's thinking of moving you all out in two days."

Ali waited a few seconds. No answer; no sign of interest. She carried on with her cigarette.

Ali pressed on. "I thought I should discuss it with you and go about it the way you prefer it to be done. In my opinion, if we send the furniture tomorrow, it would make it easier for you to move the day after. I'll ask one of the villagers to stay there and arrange the furniture before you arrive."

She inhaled deeply, looked at Ali listlessly and said, "Do whatever you want to do. It doesn't make any difference to me."

"Of course it does, Zan-Arbab. God forbid, if anything gets done 'the wrong way', you'll go into a bad mood and stay there for the good part of the day," Ali said, in a light tone.

"Well, I can assure you that no one would hear me lambaste you or anybody else for that matter. I'm not moving to the Arbab's house."

"What do you mean? Where're you going to go? I knew something was wrong. God knows I've had my share of disaster, so please don't take it as condescending when I say this shall pass. You're a strong woman, Zan-Arbab. I've always admired you for your powerful will. You can do anything when you put your heart into it."

"I don't think it's worth putting my heart into this. I don't see any place in this family for me. Not any more."

"Think about Aban. Can you imagine how heartbroken she'll be when she finds out that her beloved Auntie Pari is leaving her? Can you bear the guilt?"

An emotion flashed across her face, too fleeting for Ali to divine what it might be, but enough that he could at least see she was still in there somewhere. Maybe her stoicism was an act?

"The only reason I didn't leave three weeks ago was Aban." She crushed her cigarette butt into an ashtray. "I would be no good to her anyway."

"Where will you go?"

"I will live with my cousin Zeeba in Tehran. It's already arranged."

"How can that be better than living with your husband?"

She raised an eyebrow. He saw he wouldn't get far on this tack. "Aban?"

She softened, just a little, then her expression froze again. "It's my choice."

Images of the night before flooded into her mind. Her choice? To leave her beloved Aban? To know that Aban would believe Pari had abandoned her? This was a choice? Pari had not the strength to say goodbye to the girl. She had crept into Aban's room and whispered goodbyes to the sleeping child. It was as if the very breath was being sucked from her lungs. Pari did not know what was best for Aban. All she knew was that she could not hold a tearful child in her arms and explain why she had to leave. The pain would be too great. She really was abandoning Aban. This was the truth. She told herself that Aban's time with her would help to form her. The good times would become a part of her character as the memories faded. But the truth was she had not the strength to listen to the child call her name after her. That would surely break her.

Ali had known her for years. He had never seen her like this: beaten, lost. He felt for her but he couldn't hide his disappointment.

Pari could see it. She could see he wanted more from her. He wanted her to be the Zan-Arbab, to rise above her troubles. But it was too late. She'd had enough. She didn't have the strength left to satisfy Ali's vision of who she should be.

"I can't change your mind."

"That's right," she said, more to herself than to Ali. "He let me down. He let me down. He brought an adolescent girl he had married in secret into my house. I thought that was the worst humiliation he could have caused me. How could I know he would outdo himself? That was just the start. A prelude to poverty and homelessness. He's responsible for this disaster. And I'm responsible for entrusting my welfare to him. Zeeba is a difficult woman but she shows her heart where it matters. When she remarried she took in her husband's sister, Foti. Zeeba and I share pleasant childhood memories together. I'm not expecting a red carpet. She needs an extra pair of hands. There's nothing left for me and him."

"Have you told Arbab?"

"I will."

On a brisk November morning, after performing prayer, Pari closed her small suitcase and put her woollen scarf on. She went out to have a last look at her garden, glistening under a thin sheet of frost. The frozen morning dew embellished the leaves of her roses like tiny diamonds. She wondered if the new Arbab would keep the garden the way it looked. The first sun bade the birds chirp and filled her with remembrances of the morning when she snuck out of her parents' house to marry Yousef. And here she was; all packed, ready to leave the man she had eloped with sixteen years ago. This time the future didn't look so promising. All she could see was darkness ahead of her.

The footprints she made on the pathway were Pari's last trace in that village.

PART
2

16

Zeeba's house wasn't anything to write home about (after all, she was a teacher and her husband an office clerk) but it was in a good area. Seven minutes walk to the shops, it was a housewife's dream. Zeeba had put the down payment on the four-bedroom house from her share of the sale of her mother Shamsi's house, and with a small inheritance bequeathed to her when her beloved brother Mehdi passed away prematurely. She had assumed two-thirds of the monthly payments, leaving the rest to her husband, Rahim, to fund. Squeezing four bedrooms, two public rooms, a bathroom and a kitchen into such a small plot of land meant too many narrow flights of stairs joining three skinny floors together.

Rahim, her second cousin and junior by six years, was the most suitable man Zeeba could have imagined as a husband. He was quite upbeat and sociable, had a good sense of humour and somehow always managed to cope with her mood swings. A quality she did not ignore was that his easy manner enabled him to mix in circles above his social station. For reasons only God knew, Rahim was infatuated with her and did everything in his power to please her.

A thick moustache made Rahim look a bit older than his age. His eyes didn't betray any signs of genuine intelligence, though he had made up for this shortcoming by cultivating his manner into an affability that drew people to him. Meticulousness about his appearance and an undeniable fatherly fondness for Malous, his adopted daughter, completed his virtues: Rahim's only liability was his older sister, Foti.

Ever since they had lost their parents, Rahim had become responsible for her and with her "tough luck in the marriage department" (as he always described it), it seemed that his custodial duty was going to be a life-long activity. Foti didn't like the situation any better than her brother did. She wanted a house and a husband and children of her own. She wanted to be the mistress of her own turf and instead she had to put up with the whims of her sister-in-law.

It wasn't easy to endure the fluctuations in Zeeba's moods. Her selfishness and curt manner were guaranteed to invoke resentment, and on top of everything Zeeba made sure that everyone knew who the primary owner of the abode was.

Foti's only consolation was her room; the thirteen-by-ten-foot haven she didn't have to share with a soul. It was a place to cool her blood, to hide her secrets and somewhere to give her a sense of ownership. Besides, her window caught the view of the neighbour's magnolia tree, a relaxing sight to wake up to, while the flowers lasted.

Every morning Foti would wake up at 6:30 sharp, confused and listless for five or six minutes until she gathered the energy and concentration to drag herself up seven steep, narrow stairs to the bathroom. There was no morning prayer on the menu for her; she didn't have much faith in the God who had left her an orphan and at the beck and call of other people. And she'd noticed that the same God hadn't shown much mercy in finding her a husband now that she was past marriageable age.

A few splashes of water and the fear of being late to prepare the breakfast were enough to wake her up completely. With her hair trained and rolled up on her head she negotiated her way down twenty-one sheer steps to get to the kitchen and put the kettle on.

After Zeeba and Rahim left for work and Malous for high school, she would arrange for daily shopping and lunch preparations so efficiently that not even one minute of her cosy afternoon nap would go amiss.

Foti also assisted Zeeba in her small business. Zeeba had made a name for herself among friends and relatives with her knack for designing clothes and her ability to sew them into perfection. She truly was an artist when it came to clothes. Her best advertisement was the dresses she made for herself, the best cut clothes any woman could wish for made from bargain-basement fabrics; the cut hid the lack of quality. Her expertise of finding a way to "hem" extra fat around the bottom and belly in a woman's dress had won her the title "miracle worker".

Foti didn't mind working for Zeeba for free. She had come to learn a lot from her. She knew no matter how much and for how long she struggled, her work wouldn't come near the sublimity of Zeeba's. But she didn't care. It was the only skill Foti possessed. She could brag about it to make her feel valuable. Besides, every now and then her sister-in-law would sew her a dress to compensate for her assistance in the business.

The appetizing smell of aubergine stew wafting from the kitchen window filled the air in the alley. It was Pari's assurance that Foti was home. She opened the wooden door after the second knock. No frantic emotions, no exuberance; Foti gave a pale smile and ushered Pari to the kitchen.

"Zeeba told me you'd be coming today. I was hoping you'd arrived when I got back from grocery shopping," Foti said, calmly. "Shall I make you a cherry sherbet or you're happier with a cup of tea?"

"I'll take a cup of tea, if you don't mind," Pari said, lighting an Oshno cigarette.

Foti peeped from the corner of her eye and said, "Oh! You're still smoking."

"I know. It's a bad habit. But it's a habit that I've carried for years. Hard to get rid of," Pari replied with no sign of offence in her voice.

She took a sip from her cup and watched Foti soak the rice. *This is it,* she thought. *From now on, this is my home…no…better not to jump the gun…not home…this is the place where I'll live. I should make the best of it. There's no going back.*

"Lunch will be ready in an hour and a half. We don't have to wait for them. We can go ahead and eat ours," Foti said, wiping her mouth after testing the stew.

"That would be nice. I'm quite hungry."

"Let me show you your room. You'll be sharing with Malous. Zeeba uses the fourth room for her business. Malous has no problems sharing her room with you."

After climbing the fourteen steps to the second floor, Foti pointed to the door on the right. "That's Malous's room. The other one is mine. Why don't you go in and take a rest, I'll call you when lunch is ready."

The thick beige curtains were half-open to let air in through a small window. The other window facing the alley was shut with the help of a wire running through the handle. Obviously, the lock was broken but with the room located on the second floor there wasn't much fear of a stranger sneaking in from the alley.

Pari drew the curtains to the end of the rail to let more light in. There was a single bed right up against the wall and a dressing table on the opposite side. A wardrobe at the other end of the room faced the bed with a wooden chair placed next to it. The old bookshelf seemed ready to collapse any minute from the thick, weighty books pressing upon it. One of the books had the same picture of a heavy-bearded man as a poster on the wall. On the cover it said, Karl Marx. *That must be his name,* Pari thought. There was another poster of a man with a thick moustache in an army uniform. Pari recognized his face. She had seen him in the newspapers Ali had once or twice brought back with him from Tehran. He was Stalin, the ruler of Russia.

Why a young girl would want pictures of these two on her wall was beyond her. If Malous wanted to put up pictures of old men, she may as well have hung one of her grandfather.

Clothes thrown on the wooden chair and the bed, the mess on the dressing table, told Pari that Malous wasn't bothered about tidiness. *No surprise, anyone with so many books has definitely got no time to keep her room straight.* She opened Malous's wardrobe, found a few hangers and put the clothes away.

She took a magazine from the bookshelf, lay on the floor with her scarf scrunched up under her head and started browsing. The magazine was called *Kargar*, Labourer. On the third page there was a picture of four men and two women in scruffy clothes, two of them wearing woolly hats, all looking serious. In the description below the photo, it was explained that they were members of a labour union in a factory eighteen miles from Tehran demanding an immediate strike. Pari skipped through the rest of the magazine. There wasn't anything in it to compete with the heavy weight of her eyelids. She dozed off.

She was running along a dirty street. A crowd of people, furious, waving their fists behind her. In front of her the two men from the posters blocked her way. She looked back and forth in hope of finding a way out.

"Pari…Pari…Lunch is ready. Let's eat, then you can have a long relaxing sleep," came Foti's voice, loud enough to pierce her dream.

A glass of cold water was what she needed to bring her back to reality. She sat at the table and ate some fresh herbs: basil, chives, mint and tarragon to kill the bitterness in her mouth. Foti looked preoccupied pouring the stew over the fluffy white rice. She was diligently counting every meat cube in the pot, keeping track of how many were allowed for whom. She had a strange, and unappetizing, method of counting the cubes: turning each one in her fingers, licking the fingers after the count was done and dipping the same fingers inside the pot for a new count.

Pari chewed on more herbs and stared regretfully at the plate of food in front of her. *I wish she had put my food on the table before she came to get me, that way I wouldn't have faced this disgusting scene.*

"You'd better get started, your food's getting cold," Foti said.

Pari smiled, nodded and chewed some more herbs to hide the commotion in her head. *Don't be squeamish. Pretend it never happened. Surely, they'll expect me to cook every day? That'll solve the problem. Go on!*

The cigarette she lit after lunch helped get her mind off the food and the forthcoming indigestion.

The voices of two women broke through the window. Pari woke up. She recognized Zeeba's voice. The other was too screechy for human tolerance. She looked at the clock on Malous's dressing table. It was ten to five. *Surely the rest of them will be back soon too?*

She craved a cigarette. The nicotine would give her some energy. Zeeba was still chattering to the woman from across the alley. From the window, Pari could see that her thick, wavy hair was short and meticulous. *She's put some beef on but it suits her.* The red lipstick added a pleasant glow to her face. Altogether, she looked fine. *Life must have treated her well.* Pari watched her walk towards the main door.

"Hasn't she arrived yet?" Zeeba asked Foti.

"She was here before lunchtime. She's taking a nap. Her tiredness got the better of her."

With the kitchen door wide open Pari could hear their conversation as she walked down the stairs. "Hello, Zeeba, it's nice to see you again. It's been quite a while."

Zeeba seemed pleasantly surprised. She extended her arms, gave Pari a hug and a kiss and said: "I thought you were asleep. It's nice to see you too. Why don't you pour a cup of tea for us while I get changed?"

Foti fetched some dry pastries from the living room and offered them to Pari. They were stale. She lit a cigarette to kill the taste.

"That's too strong for me. I'll have my tea mixed with more water if you don't mind," Zeeba said as she entered the kitchen. "Foti, it's a good idea to take Pari grocery shopping tomorrow so that she gets to know the neighbourhood."

Pari put Zeeba's diluted tea in front of her. "Thanks. Have a pastry with your tea."

"I had one. That will do."

"I was thinking if you took over cooking and shopping, Foti would have more time to help me out with the piles of sewing I've laid in that room. One of them is driving me mad. It's a dress for the daughter of a friend. She's completely misshaped; small shoulders and a gigantic arse. The fabric cost a fortune. She's going to wear it to a wedding. I think her mother takes her to every single wedding in the city. She thinks that's a good way to show her around and find her a husband."

"She'd have a better chance of finding a husband if she washed her armpits more often," Foti said in a voice laced with hate. "Sometimes I have to leave the room when she tries on the clothes she's ordered."

The slam of the main door interrupted Foti's complaints. "Malous, is that you?" she shouted.

A clean-cut girl appeared at the kitchen door.

"You're home early. Either the cinemas are closed or you've run out of friends to go to the movies with," Foti said with a hint of sarcasm.

Malous walked enthusiastically towards Pari. She hugged her.

"It's been so long since I've seen you. My God, you're a grown woman," Pari said with pride. She couldn't keep her eyes off her as she poured a glass of water for herself. "I can't get over how much she's changed."

Malous's spotless white shirt contrasted with her sultry complexion. The perfect cut on her skirt (accomplished by Zeeba's expertise) flaunted her tiny waist and small, round bottom. Brown eyes embellished her velvety smooth skin and her long black hair draping and curling on her shoulders flattered her firm bosoms. Diligent deportment kept her back and shoulders straight, adding grace to beauty. Only her front teeth protruding behind sensuous lips denied her the label *beautiful*.

"Rahim might still be a while. We'd better eat," Zeeba said to her daughter.

"I don't feel hungry. You go ahead and have your dinner without me." Malous put a few fresh herbs into her mouth and said to Pari: "Have you already moved your stuff to my room?"

"Yes. I don't have much. Just one suitcase."

"Did you bring any pillows and blankets from the storage room for yourself?"

"No. I guess we could take care of that now."

Pari placed three blankets and two pillows near Malous's wardrobe. "So, is watching films a hobby of yours?"

"I don't know if you can call it a hobby. It's a good way to get me out of the house. Sometimes it gets a bit frantic in here. You'll see it for yourself before long."

"Shouldn't you have a picture of your father or your uncle instead of these hairy men on your wall? I mean *who* is that man? What has he ever done for you?"

"He's Karl Marx and he's done plenty for people all around the world with his brilliant ideas. What has my father ever done for me? I'm lucky if I see him once a year around Norouz. Last year he gave me a golden coin as my Norouz present. I was so happy. I showed it to Zeeba to let her know that she's wrong and my dad cares about me. She had a look at it, threw it on the table and told me it wasn't gold. I didn't believe her so she bent the coin and gave it back to me. He gave his sixteen-year-old daughter a fake coin."

"I don't think I could ever be comfortable with the fact that you

115

call your mother by her first name."

"It's what she wants. It's what she's taught me ever since I started talking. I'd rather call her 'Maman'."

"Do you see your half-sisters much?"

"Not really. I don't think they're that keen to hang around with me. Besides, their mother is loud and scary enough to put anybody off. I don't know how my father has lived with her all these years."

"I forgot to ask Zeeba if she'd heard from Auntie Goli. I've been out of touch, having to deal with all the problems back in Varamin."

"Zeeba mentioned a few months ago that Auntie Goli had a marriage proposal she couldn't refuse." Malous tried her memory. "Said he's a well-off man from the Caspian sea area. She's settled now in Lahijan." Then she added, "It doesn't surprise me. Who wouldn't want to live with someone like Auntie Goli. They say her cheerfulness is contagious."

"Good for her." Pari lit a cigarette and watched Malous tidy her dressing table.

Malous opened the wardrobe. "I emptied a space for you here."

"I noticed that box."

"It's an accordion. I picked it up two years ago. I take lessons once a week from an Armenian teacher, Madam Yacobian. I'm not that good at it."

"I bet you're saying that because you're embarrassed to play in front of me now."

Malous put a shy smile on her face and said, "No, I don't feel like playing now."

There was a kind of innocence and warmth in this teenager that drew Pari to her. She could see a close relationship developing.

Pari was the only one in the household who woke up at dawn to perform the morning prayer. Malous was fast asleep, lying on her belly with a book wide open next to her pillow. It was a thick book and she had read three-quarters of it already. She turned off the reading lamp next to Malous's bed and left the room to pump in some nicotine before the prayer. Pari wasn't in the habit of going back to bed after performing her religious duties. So, she put the kettle on and waited for her atheist relatives to wake up.

"It's a nice change to walk into the kitchen and see the breakfast ready on the table," Foti said. "Maybe you can buy some fresh bread tomorrow, seeing as you're up so early in the morning. I'll show you the way to the bakery today." Pari could tell that from now on she would have to take a long walk down the *Yes, sir* path. After all, she wasn't there to spend her holidays. She was there because she had lost her home, her wealth and her authority. Her impotent position and decrepit mental state didn't leave her much room for backchat. Foti wasn't a bit shy introducing Pari as the delegated shopper from Zeeba's household to the traders in the neighbourhood. She made sure they all understood that from that day on Pari was to get the same offers and bargains as Foti. She coached Pari in how it wasn't necessary to buy the vegetables fresh; she should wait a day or two so that they would be cheaper than the set price. During their fifteen-minute walk to show Pari the location of the cheapest poultry in the area, Foti explained to her how the neighbourhood drug store occasionally gave Zeeba medicine without prescription. "All you have to do is tell the pharmacist that you're buying stuff for Haady's sister. This is his way of reciprocating Haady's legal advice. Recently he had a problem with one of his tenants. Haady helped him with legal evacuation."

This was all new to Pari. She had always eaten fresh meat and vegetables. And as authoritative or dominant as her behaviour had been all her life, Pari had never possessed the audacity to ask people to do her an illegal favour; she would have been too embarrassed. *I'd better adapt to this lifestyle and learn it fast. This is not going to go away.*

On the way back Foti felt free to make use of Pari's physical strength for carrying the daily purchases.

As the day unfolded Pari got to find out about other chores that were expected of her: cooking, dish-washing and doing the laundry. Foti had become more embroiled in helping Zeeba with her sewing business, though she would still keep her task of cleaning the house.

Sixteen days passed and Pari's supply of cigarettes shrunk substantially. She was a hostage to her nicotine and as proud as she was, she had to succumb to her need. She had noticed that every time she was sent to buy something Zeeba never left the change with her. *It could be she's so used to seeing me smoke all the time that she doesn't notice my cigarettes anymore and it has escaped her attention that I need money to buy more?*

Next time Pari brought some change back she took a chance with her cousin. "I thought I'd keep the change for cigarettes."

"Cigarettes are a waste of money. I don't have extra cash to pay for blowing smoke in the air."

It was a slap in the face. She had never felt this humiliated. A fury stormed in her head. *Who the hell do you think you are? You cheap, mean, cold fish. How many times did you come to my home and I entertained you? How many times did I send loads of summer fruit to your doorstep? Now you're rubbing your stinking change into my face?* Her blood pressure fluctuated like a mad roller-coaster, she was so exasperated she wanted to cry. She knew that if she let one word out she wouldn't be able to rein in a flood of curses waiting to burst forth. Instead, she sat quietly, pursed her lips and sniffed a few times to vent her anger.

Zeeba saw it but she didn't give Pari's anger a second thought. As far as she was concerned she hadn't done or said anything wrong. Spending money on smoking was a complete waste of cash and anyone who was content with squandering money like that should have her head examined.

The next day Pari got lucky with replenishing her supply. It was almost mid-afternoon when someone rang the bell. Foti was taking her nap and that left Pari to open the door.

"Well, that's a surprise. So finally you remembered that I exist?" Pari said with a cold tone.

"Sorry, I know I should have come to visit sooner but I had a lot of things to handle. I'm here now. It's better late than never," Yousef said timidly.

"So, how is everybody? How is Aban coping with the new place?"

"She's managing. It's not like she can run about the field all day playing with horses and dogs and chickens but she's making friends with the kids in the alley. I enrolled her at the nearby school. She's got a few months to get used to the idea of having to go to a new school. She's always talking about you. She misses you so much."

"I miss her too. Tell her I think of her."

"You know you're always welcome to visit, to spend time with Aban."

"It's for the best. She already has one mother. I'm not someone she can depend on."

Yousef decided not to press the matter.

"How has it been at your cousin's house?"

"It's been all right. Everybody gets along."

"I didn't want to come and see you empty-handed, so I brought you some cigarettes."

Pari's face lit up like a little girl receiving a beautiful doll. "Just in time. I was running out. Could you bring some more when you come to visit me again? It would make my life a lot easier."

"Sure, that's the least I can do." Yousef detected the desperation in her voice but chose not to pry. If Pari had wanted to talk about it, she would have. He slipped a little cash into her hand, kissed her forehead and left.

For the first time in years Pari was looking forward to seeing her husband.

They had invited four couples; old friends. Pari was put in charge of preparing the favourite of all: dolmeh, a sweet and sour conundrum of split peas, ground meat, parsley, chives, cilantro, lime juice and sugar, and rice wrapped in steamed vine leaves.

"Do we have any ice handy? I need it for the vodka," Rahim said as he walked into the kitchen. He wore a green tie with a beige shirt. With a well-groomed moustache and curled hair he was quite spruced up for the occasion.

"Yes. There's ice for your *unclean* beverage. Just make sure you keep the vodka glasses away from the rest of the stuff. I have to wash them separately. I don't want to get anything unclean on the plates we use every day." Rahim found Pari's comment amusing. It was refreshing to hear something new and sincere, even if it was to criticize him.

"Is there anything you want me to take to the living room?" Rahim was in a good mood.

"Take the fruit bowl and check whether we need to replenish the nut supply."

Pari glanced at the clock hung lopsided on the kitchen wall. It was quarter to six already and with the guests arriving shortly, there was still no sign of Malous.

Foti entered. "I'm all dressed up. I can give you a hand with preparing the sherbet glasses."

"Good! I could do with some help." Pari was curious to examine her outfit. It had taken Foti ages to dress; she had put a lot of effort into it. She was wearing a dress sewn by her sister-in-law, black patent leather shoes and a pair of fake pearl studs. Her normally straight hair was waved and sprayed stiff. Her eyelids were like two luminous green almonds and her cheeks bore the two great red spots usually found on the faces of dolls and small children.

It's as if a twelve-year-old girl has helped her put her rouge on, Pari thought. *Poor thing, she's tried so hard.*

Zeeba came into the kitchen. "Foti, one of the tables needs dusting. Look at your face again. How many times do I have to tell you about the rouge? Wipe your face." Zeeba left. Foti took a handkerchief and wiped her face the way an apprentice might react to the advice of a master. No offence. No emotion. Nothing. She simply took a handkerchief and wiped her face.

Pari's dolmeh were ready to be served on time. She took a few and put them aside for herself before calling Foti to the kitchen.

Pari said, "I wasn't sure which tray you wanted me to use. I guess the one with the flowery pattern looks more suitable."

Foti took the flowery tray and arranged the dolmeh one-by-one licking her fingers each time and showering compliments on Pari's remarkable skill between every two or three licks. Pari ignored the ritual; she was as used to the unpleasant habit as she was ever likely to get.

She could hear resounding praise of her dolmeh through the open kitchen door and that pleased her. Pari took great pride in her cooking; she knew she was the best. Some people believe there are great cooks in restaurants, one better than the next, but Pari knew there was a level beyond which there were no comparisons. Many Iranian women were truly great cooks; many. Their pastries or stews or bread were sought after and discussed. Plates always licked clean, crumbs cleared. The tradition in her family of the little girls learning from mothers and grandmothers and great-grandmothers was so old as to have been simply going on from the beginning of time. Many such families existed in Iran and they all believed that their mother or grandmother truly was the greatest cook in the world. Pari thought perhaps they were all right. She had no one to pass the gift to, but that couldn't stop her bathing in the spoils of the gift: to be appreciated, to be acknowledged as talented in the same way that someone might acknowledge that it is day and not night. An objective truth. It gave her pleasure and she drew from it some strength.

The key turned very carefully and slowly in the lock of the main door as if a thief was doing his best not to wake anybody up. Pari stopped eating. Her first thought was of catching the uninvited guest.

Malous's head popped round the door and scanned the place to make sure the coast was clear.

"About time. Where were you? Why are you hiding?"

"I went to see a movie with a classmate. Is there any food left in the pot?"

"Everybody's having dinner over there. Why don't you join them? It's not too late."

"I don't feel like it. The greeting ceremony puts me off. Besides, they'll be getting ready for their game very soon. I'd rather eat here with you."

"I think there's some dolmeh left in the pot but Foti took all the side dishes."

"That'll do just fine."

"Say, what game is it you're talking about?"

"Rummy. It's a card game. They've got their rounds every week. The reason it's been off for a few weeks was that some of the 'hands' were on holiday." Malous raised an eyebrow. It was clear she didn't like these people, or their games.

"I didn't know Zeeba gambled." Pari didn't even try to hide the disapproval in her voice.

"It's her favourite hobby. She's good at it too. She's even taught Foti how to play so that they never go short of players."

"Does she spend a lot on it?"

"She's too stingy to make big bets. Also the group she's formed are more or less the same as her, skill-wise. Of course, sometimes she hits a losing streak. Take my advice: you don't want to be near her when she's lost more than her budget. She moans about it non-stop until your head is splitting." Malous finished her food. "That was the best dolmeh I've ever had."

"Does she ever ask you to sit with them so that you learn how to play the game?"

"Not any more. She knows how much I hate gambling. She thinks I'm too boring."

"Well good for you. You're not a bit boring in my book."

That cheered Malous up; it wasn't so often that she heard any praise of her choices. She kissed Pari on the cheek, grabbed a handful of fresh herbs and sneaked up to her bedroom.

Pari woke up with a fright. She had dozed off when Rahim's loud laughter in the corridor gave her a shake. He was seeing off the guests. It felt late; the kitchen clock confirmed it was 11:00pm. Foti brought some dirty dishes back from the living room. She looked grim.

"Ach, I lost again. I thought tonight might be a chance to win back my losses from the past four sessions."

"Did Zeeba have a lucky night?"

"You just have to look at her happy face to get your answer. You'll get to see her in a good mood tomorrow morning."

"I guess we have to be thankful for small mercies. Leave the dishes on the counter. I'll wash them after morning prayer."

Foti hadn't done a good job clearing the dirty dishes off the tables in the living room. Pari was squeamish about touching the glasses; she didn't want to get any of the *unclean* substance on her hands. The best way to screen them out was to smell each glass and line up the ones with vodka stench away from the rest. She opened the windows wide to get rid of the stale smell of food and cigarette smoke choking the air. The rummy table was still untouched. It was covered by a green blanket laid with two decks of cards, chips with different colours and a few ashtrays. She had never seen gambling tools up close before; gambling wasn't one of Yousef's sins. All four ashtrays were full, some with half-smoked cigarettes. Pari picked one up and gazed at it as if this was the first time she had seen such a thing. In a way it was the first time; the first time she'd held someone else's half-smoked cigarette and dwelt on whether she should light it or not. The thought of sinking so low made her cringe but the harsh reality of being poor wasn't about to disappear. She couldn't rely on Yousef as a source of replenishment. He was supposed to have visited her five days ago and he hadn't shown up yet. As demeaning as it was, she had to feed the needy beast inside her. And what difference did it make anyway? Her misfortune, her bankruptcy, her fall was in the open. Everybody knew she was usurped from her social rank. There was no going back. There were six, no…eight cigarettes that had only a few puffs at them. That would do for now.

18

As much as Malous wished to look like a serious-minded person who read books with incendiary material written by serious, heavily bearded intellectuals, she still enjoyed indulging herself in the soap-opera type stories of *Zan-e-Rouz*, Today's Woman Magazine. There were stories about "love at first sight", battered women who were plotting to get rid of their abusive husbands, girls running away from home and becoming enslaved; all the ingredients a teenager would find amusing.

She had an audience. Pari enjoyed listening to the soothing tones of Malous's voice telling tales of other people's lives. It used to relax her, take her to a different place where she could sit back and watch these people wrestle with their convoluted issues. Pari could smoke her cigarette feeling light, unburdened.

Of course, the satisfaction of this reading ritual wasn't exclusive to Pari. Every time a new issue arrived, Malous would be filled with anticipation of delivering yet another superb performance. She knew she was as good as or even better than the narrators of midnight stories on the national radio. Also, Pari's gratification appeased her. It made her feel wanted.

"What's that you're reading?" Pari asked

"The recent issue of *Kargar* magazine."

"Don't you ever get bored with reading this?"

"I want to be up-to-date with the news about the masses' movement."

"As a matter of fact, I do think you get bored. I've seen you read it as if you've been assigned to do a chore and you feel obliged to finish your chore before you do anything else."

"That's not true!" Malous snapped. "There are articles in this magazine that interest me a lot. Articles about the exploitation of the masses, poverty and how all the resources and wealth should be distributed equally."

"And who writes the articles?"

"Some of the comrades in the party, of course."

"You mean a bunch of rich, spoiled kids who haven't done a day's work in their lives and who think that somehow by denying God and religion, they'd be ranked as intellectuals?"

"They are well-read intellectual people. They don't talk hot air."

"They're a bunch of ignorant loud-mouths. The very people they're supposed to support are religious and believe in God. It would help if they got to know their audience first."

"They go out on a limb to arrange for these meetings and speeches. It's very dangerous, you know."

"They arrange for these meetings because they want to meet girls."

"What are you insinuating?" Malous shouted. She was hurt and baffled.

"I mean…" Pari looked this way and that. She leant forward as if to whisper, then she shouted, "they have dicks too."

"Oh, that's preposterous and obscene."

"What? It's obscene that they have dicks or that they've come up with a plan to meet girls?"

"They put their lives in danger to open people's minds. That's not fair!"

"Right. Maybe you're right. Maybe they put a lock on their dicks before joining the party." Pari laughed at her own comment but her offended opponent was still not amused. "Come on, *aziz-jan*, enough sulking. Read us one of those stories."

"The new issue arrives the day after tomorrow. There's nothing to read." Malous said it steadfastly. She wanted to make sure Pari recognized the consequences of her reckless comments.

"Don't be in a bad mood. I'm sure there's a story you haven't bothered to read yet. I don't want us to go to sleep feeling angry."

Malous hesitated. She finally picked an old issue and skipped through it. Before long, her warm voice was melting the cold air with a story.

"You chose a good one. I like it when they have a happy ending. That's what you need before going to sleep."

Malous felt pleased with herself. She switched the light off and pulled the curtain open a little. A narrow beam of light from the alley found its way through her bedroom.

"So, how did you get involved in all this business?"

"My uncle Haady. He's got a lot of friends who gather in his house to discuss these matters."

"What a shame that your uncle Mehdi passed away. He was as good a guardian as anyone could have wished for. God rest his soul."

"No matter where I am or who I become, I will never forget his kindness and love. He always had time for me. The warmth and sincerity in his eyes gave me strength. If I was ever in trouble, if I ever felt lonely, I knew who to turn to." Malous sighed. "Uncle Haady's nice to me too. I like him. He has a free spirit."

"A bit too free for his own good, if you ask me." Haady's reputation had gone beyond the boundaries of Tehran. Pari had heard about his extravagant parties, his indulgence in alcohol and how he took pride in being considered a lady's man. His wife was certainly not a happy woman. Pari didn't want to rant about his misdemeanours. She didn't want to put him down in front of his niece. His affection for Malous forged a positive balance in his messy book of deeds. It put him in the black.

Malous was fast asleep, breathing heavily. Pari thought back to the first time she saw her in Varamin. She remembered the sweet little girl that charmed everybody in the village. And here she was, ready to embark on womanhood. Pari wondered: *Would she ever know what love is? She's had too many rag-tag bits of affection thrown at her by different people. Is that enough to fill those rugged gaps that leave the soul unfulfilled? Who could tell? Even Malous herself wouldn't know. She would have to be tested by the shrewd hands of destiny.*

Yousef knew he was in trouble. He had left Pari hanging dry with a few cigarettes and anguish simmering in her blood. Naturally, he didn't expect any welcoming smiles. He felt like a sheep being dragged to slaughter. But, he had to go, Pari was still his wife.

"Very big of you to show up." She glowered at him.

"I know. I'm sorry. I didn't feel well. I couldn't get out of the house," he said, following sheepishly behind Pari and into the kitchen.

"Why? What's wrong with you?"

"I've been feeling weak. Sometimes I get short of breath and I get a sharp pain in my arm. It's as if all the energy in my body has been drained out of me."

"You should see a doctor. Is Pouran taking care of you?"

"Pouran is sick and tired of me. She's got a scroll of excuses to get away from the house as often as she can." He took his jacket off and hung it on the back of a chair.

"That's what you get for marrying someone who could be your daughter." Pari regretted saying it as soon as soon as the words left her mouth. She wasn't after a row. Besides, that was all behind her; it was old news. She looked at him; his grey beard failed to hide the thinning flesh pasted to his cheekbones. There was no trace of the vivid, gay eyes that she had fallen in love with. He looked pale and gloomy.

Yousef had no energy and no desire to squabble. Neither did he care any more. He listened to Pari's unpleasant remark as if she were talking about somebody else. He was even too tired to feel sorry for himself.

Pari didn't want to succumb to an apology but she couldn't let Yousef leave with her harsh remark hanging over him. That would have been too much guilt to handle and she was simply not up to it.

"How are Aban and Hameed getting along with school?" she asked.

"I think they like it. They've made friends."

Pari slid her hand into the right pocket of Yousef's jacket. In all the years she'd known him that was where he kept his cigarettes. She could feel two, no, three loose cigarettes. She grabbed two. They weren't the usual substantial cigarettes, ones that people with money smoked. They were thinly wrapped by Yousef. She offered one to her husband. He gave a dejected nod and took out the third cigarette from his pocket.

"Hameed is especially keen on school. I think he's got a crush on his teacher," he said. He smiled as a father does.

"How's that?" She was intrigued by the thought of a small boy falling in love with his teacher and relieved that Yousef still knew how to smile.

"I don't know. It's actually quite funny the way he talks about her. He says his teacher has milky skin with black eyes and that she always smiles. The other day he was saying that her skin is so soft."

"How does he know?" Pari lit one of the cigarettes for herself and put the other one in the inside pocket of her dress.

"That's exactly what I asked him," Yousef said, laughing. "He said when his teacher was passing by his desk he managed to touch her leg and that's how he knows she's got silky skin."

By this time Pari was laughing. "Seems that he's even more advanced than his father."

"I guess. But the good thing about it is that he yearns to go to school and he studies hard to please his teacher."

Yousef gazed into Pari's eyes. It had been a good while since he'd seen amusement in them. The sparkle in her eyes reminded him of the joyful, spirited girl he'd married a lifetime ago.

His heart sank. He'd had it all and he threw it all away. A storm of "ifs" and "buts" raged in his head. He noticed the frayed sleeves of the washed-out dress that his wife was wearing. He felt terribly ashamed. This wasn't worthy of a Zan-Arbab, but he knew that if somehow he could go back in time and start all over again, he would do everything the same way. He was who he was, for better or worse.

"How are you keeping here?" he asked with bowed head.

"I'm all right. I guess you can't expect any more when you're staying in someone else's house. Malous is a joy to be around, though. Any news? How is Banoo, Ali, Sardar? Have you heard anything? What of Sardar's camel?" She smiled.

"I hear that Sardar is in good health. The new Arbab treats him with the respect he deserves. I don't know about his camel, he must be getting his dose." Yousef smiled. "Ali treats Banoo as if she were his own mother. She insists on doing her share, she takes care of his house. Ali told me he may take a wife."

"He deserves some happiness."

"Why don't you come back with me today?"

"I'm done with that life. Don't waste your breath."

Yousef took four notes and some coins out of his pocket. He placed them in Pari's hand and folded her fingers around the money. He was ready to have a row and make her take the money if she snubbed his gesture.

"Thank you."

Her submission said it all. His wife had been relegated to performing free labour but still she would not go back to live with him. The blood rushing to his head almost burst a vein. It was like an invisible force pounding a heavy hammer on his skull. He wasn't sure if he felt sorry for Pari or furious at her. This was the same woman who had headed a whole village on her own. But her stubbornness was still there, and her will to carry on.

It's her choice. She's a determined woman. Whatever she's content with... Yousef was too aggravated, too tired and too ill to start a row. He didn't even know if he cared enough to get embroiled.

He had to leave.

19

Everyone knew about it when Haady came for a visit. He'd herald his arrival with a loud greeting and a seemingly endless supply of hugs accompanied by the world's loudest kisses. Recipients of Haady's kisses, both women and men, invariably laughed when they thought of the man, so enthusiastic, so happy to see them, as if they were the person he'd been searching for. Then he would jump into a tale of one of his cases at the court of justice. He'd recount every speech, every phrase he had used in his client's defence. His stories were always engaging, and with a vivid performance to accompany them, no one could resist the entertainment. He usually had a poem handy to spice up his endings. It didn't matter whether it was old or new. He enjoyed listening to himself. Haady had come a long way from the time when his mother would mock him for his inhibitions.

"So, I take it that you managed to get a 'not guilty' verdict for your client?" Zeeba said.

"Even the judge himself congratulated me on this one." A rush of pride ran through him. He lit a cigarette to calm himself and offered one to Pari.

"I wasn't sure you'd be home. I took a chance. God knows you wouldn't want to miss a minute staying at home when you could be out there partying, Sister."

"As a matter of fact Rahim and I are going out but not for a while."

"I need your help with a crucial matter. I need your permission to ask Malous for a favour." He prodded a few of the pastries that Pari had set in front of him then he chose one and bit into it.

"And what would that be?"

"You know Kaaveh Rabbani." Pari threw him a look. At first he was puzzled until she looked down at the floor in front of him where a speckled patch of pastry flakes was accumulating. She would have to clean up after his enthusiastic treatment of her pastries. He lifted the plate to his chin to catch the flakes and knew that it was his duty to acknowledge her skills as a pastry chef. He closed his eyes and munched slowly. Pari tried not to laugh and she filled with pride.

"Mmm…You know how important he is to the party. Without him and his ideas, we may as well lock everything up and go home, put an end to the socialist party in this country. Not to mention his charisma and his influence on young people. They look up to him. Anyway, they arrested him last night. He was in an accident. In his car. He was drunk. It's obvious that they're not sure about his identity because they kept him in the holding cell with the common criminals. If he stays there any longer even those buffoons will make a positive identification and before long he'll be a laughing stock."

"What can Malous do for him?" Zeeba asked. Kaaveh Rabbani was a legend; an almost mythical character, he bore the weight of the whole party on his shoulders.

"I'd like Malous to go to the prison to visit him. She'll pose as his niece. I want her to pass a pair of tweezers to him so that he can get rid of his trademarks: his thick moustache and eyebrows. That way he'll have a chance to sneak out as a visitor. He'll know how to engineer that."

"I'm sure Malous is capable of passing on a pair of tweezers. You can tell her the details yourself. She should be back any minute."

"I can't believe you sometimes. Why would you want to get her involved in such a dangerous game? If you don't look out for her, then who will?" Pari interrupted.

Haady snapped, "It's not a game as a matter of fact. It's quite serious. That's why we need to get Kaaveh out of there as soon as possible."

"To hell with Kaaveh or whatever the hell his name is. He should have thought about the consequences before he decided to become Stalin."

"Don't stir up a riot here."

"You're giving me a headache. I'm sure there's no danger for Malous, otherwise my brother wouldn't have suggested it," Zeeba said, matter-of-factly.

"That's right. Because you're well-known to be the most caring mother of all time. All she cares about is pandering to her brother.

And all her brother cares about is himself and his reputation as an intellectual. Between them you can't find a modicum of unselfishness and nobility." Pari bit her lip to stop her screaming out all the thoughts that were going through her head. It seemed unbelievable that they would allow this child to become embroiled in such matters. How could they think Malous should be involved?

Malous arrived shortly after her family had taken a rest from arguing the dos and don'ts of her assignment. She was delighted to see her uncle. He always made an effort to flatter her intellect and her desire to better herself. Haady made Malous feel like a grown-up responsible woman, someone capable of making her own decisions. She didn't know, and in fact wasn't bothered to know, if her uncle's cavalier attitude towards her upbringing was due to his lack of concern for her or whether he believed in his niece's judgment and her ability to do the right thing.

Haady briefed Malous on what she was expected to do. On how crucial it was for her to put on her best performance in front of the prison guards.

"The party would be proud of you, dear. I'd be proud of you. I didn't choose you haphazardly. I trust you can do this. You're the person for the job."

"You can rely on me." Malous was bloated with a sense of valour and craving for adventure. "Trust my performance. I'm a chameleon. Just tell me when and where and I'll do it."

Pari was livid. She wanted to pull Malous's hair and tell her how idiotic she sounded. *What's the use? Look at her. This girl will go to any lengths to feel loved. It breaks my heart.*

Kaaveh Rabbani's escape from jail did fulfil Malous's thirst for heroism. She was the one who made his escape from shame possible. And the importance given to her deed kept her in ecstasy for a good while.

Pari was right to be worried. Had Malous been caught she would have been ensnared within the labyrinthine maze of the justice system and who knows, maybe even thrown into prison herself. It was 1952; under Prime Minster Mossadegh there were no political prisoners, no torture, people said freedom was in the air. But she would still be aiding and abetting a crime. Haady had explained it all to Malous, but the way he'd said it made it sound like a great adventure.

He was right about the deed itself and the likelihood of being caught. The prison guards were bumpkins, villagers shipped in to perform tasks for which they had no training, with hardly an idea of what they were supposed to do, and no one to bother telling them; peasant farmers, out of work and in the big city, it was a job, they wore a uniform, turned up on time and hoped that was enough. Malous smuggled in the tweezers but she might have smuggled a great metal file in a cartoon cake for all the attention the guards paid her. Rabbani made his face naked with a thousand painful pinpricks and cursed Haady to hell and back for not supplying a razor. He walked past the guards as if he were the warden. He had the gait of an educated man; a superior man. The guards didn't even look at his face lest they felt the brunt of his anger. Had they glanced at him, even for a moment, they would have seen his upper lip, glowing red, swollen; evidence of a jailbreak almost as simple-minded as the jailers.

And now Malous was really a part of it all. The little girl with posters of her heroes plastered over her wall was now one herself. That she would almost certainly be arrested if someone should inform on her was not something she dwelt upon.

Zeeba wasn't famous for her good temper, but her recent erratic and exaggerated mood swings had even Pari concerned. She was an inch away from being utterly intolerable. Everybody tried to avoid her as much as they could. And that wasn't to give her some leeway but to dodge any disastrous quarrels. Especially Foti; her quietness around Zeeba was so diligent it could have easily passed for a religious silence. She was right to be scared too; Zeeba had made a habit of using her as a verbal punch bag whenever she wasn't in the *right mood*. It was no secret that the way she treated Foti made other people feel uncomfortable. Strangely, Rahim never made any effort to subdue this behaviour, instead citing platitudes; his favourite being, "It'll pass just like a bee's sting."

"Is Zeeba working in the sewing room?" Rahim asked.

"She's still with a client," Pari replied. "You've been handling her temper very well. It's quite amazing."

"She's my wife and I love her. It's as simple as that."

"Her tantrums are so unbearable that even love couldn't put a lid on them. Your tolerance is suspicious. Is there something I should know about?"

"Absolutely not," Rahim said nervously. "I don't want to interrupt her work. Could you tell her that I'll be gone for a couple of hours?"

"Will do," Pari said sarcastically. "You know, whatever you're hiding will come out sooner or later. I've already got an idea as to what might be wrong with her."

Pari took three glasses of lemonade to the sewing room. Foti, still dedicated to her vow of silence, was sitting in a corner of the room basting a frill to a see-through sleeve. Zeeba, with a mouthful of pins, was concentrating on finding a way to get rid of the unwanted pleats in the client's top. Pari looked at Zeeba's client with more than a little wonder. Her cousin had quite a challenge in front of her; the woman's breasts were too big and quite out of proportion with her shoulders and back. *Those things make the problems of tailoring a skirt for her gigantic bottom look easy,* Pari thought to herself. She could see the frustration on Zeeba's face and also the struggle not to seem rude to her client.

The woman spun half round to look at Pari. Her breasts followed a moment later then wobbled about before coming to an uncertain rest. Pari couldn't hold back any more. She laughed. The woman squirmed with a smile that somehow expressed embarrassment tinged with a little anger. After all, Zeeba had been killing herself for a good while trying to make her look good in that top.

"What's so funny?" Zeeba snapped. She glowered at Pari until she got an answer.

"Oh, nothing. I just remembered something amusing I had heard on the radio." Pari directed her reply to the customer.

"Well, nobody's interested. So, make a move and hem this skirt," Zeeba said curtly.

The sudden switch from a giggle to a long blank face hid no secrets about how small Pari felt. *I wonder if there was anybody in our village who wanted to strangle me the way I feel like strangling Zeeba? I wonder if I ever triggered violent thoughts in people?* And then she remembered what Banoo once said to her: *"Don't talk to me this way, Zan-Arbab. I used to be somebody. I used to be an Arbab's daughter. You never know what destiny has stashed away for you. You never know how your life will turn."*

I must have shouted at Banoo the same way Zeeba shouts at me. You don't evaluate your behaviour. You don't even think about it. Because you have a solid notion that you've got control over this person's life, you're the one with power and you poke a dagger into her soul whenever you feel like it. You don't plan on any moments to dump the humiliation on her, to stain her soul because she knows she has to hold back, because she knows she has no choice. It just comes naturally to you. And that's what's scary about us.

The thought that this scene could easily be a repeat of her behaviour towards Banoo that particular day churned her stomach. She needed now to remember some of the good deeds she had left behind in the minds of the peasants in her village. Times she had helped them out of their sorrows and pains. Times she had staved off prospective problems heading their way. She needed to remember because now she was desperate to cleanse her soul.

The big-breasted client left the house content and smiling. Zeeba's struggle had paid off. Her obsession with perfection would have it no other way.

"Rahim has gone out for a few hours. He didn't want to interrupt your work. He asked me to let you know," Pari murmured with her head down, still hemming the skirt.

"I have to go and lie down. I don't feel well. When he comes back, go ahead and have your dinner without me." Zeeba marched out without looking at either of them.

"I don't know how much more of her filthy temper I can take before I go mad and strangle someone," Foti said. "Rahim has promised me to take her to the doctor's soon. He'd better come up with a perfect cure or there will be a gory scene in this house."

"I'm no less aggravated than you are but calm down."

"I can't help it. I hate the way she talks to me, I hate the way she takes her anger out on me. That's what I get for not having a family of my own."

"I'm sure you'll get married before long and put all this behind you." Pari tried to console her.

Rahim did stand by his promise. Zeeba's nasty mood had grated even his abundant patience. The good news was that he didn't have to put up a fight to convince his wife to see a doctor; she was more than willing to tag along. It seemed as if she was certain that the doctor must have the very cure for her, as if she had this perfect notion of her diagnosis. And she had decided that now was the time to take the potion and put an end to this "nuisance".

The two long faces that left the house in late morning came back in disagreement. Rahim's bewilderment and sadness was nowhere to be seen on Zeeba's face. As a matter of fact, she looked relieved.

"Well, thank God. Your face has brightened up. I take it that the doctor had good news for you," Pari said with a trace of suspicion.

"Everything seems to be in order. Though, I have to go back for some routine tests in a couple of days."

"What's wrong with my brother? He looks like he's a nudge away from slitting his throat," said Foti.

"There's nothing wrong with him. We had a row on the way back."

Foti's curiosity tailed off. It was no surprise to hear that Zeeba had a squabble with her husband.

As perky as Zeeba seemed to be, Rahim avoided any conversations and any face-to-face encounters with the whole household. It was obvious he wanted to be left alone and everybody respected this.

Zeeba kept her appointment for the tests she had mentioned as necessary. On the day they got ready to go, her husband looked as gloomy and spiritless as a sinking ship. The dark bags under his eyes were quite indicative of his sleepless nights ever since they came back from the doctor's office. Everybody had heard their aggressive whispering during the night, but no one had figured out what they were arguing about.

"We won't be back till this evening. I'd like to stop by Haady's place and see how he's doing," Zeeba said, expressionlessly.

"Good luck at the doctor's!" said Pari, jovially, but Rahim looked at her like he wanted to kill her.

According to Zeeba, the tests were fine. Though her pronounced paleness made it seem as if they had taken too much blood out of her flimsy body by mistake. She said she needed a couple of days to regain energy after this period of physical and mental attrition and that's exactly what she did. She had two people to serve her and she took the utmost advantage of that. Rahim slept in the living room for two nights, imparting that he wanted to give her as much peace and quiet as possible.

With her convalescence out of way, Zeeba decided on a trip to the Caspian Sea for the whole household. It was a good opportunity to relax. She reckoned that two weeks away would do everybody good. The house they rented had two bedrooms for five people and a kitchen that could only fit two at a time. But its proximity to the beach compensated for the cramped space and left everybody genuinely satisfied. Pari couldn't even remember the last time she had made a trip to the Caspian Sea; it seemed to have occurred in a different life. But she had no problems recalling the peaceful feeling that seeped through her from tip to toe every time she sat on the beach being hypnotized by the waves. How she envied local people for waking up to this gift of God every day. Pari was aware of the main reason for her being a part of the Caspian Sea trip: to cook for everybody. But she didn't care. The fact that she could spend her spare time sitting restfully on the beach was enough for her.

Rahim had started to come out of his shell and be more like his usual self. Zeeba made a firm effort to spend time with her husband. Every day they visited the neighbouring village to buy homemade products then they'd have a dip in the sea.

Pari was burying her feet under the sand when her cousin joined her in the mid-afternoon. She had resorted to the shade of a large bush so that she could prolong her resting time at the beach.

"Rahim's taking a nap. I thought I'd get out for some fresh air."

"He seems to be cheering up finally," Pari said while Zeeba was forging an impression on the sand comfortable enough for her bottom.

"I've been spending a lot of time with him trying to make him realize that I care."

"Why is it that all of a sudden he needs confirmation that his wife cares about him?"

"Well, because of the bad patch we went through recently. You know, with me snapping at him, pushing him away."

"Don't I know it. And if I may add, he wasn't the only one either." Pari was pleased to voice her complaint. "Now that, apparently, it's all behind you, what was the problem in the first place?"

"I was pregnant," Zeeba said, slipping sand through her fingers.

I knew it. Her tiredness, lack of appetite, her moody behaviour and also Rahim's incredible tolerance of her devilish temper.

"Aren't you going to say anything? Are you that much in shock?"

"As a matter of fact, I'm not in shock a bit. I had reckoned that you must be pregnant. It's just that I never told anyone about it."

"How did you know? Did Rahim spill the beans?"

"Of course not. Don't worry, he obeyed your instructions. I wasn't born yesterday, you know. I can recognize a pregnant woman when I see one. So the tests you went for that day were really to have an abortion?"

"I had made up my mind and couldn't be bothered to be judged by anybody."

"If one of the people you're talking about is me, and I'm sure that's the case, I have to say that I'm not in a position to judge anyone else."

"The way you said it sounds like you've got a guilty conscience."

"I'm not sure if I feel guilty. It's just that by what I've done I could easily be exposed to other peoples' judgments. Back in our village whenever any woman went into labour, they would come and get me to supervise the birth. I don't know, maybe they thought my presence, my decisions, would make everything better. One night in autumn I was asked to help the midwife with an eighteen-year-old woman who was about to give birth to her first child. The delivery took place with no complications. It was rather fast. The problem was the baby itself. It was completely deformed. It had no arms or legs and two nostrils for a nose. Poor little thing, it didn't even seem human. My shock was too grave to even notice whether it was a boy or a girl. It was the most grotesque thing I had ever seen in my life. Right there and then I made up my mind and declared that the baby was stillborn. There was no way I could let that young woman see it. The midwife played along and confirmed that the baby was dead. The poor girl, expecting to hold her baby in her arms, started crying. I took a blanket, wrapped the creature in it and rushed out of the room. The midwife followed me after a few seconds. I told her that although it was almost breathing, there was no chance it could survive. So, I took it to the backyard and left it under a box. After an hour I checked to see if it was still alive. It had stopped breathing. I dug a hole in the backyard and buried it. As planned, the mother never found out about the horrific state of her baby."

"That baby was going to die anyway. At least you protected the mother from scorn," Zeeba said, unmoved by Pari's confession.

"Well, that's what I thought at the time. But it's not so black and white as we would want it to be. She was the mother after all. Maybe

I should have given her the right to see her baby and choose for herself what to do with it."

"As far as I'm concerned she's indebted to you. You made life easy for her. You decided for her. Now I can see why everybody wanted you present at the delivery."

"I take it that Rahim wasn't on board with aborting your pregnancy?"

"No, he wasn't. He wanted a child of his own. But I'm the one who should be comfortable with that. I'm the one who carries the baby for nine months, not to mention the problems after they're born. I wanted to have an abortion and he did as I bade him."

"Not many men would have put up with that; completely ignored. No wonder he looked depressed."

"He'll get over it before he knows it and then he'll thank me for saving his freedom."

Pari lit a half-smoked cigarette. It wasn't her usual roll-up, no-filter material. And it had a lipstick mark on it; something that certainly didn't fit in *her* lifestyle. She smoked and inhaled every molecule of it right up to the butt. Ever since she had moved to her cousin's house and had to adopt a monkish way of living, cigarettes had become as precious as saffron; every strand of tobacco had to be handled with care and every half-used cigarette was to be treated like a trophy. After all, they didn't grow on trees.

Pari saw no point in wasting her breath arguing with her cousin. The baby was gone and Zeeba felt satisfied with her choice.

A little person in her little reign exalting her authority and domination. How pathetic and small she looks. But, isn't that what almost everybody's after? Just a sliver of power between you and other people? A sliver that's forged by awe or intimidation or love and allows you to sway them whenever you desire. To shape their feelings into a mould that suits your purpose and leaves them baffled as to whether they've done something wrong.

"How does Malous feel about this? Or have you not told her yet?" Pari asked, smoke streaming out to accompany her words.

"I've already told her. She didn't show any reaction. I guess she's not bothered one way or the other."

"Well, her days of yearning for a brother or a sister as a playmate are long gone and she's definitely not at an age to want a baby drilling her head with constant crying," Pari said.

"Like I said, my decision was best for everybody." Zeeba said it like she was describing a victory long past.

CHAPTER
21

The excitement in Malous's voice hinted at who the person behind the door ringing the bell might be. Her uncle Haady had come for a visit. No matter how down she felt, a dose of Haady's encouraging words always delivered enough joy to last the rest of the day. It wasn't just the words themselves, it was the way he embellished them with his gestures, the firmness in his voice, his earnestness, that gave his stories life. And he didn't need to make any special effort to bring his performance to life, he was well-practised in influencing people; he was a lawyer and a good one at that. Maybe his mother's constant ridicule of his lack of articulacy, his lack of confidence, as cruel and harsh as it seemed at the time, had been a spur, although Haady's recollection of her memory brought no warmth or gratitude. He hardly ever talked about his adolescence and his mother's place in it. And if he did, it always left the listener with a sense of ambivalence; too many lines to read between and enough hurt to engulf mere empathy.

Malous took Haady by the hand and to the kitchen, where Pari was hard at it preparing the evening meal. "I've come to treat myself to your famous lamb," he announced as if he were proud of himself for praising Pari's cooking skills.

"We were going to have soup and bread but I expect now the menu has changed," Pari said with no trace of amusement in her voice.

"I heard from a friend the other day that Yousef is quite ill. What's wrong with him?" he asked, almost conspiratorially. Insignificant illnesses, colds, sickness, could be taken head on but the prospect of something grave was best approached from a different vantage point.

Pari scanned the room. She listened until she was sure the coast was clear then returned to her cooking and spoke in a tone that belied her caution. She was no master here but she still had business that was her own and she'd broadcast her own business when she was good and ready. "I think it's his heart. I'll make time to visit him soon."

"Poor man. These past few years have been so hard on him. It's not easy to lose what you worked for all your life."

"You reap what you sow," she snapped. This was a husband who had doomed her to a life of neediness. There was no shred of mercy in her voice.

Pari's outburst alarmed Haady enough to know that he should leave her with her thoughts and go find his sister. He cocked his head to Malous. She cringed a little at her uncle's ability to set Pari off in such short order. She led him away to her mother's work room. She would apologize to Pari later for her uncle's clumsy remark and she made a mental note to instruct him on the life that Yousef had enforced upon his wife.

Zeeba was busy directing Foti on a job that was due for delivery the next day. She had the impatient demeanour of a great chef or perhaps a surgeon when instructing a student or informing a layman on the intricacies of some imperative minutiae. Zeeba found it hard to understand why others could not understand what she found so simple. But she would give no one, least of all Foti, any leeway on matters of dressmaking. She was unable to hide her disdain for the stupidity of others in these matters while harbouring deep pride that her own knowledge towered so far above the knowledge of others as to ensure they were always mistaken and she always correct. If her knowledge of dressmaking had been a mountain, to poor Foti it was a brick wall built high; an endless, hard, unscalable wall, an insurmountable obstacle without beginning or end. Always it seemed to Foti that Zeeba had her by the scruff of her neck, pushing her face into that wall.

She wanted Foti to religiously apply the meticulousness, the attention to detail that the world expected from Zeeba's sewing work. Although Foti's apparent low level of intelligence wasn't a secret, it still made her so frustrated that, after all these years, Foti still hadn't mastered the basics and couldn't be trusted to finish a job on her own.

Haady watched the two women for a moment. Poor Foti, with that expression telling of fear and constant apprehension, and always trying so hard. His sister, in her own world, a true artist but with the patience of a tyrant; always boiling and ready to blow.

Zeeba stood back to try to see how she could save the mess that Foti had made of a particular dart that she had explained and demonstrated a thousand times when she caught her brother standing at the door silently smiling, watching them work.

"Ah, there he is! I've heard rumours about you and I'm hoping that there's no truth in them." Zeeba spoke the way a sister would when she suspects her little brother of doing something naughty.

"It depends on what you've heard."

Zeeba directed him to the living room and sent her daughter to fetch tea (that would leave them with some privacy). The overpowering aroma of the smoke from his ever-present cigarette hung in the air but Zeeba didn't mind; revulsion to odours and tastes imposed by her pregnancy had passed.

"So, what's going on between you and Jamal's wife?" Zeeba was prying. The seriousness in her face told of determination to conduct a successful interrogation.

"What do you mean?" Haady might as well have been a sheep trying to escape its destiny in a slaughterhouse. His sister could always open him up.

"What I mean is that Jamal is your friend. How can you bring yourself to look at his face any more?"

Haady replied with a puff on his cigarette but he knew it was futile to resist; she would never let go. Of course, in reality he enjoyed talking to his sister. She had always been his confidante.

"Well, what can I say? It's not like you plan to fall in love with someone."

"Hold your horses." She placed one hand on her hip and flapped the other at him dismissively. "Fall in love? I think you mean fall in lust. You fell in love with your wife, remember?"

"Yes. And I still care about her. I don't have any complaints about my wife."

"So, how could you see another woman behind her back?"

"I don't know. Hoori touches places in me that I never knew

existed. Granted, she's beautiful. But it's not just that. The way she moves her sublime body mesmerizes me. She seems to radiate an energy, a brightness. She brings joy."

"You've lost your mind. You're talking like a fourteen-year-old teenager in heat."

He shrugged. *Obviously she didn't get a word I said,* he thought. But, what did he care? He wasn't the least bothered about his sister's opinion, or anybody else's. Haady couldn't remember the last time he changed a single thing about himself for other people and this wasn't going to be an exception.

"Does your wife know?" Zeeba asked because she had a feeling his wife did know, as do, she thought, all wives with unfaithful husbands. Either the husbands betray themselves with their behaviour or they never cared enough to even try to hide their infidelities. Zeeba believed that all men had to be unfaithful. It was their nature, but when the time came, it was their character that mattered. Whether they'd blunder deliberately to clear the way for more, or whether they'd hurt their wives for pure entertainment, or whether they'd be discreet; holding their first wives with some esteem, an unassailable place for first loves or first promises. That was what decided matters for her. She'd be the second wife of no man and she'd play second or third fiddle to no woman. The women would never talk about it openly but they all knew that some of them welcomed a second wife, even a third or fourth if the husband was a good-enough provider. The younger women could take care of the awful bedroom business, the bearing of children and the bearing of the husbands; mostly worse than children. First wives got the best of men. First wives felt the first blush of love. Men feel love. They feel it the first time. But when they get to know it they go mad for it. They need to recapture it again and again.

"Someone told her. She wouldn't tell me who." He shook his head with disdain for the Judas who had upset his almost perfect life. "She confronted me the other day and I didn't deny that I'd been seeing Hoori for a few months already."

"How did she react?"

"How do you expect her to react? She burst into tears. And yes, of course she asked for a divorce. I have to admit that her civilized manner, under the circumstances, impressed me quite a bit."

"Impressed *you*? I'm sure she'd be proud to hear you were *impressed* by her. She's too good for you. Like a nice red apple in a crippled hand, as mother used to say." Zeeba wanted to hurt her brother.

Foti's arrival with a tray of tea and biscuits brought Haady an opportunity to end the conversation. He'd expected a little understanding on this matter from his sister. He'd met a woman and fallen in love. It happened. She didn't have to be so cruel about it. It's not as if he wanted to hurt his wife. He still loved his wife. At least he still loved her but in a different way. In his eyes she was still his friend. What could he do? He was powerless in the face of love.

He popped two sugar cubes in his mouth and took a sip. The tea was bitter. There weren't enough sugar cubes in this world to sweeten the bitter mood his sister had forced upon him. He had no escape from the nagging words of his mother. Now, from the grave she was possessing his beloved sister to torture him. Even death refused to quiet her.

He shuddered. The warmth of his new love was not enough to dispel the icy wind that blew through his sister from his mother's cold heart. He still feared her. When it came to his mother, he was a rank coward, and he knew it.

And he was deeply embarrassed by that.

"What happened to Malous? She was supposed to take care of the tea," Zeeba complained. She thought her daughter had tried to dodge her chores to make more time for her entertainment; an unacceptable violation of Zeeba's strict house rules.

"I asked her to dash out and get me a bobbin of lilac thread." Foti's nervous admission brought a look from Zeeba. Foti wouldn't stop staring at her cousin, Haady. She had guessed that the sourness in his face was a result of a discussion about an infidelity. She wanted to study every angle of fury, and she detected the agony of second thoughts on his face. She could see it all, written there. They thought she was stupid and maybe she wasn't as clever as them but she had eyes to see well enough. This was the man that for years she had yearned for. Her adolescent fantasies of becoming his bride and wrapping herself around his firm body hadn't subdued a bit with the passage of years. She could still imagine tingles on the tips of her fingers as she ran her hands through his thick, black hair. Foti had lost track of the number of times she had imagined carrying his child in her womb. And the longevity of these imaginings made the make-believe life in her belly and the make-believe life in her head more and more real. She was *married* to a man who'd been repeatedly unfaithful to her; marrying his first wife then the *other* women, ignoring her emotions for so many years. But she had vowed to forgive him, till death did they part.

"Would you like a handful of the white berries I bought yesterday? They're really sweet and scrumptious." Foti knew his favourite fruit. She didn't take her eyes off him. But he wouldn't notice. He never noticed her staring at him until she had mapped every hair, every line, every blush, every tiny blemish on his face. She knew when he was sad inside or happy inside, although he never hid his happiness; one of the reasons she loved him so. But she could tell when he was lying, always.

Haady gazed through her with disengaged, cold eyes. She was invisible to him. He shook his head as if saying no to some other, more distant question. There was joy in her eyes. He finally noticed her. "What's she so happy about?" he asked Zeeba, as if Foti were in another room.

"What's the point of grieving over spilt water?" Foti said to him, as if she were a part of the conversation Haady and Zeeba had conducted in private.

"I don't know what you mean," he said, almost with amusement.

"Well, the sooner you accept your marriage is over the better. Anybody who knows your wife knows that she would never go along with an unfaithful husband."

"Have you been eavesdropping all this time?" Haady snapped.

"Your voice is loud enough for the next-door neighbour to hear about your troubles, especially when you're irritated." Foti said it like a knowing wife. She resented the way he'd roar at her as if it were his prerogative.

Her swift retort shut him up. He was aware of his voice. It was a double-edged sword; impressive in front of a judge and jury, and apt for a recital of one of his poems at a gathering, or even when praising or engaging in flattery. And thanks to his vocal assets, a circle of neighbours had a list of subjects to gossip about.

Foti couldn't hide the thrill she felt when a plan bore fruit. The realization that her scheme had come to fruition filled her to bursting point. It made her feel good. It made her feel clever despite what anybody said about her. The thrill of hitting the target and satisfying her desire to be smart was overwhelming.

"She might still take me back. You never know!" Haady said.

"No. There's no going back," Foti insisted.

"How do you know? You're not in her mind."

"I saw it in her eyes. I did."

"Did you now? Would that be when you spilled the beans about me to my wife so that you could ruin my marriage? You nasty creature!"

"It...wasn't me! Who said it was me?"

Her cover was blown.

Zeeba broke into the row. "What did it have to do with you anyway?"

"She's a nice woman. I like her. It wasn't fair on her having another woman take her place behind her back."

"Since when did you start caring about fairness for other people? We both know your shell's too thick to break out of."

Haady lit a cigarette to calm his nerves. The whole thing had made him too flustered. Even a pipe of opium in that house wouldn't release him from his frustration. He needed to get out. He left muttering a faint goodbye to his sister.

Pari tried to calm the squabble. She went to Foti but Foti would have none of it.

"I like her and that's why I told her about Haady and that slut. You can believe what you want." Foti wouldn't give in.

"Look! We both know about your ulterior motive. You'd better get this into your skull. He's not attracted to you and he'll never marry you. Believe me when I say I have no problem whatsoever with him taking you as his wife. But the chances of that happening are about as slim as the chances of a snowball surviving in hell. So, stop stirring problems!"

Foti pouted like a baby on the verge of a tantrum. Zeeba's words were acrid and distressing. She wished they weren't true but she knew that nobody had heard of a better rate of survival than zero for a snowball in hell.

"Why don't you go and get some fresh air? It'll make you feel better." Pari felt sorry for her. It wasn't an unreasonable desire for her to have her own house, her own family, to dictate her own rules in the household instead of being dictated to, to experience the simple pleasures of family life that people with families take for granted. It wasn't even her love (or maybe really her lust) for Haady that had kept her from settling. She would have settled for anyone with a career and reputation who proposed to her. She had turned down offers in the past, when she put a higher price on herself. But that was the past. No one had stepped forward to ask for her hand, in a very long time.

Pari couldn't imagine why. Maybe the way Zeeba talked down to her in public had ruined any chance of her establishing a proper image for herself. Maybe she reeked of desperation? Or maybe she was simply doomed to stay single for the rest of her life despite her struggle to find a way out.

Isn't life full of people chasing what they think they want? And when they get it they're not sure of what they wanted in the first place. They covet what they don't possess, what they're not allowed to possess and what they would not have wanted to possess had it not belonged to someone else. Haady coveted a woman who belonged to another man. Foti covets a man who would never consider her a soul mate. And what about me? What do I covet?

"Why is everyone angry?" Malous's question shook Pari out of her thoughts.

"No reasons you would want to ruin your day with. Come and give me a hand in the kitchen."

22

It was comforting to be back home. The secure, impregnable, welcoming place that she remembered as her home; away from the wreckage, the damage, the broken feelings. It was good to be back in her temple, her garden, the place she resorted to when she felt the need to screen out the irritations of life. How much she missed grooming her colourful roses and populating the edge of the garden walls with vases bursting with geraniums. She had always felt proud when Yousef complimented her on the job she had done with their backyard haven.

"You have magical hands. This isn't a garden. It's heaven. What do you give these flowers? They look extraordinary. Maybe you nurture them with some unholy potion!" Pari hadn't seen him for months and there he was, as lovely as the day she fell in love with him; groomed and poised, using his charm to flatter her.

"How did you know I was here? You haven't been to visit me for months."

"I know. I'm sorry. And believe me if there was anyone I would have liked to see, it was you."

"Well, have a seat! I'll make you a mint sherbet, the way you like it."

"I can't stay. I only came to see my woman again before I leave."

"Where are you going?"

His image faded. Pari rubbed her eyes until they were sore. There was no use. Everything was faint and blurry: her husband, her flowers, her pond with the goldfish in the middle of the garden. Her frustration, her striving to see lasted until a beam of light stroked her eyes. It was morning already; not a good one. She had woken up to a clobbering migraine and a pounding heart. Her mouth was as dry and bitter as the thought passing through her mind: *He's gone.*

She felt saddened. Despite the desperate events of the past few years of her life with Yousef, she couldn't brush away the pleasant memories she'd amassed being married to him. His sense of humour, easy-going nature and alluring traits gave her so many delightful moments; moments she could escape to whenever she despaired of her life at her cousin's house.

We were a good team until the madness and obsession of passing on the family name, having children, demolished our livelihood. Pari rolled over on her side. Here she was again on the verge of an explosion with all the thoughts that she had run through her mind a thousand times before. Only this time they sounded like a broken record with no impact. *Was that really the reason? Having children? It's all horseshit! We are who we are. We show what we're capable of when we're presented with difficult conditions. Up to then we don't know ourselves, never mind anybody else.*

She couldn't take this one-way row any longer. She got up to perform her morning prayer. Pari needed to pray; to see her husband's soul to the other side with blessing and mercy, to cleanse her soul of any resentment and to wash away the guilt she felt for ignoring Yousef during his illness.

She woke Malous up and headed towards the kitchen. She mulled over the when and how of visiting Pouran and her children in-between making tea and replenishing the sugar jar. *I could go today. I should go today. He was my husband and I ought to find out what happened to him.*

Pari didn't notice the first bang at the door; she was too busy talking to herself. The second bang was determinedly loud enough to interrupt the buzz in her head. It was too early to knock at people's doors. Maybe she was mistaken? Maybe it was Malous slamming her bedroom door? On the third knock she went to answer it.

"I didn't expect to see you here, especially this early in the morning." Pari marched back towards the kitchen. "So, when did it happen?"

"You know that Arbab passed away?" Ali was stumped. He knew that Pari hadn't seen her husband for a good while.

"Yes I did. When did it happen?"

"But, how did you find out? Did anybody come to tell you about it?"

"No…I just knew." Her tone gave away her reluctance to talk about her knowledge.

"He passed away yesterday. The burial ceremony is in three days so I've come to get you, Zan-Arbab."

"Did he suffer?"

"He'd become very feeble and debilitated during the past month. He couldn't eat properly. To be honest I think he refused to eat; he had lost his will to live."

"I should have gone to see him," she muttered.

"The day before his death, I went to visit him. All he said in-between gasping for breath was: 'I wish Pari was here. If she was here with me, I wouldn't be in this pathetic state. I wish she was here'." Ali sighed. He felt pity for his Arbab. "He had it very hard ever since they moved to Tehran. There was no trace of joy left in his spirit. Poor man."

"How are the children taking it?"

"Of course, they're both heartbroken that they won't see him any more. They didn't get to spend much time with him over the past two months. He was mostly in bed. Maybe that softened the blow, a little."

"Aban must have grown up a lot since the last time I saw her."

"Well, she hasn't forgotten you. That's for sure. You must have carved some impression on her."

"I guess the truth is that when you genuinely love someone, they know it. They carry your love with them wherever they go. It's one of those things with no concern for time. Aban knows that I've always loved her and I'll carry on loving her."

The elongated faces of the kitchen occupants sparked the suspicion of Yousef's death. Zeeba and Rahim had known of his illness for a while. And Ali's presence at that time of the morning could be for no other reason than to announce Yousef's passing.

"So, his heart gave out?" Zeeba asked without surprise.

"Yes, ma'am. Yesterday," Ali responded, clutching his hat.

"When's the funeral? We'd like to go to his funeral." Rahim realized he'd spoken too soon when he noticed his wife's alarmed eyes fixed upon him.

"It's okay. You're too busy. I'll go on my own." Pari had known Zeeba long enough to be sure she wasn't one for wasting her time at unentertaining occasions unless her presence somehow reflected upon her.

"When do you think you'll be back?"

"I won't stay for more than a week."

Pari packed her dusty bag with the only black dress in her possession (that she used to mourn the martyrdom of the Prophet's grandchild every year) and the pair of black shoes Zeeba had given her when she first walked into her house.

Zeeba was waiting impatiently at the bottom of the stairs. Pari had hardly got to the bottom step when Zeeba blurted a few words of condolence then sped off in the direction of the backyard.

Before Pari got to the front door Rahim placed a ten-touman note in her hand and folded her fist around it.

Pari stayed for more than a week. In fact, she stayed for eleven days; not that she had any hidden plot stashed in the corner of her mind before she left her cousin's house.

She didn't want to be at the funeral in the first place. Even Ali's delivery of her husband's last words hadn't sparked any feelings of mourning. She simply recoiled from the whole scenario of giving him away to the underworld. She still hadn't spruced up her messy sack of emotions; a little bit of love, a lot of despair, some anger, some concern, a patchwork of feelings she hadn't dealt with for years. He was a part of her life; the moaning part. The part she would grab and beat up on without taking breath whenever her work and toil went unnoticed, whenever she had to swallow her anger, whenever she could take no more. And now he was gone; she wasn't sure if she could beat up on a dead person.

And she felt nervous about seeing Aban. She had abandoned her. Aban had every right to hate her. The thought of Aban ignoring her, dismissing her sent a shudder through Pari. How could she ever have explained to Aban that she simply didn't have the strength for furtive, sporadic meetings; a hundred goodbyes to break both their hearts a hundred times?

The room in which Yousef took his last gasp was too dark. Pari pulled the curtains open. Everything in that rectangular space shouted of sadness and despair. Maybe the room was better off with the curtains shut? His ashtray was packed with cigarette butts. Its stench a clear sign that it had been abandoned for a long time. His blanket reeked of smoke with holes marking cigarette burns. His half-empty glass of water had kept its space under the wooden bed. An apple core and an ice-cream spatula next to it had left a trace of the occasional visit of his children. By the look of his room, no one could have imagined the days of his mastership, the glorious days when he was an Arbab.

"I thought I'd give this room a good clean after the funeral." Pouran fidgeted. "The children will be back from school before long. I thought it would be a lot easier on them and me if they went to school and stayed away from the house."

The youthful vigour that she brought with her the first time she stepped into their home in Varamin had long faded. Her perkiness was replaced with an implicit indifference that she wore like an old coat. Pari couldn't spot any joy of life in those once-sparkling hazel-green eyes. They seemed dull, almost wooden.

"Sounds reasonable. I'm looking forward to seeing them." Pari tried to show some tenderness. She meant it.

Pouran's offer of tea and dry pastries was the right means to break the ice. After all these years she still felt rather uneasy around Pari. How could she feel close to an older woman who treated her like a snotty schoolgirl? Her presence had always been so powerful and dominating for Pouran, no matter where and under what conditions she happened to see her. This was the woman who kept the title Zan-Arbab and remained the sole Zan-Arbab even after the reign was lost.

"Aban often talks about you." Pouran's attempt to flatter Pari was rather hopeless. Pari could sense the spiteful rivalry of a mother who had no choice but to surrender to the forged holiness of a strange woman her daughter had built a shrine to.

"I often think of her. She has a special place in my thoughts." Pari was aware she hadn't made it any easier on Pouran. "You realize no matter how much Aban appreciates the times she spent with me, the times I took care of her and showed her tenderness, deep inside she knows you're her mother, her flesh and blood, and I'm just a stepmother. Blood attracts blood. That's something no one can take away from you. It's yours and will always remain yours."

The gravity in Pari's tone made her words sound real. She never meant to steal anybody's child away; she seeded true love and kindness, creating an untouchable, timeless place in a human being's heart.

And at that moment she was willing to bend over backwards to show some of that kindness to the fragile woman sitting opposite her. Pari did feel sorry for her. She'd been forced to exchange her youth and fertility for the promise of a wealthy life. And she was cheated out of her contract. She was a simple teenager who gave herself to her future. And what a bleak future that had turned out to be. Squandering her youth on a man older than her father, bearing two children by him and spending the rest of her marriage with an ill and bankrupt husband, in relative poverty.

"Aban and Hameed didn't see much of their father in recent months. I had to take care of two irritated children and a dying husband." Pouran felt more comfortable talking to Pari. "I know it will sound callous to you but in a way I'm glad it's over. It was too much to take."

"I can imagine how difficult it must have been. I don't think you're being nasty by wanting it to be over." Pari didn't have to contrive sympathy for this husk of a woman. She empathized with her pain. "As a matter of fact, marrying you off to someone the age of your father was a crime in itself. I hope Yousef asked for forgiveness for ruining your life before letting go of this world. Who will take care of you now?"

"My uncle said he will provide for us until I find a husband." Pouran was overwhelmed by a sense of relief and gratitude to Pari. She had opened up to her relatives time and again to unload some of her ragged loneliness, to weep about her wasted womanhood, to moan about eking out her daily budget. But all she'd heard was advice as to how she should abide by her marriage and how she should keep her head down and cope with *all* of the ups and downs. She could hardly recall a single "up"; and this made her feel guilty. She desperately wanted to remember something good about life with her husband. But she could not.

"Where does he live, your uncle?"

"In the south. Kerman."

A familiar chill coursed through Pari's veins; the cold that dulled the pain of separation. She had no right to mourn over a parting that had already taken place. But Kerman was so far away. She would surely never see Aban again.

And then Pouran started. An explosion of words, with no hiatus, out of a face purpled by the desperate need for oxygen. She recited a diary of how she yearned, nightly, for a loving, lusty kiss on her neck, a run of appreciative fingers through her hair. She wept about being a servant and not a wife; about how she had to care for a sick husband and how she had missed the joys of youth.

Pari's trance was interrupted by a kiss on the cheek. Aban circled her arms around her neck and milked as much of Pari as she could. Hameed shied away, waiting for persuasion to become friendly with the familiar woman that had vanished one day and now sat in front of him as plain as day. A bar of chocolate paved the way to fond remembrance.

"So, how do you like school?" Pari asked Hameed.

"It's all right."

Hameed shrugged and took a big bite of his chocolate. "Will you take me to school tomorrow?"

Pari would end up accompanying him to school for the next ten days. It was a welcome change for Hameed and a hidden pleasure for his stepmother. She got to enjoy the purity and the unpretentious liveliness of two human beings for a while; something she had almost forgotten about and now that she had tasted it again, she wanted to keep it for all the time she could spare. Lack of jealousy on Aban's part made her stay even more of a happy experience. All Aban desired was her presence in that house. As long as she could have her, she was content sharing her with other people.

Yousef's funeral was by no means fancy or extravagant. Pouran needed the money to eke out a bearable life for her children. That money could support them before any philanthropic hand-outs from her uncle would find their way through her door.

Ali had taken charge of the ceremony, making sure that the two remaining women in Yousef's family, the odd combination, suffered no discomfort on that day. Standing next to the bare dark hole, the grave that held the shrouded body of Yousef, Pari said a special prayer for his soul. During her prayer she begged God to grant him a comfortable journey to the other side. Pari was trying to bury the spite and the fury that she had dragged with her all these years deep into that hole with him. She needed to let go of the dark cloud hanging over her. She needed to cleanse her soul.

Some of the villagers had come to see their Arbab off to the other world. Though after the burial, when everybody went back to Yousef's place to dip into the sending-off lunch, it became apparent that many of them had travelled from Varamin to see Pari, their beloved Zan-Arbab, again.

She saw Sardar and enquired of his camel. She saw Banoo and learned that she was content living in Ali's house. Ali had a wife. Knowing of the Arbab's illness and Pari's ill fortune he had married without fuss. Pari was thankful that fate had spread its favours evenly. Ali had suffered in this life so much, he deserved a little peace.

The pleasure of being liked and remembered was too overpowering to hide; Pari's face was brushed with gratitude. She allowed herself, for a little while, to relive the great memories of the good old days. Years barren of regard had made her insatiable.

She did not want the day of her husband's funeral to end.

CHAPTER

23

Pari didn't expect to be greeted on her return, having stayed away for longer than promised. Foti delivered a heavy "good morning" when she opened the door for her. She wasn't the slightest bit pleased about having to help Zeeba with the sewing work and taking care of the daily chores on her own. Having first-hand experience of the frequent unreasonable demands of her cousin, Pari couldn't blame her for being cross.

Foti shuffled towards the kitchen, which somehow implicitly invited her back to her usual spot.

"You must have enjoyed your time over there. Was it really a funeral or a prolonged party you couldn't miss?"

"I hadn't seen the children for a long time. I had to spend some time with them. Especially at a time like this, with their father dead."

"I didn't know you were coming back today. I've already prepared the ingredients for today's soup. Do you think you can take charge of dinner?"

"I'll unpack and get about it right away."

Malous's room was a mess. There were clothes everywhere; on the bed, on the chair, on Pari's mattress. There was a handful of books on the floor next to her bed, some of them wide open, some closed with papers half sticking out covered with hand-written notes that resembled lines of ants.

She must be studying for the end-of-year exams? Not that she clears her room regularly anyway but it's usually nothing compared to this mayhem.

Pari started cleaning up. It wasn't her first time; she knew where to put each item. Her school books on the third row of the book shelf right above the "intellectual ones". All the papers on the first shelf next to the magazines and her clothes stashed back into the wardrobe with no fuss attached to location. The only irregular items were a couple of brochures regarding a nursing school. Pari skipped through them. She didn't notice anything that would particularly lure her attention. Besides, she was wanted in the kitchen. *They can stay with the magazines for now. She can shift them later if she wants to.*

Pari's return to her daily duties alleviated the bad mood Foti had been brewing for eleven days. By dinnertime she was bearable. Pari had already made herself ready for the sarcastic comments of her cousin, the inquisition into why she was late, the speech as to how stranded they were without the extra hands. She'd gone through the questions and answers in her mind beforehand and had prepared a list of acceptable replies to make the pain of the procedure pass as quickly as possible.

The soup she cooked cooled the aftermath of the interrogation. For years her almost magical culinary skills had calmed and soothed mental and physical strains, and the foul moods associated with them. The first spoon in the mouth cast a spell on the stomach that somehow found its way to the soul. No one knew how but no one could deny it; her food was delivered from heaven.

Malous arrived in the middle of the eating meditation. She sat with more than a little uneasiness. For the last eleven days she'd had to listen to every sideways comment on Pari's absence, but she bit her lip. She knew that Pari was more than a match for Foti's empty complaints, and even her mother's overblown pronouncements on the terms to which she'd condemn the accused would surely meet a more animated opponent in the flesh. But here they were; all sitting silently, almost still. Only the occasional slurp to catch a stray morsel of bread, or perhaps a drip of soup escaping the side of the mouth to disturb what looked for all the world more like prayer than dinner. Pari gave her a knowing wink then she poured some of the enchanted soup into her bowl with an invitation to join the circle. A wave of pure pleasure passed through her as she watched them all, bliss written upon their faces.

Malous helped Pari to pile up the dirty dishes in the sink but stopped short of offering to wash them. She'd never made a habit of spending too much time in the kitchen. Spending too much time in a place gets people used to having one around and consequently raises their expectation and, if one is not careful, pretty soon they get to wondering as to how one could become more useful.

She followed her mother to the sewing room. Malous picked up a skirt and started hemming. Zeeba couldn't hide her surprise. It wasn't every day that her daughter showed any interest in labour.

"What's possessed you to sit here and give me a hand?"

"Is there anything wrong with that?"

"I guess not. How come you were late today again?"

"I went to watch a movie after school with a classmate."

"God Almighty. Are there any movies left that you've missed by any chance? Or maybe you watch them ten times in a row?"

"I watch some of them twice. I enjoy watching movies."

"How are you coping with your exams? You don't think you'll fail any?"

"No. So far I've managed just fine. The course consultant has asked the whole class to hand over the questionnaires by the end of this week. We have to let her know if we want to continue the remaining year to get a high-school diploma or to head for a profession and apply for an apprenticeship." Malous didn't notice any reaction in her mother. She looked like someone waiting for the punch line of a joke she'd heard before. "I've decided to go to nursing school. I'd like to become a nurse and I've filled in my questionnaire accordingly."

Zeeba's reaction was as quick and aggressive as a cheetah pouncing on her prey. "You what? You've decided? Who are you to decide?"

"I'm old enough to decide my own future."

"Oh really! Since when? I let you get out more than your classmates are allowed to, I give you freedom at the expense of being considered too lenient and non-caring and all this has gone to your head. Well let me enlighten you. You're nothing without me and you do what I tell you. Don't you think for one second that you can live under my roof and do as you please." Zeeba's face had turned a shade of mauve.

"I don't understand. What's wrong with becoming a nurse? What's wrong with taking care of people?"

"I didn't bring you up to empty toilet pots and wipe the shit off people's arses."

"What are you talking about? Nursing is a decent profession. You should be proud to have a nurse as your daughter."

"Proud? While you're living in my house you'll do as you're told. You'll finish high school, go to university and get a degree. That's the kind of daughter I want."

"But…"

"I don't want to hear any more rubbish. I said my piece and that's the end of it."

"No, it's not the end of it. As a person, I have the right to think for myself. I have the right to make decisions for myself."

"Sorry to break the news to you but your slogans aren't worth the paper they're written on. They don't apply in my house."

"You have no principles. You pick and choose what suits you at the time."

"You want principles, I'll show you principles! You're going to pack your bags and head for your father's house. I'm sure it doesn't make any difference to him what kind of a daughter he's got. Go on! Move it! On your way!"

The commotion attracted the rest of the household. By the time they got there Malous was leaving the room looking like a beaten dog with her tail in-between her legs. Foti was the first among them to broach the question. She had to satisfy her curiosity. Any trouble in the house was fun; especially when it was between Zeeba and her daughter. That way Zeeba was certain to suffer.

"What happened here? What has she done?"

Zeeba didn't even lift her head. "She's going to stay with her father." She carried on basting a hem with great long stitches that could hardly hold the weight of the cloth.

"With her father? Since when did she become a fan of her father?"

"I don't want to talk about it. I'm too angry. Leave me."

There was no refrain, no attempt to talk her round. Zeeba was a ticking bomb waiting to blow and nobody wanted to be the one lighting the fuse. Pari followed the long-faced teenager to her room. She was sure that a bit of a pep-talk would put her mind back in order.

"What's the trouble, *aziz-jan*?" She stroked Malous's hair.

"The trouble is her as usual. The fact that she believes she can order everybody around."

"I still don't know what's going on."

"She's thrown me out. That's what's going on. Her own daughter. She's kicking her own daughter out."

"What have you done, *aziz-jan*? What did you do to make her this angry?"

"I told her that I've made up my mind to go to the nursing school as of next year instead of finishing high school and she wouldn't let me. It's beneath Her Royal Highness to have a nurse as a daughter."

"Well, if you finish high school you're presented with more choices in the future. You can study whatever you want at university. I won't argue when you say Zeeba's a dictator. I know how little regard she's got for other peoples' opinions but she has a point insisting on you getting your high-school diploma."

"Thanks for the support."

"Let me go talk to her. I'm sure she didn't mean it. I'm sure she doesn't want to send you off to your father's house."

Pari decided to give Malous some space and went to plead with her cousin. She didn't believe that Zeeba was determined to send her daughter away to Amir's place. *It's a mother-daughter squabble and in the end it will amount to nothing important.*

Despite her fear of setting Zeeba off, Pari barged into the sewing room, on a mission.

"For the love of God. She's just a schoolgirl."

"That's not what she thinks. She's adamant that she's old enough to decide for herself. Well, I'm giving her the opportunity to do so."

"You're talking like a schoolgirl yourself. Just tell her you didn't mean what you said. And later you'll talk the matter over. You never know, you might change your mind about the nursing school."

"I will not change my mind about the nursing school and don't you ever, do you hear me, ever give her the impression that I would agree with her stupid plan. I will not have her clean people's shit and pretend to myself and everybody else that she's achieved something."

Pari kept silent for a few minutes to gather her nerves. She had seen Zeeba in such a state before; she was sure there was no changing it.

"Fair enough. But you don't have to send her away. I'm sure the thought of staying at her father's house with that monster of a stepmother has sent enough shivers down her spine to soften her."

"That's not my concern. I'm serious about sending her off to Amir's place. She's got to experience this fear first-hand so that she'll never talk back to me in the future."

"That's not fair. How could you be so heartless? Amir doesn't want her, he never asks about her. And as for his wife, I don't even know if I need to waste my breath talking about that witch."

"She has to learn to appreciate what I've done for her. She has to learn not to take her life with me for granted. I've done everything in my power for her without the slightest help from that bastard. I even aborted a baby so that she doesn't feel that I've lost interest in her." Zeeba pulled at the cloth in her hands so fiercely the loose basting gave way, then the cloth tore into two pieces. She held them up, as if in evidence. "And this is how she pays me."

"Don't you blame the abortion on that girl. We both know it had nothing to do with her. That's unforgivably cruel."

Pari had so much to say. She was bursting with a pile of distilled gripes and hatreds from petty to grave, and she wanted to spill them all now, but she kept them inside. She knew that they would turn inside her then come back and haunt her in the shape of high blood pressure and acute migraine. But there was no point in arguing with Zeeba. There was never any point in arguing too much with her unless you were ready to pack your bags and leave. Zeeba's belief in herself seemed to transcend every logic, every reason, every truth under the sun.

By the time Pari left the sewing room, Malous was already standing at the staircase with her travel bag in her hand. She looked like a pitiful orphan, the trepidation at the horrors and hardship of the new foster home she was allocated to written upon her face. Malous knew her mother well. She knew she had no option but to walk out through the door. The only hope she carried with her was a revival of mercy in Zeeba's heart as to the duration of her sentence. It was comforting and easy to live in a fantasy world from time to time where she would pretend to herself that she had a father who wasn't around but must have thought of her often. But like a girl playing with her doll's house she was aware that the whole thing was just a fabrication of her imagination. If her father cared about her then he cared in a very strange way.

Pari didn't even bother to try to tell her that things wouldn't be as bad at her father's. She simply didn't have the strength to tell a lie that would surely be exposed as soon as the poor girl arrived at his house.

She stood at the doorstep until Malous disappeared into the main street.

Then she was gone.

CHAPTER

24

Malous's absence hardly made a dent in the everyday routine at her mother's home. After four months still nobody acted as if Malous was gone. Their apparent indifference saddened and infuriated Pari. She talked about Malous constantly, concocting scenarios of her "difficulties" at Amir's place and her undoubted desire to come back, hoping that she could find some sympathy, a little mercy. What she faced was less than apathy: a monotonous munching noise at the dinner table or the uninterrupted hum of the sewing machine, or simply silence. They were completely deaf to anything concerning Malous, whether fabricated or real.

Zeeba wasn't in the dark about the state of her daughter. She'd received intermittent news about how she'd lost weight, about her commencing the nursing school and about how she'd been worked to the bone for every grain of rice she ate. But in Zeeba's books Malous hadn't seen hardship enough; there was no sign of remorse, nothing to suggest her daughter might see the error of her ways and beg her mother's forgiveness.

Zeeba had other matters to hold her interest. Her brother's divorce was finalized; to no one's surprise. He brought his new wife into his house two months after that. They didn't arrange for a fancy ceremony. After all, they had both left their previous marriages under *peculiar* circumstances and had little reason to flaunt themselves.

Haady wanted his sister to start her relationship with Hoori on the right foot. As much as he tried to deny it, his sister's opinion of his wife, his life and what he did with it mattered to him. He also had the notion that Zeeba's approval would give him a "free" life. He always railed against Zeeba's interference but deep inside he knew better than to ignore her.

To engineer a good start, he took Hoori to his sister's for frequent visits and made it crystal clear to her that kowtowing to Zeeba would help strengthen and prolong their marriage. It made sense to him that the more his sister saw of Hoori the sooner she'd be accepted as a part of the family. But Zeeba was no easy nut to crack. The way Hoori had become her brother's bride hadn't endeared her to Zeeba one bit. The bother and the stress that she caused had already brewed a big pot of resentment on Zeeba's fire. And all things being equal, Zeeba preferred her ex-sister-in-law. She saw her as a different class. She was educated and gentle and from a "good family". Even Zeeba's hawkish scrutiny couldn't poke any holes in the content of her character. Until something miraculous changed her mind (and that was difficult to envisage), she would perceive Hoori as nothing but trouble.

Haady's knock at the door announced yet another visit. Pari noticed a box of pastries as the door opened. She was certain that the sweet content of the box was a messenger of some news; enough to be heralded with fresh pastries.

It was a Friday afternoon with no pre-arranged dinner plans or rummy sessions; plenty time to spare for the preparation of dress patterns for new clients. Pari led them to the sewing room (she didn't want to pass up the opportunity to hear the news first-hand).

"Why did you bring them here? Let's go to the living room." Zeeba smiled, somewhat dubiously, at the pastry box.

Rahim and Foti were comfortable in their seats in the living room, completely unbothered by each other. Rahim put his paper down and shook hands with the guests.

"Is that cushion finished yet? Don't forget to sew the pink pearls on the left corner." Zeeba made sure that Foti didn't stop working to hobnob with the visitors.

"So what's the occasion?" Zeeba asked, looking at the pastries.

Hoori tilted her head, trying to look charming and meek as a prelude to her announcement before her husband cut in: "Hoori's pregnant! You're going to be an aunt."

The momentary silence felt like hours. Zeeba was ambushed by a hoard of conflicting emotions. She wanted to see her brother's child, she would care for his child as much as she adored him. But she had a problem with the mother-to-be.

"Well, well, congratulations. May you always bring good news with you." Pari opened the box and offered the pastries. Hoori's expression imparted her gratitude for Pari's timely ice-breaker. Haady, unaffected by her cheer, was still waiting for his sister's reaction.

Rahim was next to congratulate them. His pause to gauge Zeeba's emotions had become uncomfortable.

Finally, Zeeba spoke. "It's nice to be an aunt. I'm looking forward to seeing my nephew…or who knows, my niece? Congratulations!" She phrased her sentence with enough easiness to make everybody (including herself) believe that for the time being she was happy about Hoori's pregnancy. Certainly, problems would arise as Hoori was patently unfit to be a mother but she could always deal with them as they appeared along the way.

Foti's lack of cheer didn't catch anybody's attention. She had known throughout her adult life that her chances of developing any romantic relationship with Haady were as likely as Hoori getting struck by lightning. But as long as there were chances, there was hope. Now, with a baby on the way, she could feel her hands letting go of the grip of that imaginary and fragile branch of hope.

She stared blankly at them. The dimensions of the room had changed. They looked miles away from her, so distant, so detached. It wasn't as if she had ever seen herself as an integral part of that household. It wasn't as if she had ever got the chance to nestle into the warmth of acceptance and moral benevolence. But the distance she experienced at that moment immersed her in despair. She was drowning in helplessness and self-pity, completely invisible to the people around her. They were from a different world, somewhere she didn't belong. They had everything. They had sucked up all the happiness in this world and had left nothing for her. And sinners they were; they didn't savour their happiness. Here she was, starved of life's pleasures and there they were; served with enchantment on a silver plate and squandering every bit of it.

She took her share of the pastry, grabbed the cushion she was working on and left the room with the excuse of having to complete her handiwork.

Hoori's pregnancy kept Zeeba at bay. Not that Zeeba ever gave her the impression that their differences were mended but the noticeable reduction of sarcasm was a godsend to Haady. He was enjoying the absence of bickering and wouldn't change it for the promise of Solomon's wealth. Pari made an attempt to elicit his sympathy for Malous, to get him to talk to his sister. If there was anyone who could touch her mercy, it was Haady. Zeeba had a soft spot for her brother. But he wasn't about to rock the boat, not for anybody's sake; even a temporary relief from Zeeba's stifling chain of reproach was to be appreciated.

Foti had become inhibited and even more bad-tempered. The slightest thing would strike her nerves and make her boil. She seemed to reserve her facial expressions for Zeeba and her breathless shouting for Pari. Her behaviour had stretched to beating on herself, pounding her fists on her head and pulling out her hair as if possessed by a djin. Even Zeeba had taken the situation seriously by getting out of her way. Pari took on all the household chores to evade any possible friction. Nobody knew for how long her madness would linger. The cause of it was irrevocable and the cure for it unattainable. They all had to suffer it until she either came to terms with reality or some miraculous event diverted her attention.

The slamming door jogged Pari out of her trance; it was Foti's way of announcing her foul mood on arrival. Pari felt trapped in her seat at the kitchen table. *No surprise, she'll barge in nagging about some ridiculous thing, waiting for the wrong answer to start a row. God, I don't know how much longer I can take this before I head for the madhouse.* She stopped peeling the carrots and waited with a kind of dread. As Foti's steps came closer, she surrendered a little more, ready for a squabble about nothing, initiated by a frustrated woman half-mad. But the footsteps rushed by the kitchen door without hesitating. Pari was so ready for the whole scene that she almost felt betrayed by Foti ignoring her. She waited a while, to see if Foti might appear, until a strange, pounding noise from upstairs put an end to her patient wait. This was too bizarre to ignore. Pari rushed upstairs hardly able to imagine what poor Foti might be up to.

Foti's state was disastrous. She looked like she'd been attacked by a pack of wolves. Her shirt was ripped open with buttons missing. The expression on her face was a mixture of fury and fright; like an animal caught in a trap. She threw herself from her bed and onto the floor as hard as she could, then dragged herself up, determined for another jump.

"In the name of God, what are you doing?"

Foti ignored her and made another painful jump.

"Have you lost your mind? Why are you hurting yourself? Stop it!" Pari wasn't sure whether trying to restrain her might make things worse, so she tried to reason with her.

"Shut...up! Shut up!" Foti grabbed a wooden coat hanger and started to beat her stomach, cursing everything under the sun.

"I beg you to stop. Please have mercy on yourself. Please calm down. I'll make a glass of gol gavzaban for you. That will help you relax."

"Gol gavzaban? That'll do it," she said, her eyes almost popping out of her head. Then she threw herself down again, this time her head make a sickening thud as it hit the floor.

Pari's attempt to talk Foti out of her madness had simply fuelled her rage. She lashed her stomach with the coat hanger again before falling against the wall then she slid down it as if suddenly she'd turned to liquid, her strength completely drained.

"Get out of my room," she gasped so breathlessly, it was almost silent.

Pari couldn't bring herself to abandon her but she had no idea what to do. No, it wasn't that she had no idea what to do. Pari knew perfectly well there was nothing in this world that she could do. She was helpless.

"Are you deaf? Get out of my room." Pari left almost in as much pain as Foti herself.

Every hour that Pari waited for Zeeba to appear at the front door felt like a whole day. She was stranded. There was no way she could go back to Foti's room without risking a broken bone. And yet, she was worried sick that Foti's lunacy would place her in a hospital. The only thing she could do was to listen. She sat on the stairs and honed her hearing into every little sound from Foti's room. Her neck started hurting before she realized how much she had crouched and contracted her body to let her ears find a better reception.

Time passed and there it was again. A dull, thudding sound, then Foti wailing and cursing, sent a shiver down Pari's spine. She was determined to go back in, even at the risk of a broken head. This was too much to bear. She had to put a stop to it. She marched into the room and grabbed Foti from behind just as she leapt, taking them both into a crash landing on the floor. Pari was always proud of her physical strength but Foti had the strength of a madwoman. After what amounted to a wrestling match, they were both depleted, both ravaged by helplessness and exhaustion.

"What's happening here?" Zeeba was standing at the door, baffled.

She raised her voice at the lack of response. "Is anybody going to tell me what the hell has happened here?"

Foti had neither the will nor the energy to speak. She kept her head down and released herself from the tight tangle of Pari's arms.

"She doesn't feel well. Maybe you can talk to her." Pari got up, straightened out her clothes and left somewhat unsteadily; she staggered a little against the wall, looked at Zeeba, fixed her hair, then carried on to her room.

She poured a cold cup of tea to wash down two painkillers. A migraine was imminent. She could feel blood pumping tightly through her veins. *God, she must be possessed. For the life of me, I have never witnessed such insanity. It's too much…even for her.*

She went to the backyard and sat by the pond, in desperate need of some fresh air. She splashed ice-cold water from the pond's tap onto her face. No smoking though, she had quit her old habit a week ago and the memory of her last cigarette seemed as distant as her first encounters with the habit that had been a friend to her for so many years. She had no fear that thinking about it with fondness would lead her back to it. She could remember, quite clearly, how she had started.

She took her first puff thinking nothing of it; she had lit a cigarette for her father. Then, little by little, this small participation turned into a fully fledged membership feeding a sixty-a-day habit. No one could remember Zan-Arbab without an Oshno cigarette between her fingers. She never thought anything of it; her father smoked, her husband chain-smoked, as did almost all the villagers. Above all, her supply was abundant.

She remembered puffing away her troubles with every luscious breath. She remembered the bonding power of a cigarette in a circle of friends telling stories. She remembered how a smoke offered a prop when she wanted to rekindle a friendship after an absurd row, and she remembered, bitterly now, how all the warm memories of her Oshno cigarettes were replaced by the nightmare of addiction. Pari had become a beggar rummaging through ashtrays after the weekly rummy session at Zeeba's place; a pathetic creature crippled by what was once a pleasure. There was no point brooding over Zeeba's miserly attitude to purchasing her cigarettes; maybe it was reasonableness on her part? Pari had to be practical about it. She knew herself. She had no time for self-pity. She had to sever the addiction, to see off the rotten cause of her indignity, to end her pride's erosion.

One early morning after prayer she refused to light a half-smoked butt she had found while sifting through an ashtray like a rat riddling a garbage bin.

She knew only one way to relinquish the unwanted, to break away from that which caused misery, and that was to chop it off with one strike and never look back. Pari beat cigarettes the way she beat opium. She went from smoking sixty cigarettes a day to none.

"I need your help." It was Zeeba. Pari jumped.

"How is she? Has she calmed down?"

"I don't give a damn how she is."

"What do you mean?" Her response sounded too callous even for Zeeba.

"What I'm about to tell you, I don't want it to get out of the boundaries of these four walls. The stupid whore is pregnant."

"But…" Pari was speechless. She was trying to gather her thoughts, to organize the filing cabinet in her mind and think of a time that she suspected something out of place, something that didn't tally with Foti's usual behaviour, usual madness, usual temper. It didn't make sense. How could she be pregnant? She wasn't even going out with any one secretly. Pari knew that because she knew Foti: She wasn't clever enough to hide such a thing from her or Zeeba. So, how did it happen? When did it happen?

"Who's the father? Did she tell you?"

"Did she tell me? Of course she did. After the scandal she's brought about she'll do as I tell her."

"So, who's the father?"

"Rahim's friend. He proposed to her a long time ago but she declined, God knows why. Apparently he hadn't matched her expectations. Stupid bitch. She should have got married to him. It would have saved us all the embarrassment. The way it appears, she didn't seduce him, she almost raped the poor fellow. Now, officially, she can't get married. Who wants to marry an old maid who's lost her virginity?"

Zeeba looked like a steam cooker about to blow. Her veins were sticking out of her temples. Pari was diligent not to let out a peep. She had no plans for being the one who paid for someone else's mistake.

"We have to take her to the hospital. The termination has to be performed in a proper and hygienic way. She's done enough damage beating herself up. You have to stay with her tonight. We'll see for how long she'd need to stay in the hospital. I'll make up a story about her health. I don't want anyone to find out, not even Haady and his wife. We'd have to pack our bags and leave this city if any one finds out the truth."

"I'll go and pack a bag for her. Are we going to wait for Rahim?"

"Of course, we'll need the accompaniment of a man when we get to the hospital."

Foti was crying quietly in the dark. She had drawn her curtains tight, as if she had planned never to see even a spark of light ever again. Pari took out some underwear and a couple of shirts for her without uttering a word. Sometimes silence was best. Besides, what was she going to say? *Don't worry? Although contrary to tradition, religion and the whole way of life in this country you gave in to lust and opened your legs for a stranger? Never mind. All your troubles will be over soon and everything will be fine.*

The slam of the front door added an accent to her crying that made it even more heart-breaking. Her brother was about to hear the news. Pari stayed with her for a while but the absence of the expected commotion made her head downstairs to make sure no frightening surprises were in store. She saw Rahim's face but did not look directly at him, as if she could pretend that she had no notion of what had happened. The atmosphere was uneasy and edgy and the incredulous expression on Rahim's face didn't exactly smooth the way. He seemed more disappointed than livid. He had the look of someone betrayed. Pari thought she could even detect a hint of pity. Maybe that was what was really needed: pity. Maybe that was what was missing from Foti's life; someone to feel sorry for her?

"Get her downstairs. We're leaving now," Rahim said, without emotion.

All the way to the hospital, no one exchanged a word. No one wanted to break the holy silence and possibly open Pandora's box. Maybe if they kept silent about it, somehow it would all disappear, simply vanish?

They sat with the other families in the waiting room. Fear and hope etched into their faces, they could be there for a son or a daughter, or a mother, father or a friend. Perhaps an accident, maybe a disease or a stroke or a hundred other ailments of which Zeeba and Rahim might be envious?

But they would be silent. In the still hours of the night someone might venture to ask what the problem was but neither Zeeba nor Rahim would indulge in any such chit-chat. Poor Foti would certainly live. She was in no mortal danger, although the other relatives in the waiting room might have believed so from their expressions.

After a few hours of silence it became apparent that nobody was about to enquire, nobody to poke and prod and wonder why they were there.

Pari had a chair to rest on all night and keep Foti company. It was lucky she didn't have to share her room with another patient. She didn't have to dodge any intrusive questions or get involved in any boring small talk.

"It was a boy, you know. I heard the doctor telling the nurse that it was a boy." Foti sounded calm and unaffected.

"I...don't know what to say."

"I know what you want to say. That I'm a whore and I finally showed my true nature...But I don't care."

"Best not to talk about it."

Pari fought back the tears. Poor Foti. The poor child. Pari knew better than to conjure the child in her mind's eye; to feel her own pain as she watched it wean and play and grow to maturity in a fleeting moment.

"Getting pregnant put me in trouble," Foti grunted.

Maybe it was the medication but Foti seemed unaware now of the phantom child. She had tried to kill it by throwing herself to the floor, and it seemed she mourned a future that might have been hers in another life. In another life she would bear the child and all would be happy. The same woman. The same lover and father. The same child. Brought into existence by the whim of a man who might have loved her, in another life.

Poor Foti; she thought she had suffered but this was just the start; simply a prelude to the bleakness that her life was about to become.

Pari felt an uncomfortable contempt for her at that moment. Pari had always respected and been obedient to her religion and customs, though when it came to others she left room for tolerance. She knew Foti could not give birth to this child, the fruit of lust, not marriage, but she couldn't help being angry at Foti for not caring enough, and she couldn't help despising the world for its cruelty. Foti's spinsterhood came with a crushing mixture of oppression, rejection and no chance to live life the way she wanted. It was too much baggage to carry, too much of a load to ignore. She had been a volcano brewing for years, ready to burst, burning everything in her way. Years and years of yearning to be accepted on her own terms, to assume control over her actions, had accumulated in her a boiling lava of mutiny.

Pari carried on with her silence. There was nothing she felt like saying to Foti.

Foti regained her energy after two days in hospital. She went home with the notion that now she had given more control of her life to Zeeba than ever. They had all taken a tacit vow of silence over the incident but there was no doubt that she would be brushed with blame every time she took a wrong turn. She had exchanged the expiry of virginity, the experience of sexual intimacy, for Zeeba's absolute dominion. But no one could undo the past.

Pari had just finished washing the curtains of the living room as part of the house cleaning before Norouz, the new year. She needed to refresh her strength with a hot cup of tea. The knock at the door didn't thrill her. The last thing she wanted was a visitor to slow her down. She had a marathon of housework to accomplish before the first day of spring. It crossed her mind to ignore whoever it was but she dutifully diverted her path from the kitchen and opened the door.

"*Aziz-jan*, what a great surprise! Don't be shy. Come in. It's your own house after all."

"Is anybody home?" Malous left her bag in the corridor.

"Your mother and Foti have gone shopping."

Malous had changed. She had lost weight and the two dark bags under her eyes did not speak of a relaxing time. Her skin had the dry, darkened pallor of the malnourished. She seemed tired and drained.

"Are you hungry? There's fresh bread?"

"That would be nice."

Pari cut a chunk of bread and put it next to her plate. She poured a cup of tea and joined Malous at the kitchen table. She popped a sugar cube into her mouth.

"Been doing a lot of walking?"

"Huh?"

"Your shoes look like they're ready to bark."

"I didn't have any money to pay for the bus fare. I have to walk to get to school, or anywhere else for that matter."

"You mean he didn't even spare a bus fare?"

"He never offered and I never asked."

"How is nursing school?"

"It's all right. I've learned some useful things. But I don't want it enough to bear the misery at my father's place any longer. It's a nightmare. It's like waking up in hell every morning knowing that no matter how much you try everything will crumble down on your head by night time." She talked like an inmate just released from a penitentiary packed with unpredictable lunatics, as if she were dramatizing her story. Staring off into space as she spoke. "I don't think I've ever met anyone as penny-pinching as my father in my whole life."

Pari nodded in agreement.

"At least now that I've lived there for a while I know that he treats all his children the same. He doesn't care about a single one of us. It's as if we're another mistake in his life. And for heaven's sake, what is that woman he got married to? God, she is truly as low as they come. It's a madhouse, that place. It's as if she lives for stirring a fight. Saying that she's rough is an understatement."

Malous shoved the last piece of bread in her mouth. She looked ready for more.

"There's yogurt you could have. I made it myself. Do you want some before dinner's ready?"

"That would do nicely." She poured a cup and left it on the table to cool down.

"Did anyone miss me at all?"

"I'm sure they did."

"You don't have to lie for other people, you know. I'm a big girl. You don't need to pretend in case you hurt my feelings."

Pari responded accordingly. She didn't pretend. She kept silent and that spoke for itself. Malous was right. What was the point of brushing the truth under the carpet? After all, it wasn't as if her childhood was embellished with undivided attention or devoted concern from her mother or any member of her family. It wasn't like she was new to this.

Pari looked at her. She didn't look like a *big girl* who was ready for the truth. As a matter of fact she looked like a little girl who wanted to be smothered in good news. She looked like she preferred to be lied to. She needed to hear how much she was missed, how no one could fill her empty space, how irreplaceable she was. At that moment Pari detected that she was always going to remain a little girl yearning to be wanted, no matter how old she became. There was a gap in her soul wanting to be filled regardless of time, regardless of age, regardless of where she ended up in life. As much as she despaired of her mother for her shortcomings, she still needed to be the most precious thing to her, to know that nothing would ever replace her. Pari could see that even having children of her own one day would not heal this gap, that Malous's love for her children wouldn't cure her bruised soul.

"Did you hear that you're going to have a cousin after all?" Pari was desperate to change the subject.

"None of my father's relatives knew about it."

"Hoori looks exceptionally beautiful. Being pregnant suits her. She's really looking forward to having this baby. She doesn't have any children from her previous marriage."

"Did my uncle ask about me at all?"

"Yes he did. Every time he came for a visit." Pari didn't hesitate for a second to lie.

"So, did they go anywhere out of town without me?"

"No. Nowhere. Nothing much happened while you were away. Just the usual rummy session and the odd nights of gambling in their dive, the hotel they usually go to."

"Hopefully she's lost some money." Malous wanted her mother to pay for abandoning her; even a few touman in a sleazy card game would be better than nothing.

"Some winnings and some losings. Just the usual. If you ask me she does it more for hobnobbing than gambling. I guess she finds people that gamble more fun to socialize with."

"I have to admit I like a few of her friends."

"I have to get on with my work, *aziz-jan*. I've a ton to do. Lost time isn't something you can get back."

"Can I give you a hand?" Malous said, following her to the backyard.

"I have to hang the curtains. You could help."

Helping Pari with the housework made her feel at home.

"I'll go and get more pegs." Malous went to the kitchen.

Zeeba was standing behind the kitchen door, her arms folded, her head slightly cocked to one side. She wasn't even feigning an excuse to be there. She still had her handbag in her hand. She might have been standing outside a store waiting for a taxi. Her eyes were cold, hidden, far away. She didn't care. Or rather, she cared enough to creep about the house and eavesdrop but she didn't care enough to try to hide it.

"Oh, we didn't hear the door close." Malous's voice was shaking. She was shocked at the dark figure behind the door, but the realization that it was her mother chilled her even more. This woman had condemned her merely for being impetuous. Malous knew that she had to obey her as if she were a mighty tyrant. The consequences of even the slightest dissent would far outweigh the crime.

"You've forgotten how to say hello?" Zeeba turned her face in expectation of a kiss.

"Of course, Maman." Malous pressed dry lips against cold cheeks. "Pari tells me you've all been doing well?"

"Yes. I expect you've been doing poorly. That's why you're back?"

"I didn't have a good time over there."

"All the huff and puff about your beloved nursing school wasn't worth it after all?"

"I'm going to go back to high school to get my diploma."

"I'm glad you're back to your senses." Zeeba took some money out of her purse and handed it to her daughter.

"Buy yourself a decent pair of shoes. These are embarrassing. Your father never changes, does he?"

Pari had waited for Malous's return long enough to realize that she must have bumped into her mother in the kitchen. It was time for her to come back home. She carried on with the curtains and hoped that Zeeba would be gentle.

Malous stuck her head around the door.

"Sorry, I have to leave you here on your own with the curtains."

"What's your excuse?" Pari smiled. Malous seemed happy.

"Shoe shopping. I'll try not to take long. I wouldn't miss your dinner for the world."

Foti seemed calm. Her normally foul temper almost evaporated. Perhaps a sexual experience or, more likely, a brush with intimacy had been all she needed? She would never marry now. She could never marry. But she had been taken by a man. She would not die a dry old spinster. It was enough.

Her calmness though hadn't fooled anybody about her malevolent feelings towards Haady's wife. What she felt for Haady was obsession; obsession to be married to him and bear his children, obsession to get embroiled in his world of intellect and becoming a part in the circle of trendy people he hobnobbed with, obsession to submit to him and take care of him.

Malous sensed the change of atmosphere but didn't bother to search for the source. The calm suited her just fine. Her desire for confrontation was spent. It wasn't worth it. With everybody minding their own business she had more time to spend on things that interested her. She immersed herself in school work, and retook her place among her circle of friends. She implemented her heavy movie-watching regime. She read books; the "intellectual ones", behind Pari's back, and she read the novels and the biographies with Pari. She loved it that Pari looked forward to their nightly story reading. Sometimes she read from her own writings; essays she was assigned to do by her literature teacher. Pari was amazed at the extent of her vocabulary (Pari said her words were as "clear and fresh as a mountain spring"). Sometimes she recited from a movie she'd seen.

So passionate were her renditions of the films that Pari would close her eyes to listen and later she'd swear blind that she'd actually seen the movie. Malous was both a daughter and a sister to Pari. She would watch her with a mother's pride but when Malous told her stories Pari turned into a girl. She remembered the future she saw for herself, she remembered herself. Malous's passion for movies and stories and for life was contagious and irresistible.

"You're a born storyteller, *aziz-jan*. You're a natural," Pari would say, as much to elicit another story as to advise her of her gift.

Their enthusiasm for stories had woven a strong bond between them; something that they weren't entirely consciously aware of. It was pleasant for Malous to share her interests with someone else, especially someone who cared about her. It made her feel fulfilled. Entertaining Pari every night made her feel good about herself. To Pari the stories were a drug, and with her addictive personality she didn't need much persuasion to get hooked.

Going back to Zeeba's place meant a return to Madam Yacobian's music lessons, and the accordion. Pari listened to Malous practise and improvise and, of course, Pari wildly overstated her abilities. Malous was a fine musician but listening to Pari speak of it, people might think a great maestro had risen from the grave and taken the form of a teenage girl.

Nevertheless, Pari's obstinate belief in Malous's abilities managed to banish the nerves that once plagued her performances. It was as if the woman's strength of will had a power in itself. Malous was more than a little surprised when music that once was difficult seemed to play itself. She no longer cared whether she was playing well or not, it was a joy to play, to return to that state which made her fall in love with music in the first place. Pari had taken her back there, and she had allowed her to bring a lifetime of discipline and practice with her.

Malous hadn't let go of her weekly attendance at the socialist party meetings. She still read their periodicals and sometimes wrote a letter to the editor if an article grabbed her attention. Whether a phase or not, politics had become her religion. It was the religion of anyone who wanted to call herself an "intellectual". It was a ladder for rising above everybody else with the possibility of righteousness without hocus-pocus at the top of the ladder. And to prove that she functioned within the rarefied air of the intelligentsia (albeit unacknowledged), she had read every book she owned…twice. That she hadn't really understood a word of Karl Marx's theories or Lenin's interpretation of those theories didn't deter her at all from believing herself to be a part of some secret socialist intellectual elite. What mattered to her more than the actual content of the theories was the certainty of the creators of those theories. She had given herself over to these men, these saviours. She knew she would follow them until the day she died.

Pari always watched for her expressions when she came back from the movies. Most times Pari could guess what kind of film Malous has seen merely from the expression on her face as she entered. Tonight she was sad. No. Worse than sad. She looked inconsolable. "So sad, *aziz-jan*?"

Malous couldn't hold back any longer. She cried like a child who'd lost her dog.

"Oh my God, what's the matter?" Pari felt that old familiar tightening in her chest. News of a death. Someone close, but who? She gripped at her chest. "Did anybody die?"

"Comrade Stalin died today."

"Comrade Stalin? Comrade Stalin? Thank God." Pari put the back of her hand to her forehead. She might have been acting out a scene from an old black and white movie; the heroine feeling faint.

Malous looked at her like she was a monster.

"For a second I thought maybe your father was de…I mean I thought maybe something bad happened."

"I wouldn't have cared so much if my father died instead of Stalin."

"Bite your tongue. You'll be an orphan if your father dies."

"I feel like an orphan now."

"We should care that Stalin's dead? Did Stalin do anything for you lately? Let's all sit and cry for an infidel who killed so many without mercy."

"I'm not going to stand here and listen to you insult a great man."

"Suit yourself." Pari shrugged. "Dinner's ready in an hour." Pari's slow shuffle to the kitchen made Malous feel slightly ridiculous.

Malous was serious about her loss. There was no accordion practice, no story reading that night. Pari couldn't fathom why she should be punished for the death of some Russian army man.

The next day Malous wore her only black shirt with a long black skirt that Zeeba had made for her.

"Aren't you going to wear your school uniform? They won't let you in with normal clothes."

"I'm not wearing normal clothes. I'm wearing black because someone close to me is dead."

"Well, I don't think your deputy principal will be amused to hear you're so close to the great Stalin."

Malous drank her tea and grabbed her school bag, clutching it to herself with one hand as she threw back the tea Pari had made with the other. She refused to look at Pari.

"Has your mother seen you leave without the school uniform?"

Malous left without a word. She knew Pari was right. They were going to stop her entering the school wearing ordinary clothes. But even the principal herself couldn't object if she told her that her father had passed away. It was a clever story. On the way to school she toyed with the idea of her father dying. What if he did die today for real? What if she went home and heard the news that she'd never get to see him again. And that's it. He's gone forever.

She wouldn't wish dying on him but if he did, it wouldn't be the end of the world. She felt sorry for herself. It wasn't supposed to be like that. She was supposed to be filled with grief and emptiness at the thought of her father's loss. Everybody she knew, all her friends at school would be sorrow-stricken if they lost their fathers but not her; and it didn't seem fair. She wanted to feel grief too; to feel a sense of bereavement. She wanted to be a part of "normal" society; the one that mourns for the loss of their loved ones. It wasn't fair that she had an uncaring, mean egotist for a father.

The thought of not being able to feel much got the better of her. Surely even cruel fathers are mourned by their daughters? Her father wasn't even cruel, at least in the sense that he never knowingly tried to hurt her, he was just selfish, self-absorbed, he couldn't see past himself. Surely that's not cruelty that warrants no daughter's tears in death? She dived into her memory to try to find a moment when she could know that she felt, really felt. At once, her mind trammelled her into the realization that the great Stalin had passed. A vision of Pari with one eyebrow raised banished Stalin and a faint remembrance entered her consciousness. At first it was just a feeling, a horrible feeling of enormous emptiness. It was hard to breathe, as if all the air had been sucked from the room. Then a portrait of her uncle Mehdi, who had passed on when she was younger, floated into her mind. The vacuum was filled with warmth. She was small when he passed away but the kindness he left behind still felt fresh. A memory of sitting on his lap; laughing, him stroking her hair, telling her stories. She was overwhelmed. It was as if someone had woken her from a slumber. She burst into tears, this time real tears and this time from the heart. She mourned and wailed for her uncle with whom a part of her heart still remained forever in love. The unconscious, unselfconscious feelings of a child, her love for her uncle was at the same time warm and secure and cold and empty; the memory of him inseparable from the memory of his absence, his parting, his abandonment.

Malous felt lifted by self-discovery. This memory would be her drug. She could send this memory, of true love, coursing through her veins when the need arose.

Malous was stopped by the deputy principal for not wearing her school uniform. She explained that her uncle was dead and how the whole family was grief-stricken. Her performance was real enough for anyone to accept her statement question-free. After all, she truly believed in it herself.

CHAPTER

26

Midsummer summoned a few anxious events in Zeeba's household. Haady's first child was born. Hoori gave birth to a beautiful boy. They named him Neema; of course, Haady's choice, after Neema Youshij, the famous Iranian poet. Haady even managed to make the name of his own son a *statement* about himself. Given the choice, Haady would have preferred a daughter. He believed girls brought with them fewer conflicts, fewer intrinsic problems. He believed himself to be too evolved to care about a son to carry his name. Family names were unimportant, fodder for gossiping fishwives. He believed that most people were backward, bumpkins who would believe anything. What interested Haady was altogether more rational than an imagined eternity through a name. Haady simply wanted to control his family and women; daughters were easier to control than sons. Haady wanted the quiet life. He wanted peace at home. He wanted peace to write his poetry, to drink, to get drunk on occasion, without any interference. A son, a teenage son, might, in time, make his life difficult. But the boy was healthy and beautiful, the centre of everybody's attention, and who could tell what the future might bring? Maybe a son was best?

Zeeba was genuinely happy about the birth of her nephew; maybe a bit too happy. Pari could recall when Zeeba gave birth to Malous. Granted, she was cheerful at becoming a mother but Pari hadn't detected purity in her happiness. Zeeba *knew* the grass *really was* greener on the other side and she had applied this dictum to every aspect of her life; even her own child. Pari couldn't fathom why Zeeba chose to covet others when she had a perfect child of her own to love. *It's sad that Zeeba cannot know love, but not everyone knows the art of happiness. Maybe there has to be a talent to find the way to true happiness? Maybe it's too deep an insight for some?*

Foti didn't show any emotion. She went with the crowd; she laughed when they laughed, she sweet-talked when they did. Seeing her suppressing her feelings wasn't something Pari felt comfortable with. It would have been better if she had had a howling and wailing session, like the ones the old women had when their beloved sons died; they would pound their fists on their heads and laps cursing everything and everyone under the sun then, suddenly, they'd stop. They'd go calm for several days, in a trance. Foti piled up her resentment inside until it fermented into a kind of bitter venom that she would release little by little towards anyone she could get her hands on, anyone unaware, vulnerable. Pari suspected her of fiddling with the stew Malous was learning to cook. She always did everything perfectly; she would wash and cut the herbs ahead of time. They'd be dry and fragrant come time for the pot. She refused to add a grain of salt without Pari's approval. She cut the meat into neat cubes; no trace of fat. She washed the rice many times, then she left it to expand in water; not long enough would mean roughness to make the Persian palate shy. Too long and the rice would be waterlogged, even sticky. But Malous's rice was perfect; light, so fluffy it might float away. Her tahdeeg, the crunchy, toasted rice at the bottom of the pot, was even better: crispy and light, seared in the centre and becoming thinner around the rim. Presentation was almost as important as taste and her rice invariably looked good. Always she used the best saffron, but not too much; just enough to lift the aroma and infuse the surface of the rice with little yellow-red clouds of intense flavour.

Her ghormeh-sabzi, herb stew, was almost as delicious as that of her teacher Pari, but there were occasions when the taste did not match the preparation. Of course, this elicited some disapproving looks from her mother (who only needed to know that Malous's cooking was "hit-and-miss"), but more importantly it shook her confidence a little. Pari knew that the food had been tampered with, especially since now that she had stopped smoking she knew exactly how something was going to taste simply by examining the ingredients. Someone had tampered with the food. Not in any way that could hurt; just a handful of doubt thrown into the mix. Pari didn't tell Malous about Foti. "Sometimes some salt is saltier than other salt," she'd say and laugh.

Malous did her best to juggle studying and her party meetings, writing and watching movies. She wasn't one of those students that read a book once and came out all shiny and happy. She needed hard work. She didn't have a broad kind of intelligence she could apply to any subject. Some subjects: history, music, literature, were easy, others: mathematics and religion, she found difficult. In truth, she was prone to too much analysis; she could hardly get past a single idea without an overwhelming urge to test it.

The high-school diploma was easy enough but university matriculation was another matter. She felt sure she had studied hard enough, regurgitated enough information, but no, she missed by a single percentage point. It was too much to take. After the appalling experience of dropping out of high school and getting exiled for eternity (as it seemed to her) to her father's madhouse, she couldn't find the stamina for another attempt at the matriculation. Zeeba's house was no place to rattle about in an idle existence. She would have to get a job. She'd be forced to enter a vicious circle. She would have to take a menial job. It would discourage her and make her feel hopeless. She was too exhausted for that type of struggle. She was just too tired to fight. She needed help and she didn't care if the devil himself offered a hand; she'd take it.

Zeeba was as desperate as her daughter to find a way through the university's gates. She struggled to come up with the right plan, to spot the right person to solicit. A failure of a daughter trying to eke out a living in a menial job was unthinkable. She needed to be able to present Malous as evidence of her superior parenting skills. She had made an extraordinary social leap in a society where a woman's place was a direct extension of the man in her life, be it husband or father, or even brother if the poor woman became an orphan without finding a husband. She was climbing the social ladder on her own; her place was more than simply a reflection of her husband's. Her daughter thought her a snob, but she knew better. She *was* better and the proof was a daughter as headstrong and courageous as any son could be. She was born to be better than her peers. There was no room for doubt, and she would do anything in her power to realize her destiny.

The prospect of failing to get her daughter into university was the spur she needed. She wanted to be a woman powerful in her society but she knew she was not, yet. Even so, her social circle certainly contained a path into university admissions. There was always someone willing to help a friend. There was no real corruption to deal with; no bribes or secret trysts; no fear or guilt, no risk. Friends of friends would be enough. And, she told herself, Malous was a very bright girl; they'd be doing well to have her as a student. It's not as if she wasn't university material; only a percentage point away?

It wasn't long before one of Rahim's friends introduced them to a *friend* in the ministry of education. They played on Malous's forte: writing and literature. They went through all the motions: meetings with lecturers and professors. Somehow it was made to look real, concerned parents fighting for the education of their daughter. But it was all a dance. Had they been regular parents without any contacts they would have been told by a bureaucrat that children must pass the exams to gain entrance and they can never make exceptions. Where would they draw the line? Malous was in. She was accepted as a student in the department of literature. Nobody would ever know that strings were pulled. And even if they found out, a single percentage point?

It was as if she were lifted into heaven. That she had entered "by the back door" hardly registered with Malous. She was too relieved to care about the manner of her achievement. She was the first woman from their family to enter higher education.

All she could think about was the new people and the new life that she was about to encounter. She fantasized about the prestige that went to a woman graduate and she was going to push herself to the limit to garner it, even if it meant she had to give up on her party meetings or cut back on her movies.

Pari soaked up the unusually warm atmosphere at Zeeba's place. She had the notion that before long there would be a storm to steal away the temporary calm in that house. She listened to Malous's long tales where she imagined all of her friends at university. Malous was going to become part of a new intelligentsia in the country, a group of intellectuals who even welcomed women to their ranks. Malous had it all worked out. The world was changing and Iran was changing, and she would be at the forefront: a woman in politics. Pari hoarded every story Malous read to her at their nightly sessions. She knew that soon Malous would be off and it would all end. She knew that Malous would continue to tell her stories but she would have to tell them to a journal. Another happiness was about to pass from Pari's life. At least this time it was for the best; for Malous. But that knowledge did not make it any easier. The nightly story sessions were all she thought about during a busy day of hefty work. She looked forward to it the same way a factory worker anticipated her five-minute cigarette break.

Zeeba started sewing a whole new wardrobe for her daughter. And she didn't stop at clothes. She went after her eyebrows with a pair of tweezers. High-school girls were forbidden from plucking their eyebrows, but those days were behind her now. Zeeba had the idea that if she didn't pluck her daughter's eyebrows then there might never be a wedding at all. Who knew? She might meet a suitable man over there. Universities were full of lonely professors who needed a good woman. Zeeba figured that if Malous were to arrive at university with plucked eyebrows then everyone would just think it was natural; at least men would never notice, and that's all that mattered. And it would give her an edge.

Malous didn't really put up much of a fight. Plucked eyebrows made her feel beautiful and independent. The women would be jealous and the men oblivious. Her eyebrows gave the two of them a rare bout of togetherness. Zeeba chased her in earnest and, as Malous complied in being caught and *plucked*, Zeeba enjoyed a taste of the relationship that still might be theirs.

Zeeba thought it best if Haady and his wife, Hoori, moved near to her house so that Neema had more people to look after him. She decided to employ her usual tactic of attrition until Haady gave in. In truth, there was hardly any fight in him. So used was he to eventually giving in to his sister's demands, he agreed over a single cup of tea. Hoori could see the disastrous plague of trouble creeping over their lives but her opinion was of no importance next to Zeeba's. Their new home was close enough for her sister-in-law and her gang to poke their noses in whenever they deemed it right. From the start they imposed their unwanted help on her and had no tolerance for lack of gratitude. Haady and Hoori and little Neema moved into a house less than a kilometre away but they might as well have been ensconced right in Zeeba's living room. Foti was especially satisfied with the situation; she could pop in unannounced to monitor their state of living and report back whatever she calculated might best cause a rumpus. Foti even concocted a plan to offer her services as a child minder in order to rummage around the house more freely with Hoori out of the way. Hoori knew what was happening but she had no resistance. She would have gone mad if she had been stuck indoors every day with Foti complaining or Zeeba directing, or even Pari helping. Hoori's life was no longer her own. The best she could do was take advantage of Foti's offer in order to grab a few precious hours for herself.

Foti opened every cupboard, every wardrobe and drawer just to see Hoori's belongings. If she saw a dress that caught her eye, she'd put it on to have a taste of it. Her surveillance was so thorough that she could have submitted a report of the number and probable value of Hoori's clothes, the brand of her make-up and the details of her kitchen utensils. It didn't matter how many times she'd poked around in them; she'd repeat her search pattern at every visit. She didn't want to miss any recent purchases. Everything had to be accounted for.

Foti was a more than able spy. Zeeba was more savvy about when and how to use the information Foti gathered.

Pari half-hoped looking after a baby, a pure and innocent being, would help soften the ragged edges in Foti's soul. Neema's mere proximity might open a new horizon, a new way of perceiving life for her.

"So, how do you like taking care of Neema?" Pari thought the best way to find out was to ask.

"What do you mean how do I like it?"

"I mean do you enjoy caring for him?"

"Enjoy?"

"He's a beautiful baby. One of those you can't get enough of."

"He's beautiful and he shits a lot. He won't stop bellyaching when he has a bellyache. His screams drill right into my head." Foti drilled her finger into her head to make sure Pari understood exactly what she meant.

"Oh, I thought you'd like him by now?" Pari hardly knew what to say. She'd expected some resistance but this was too much like the horror films Malous would watch and regurgitate in all their gory detail into the small hours of the morning. Foti was a little scary.

"I didn't say I dislike him," Foti grunted. "I have to take care of him. Don't I?"

"I can come over from time to time so that you won't be forced to sit with him as frequently."

"No thanks. I can manage perfectly on my own." Foti panicked a little. It had taken her a while to establish her scheme. She didn't want to see it interrupted or interfered with. It didn't matter how annoying it was to look after Neema. Neema was her ticket into Hoori's house, it was the only interesting thing in her life and she wasn't going to let it slip through her fingers.

Pari didn't understand Foti. The woman was impervious to the charms of children. She almost didn't even see them. Some might conjecture it was because of her bad experience but Pari knew better. Pari never tried to pretend that taking care of a baby was a joy, or that a woman would be an angel to watch over children. Pari saw it as a transaction: an emotional exchange between two human beings. One, the mother, offers care and support and the other, the child, peace and purity to relieve a disturbed soul. Pari wasn't ashamed of admitting this ulterior motive as the main reason for taking care of another human being.

What Pari didn't know was that Foti had already come up with her own way of soothing her troubled soul. The time she spent lurking around Hoori's house going through her belongings was her quiet time out of Zeeba's house. The added bonus was the pleasure of stirring trouble for Hoori.

There was no shame in conjuring up difficulties for the unwanted newcomer; especially when she had an accomplice to approve of her action. Zeeba demanded comprehensive reports and Foti was always ready and delighted to provide details.

It wasn't long before Pari overheard one of those reports. It was a house too small to bear secrets for very long. Besides, it didn't bother Foti a bit to have her scheme revealed. In fact, Foti's reports were almost pure fiction. She concocted stories and facts to damn Hoori, and she seemed to believe in them herself as if they were real. Hoori was a mischievous woman in her book and even if she hadn't committed all the crimes in Foti's list, it was just a matter of time before she fulfilled Foti's predictions.

Pari was happy to stay out of things. This wasn't her village. People laughed at her here as if she were an eccentric. She felt for Hoori and the treachery she had invited into her own home, but Hoori was a grown woman. In Pari's village she might have acted as Solomon in a matter such as this but it was even better for the woman under attack to fight her own corner. Anyway, Hoori had done her fair share of wrecking the homes of others and perhaps this was her reward?

What caught Zeeba's attention was Foti's discovery of the number of times Hoori had prolonged her customary grocery shopping. She was itching to find out what Hoori was up to. Zeeba felt her lack of trust was vindicated. It was just a matter of time for her sister-in-law to slip up and show her hand.

Zeeba didn't spare any tact to approach the subject. She put it to her brother outright the very next time she met him. This was always her way: to say what she wanted whenever she felt like it. She had no patience for consideration or subtlety towards people she deemed beneath her. She was tactful enough when dealing with *important* people but that was it; everyone else was fair game.

"Your wife's having a good time since Foti started baby-sitting for her?"

"She didn't force her into taking care of Neema. You offered. You almost shoved it down her throat." Haady couldn't be bothered with her sarcasm.

"Touchy today?"

"Yes."

"What I see is my brother under his wife's thumb."

"Please. Compensating for Mother's belligerence?"

"Don't you take that tone with me!"

"Haven't you anything better to do than talk behind Hoori's back? What has she ever done to you?"

"I look out for my brother."

"Look out for me? No thanks, I'm fine."

"You're blind."

"I don't know what you're talking about."

"Ask your wife. Ask her where she goes every other day in the afternoon."

"You're watching her?"

"You should be more aware of your wife's whereabouts."

Haady looked at his sister and felt a tangible shiver run down his spine. His silence seemed to Zeeba evidence that he hadn't understood her.

"She started seeing you while she was married. Her husband only found out about you two when she asked for a divorce. To be honest, what kind of a man was he? A pushover, probably ever since he was born. No real man would stand for it."

Haady was still silent and Zeeba still convinced that she had to make him understand.

"What I'm trying to make you realize is that I don't see why she would turn into a holy nun all of a sudden. I know you'd like to think that it was 'you' she chose but the bottom line is 'once a tart, always a tart'. Why would she stop at you? Who's to say that she wouldn't meet someone else or that she wouldn't look to meet someone else?"

Haady's face was ashen behind a faint mist of cigarette smoke. Eyes bloodshot, his expression became scary enough to make her stop.

Haady left without saying goodbye. He was overwhelmed by the fear of humiliation. He had developed a peculiar sensitivity to it since he was a boy, since he became aware of himself, since he first felt his mother's bite. The thought (that his sister had successfully planted) of his wife touched by another man tormented him. But he could live with betrayal. He could get over it and move on. There were other fish in the sea. What dominated his psyche was other people's perceptions of him. This would make him look foolish. Nothing in this life mattered to him more than the opinion of others. The idea that people respected and admired him was too much to lose. First, he had to find out the bitter truth from his wife.

When he got home his dinner was ready to serve. Hoori gestured repeatedly to the table to direct his attention to the result of two hours' work in the kitchen. She took offence at his lack of interest.

"What spoiled your day? Miserable?"

"Are you seeing someone behind my back?" Haady looked tortured, on the verge of tears.

"For the love of God, what are you talking about?"

"I'm talking about you in the afternoons every other day."

"Who told you that?"

"It doesn't matter."

"Yes, it does matter. It was your sister. Wasn't it? Mrs Troublemaker. She offers a hand with babysitting but the truth of the matter is that she sends her minion here to spy on me."

"Don't divert the subject. I'm still waiting for an answer."

"You want to know where I've been going? This is where I've been going." Hoori pointed at the dinner table. "I've been taking cooking classes for an ungrateful husband."

This was just about as stupid as Haady had ever felt. He knew from the tone of her voice that she was telling the truth. Zeeba's accusations were almost lunatic and he'd been taken in by them.

Hoori folded her arms in a gesture that said maybe he'd better just eat and stay quiet.

Further evidence of his wife's innocence was to be found in the stew she had made. Haady ate and he vowed to himself never to doubt her again.

Foti's babysitting became less frequent after her failed plot to stir trouble at Haady's house. But Zeeba hadn't given up on looking out for her brother; she didn't like the woman he was married to and she wouldn't trust her even if the Prophet himself vouched for her. Zeeba was patient. Her certainty in her ability to grasp the right event, the right moment to expose the crooked nature of her sister-in-law was impregnable. She decided it was best to send her reporter less often to Haady's place. It demonstrated good faith and a kind of apology by pulling back. She ought to give Haady some space, some time to shake out the grim dust of the memories of their last conversation. Foti was back on track helping Zeeba with her sewing business.

27

Malous's first day of higher education was upon them. No matter how much Zeeba tried to seem calm about it all, the pleasure of sending off her daughter, the first woman in the family, to university made her almost burst with pride. She had already put off some of her orders to finish Malous's clothes on time. And it was worth it.

Pari and Zeeba were standing in the corridor waiting to see Malous off. They looked like a couple of enthusiastic mothers ready to take their child to the first day of school. They studied her from head to toe as Malous walked down the stairs. Zeeba was looking for any flaws she had missed while making her outfit, Pari in admiration of her clean-cut appearance. Her thick, wavy hair draping on her shoulders framed and partly obscured the suggestion of firm breasts accentuated by a high ribcage. Zeeba had tailored her blouse so delicately that, at rest, it might have been described as loose or even baggy, but the slightest movement seemed to pull the material taut against Malous's body. There was no ignoring her tiny waist that led smoothly to a full, round bottom. Zeeba believed that women's clothes should be as sensual as possible but never coarse, never tacky. The trick, she believed, was making it look natural. The woman should look sexy as if it were in spite of the clothes she was wearing, not because of them. Any woman could turn a man's head with a progressive display of skin or curves, but if the man could be led to believe that he had to look for the curves, that he alone could divine the true woman beneath the garments, then the clothes had succeeded. Zeeba knew that Malous would never flaunt herself so she had made sure that the clothes certainly would (and she knew her daughter, like any young girl, no matter how *serious*, secretly wanted it that way).

She examined her daughter's face with the scrutiny of an army sergeant inspecting the face of a new recruit. She was satisfied with her eyebrows; the thick, hairy caterpillars that almost met had been replaced with two finely drawn lines. Malous looked thoroughly grown up but her eyes, betraying her innocence, added more still to her attraction. It was as if the obscured, unformed beauty of little Malous were magnified and focused. She was quite striking.

"Thank God for the demolition of the hijab years back. Otherwise, you'd be covered in a black shroud going nowhere," Zeeba boasted as if she'd had a hand in it.

"That's not true!" said Pari. "We had women teachers when we went to school. They weren't sacks of potatoes. They were women working, weren't they?"

"Yes, I know. But you can't deny the fact that getting rid of the black shroud opened many more doors for women. Society's attitude changed towards them. Now nobody thinks twice about women holding jobs outside of teaching."

"I still remember the humiliation of having my scarf pulled off my head by a bunch of hooligans calling themselves the police."

Malous interrupted. "I'd like to participate in the conversation but I'm afraid I'll be late. I have to rush."

Going to university was the best thing that ever happened to Malous. She was sociable by nature, she enjoyed being a part of a crowd, belonging to a group of people that could distinguish themselves with a name or title. And now being a student and all, she was sure her mother would cut her even more leeway to find her own friends. She felt like she was on the cusp of a great adventure, looking out across a panorama of freedom and choices. It made her feel like she had all the time in the world to take part in any activity that took her fancy. Who knew, she might have hidden talents? Locking herself in a room to study and try to outsmart everybody else was the last thing on her mind. A passing grade would do; something that would leave her time to explore other aspects of her new life was more than agreeable.

By her second term, she'd become a permanent member of the theatre group; and she was good at it. Perhaps it was in her genes? There was no argument Zeeba could lose if she applied her acting skills to it. And many of her uncle's court wins were more a result of his passion than the strength of a case. Malous felt at home on the stage. There were no nerves, no stage fright to tarnish a performance.

Pari's prediction regarding their nightly sessions hadn't exactly come true. Apart from the odd nights that she was occupied with university work, Malous continued reading to her. She had even expanded her selection to poetry. Pari had heard many people recite the Hafez but none so expressive and full of emotion.

Malous told Pari everything about the friends she'd made and the people she was planning to befriend. She told her about the play they were working on and she even persuaded Pari to read lines with her. She talked about the male lead actor and the interest he showed in her. It made her a little uneasy. She wasn't interested in him and didn't know how to fend off his attention tactfully. He was handsome enough, he had talent and probably a bright future but superficial or not, he hadn't passed her height criterion. He was short. She could never see herself with a short man. So, by default, he was beaten before he started.

Pari was of no particular help when it came to advice on how to behave around men. Her suggested tactic of telling him straight that she wasn't interested and that he should leave her alone wasn't exactly compatible with Malous's personality. But Malous was a good listener, and she made Pari believe that her advice was full of useful wisdom.

Her group assignments were often a topic in their list of nightly conversations. Pari was keen on hearing stories of other people; gossip. It was all the more enjoyable that Pari knew none of the characters involved; no guilt.

"Today, we had to hand in a suitable subject for our assignment. It's due by the end of term. I've been teamed with a boy, I think a couple of years older than me. He's from Yazd."

"He's away from his parents?"

"He rents a room."

"Did you have to group up with a boy or you had a choice?"

"Well, the number of men more than outweighs the number of women. So, it's not like you have a choice. But I don't mind working with this boy. He's very cooperative and easy to talk to. I don't feel like I'm on my guard around him."

"So, what's the subject about?"

"The assignment's for our social studies class and we've chosen to do research about prostitutes and their lives."

"Prostitutes? Whose bright idea was that?"

"I put it to him and he thought it was an interesting subject."

"I bet he did."

"I see what you're getting at but he's not that type."

"Really? He's a man with a thing between his legs, isn't he?"

"Why do you always have to look at everything in a superficial way?"

"Superficial! It's all they care about. It's everything to them. You should always be aware of that."

"Well, I'm happy with my subject and I'm sure we'll do a great job with our research."

"So, how are you going to find out about prostitutes' lives? Are there books written about them?"

"The best way of gathering information would be interviewing them in person."

"And I hope you assure me right now that the boy's going to take care of that."

"We decided that a man could get into a brothel disguised as a client and gather all the information we need."

"It's a relief to know you haven't completely lost your mind."

"I've got high hopes for our research. It's a fascinating subject. Everybody's curious to know about the ins and outs of these people's lives, right? You're interested for one, aren't you?"

"I guess I am. But I'd rather someone else did the investigation. I don't like it when a subject like this is too close to home. These are not ordinary people."

Malous's plan started off on the right foot. Her classmate Taymour went to the brothel pretending to be a client. He was instructed by Malous, who had somehow assumed expertise in such things, to record everything from the minute he went into the place to the minute he left.

The oppressive atmosphere hit him as soon as he entered. Dim lights, a smell of damp, narrow corridors leading through swing doors to more corridors. He felt miserable, dirty; he wasn't a client and he wondered how desperate a man had to be to endure such a place. He reeked of nervousness. His shyness seemed to clamp his head at a forty-five degree angle, as staring down at the floor he muttered to the brawny man sat behind a very low desk that he wanted to meet a girl. His mouth was dry, he wondered whether there was something else he should have said, some kind of code men use to order their whores. The man shouted a name. Taymour raised his head high enough to catch a glimpse of the man's foul and crooked teeth. His breath seemed to fill the whole room, it was inescapable and it churned Taymour's stomach. A woman at least ten years older than Taymour entered the hall. He didn't know how to react. Was he supposed to be polite and greet her or just follow her to wherever she took him?

The man with the foul breath shouted something at the woman as she led Taymour into a room. He laughed. The woman looked at Taymour and smiled; not a kind smile. The man shouted again, a name, but Taymour didn't catch it. He was so nervous his knees would certainly have knocked together if he allowed them to get close to each other. He stood, planted, as if on a small space at a great height. The woman disappeared into a back room and appeared with a young girl. She looked as shy as her customer. Her uneasiness seemed to cause an intense contraction in her body; as if she had just walked into that hall from the cold of Siberia. The older woman murmured something and pushed her towards the assigned room. A burst of laughter broke outside after she closed the door behind them.

The room was dark and small. A filthy curtain with what looked like cigarette burns offered at least some privacy. Taymour retched at the stench of feet and other body odours that hung solidly in the air. He asked the girl to sit on the single bed that was pushed against the wall. He sat on a stool at the other side of the room. The girl clutched her dress and kept her head bowed. She was shivering like a beaten dog. Her eyes were shut tightly, as if waiting for her sentence to be administered. It was dark but he could see that she was slight and very young. She was trying desperately to hide her face. As his eyes became accustomed to the light he noticed that the skin on her feet looked harsh, weather-beaten. He felt ashamed of himself staring at her breasts that seemed too large for her small frame. He dispelled his base instincts and tried to get down to business.

"What is your name?" he asked gently.

"Zahra, after the Prophet's daughter." She burst into tears and started pounding her chest.

Taymour rushed towards her. He almost touched her shoulders to show sympathy, but instead he held his hands about her shoulders, as if she had an invisible force field around her.

"I didn't mean to upset you. I'm sorry. I'm sorry."

She lifted her head for the first time. Dark brown eyes, exposed, vulnerable. She wiped at her red lipstick with the back of her hand leaving a smudge on her cheek near a cluster of red spots; a mild rash, perhaps acne, she was young enough, spread on both sides of her face that she tried to cover with her hair. Cheap make-up plastered on a teenage face was not successful in masking her innocence.

"My mother called me Zahra because Zahra answered her prayers when she went into labour with me and saved us both. Look how I'm paying them now." Her face was a pool of tears. She used the frill on the bottom of her dress to wipe her nose.

"I'm not a whore. I swear to the Prophet himself, I'm not a prostitute."

Taymour sat on the floor near her legs. She moved them away; he would surely grab at them any minute.

"Relax. I'm not here to jump at you."

"You mean you're not going to touch me?"

"I'm here to talk."

Zahra was baffled. Ever since her first day here she was told that the whole purpose of her being was to satisfy men; whatever they demanded. The older woman had already told her that all she had to do was to sit on the bed and let them do what they wanted. She was to show no resistance, unless they hit her. In that case she should inform the master and he'd take care of it. If they gave her any tips she was to hand them over to the master or she'd be punished.

"Honest to God. I'm here only to talk."

"Why would you want to talk to me? Don't you have any family, any friends to talk to?"

Taymour couldn't help laughing. She was right; it sounded stupid that a man would pay to talk to someone.

"I'm a student. I'm doing some research about the lives of women in this business."

"I have nothing to do with this business and my life is a hell in this place."

"How long have you been living here?"

"I'm not sure. Could be a month. My parents must think I'm dead already."

"Where are you from?"

"Lalejin, a village near Hamedan. I lived there with my parents and my two brothers."

"How the hell did you end up here? Did you run away from home?"

"No. Why would I run away?"

"I don't know. Maybe someone in your family treated you badly?"

"They were all nice to me. Once my younger brother beat me because a boy said something rude to me. He said he wanted a bite of my bottom. My brother was so mad his eyes were bloodshot. He said he didn't want a sister that people would talk dirty to. But he didn't hit me to be nasty. He cares about me."

Taymour started to see the gulf between them. How could he reason with her? This, being beaten by her brother, she took for love.

"How old are you?"

"I'll be sixteen by the end of autumn."

He could tell she was very young. But hearing her actual age somehow made it more sickening, more frightening.

"A week before I was brought here my parents were talking to a distant relative. They had asked for my hand. Their son works in a factory in Hamedan."

"Did you go to school?"

"I went to school for four years. After that I stayed home to help my father make ceramics. I can read and write and do the mathematics."

"Going back to my main question…" A knock at the door brought them back to the reality of where they were, and why they were supposed to be there in that depressing, dirty room. The older woman warned him that his time was up. Taymour had to go whether his business was over or not. A shadow of hopelessness covered Zahra's face. She looked as desperate as a child left with strangers, watching her parents leave. She couldn't stop weeping.

"I'll come back tomorrow."

Zahra pounded her fist on her lap crying her eyes out.

"I promise. I swear on my mother's life I'll return tomorrow."

On his way home, he could think of nothing but Zahra. The last image he registered in his mind was the sight of her trembling like a lamb.

Malous clamoured to know about it all the next day. The prospect of first-hand stories about such a place almost made her faint with expectation. She had heard or read in women's magazines about these places: Did the women really have no shame? Were they covered in heavy make-up? Did the pimp invite him in or the madam?

But Taymour wasn't up to talking about it. At first she thought he was just being coy. Then she wondered whether he didn't do a little too much research and now he felt ashamed to speak of it. But the more she pressed the more withdrawn he became.

Finally, after she reminded him that they needed to produce a paper or they would both fail (which had no effect at all on him), she promised that anything he said would be kept in trust. It seemed to Malous that Taymour had experienced something that went beyond her ambitions for good grades and a little excitement.

He told Malous that he met someone in there. Hardly more than a child, innocent, a victim. He didn't tell Malous everything; just enough for her to know that this was serious. Even mentioning Zahra's name felt like a betrayal. The old hag he had expected to first fear then mock then write up as a subject, a non-human, had turned out to be a helpless girl.

Taymour convinced Malous that it was best to finish the interview with no diversions or distractions. Malous felt bad that they had stumbled into something more than they had bargained for but Taymour's girl was still working in a whorehouse. There was nothing they could do to help, outside of documenting her plight and hoping that someone might take notice. Taymour made a case for himself as the diligent researcher. He had to go back to finish the work. Malous could see he was torn so she pretended to believe him. He was going to prepare a list of questions and then, with Malous's help, he would collate the answers and write the results, in spite of himself.

Taymour went back to the brothel the next day. The halitosis man welcomed him. His grotesque smile, his satisfaction of a repeat customer, churned Taymour's stomach. Taymour asked for Zahra and in a minute they were both sitting as they had been the day before. The girl could hardly believe he'd come back to see her.

The old woman had sniffed at him suspiciously; she couldn't understand his keenness for a shy girl. Certainly the older men loved a girl but the younger men usually went for women. This one was up to something.

Taymour got the notion that his time as a customer was almost up.

Zahra couldn't wipe the smile off her face.

"I believed you yesterday when you said you'd be back. I thought I might be a fool but I believed you."

"We don't have much time. I think your madam is on to me."

"As God is my witness I did not say a word."

"How did you end up here?"

"I was snatched from my village. On my way back from Asghar-Aga's shop. I was to deliver two baskets of eggs and bring back a bag of rice with me. A woman came close to me and asked me how to get to Hamedan. She wasn't local. I'd never seen her before. I told her how to get to the main road. I pointed in the direction and told her about the bus stop, but she started crying. She begged me to walk with her to the main road and take her to the bus stop. I felt sorry and accompanied her to the road to Hamedan. As soon as we got out of the village boundaries two men appeared in a white car. They jumped at me, tied my wrists and legs. I begged the woman to help me but she just watched. Then they shoved a hankie in my mouth and tied it behind my head. They flung me into the back seat and said if I made a peep they would kill me. They drove off. That night they kept me in the basement of a house. Next morning they drove to the city and handed me to the man that let you in. He gave them some money and told them 'not to stop their good deed.'"

Zahra started crying. "I've been stuck here ever since. They don't let me go out. If my parents, my brothers find out where I am, they'll skin me alive." She bent down and wiped her nose on the frill of her dress.

"I pray every night to Zahra. I beg the Prophet's daughter to help me, to get me out of this hell. Even she has shunned me. It wasn't my fault that I ended up here." She said it as if she were imploring him for forgiveness. As if he were a holy man and could mediate a rescue package with the Prophet's daughter.

"Has he raised his hand to you yet?"

"The madam slaps me. When they brought me here I wouldn't stop crying so she slapped me and told me she'd make sure I got a good beating if I didn't stop. The first time they put me in a room with a man and he tried to touch me I kicked and screamed. The man got angry and complained to the madam. She slapped me several times. But I wouldn't give in so she stayed in the room with the customer herself. After the man left she told me I'd get used to it, I'd start to like it. She said I could be popular and get a lot of attention."

She blew her nose then stared into Taymour's eyes.

"I don't want that attention. I want out of this nightmare."

Taymour paced the smelly hovel back and forth a few times. He'd spent so much time formulating a story to convince Malous that he had to come back; he'd neglected to find a plan for Zahra. What was he to do? Go to the authorities? The authorities were probably involved themselves. Should he try to fight his way out with her? But he was no fighter. These people were criminals, used to violence. What should he do? What could he do?

There was no possibility of walking away from this. He was scared to admit it to himself but he had fallen for her. Her openness, her innocence and her troubles had lured him. He had to get her out of that place or he'd be haunted by her image for the rest of his life.

"Have you any money, hidden somewhere?"

"No. All they've given me is food. Why do you want money from me?"

"I'm not asking you for money. We have to get you out of here, and for that you need money. I'll get hold of some money."

Zahra could hardly breathe. Was he really going to save her?

"Do you swear to God that you'll get me out of here? No matter what?"

"We have to think of a plan."

Zahra whispered phrases of gratitude under her breath. Her

prayers had not been in vain. Her mother was right when she said the Prophet's daughter would never let them down.

Suddenly, the reality of freedom hit her hard. Escape was her dream. It kept her alive to believe she would soon return home. But she was disgraced. A whore. Her father could never lift his head if his daughter were found to have been living such a life. She could never marry. Who would want her now?

"I've no place to go." She felt nauseous.

"You've got your family. They must be worried sick."

"They'll never take me back when they find out." Her lips were quivering.

Taymour was so obsessed with coming to terms with his feelings for her, his desire to set her free, he hadn't considered the aftermath. Even if he did manage to get her out, what then?

"Look, first things first. Let's not lose heart over what will happen with your family. I've got an aunt. Actually she's my mother's aunt; a very kind and understanding woman. I'm very close to her. I'm sure you could stay with her for a short while until we decide about what you ought to do."

The prospect of a safe haven calmed her. The Prophet's daughter must have sent this man to save her. She might help her again, provide some means to get her back to her parents, to the bosom of her family, secure as the only daughter, protected by her two brothers.

"Are you with me? You're not listening, are you?" Now Taymour had a plan and he had to make sure she followed it to the letter. "Timing is very important. We have to move fast. I'll leave this box of matches and my watch with you. Care for them with your life. The night after tomorrow I want you to set fire to the curtains in your room, at nine o'clock sharp. You can tell the time with a watch?" Zahra nodded. Taymour worried about the timing but he might need a day to get the money, and leaving it for two days might arouse less suspicion. "Then I want you to scream as loud as you can. Everyone will rush to get out of the building. When they do, I want you to go into every room in this place and set fire to the curtains. Set fire to everything you can get your hands on. Then get yourself out of here. They'll probably all congregate out there in the street to watch. Go to them. Make them think you're with them. Ask if everyone got out, that sort of thing. Then walk away, walk to the end of the alley and round the corner into the main street. I'll be waiting. Nobody will notice. They'll be too interested in their own skins, and the fire. I'll be waiting. Do you hear? Do you understand?"

Zahra nodded.

He rummaged through his pockets to find his matches. He shook the box. Plenty. Almost full. He wound his watch and gave it to Zahra.

"You have to remember to wind the watch every day. You turn this button round and round until it won't move forward any more."

She listened diligently. She devoured and memorized every word that came out of his mouth. For the next two days she would recite the plan over and over in her mind. She had seen her mother repeating a Salavat, a prayer to the Prophet's soul, more than a hundred times to have her request to God come true.

Taymour made her reiterate all the details in the plan. He didn't want to leave with any doubt in his mind. These people were ruthless. He couldn't afford any mistakes.

"Two nights. Until then try not to draw attention to yourself."

"God blesses your soul. God blesses your soul."

He told Malous none of it. For the next two days he stood firmly by his story that his blueprint was turning into a comprehensive report, that he needed time to complete his work. He convinced Malous that her interference would only delay their project and she ought to be patient and give him some space to implement what he'd promised to submit. Malous was puzzled but she tried not to think of what the problem might be. Any time she entertained a possibility outside of his claim that he needed space to get on with it, she recoiled at her own ability to conjure up scenarios that did not show Taymour in a good light. She felt guilty for projecting the man into her own wild fantasies and decided she had better not push him too hard. As long as they could come up with a decent report that provided a passing grade, everything would be fine. She gave up the idea of anything exciting happening to her. Perhaps something exciting had happened to Taymour but if it had he wasn't about to share his adventures with her. The many times her mother had cursed all men now seemed a little less mad than she had imagined.

Taymour was a man. Taymour went into a brothel. When he came out he had changed. Maybe her mother was right after all?

When he wasn't lying to Malous Taymour was trying to figure out exactly who it was who had arranged for a movie-like escape. This wasn't like him at all. The question that tormented him was this: was his decision to offer to rescue Zahra due to his attraction to the girl or would he have helped her anyway? If she had been ugly or old? If she had put him off in any other way: her smell, her appearance, her manner of talking? Would he have jeopardized himself to change the dreadful future of a complete stranger? What if he were married? Would he do such a thing with a wife and children at home? But what if it was fate? What if it was his destiny, that this had to happen to him now, unencumbered? What if this were a test? But how could he pass a test if it was all simple attraction? If he felt drawn to this girl who, exactly, was he helping? Did it matter? If she were free then intent would not matter.

All he knew was that Zahra or rather Zahra's case had hit the spot. His urge to release this vulnerable girl had taken over his being, perhaps his sanity. Her escape would be his liberation. Liberation from the obsession he'd developed about her situation.

Taymour ducked out of attending his classes on the second day. He couldn't face talking to anyone. He hardly ate. His walks around the busy streets of Tehran measured enough to have taken him to another city.

On the second night he went to the promised spot near the main street with most of his savings bulging in his pockets. His palms were dripping sweat. Every passer-by was Zahra. His heart was pounding and leaping at every young woman that passed. He stood waiting, hallucinating, shaking with fear. His lips were dry, his mouth parched. There were still a few minutes before the show was scheduled to start.

He checked and rechecked his watch. It seemed like days passed and they might as well have. Twenty minutes was too long. The place should be ablaze by now. She should be beside him walking away calmly. He turned the corner into the alley where the brothel was and he could see the flames licking the windows. The door was still shut. He paced back and forth like an expectant father. He could take no more. He walked briskly to the door and banged on it, hard, he shouted Zahra's name with every painful thump.

The door opened and the pimp's face, even redder than usual, appeared. Zahra popped out from behind him. He grabbed her shoulder to steady himself.

"I knew it. I knew you were up to something." His eyes locked onto Taymour's. He pushed Zahra out of the door and leapt at Taymour. He punched him with serious intent. Taymour rocked backwards, as two more thugs came out of the door, spluttered, looked at their boss then joined in the attack. Taymour curled himself up into a tight ball on the ground; their kicks rolled him from side to side. Zahra was scratching her own face and crying.

"Run! Get out of here!"

Zahra pounded her head.

"Go! Go!" he shouted.

By now a crowd had gathered to watch the fire, and the added horror of three men trying to kick someone to death. The breathless punches and kicks lost intensity. The pimp ordered his two accomplices to stop. Taymour slowly let his guard down. He opened up the shield of his arms inviting a direct kick in the face. The last time he'd tasted blood was in the dentist's office. Now he felt like he'd drunk a pint of it. With the faint vision left in one of his eyes he looked for Zahra in the crowd. There was no sight of her.

He heard a dull sound whispering before he passed out.

After four days he turned up at university with an explanation for Malous. She was appalled at the sight of him. She had pictured, in her mind, a lazy skiver procrastinating, but he was frightening. His battered face and emaciated body shocked her and darkened her heart. The sorrow in his eyes left her silent.

She was all ears. Taymour related his sorry tale. Malous was both impressed and alarmed that he could so suddenly become so involved.

They never turned in the report and they never worked with each other again.

28

By her third year, Malous had become a familiar figure in her faculty. She'd gained a reputation among the academics for an assertive writing style and, among the men on the faculty, for her curves and curls. The idea that she had talent as a writer and that people who were supposed to know about such things had said so, added steel to her ego. The thought that her talent was a matter for envy among her peers was something she savoured. It immersed her in an imaginary world where no one could put her down, where she could comfortably take respite from her shortcomings. The weaknesses she'd been reminded of all throughout her life did not exist in her writings.

Her relationship with Pari had become ever deeper since the start of her higher studies. Pari was the best listener she knew. She would blurt out comments and provide verbal annotations that would send Malous into hysterics; and that made it even more fun to tell tales of her busy life at university.

Pari always had more time for Malous than had her own mother. Zeeba could hardly fit her daughter into her busy schedule. Juggling her teaching job, her sewing business and her card-playing nights was not easy. She was not blind to the steadfast bonding between Pari and her daughter. As jealous as she sometimes felt she could not blame Malous for being drawn by the comforting easiness of Pari. There were times when she herself needed to resort to this refuge of tender security. Pari was the supporting rock she leant against when she yearned for sympathy and absolution. The happy memories of her childhood with Pari still had a place somewhere in her mind, but perhaps had grown dusty and blurred and, sometimes, in need of refreshment. She was never unaware of Pari's gift to heal a troubled soul, neither was she unaware that this gift had been denied her. But she reckoned she had done *her* bit; she had helped to get Malous into university and that alone was enough.

Pari had heard all about Malous's classmates, the ones she didn't care much for and the ones she respected. Malous enjoyed telling Pari of the boys she had heard were interested in her. She certainly wasn't interested in them but it was fun to have admirers.

"You'd better choose one sooner or later," Pari would say. "By the time you finish school and get a job, you'll already have a big head, pinning faults and shortcomings on every poor boy that comes near you. Believe me, the older you get the more difficult it'll be to find the *right* man and you don't want to turn into an old maid, dear."

She had also noticed the fascination Malous had with plunging herself into difficulties on her course. Malous seemed determined to build up her literary muscles. Essays and short stories were her forte but she had taken poetry because she believed herself to be useless at it. She believed poetry to be too fanciful, kind of half-baked. Truth be told she believed she was unable to bare her soul in her poetry and when she tried to rhyme, she couldn't shake the memory of her uncle Haady who seemed almost to speak in rhyme. She surmised that she must simply lack rhythm.

A classmate, Sina, a man, and interested in her, certainly had a knack for asserting his thoughts and emotions through the same *half-baked* prose style she was too wary to touch. His sense of style and impressive delivery had taken the class by storm. Not only a poet but quite the performer, it was difficult to tell which complimented which the more. He was almost a throwback to the old storytellers, who still plied their trade in villages all over Iran. Even when the meter was missing or the vowels failed to match he'd add a rhythm to his words, from an almost liquid, lyrical timbre to a sound more like rapping on a table than a human voice, which at once fused meaning and syntax into images and ideas that would plant themselves deep into the mind of the listener. His writing was as complex and intricate as he seemed to Malous. A thinker, not a political animal but an artist, an original.

And this poet, this young man with the world at his feet, seemed interested in her. Malous was dazzled that someone only a few years older than her could formulate and transmit such deep perceptions and musings on the world around him. She was flattered by his attention. She told herself that a person as discerning and thoughtful must see something special in her. She was certain that should he approach her, she could never reject him. It was the first time she'd been so curious about a man that she even considered making the first move and introducing herself. But she stopped short of such drastic action for fear he'd be overwhelmed; better to wait.

Sina was not shy. Neither did he nurture fantasies about an everlasting relationship with Malous that would culminate in marriage. He'd developed some curiosity about this female classmate who was so natural. In her company he could almost swear he felt a physical warmth emanating from her. Just as she wondered at his skill with words he wondered at hers with ideas; forthright, to the point, always passionate, she too was kind of an artist. Then, of course, there was her body. He was a simple male and therefore unaware that it was the skill of the mother that allowed him to *see* her body. Or at least to him it seemed that he could see it for there was not an inch on show; no plunging necklines or immodest hemlines, nothing there exactly and yet there it was anyway. Were he a lesser man he might even have pretended to himself that he was interested in her mind alone. But he knew it had to be at least fifty-fifty. Beautifully written, quirky essays on the possibilities of an Islamic interpretation of communism were one thing but the way her breasts seemed to stick to her blouse when she stretched her arms or put on a coat was another. Nevertheless, he wasn't about to jump through any hoops. He wasn't going to concoct any schemes to conquer, neither was he prepared to acquiesce to the constant moan of the young Iranian woman of marriageable age.

His first attempt at an overture was crafted simply at the tail-end of an advanced literature class. "Have you been to the new bookshop in Tajrish Square?"

Malous was caught off guard. She muttered something only to realize a couple of seconds later that she hadn't made any sense. As usual, she'd been listening to the lecture. When he'd sat next to her, her heart missed a beat. But that was an hour before. She'd long forgotten the man beside her, so immersed was she in an idea she was trying to warp into her philosophy, because that was her way. New ideas, new ways of seeing had to be folded neatly into her world view in order that she could exploit them and make sense of them.

She extricated herself from her thoughts. "No. But I've heard about it. I've heard they stock books you can't find anywhere else."

That was better, now she sounded calm, in control.

"I'd be surprised if there aren't intelligence agents lurking about the shop to check what people buy. You know, the *forbidden* books." This was a good start. To get the word *forbidden* into their first conversation was pretty good going. He hardly knew what he was talking about and while he wanted her to take the bait he hoped she wouldn't quite swallow it.

"I wouldn't mind getting my hands on some of those books. Anything that's forbidden must have some value." She made an effort to lubricate the wheels of their conversation.

She took the bait. Why not? Maybe there would even be someone who looked like an intelligence man, an agent of the Shah's SAVAK, in the shop that they could join forces against? "I was planning to go there today, late afternoon. If you don't have any classes we could go together."

"I don't know exactly where it is." She knew exactly where it was but she was a fine actress when she had to be.

The bus ride was suffocating, with too many school kids and students and tired workers heading home, and all seemed to be smoking three cigarettes apiece; even the kids. It was a warm day. She'd thought of Sina when she decided it was warm enough to go to town without a jacket. She had not bargained for a bus full of schoolboys. One of them, perhaps on a dare, had leant over to her. He was no more than thirteen and had to stand on tip-toes to get to her ear. "You have the most beautiful chest I have ever seen." Malous's face beamed red and the effort to cover the objects of their desire with her folder only seemed to make it worse; or better, for the schoolboys, who were now chattering like monkeys, all stared right at her, right at her breasts. The disapproving cluck of an old woman had no effect. Malous had never got used to it. All through her adolescence it was the same, silly boys, even men, leering, talking at her, butting into her life. Sina knew well enough to stay out of it. If he intervened the boys would only get worse. When the bus pulled up at their stop Sina let her run a gauntlet of cavalier teenagers. She marched through them with her head held high, and her folder held against her breasts. Sina couldn't help admiring her. A few years ago he would have been one of those boys, now he was above that kind of behaviour, at least to an extent.

You wouldn't have known the reputation of the bookshop by looking at it. Small, dark, it had that strange cloying presence of something between an odour and an ambiance, a mustiness that spoke as much of the population of the bookshelves themselves as the people browsing them. Not surprisingly, there was no specific section for "forbidden books". Although, almost unconsciously, both of them spent the first few minutes checking the shelves for clusters of contraband. Of course, they'd all been categorized among the other books under the author's name and genre.

Malous drifted into the philosophy section, pulled by names she knew couldn't be found in a regular bookshop. Names that only people who were after "trouble", who yearned to know more, looked for. On the philosophy shelves there were some titles written by the fathers of the Soviet Union's revolution. She knew them well, copies were sitting on her own bookshelf at home. There was a copy of *Das Kapital*, a book she'd tried to read three times and still found it unintelligible. She was never sure if it was the book, her, or the translation that was at fault. Now she ignored the book, pretending to herself that she never saw it.

She found Sina browsing the fiction section. He had a pile of books cradled in his arm. He looked so relaxed, at home, as if he owned the place. He took two books from his pile and placed the rest back on the shelf.

"You've already picked yours. Can I see them?" She was intrigued to know where his literary tastes might lead. He held up the books. One in each hand, as if he were about to try to sell them in a street market. She could only recognize one of the authors, Ignazio Silone; *Bread and Wine*. She took the other book from him. "*Animal Farm*? I haven't heard of this one."

"You can have a loan of it after I'm done." He smiled. "Did you see anything you want to buy?"

"There is one I found in the poetry section. One of Neema Youshij's." She told herself that she really did want to give poetry a second chance, but if they arrested her now, she'd have to tell the Shah's secret police the truth; she wanted to impress Sina.

"Well, I guess we're all set. There's a pastry shop nearby. Do you fancy a cream cake?"

"Maybe some other time? I have to buy some cooked beetroot. Do you want to come with me to the vegetable market?"

There was a silence. Only a moment, but a moment too long, nevertheless. Maybe turning down his offer was wrong? But she really did need to buy beetroot. She frantically searched her mind for the right thing to say to rescue the conversation.

"Have you lived in Tehran for long?" Sina was kind. He smiled as he asked the question, to let her know how he felt.

"For donkey's years. Born and bred. My parents were born here."

They stepped out of the bookshop and walked towards the bus stop. "My family's from Shiraz. I was born there. We moved here when I was ten years old."

"Shiraz? No wonder you like poetry. You were nurtured in the land of Hafez."

"I don't think you have to be from his land to become infatuated by his poetry. I don't think anyone can escape its spell."

"Do you allocate much time to poetry or do you write the occasional poem here and there?" Now the conversation was going well. Impersonal, but flowing. Her invite to a vegetable market was cast away in favour of poetry and common pleasures.

"Poetry's a part of me. I take it everywhere I go. I could no sooner write the occasional poem than a fish could take the occasional swim. It's a way of living."

"Probably you've amassed a book of them." Malous blurted it out simply to keep on the subject.

"As a matter of fact I've already composed two books."

She was impressed. She was fascinated by his work but she certainly didn't expect such dedication. But then another feeling made its presence felt, around her shoulders, her lower neck. Not a tickle, more like nausea but one can't have a nauseous neck; she was uneasy. Of course, she knew what it was, it was the same feeling she got whenever she discovered a writer she loved was younger than she thought, or that the writer turned out to be a woman. No matter how much she loved to read, the more she enjoyed reading the more envious she felt of the writer; someone who had done it, written it, published it, and now she was reading it, and she and her friends talking about it. It was fine when the writer was dead or old, but someone young, perhaps female? It made her aware that she hadn't written anything. She told her stories every night to her beloved Pari and she wrote her serious essays for class but she had never written her *Pari* stories down, or read them to the class, or subjected her stories to the scrutiny of her peers.

She envied him. She did admire his talent, his depth, his seriousness, his zeal. But she couldn't help comparing herself to him; and there wasn't much comparison. She'd been too busy being proud of her writing skills to actually get down to some serious work. Maybe she was waiting for her muse? Maybe she hadn't met the right conditions to shake her awake, to ignite the crucial spark in her spirit? Maybe she wanted too much? Maybe she thought herself unworthy of creating a work of art? Something important? But then, maybe she was just lazy?

The thought of committing herself to something as serious as a book; a tangible object that everyone could read and judge, frightened her.

Sina knew she was somewhere else, lost in her thoughts. He made an effort to ease her back into the moment. "You're so quiet. Did I say something to offend you?"

"No. Not at all…"

"This is my bus." Sina stepped onto a bus that seemed to have appeared from nowhere. "I'll see you tomorrow?"

Malous nodded and smiled and, before parting, she put on her broadest, most honest smile; her most special smile.

She didn't care if he saw her, she didn't care if anyone saw her. She was rooted to the spot, staring at the bus as it bullied its way back into the thick column of traffic. He might have thought, anyone might have thought, her a love-struck young thing, already pining for the boy who was with her two minutes ago; the pain of youthful obsession? But, and she wasn't going to lie to herself, even though Sina was a part of her thoughts, he was more a part of her thoughts for what he represented than as an object of pure desire. She headed back to the station to catch the next bus to her cinema. She needed a film. She had too much on her mind.

A movie.

She'd seen it before. Never mind, she'd watched plenty of movies again and again, like old friends telling the same tired jokes, touching the same places, soothing, healing. But tonight the movie didn't do the trick, it was like plain white wallpaper, silent, meaningless shapes, light drifting here and there, bright, dark, yellow, red, green. What was wrong with doing what she was doing anyway? Just because she'd met someone who'd written two books? He said he lived his poetry, he said it was like the way religious people are with their God, he was in it always, there was no distinction between his writing and the rest of life.

Thinking about this made her feel even more inadequate. Clark Gable pursed his lips; a raised eyebrow seemed to make his ears even more pointy. Who said she was supposed to write stories anyway? Politics was what got read in Iran. Politics was the drama of the people. There was nothing in Shakespeare that could compare to helping a political figure escape from prison when you knew you might even be arrested for it.

The thought that she might really have been arrested shocked her. When she'd helped Kaaveh Rabbani it seemed like a game, a lark, serious, important, but she never really thought about the reality of what she was doing. Perhaps that was the only way one could do something like that in the first place? Maybe courage can never be courage if it knows itself? Sure enough, Clark Gable grabbed his heroine by the waist, there was a gasp behind Malous, then the sound of laughter, muffled. She turned her head and three women looked like they were about to wet themselves as a fourth made a mock-angry face. Clark Gable was pretty popular with Tehrani girls, or just about any girls anywhere for that matter.

She had helped a political figure escape from prison. She had taken a risk. Sina had written two books of verse. She wrote about politics. But then, as the heroine melted into Clark's arms and the women behind her sighed as one, she remembered that she didn't write about politics at all. She wrote exactly what she knew would get her through university most efficiently. She shaded her polemics according to the class, or more particularly, the lecturer. If she ever wrote what she really believed, they'd surely shut her down. There would be no graduation if she stepped over the line. It was this very tightrope trick that she mistook for writing. Had she just posed as a government lackey and written accordingly she would at least be committing the kind of fraud that can forge great writers, but she was spinning a thin, sickly version of herself in her diatribes.

And on top of it all Sina was dashing. He looked young; very young, but perhaps that was as much his soul shining through than his actual looks. His face was filled with a presence, an honesty that now infuriated her. She was attracted to him. She was jealous of him. She wanted to beg his forgiveness for thinking such things and she wanted to punch him in the nose. He was svelte, fragile even, but he had the look of someone who could not be budged, either physically or spiritually. Malous wondered whether he was composing something now? Perhaps something about her? Perhaps something about their day together? What would he say? Could he know? Was she so obvious? He stared so deeply, could he see her thoughts? Feel them? Perhaps feel her envy? Maybe it was in her voice? But she didn't always feel envious. When she looked at him she wanted him to kiss her. Not like Clark Gable kissing a sack of potatoes, but seriously, as an equal, a friend, a lover.

Missing dinner was a frequent enough event, now that she was a student, but she could always rely on Pari for a meal with no emotional strings attached.

"Missed dinner again? Here, I kept this warm for you." Pari unravelled the tea towel that wrapped the small porcelain herb dish. She placed a fork and spoon beside the plate and sat; she always kept Malous company when she ate alone. Now it was time for gossip.

"I went to the cinema."

"If all their customers were like you, these picture houses would make a fortune. Did you go on your own or were you with…a friend?" She raised an eyebrow playfully.

"I went on my own. But I went to the new bookshop in Tajrish with one of my classmates. With Sina; I meant to tell you about him." She jammed a huge spoonful of ghormeh-sabzi into her mouth and tried to act as if everything were normal. Really, she wanted Pari to know, but she didn't want Pari to think she was so keen to tell her everything right off.

Pari sniffed, the way she always did whenever she was either uneasy or delightfully suspicious.

"So, is he after you?"

"No. Nobody is after anybody. We just went to a bookshop and walked back to the bus stop. That's all."

"Well, you can believe what you like but I'm not so easily fooled. He's testing the water. I take it he's not short otherwise you would have turned him down right away?"

"Is that what you think about me? You think I'm that superficial?"

"Super what? It doesn't matter what I think, dear. What I said is what I know. And what I know is true."

"He's not short." Malous tried to eat without laughing. Of course, she wouldn't have been seen dead with a man shorter than her. It was one of her little foibles. Never in this world would she end up with a man shorter than she was. All the money in the world and all the looks in Hollywood couldn't overcome the shortcoming of a short husband.

"How come he didn't go to the movies with you?"

"I didn't tell him I was going. I wanted to watch the movie on my own."

"Good for you. You don't want people to think you're an easy catch."

"I'm not any kind of catch. And besides, I don't want Zeeba or anyone else to know about Sina. I don't need an interrogation every time I get home and I've got better things to do than provide a report about a friendship." So engrossed in her conversation, Malous had followed her first over-laden spoon with another and another. She'd been eating for a couple of minutes and already she was at the bottom of the dish. She unwrapped the second tea towel and took out a slice of bread; it was still warm. She mopped up some juice and wrapped a few kidney beans into the bread then stuffed it into her mouth. "Sometimes…" As she talked, Pari could see the contents of her mouth swilling around. Pari smiled, it reminded her of when Malous was a toddler, so natural, so sweet. "…I get the impression that all Zeeba's worried about is marrying me off."

"Of course. You say it like it's wrong. No one wants her daughter to miss out on having her own family."

"Usually that's the case. But when it comes to Zeeba, I'm not sure whether she worries for my sake or for her image."

Pari's silence submitted the clearest reply; probably a bit of both.

CHAPTER
29

During the weeks that followed, Malous opened up more and more to Sina. He heard about her upbringing, her best friend and confidante Pari, her uncle Mehdi, who'd shown her the purest kind of love, and her grandmother, who showed no one any kind of love. Malous told him about her fatherless childhood and how she'd always felt his empty space. But she stopped short of criticizing him; what he hadn't done for her was between her and him. After all, he was her father.

Malous had finally found a second audience member. She read her writing assignments to Sina and devoured every word of encouragement or criticism that came out of his mouth. Essays prepared for the advanced literature class were now auditioned, and improved, by Sina before being unveiled to the class.

He went to see her strut her stuff on stage at the dramatics society. She was not half bad as an actress either. Sina was impressed. Her prose had seemed to improve when she bade it; it was as if she'd been set free. Her dry polemics gave way to stories. First serious, trying to take the weight of her political rants with them but soon they became playful, absorbing, without a trace of the preachy tone that had infected her previous work.

Sina was from a military family and they had been transferred to Tehran by the army when he was a child. His father had worked all his adult life in the army. He worked his way up from lowly clerk to secretary then, after he completed his own university education, he landed a job as a lecturer with the rank of captain at the military academy. His mother was married off in her late teens and had since been taking care of her three boys. Sina's father loved poetry and literature himself. People were generally surprised to find a career army man spent much of his free time in the company of a good book. Although first, and always, a soldier, he was a quiet man with no head for trouble. When home he resorted to his sanctuary, a corner of their living room, his back pressed against two medium-sized overstuffed shelves, his hubble-bubble burning the air with the fragrance of flavoured tobacco, sometimes orange, sometimes apple; the smell was a talisman to Sina, a sensual confirmation that all was well in the world.

Sina loaned his newly bought book to his classmate a few weeks later, as promised.

"Finally finished it?"

"To be honest, I haven't even read the first page yet. I left the book with one of my friends and now that he's given it back I thought I'd lend it to you."

"Are you sure you don't want to read it first?"

"I can't take it home. If my father sees it there would be trouble. The last thing he wants to see is a 'forbidden book' in his army home. We live on an army camp. What if one of his students or a colleague saw it? It's dangerous for his career. I'd be reckless to let the book into our home. I always read books like this outside the house. And right now I have a project to do."

"Your father would have a heart attack if he saw my inventory."

"Your family's got no problems with that?"

"Not at all. I used to write articles for *Kargar*. My uncle knows a lot of people from that side, if you know what I mean. As long as nobody tells on us or makes us into a target for the intelligence people, I can easily hang on to my book collection. Otherwise, I'd have to burn them all."

"It must be wonderful reading what you want whenever you want to."

"And better yet, to talk to other people about them. I used to go to the socialist party meetings. Not any more; nowadays it's too risky. But I still have discussions with my uncle." Malous hesitated for a few moments and then disclosed the idea she'd been toying with since the start of their conversation.

"I can talk to my uncle. I'm sure he wouldn't have any objections to you using his living room to read your books. He and his wife are a couple of serious party-goers. They usually leave their son with us. I could babysit at their place while you're there reading. Anyway, he's very easygoing, I have no doubt we can come up with an arrangement."

"The idea sounds very strange to me but I guess it would give me a couple of hours of freedom."

Malous broached the subject on a Friday. She guessed it would be more appropriate to discuss her idea with Haady on a weekend when he was relaxed and away from the commotion of his workplace. Hoori was busy tidying up the house. No matter what anybody claimed about her, no one could ever accuse her of being a slob. She would rather have died than present herself or her abode in a slovenly manner. Her taste in interior design gave the visitor a sense of calm and class. Everything in her home was fresh and pristine. She took pride in buying the first vegetables and herbs of the season to cook fancy meals, and always the public rooms were adorned with a vase of aromatic flowers, meticulously cut and arranged.

Walking alongside her guest, Hoori ushered Malous into the living room. Before her uncle's arrival they spent enough time talking face-to-face for Malous to notice a change; her breasts were smaller than usual. She later found out second-hand through Pari that she inserted socks in her bra. Obviously it was Foti who was the source, ready to plead before a judge as to the accuracy of the gossip.

Haady welcomed his niece. As always he had a cigarette hanging from his lips and he puffed and inhaled without releasing the thing. He listened to her request that her new friend be allowed to read the forbidden literature within the safety of Haady's home; and she filled him in on the reasons for such a request. Sina was a nice boy, and while his father was a soldier, he too was something of a poetry aficionado but Sina would not put his family in jeopardy. Haady enjoyed the flattery she rained upon him; he was so free-minded and easygoing, a person she could rely on. Haady didn't see any harm in letting Sina use his couch to study the books he would otherwise hardly have a chance to read. The person Malous described sounded civilized and responsible and with Malous present in his house at the same time he could count on a double assurance.

"You know I ought to tell your mother about this arrangement." He couldn't help teasing her. He knew Zeeba would certainly disapprove of anything that happened behind her back, without her consent. She wouldn't mind what the books were, just that she was being left out of the equation.

"I prefer to tell her myself. I'm not looking for any trouble and I don't want her and Foti talking behind my back. Like I said, I didn't decide to bring him here so that I could hide him from Zeeba. It's just that in our place, there would be too many noses sniffing at him. How could he enjoy a book in such an atmosphere?"

Pari was the first person in the household to find out. She didn't like the idea. It wasn't proper for a girl to be in the sole company of a man, completely unattended. Above all, Pari cared about what people would say should they ever find out that a girl accompanied her male friend in her uncle's house with no supervision. It didn't matter that the purpose was an innocent book-reading session. People took pleasure in gossiping about "misguided" young girls.

"Honest to God, I don't have the slightest clue where you get these ideas from?"

"What's wrong with helping a friend?"

"Don't you remember the results of the other great idea you came up with? The one about researching the lives of prostitutes?"

"God forbid if something I suggest goes wrong. You wouldn't let me forget for the rest of my life."

"You tell me, who's going to see this as a decent deed? Everybody would think you're doing this to have some time alone with him. And besides, he's a man…"

Malous jumped in before Pari got a chance to finish her sentence and get to the point.

"Not again with the speech about 'he's a man and he's got a thing between his legs'?"

"Well, it's true. He's got one and you don't know him enough to trust him. Even if you did, it wouldn't make any difference. People commit acts under certain conditions that would even surprise themselves, never mind others. Whether you like it or not I'm going to stay with you two at your uncle's house."

"You're just too harsh on people."

"Maybe if you live as long as I have, you'll learn a thing or two. Then you'll see things for what they are. Anyway, your uncle should know better. What was he thinking, accepting your plan?"

"He's an open-minded person and he trusts me."

"He's too open-minded for his own good if you ask me. All he's bothered about is keeping his image as 'Mr Make Everybody Happy'. What he cares about is staying popular for as long as he lives."

Malous wanted to end the discussion and read a short story out of Pari's favourite women's magazine to her. She wrapped up their conversation. It didn't matter what Pari thought. She loved Pari, but this was her own life, she had to live it herself.

"Please don't speak of this to Zeeba. I want to tell her myself. Will you promise?"

"You know I wouldn't tell if you ask me not to. Why don't you make everybody's life a little easier? Just bring him here instead." Malous looked at her suspiciously. "Yes, to keep an eye on him. Why not?"

"Because it would be a waste of time. The first time he comes here and gets pestered by everyone prying into his life, into every detail about his family, he'd think my suggestion was some kind of marriage plot."

Pari couldn't argue with her reasoning. It was true; no one could dodge Zeeba's artful interrogation. Before they knew it they were trapped in a web of self-consciousness. A couple of hours with Zeeba and they were apologizing for themselves and their sins and ready to beg for mercy. Zeeba was quick in making up her mind about people's rightful place in her society, in her life. And if their selected rank was close to the bottom, she had no qualms striking them with any weapons at hand, from innuendo to sarcasm.

When she saw Zeeba in action Pari thought often of something her mother used to say; *Some people cut off your head with a sword and some cut it off with cotton wool.* Zeeba's method favoured cotton wool and she was no slouch at it.

Zeeba felt betrayed when she heard about her daughter's plan. She took deep offence that Malous preferred to take this boy to her uncle's place rather than introduce him to her, her own mother. Her daughter was treating her like a second-class citizen.

"Who the hell is this man? How come I haven't heard anything about him?"

"I just told you he's my classmate and that…"

"I'm not deaf. He's your classmate. So what? I don't know what kind of a person he is. I don't know his family. For God's sake, I

225

didn't know he existed until five minutes ago. What do you expect me to say?"

"Pari said she would stay when he's at uncle Haady's place. That way there won't be any talk."

"Pari said? So, you told Pari before you told me? I expect you've told Pari every detail? So, what is this? You and Pari have got a secret society?"

"I didn't mean to hurt you. It's not as if I went out of my way to tell Pari so that I can annoy you."

"You went out of your way to value her more than me. Someone shares a room with you and all of a sudden she's your best friend. All of a sudden you trample on your own mother."

"She's not just someone, she's your cousin."

"Don't you dare talk back to me. You're your father!" Zeeba said it as if it were an answer to a question she'd been wrestling with but she wanted to hurt Malous, to hit her weak spot. "Half of you is made of that bastard Amir with all the shit attached."

"You still chose him for a husband."

This ignited even more fury. "That was the biggest mistake of my life. Thank God I had a family to drag me out of that hell. And if it wasn't for me you'd be wiping shit off the shoes of his wife and children. If it wasn't for me you wouldn't have had a high-school diploma never mind an acceptance at university. And what I get in return is an unappreciative big mouth who treats me like a second-class citizen. And as for your beloved Pari, if it wasn't for me she'd be wandering the streets of Tehran from one relative's house to another without even a roof over her head. I saved her. I took her in and offered her a place to stay. Instead of telling me everything that happens in this house, she's become the entrusted keeper of your secrets." Zeeba's breathless rant didn't leave any room for Malous to cut in. "What I want to know is what has she ever done for you? When did she become your sacred mother? I can't deny that you two are well-matched. You're both like cats, both ungrateful. You've both forgotten where you came from. Well, from now on when you need something, when you're stuck with a trouble, don't come running to me. Run to the arms of your new mother. See what she can afford to do for you."

Malous's head felt heavy. The blood seemed to rush into it and stay. Any more of her mother's ravings and she'd have blood gushing out of her eyes, her ears, her nose, anywhere the red boiling fluid in her head could find an outlet. She felt trapped. Trapped in the middle of a circle of hyenas, every one of them responsible for her fears, her cracked self-confidence, her miseries. And every one of them expected something from her. What was it they demanded from her? Why couldn't *she* be appreciated for being born to their family, for being the newcomer who'd be perpetuating the family blood? Why couldn't *she* be cherished simply for being the product of nine months of hard work and hours of torturous labour? Or simply for being someone's daughter?

She was too hurt and too aware of her self-pity to burst into tears. The dryness in her throat ignited a burning sensation that extended right to her stomach. She felt suffocated by layers and layers of acrimony saturating the air. She ran upstairs to her room. After a couple of minutes, a dull thud dragged Pari out of the kitchen, worried that Malous might be hurting herself. She'd managed to stay in her corner without any interference or mediation between Malous and her mother.

Pari stood next to her mattress and blanket unravelled at the bottom of the stairs. She looked up to find Malous leaning over the banister, her face brushed with the colour of fury. Malous stopped herself from looking at Pari.

"There!" she screamed at her mother. "Are you happy now?" Zeeba didn't say a word. She had no intention of encouraging her daughter's performance.

The slam of the door was a clear indication that Malous was not about to explain or justify her actions to Pari.

Pari rolled up her mattress and blanket, placed them on her shoulder and dragged her load to the shed in the backyard. She'd *officially* been demoted to a servant; servant to a family that could have never afforded one. A servant with an affluent family was always given her own room, her own furniture, her own rights. She was paid, fed and clothed. She earned a living serving her employer and she was shown respect within the boundaries of her job.

Pari had been stripped of her shared room, her questionable

respect and her precarious rights.

That night Pari cried enough tears for all four people in that household. She didn't know what to think. She felt as abandoned as a child left at some auntie's house with the empty promise that her parents will come back for her. With all the ups and downs in her life, losing her husband to a teenager, losing her domain, her social status, her pride, she'd never experienced such a deep wound. Maybe it was the suddenness of Malous's action that shocked her so gravely? Maybe she'd built a shrine to someone who hadn't been around for long enough to have her character tested? Maybe she put too much faith in having found herself a resort, a person without a ragged soul, to seek comfort with? Maybe that was the price to pay when she offered her whole trust to one person. It was heartbreaking when she parted with her stepdaughter. It was harsh when her husband presented her with the result of his infidelities. But somehow she was in control. Somehow she'd kept her head above water. Now she was dependent on Malous's supply of oxygen.

This was the first time she'd nurtured such a relationship with any person. Pari saw her as a daughter, a friend, a guardian. She saw her as a safe haven, someone to sooth her troubled mind. Not that she ever complained about her troubles, or the source of them. The foundation of their relationship, the comforting ritual of reading tales, the unspoken satisfaction, the hidden bliss of being the only trustworthy person Malous had ever known gave Pari a sense of purpose. Malous made her feel wanted again. She had kept her going.

The next day, Malous skipped the morning visit to the kitchen to avoid her victim. She made up a story for Sina about the busy domestic life of her uncle and what a ridiculous idea she'd come up with in the first place. Malous watched the same movie twice and she couldn't even pretend to herself she enjoyed the film. She was afraid to go home; ashamed to face Pari.

Pari had kept her dinner warm as usual. Malous's reluctance to enter the kitchen left Pari in no doubt that she'd better get back to her doomed little hovel, where she belonged. No point shoving herself down the girl's throat. Pari thrust past her without acknowledgement. Too much pain for small talk. She was too low to feign resilience or forgiveness. Perhaps it was best not to glance at the face of the friend who betrayed her? That way she could always recall the other face, the one she spent such good times with.

Malous hadn't talked to anyone at home since the mayhem. She needed to act, to bring it to a head. She wouldn't even care if it ended with an emotional bloodbath; she needed to end it.

As much as Malous was reluctant to admit it, her little room at night felt empty and unfamiliar, somehow smaller with Pari's absence. Pari's presence, her candid remarks, the soothing voice that dispelled fears, had filled the room but at the same time made it seem larger, warmer. After her uncle Mehdi's death, Pari had been the only source of sincerity she'd experienced. And she feared it might now be gone forever.

Malous was angry. She was angry with herself for showing such a knee-jerk reaction to Zeeba's comments. She was angry with Pari for making her feel guilty. It made her livid to know how nasty she could be; a blight upon her own soul.

Being angry with her mother wasn't an issue any more. She was always mad at her. It had become a part of her life. She'd declared it so many times to herself it had become something that existed by default, something that had lost its colour, its taste, its meaning.

Her fury with Pari was different. It meant something; something real. Pari's friendship had put her in this terrible spot. Her friendship had made her look at her own soul and see the ugliness of it. Her friendship revealed what she was capable of. It exposed how easily she could pass on the injustices thrust upon her. Her friendship had distorted the balance of justice, the balance of right and wrong in her life. In the world of justice she was the victim, the oppressed, she was the one hard done by. The people close to her had let her down. But now, she'd turned the tables and she didn't like the change one bit. She wasn't the soft-hearted angel she had assumed herself to be. She could act skilfully as an oppressor, should the conditions require.

It had to be Pari's fault. The unhappiness she'd felt so deeply for the past few days had to be Pari's fault. The hurtful comments she heard from her mother were because of her. Pari wanted her solely for herself. She'd kidnapped her. She'd kidnapped her trust, her affection, her companionship, not even asking for ransom from her mother. Pari was the reason for her bizarre outburst. Pari was the reason she'd ceased to be satisfied with herself, with her personality, with her decisions.

Malous spent a week juggling reasons, interpretations, blame, guilt, and endless ifs and buts in her mind. She felt suffocated. She felt out of place, like she didn't belong. She hadn't had a word of conversation with anyone in the household. She may as well have lived in a dormitory with other students who weren't particularly interested in her. In times of trouble, Pari was the one who approached her and brought her back to the land of living. In times of trouble Pari was the hope herself.

She knew she had been wrong. She had been unfathomably cruel but maybe it was a simple aberration? Maybe she was better than she seemed to be? She became obsessed with the idea that she had to sort things; to get Pari back. Malous stood on the staircase and peeked into the kitchen the way she used to when she was younger. Pari was there, pouring her last cup of tea before bedtime. She was determined to put an end to Pari's exile. She needed to make peace with herself. She needed to wash the stain of Pari's broken heart from her soul.

She crept into the kitchen, pulled up a chair and sat on the other side of the table. Pari gave her a blank look. On another night, in a different time, she would offer her a cup and they'd talk up a storm about nothing in particular. But not this night, not now. Pari took a sugar cube and sniffed, before putting it in her mouth.

"I'm going to have a couple of dates. Do you want some?"

"No thanks." Pari didn't look at her.

"I'll take your mattress and blanket back to my room. Is that all right with you?"

Pari didn't answer. She'd been ignored for too long. She didn't feel like talking. She had no energy left. Nothing left to give. Malous could see the pain etched into her face but still she stubbornly refused to acknowledge her part in its making.

"I didn't mean to hurt you. I know I went too far but I didn't go out of my way to hurt your feelings." She was sincere, Pari could see that, but she couldn't understand it. How could Malous have done such a thing and not know what she had done? But there it was, a trick of the light? No. She had changed. To anyone else it would have been imperceptible but Pari knew every inch of this girl. And this girl had changed. Her face had changed. No, not her face, it was the way she held herself. Her lips just a little more pursed, her shoulders, folding in on themselves, downwards, heavy. Her manner, identical in every way one could see but now with a tightness, a barrier. She had become more like her mother. Or maybe she had simply let some of her mother's blood take shape? Maybe she'd been holding back? Pari wouldn't admit it to herself but there was a part of this girl that she had formed and that part was gone, or if not gone it was too far away to see, and in its place was her mother. Pari would never scold herself for not being grateful enough to Zeeba for taking her in. They were her family and they were her jailers. How wonderful it could easily have been. But Zeeba needed power and Pari was all the domain she could have for herself.

It felt like a death. Her beloved Malous had died.

Pari waited for the apology but none came. Everything was gone anyway but an apology might at least suggest this person, this new Malous, was not a monster. Perhaps she thought herself too young and too proud to say sorry? But how could she not gauge her crime? She truly was her mother's daughter. It made no difference to Pari. She was closed now. Closed to Malous. Closed to anyone, everyone, the world.

"I'm going to take your stuff back upstairs," Malous offered in response to Pari's silence. She left the kitchen to prepare Pari's sleeping corner in her room.

Pari washed the last of the dishes then headed for Malous's bedroom. This was the reality of her life. There was no magic change, no magic diversion waiting for her down the road. There was no magic. Her life with Malous seemed like her life but it was imagined, it was only in her head. There were no children, no grandchildren, no nephews or nieces, no one to love. She was alone as she had always been but now her loneliness was palpable; it hung in her heart like a cold rock.

But she could not survive completely alone. This person who had taken the place of her precious Malous, she was the best candidate; she had the most potential to be something of a friend. Pari forgot her feelings. They submerged themselves; sunk as if they had never existed. Even the remembrance of such pure love would have been too much to bear, so she became someone who had never loved, just as her precious Malous had become someone who would never love completely.

Malous's retreat from her proposed plan to create a safe haven where he might read the forbidden literature didn't sour her relationship with Sina. He hadn't taken it seriously to start with. He never cared to ask why Malous changed her mind. He could guess for himself. It would have been quite out of the ordinary if Malous's offer had borne fruit. He had met some broad-minded people in his life without any hang-ups over boys and girls socializing, but his classmate's idea was a bit over the top for any family. Anyway, reading his books in peace wasn't his main priority. He had to get a job. He'd taken enough from his father. It was time to pay his way. Tight on time to spare, teaching was the best choice to pursue. The applications for a part-time teaching job seemed to take forever, each one ending up with a rejection on the same theme: "We'll be in touch," they'd reply, as if all he had to do was wait, but he soon found out it was just a way for someone to believe they weren't being nasty. He'd rather have had it straight: "You're too young. You have no experience. Are you serious?" He needed the job for the money and he knew if he kept at it there was bound to be a position that would open up somewhere as women fell pregnant and men retired. He knew he would get a job and he didn't allow any of the replies to discourage him in any way. Finally, he landed a part-time job in a boys' school teaching Persian literature.

Sina had already started his third book of poetry. Again, he impressed his teachers. The professor of Persian literature personally introduced him to the Society of Writers and Intellectuals, a club where the good and the great of modern Persian literature mixed with the bright young things. Mostly they were fine writers but cognizant of their place in society, with families to feed, they lent heavily on that part of their talent which could elicit emotion without eliciting attention from the authorities. If they *had* to write something that would offend the believers then they would have to do it with subtlety. Wrap it up in layers for different readers, different audiences. There was no fighting to be done. There were no heroes; only writers. Heroes in literature, the kind that stand up to oppressive regimes, cannot survive until the groundwork is laid. Long before then, long before the young and the angry get to take their turn, there is only the writing. Putting down on paper exactly that which was intended using the raw materials at hand. Sina was the kind of talent a teacher would take pride in; and his writing demonstrated no signs of controversy, a fact that made a proud professor's job a lot easier when he was asked to bring young writers to fruition without controversy.

Malous was always encouraging. She adored his work and made sure he knew about it. She envied his talent, and she kept that to herself.

Malous had been toying with the idea of inviting Sina over for an afternoon. She could put an end to Zeeba's groaning about when she was going to meet the *hidden* friend of her daughter. It would also show Sina how valuable she deemed their friendship.

To make the bumpy road of introducing Sina to Zeeba as painless as possible, she made a list of Dos and Don'ts and begged her mother to abide by them. Not that she thought Zeeba would obey her rules but the list was an indication, a proof, a declaration of Malous's knowledge of Zeeba's intentions for everybody in her household to witness.

It wasn't difficult to persuade Sina to visit. He was curious and interested to observe her in her domestic environment. The concept of meeting the people who had a hand in her upbringing, comparing their differences and similarities and gauging their level of acceptance of someone like him, seemed mildly attractive.

Pari made sure she was first to the door. She wanted a good look at the man she'd heard so much about. She prided herself on her ability to evaluate her subject in a matter of minutes; quite an achievement for someone who avoided eye contact with men. Her mind was set as to what a man should or should not look like. She had a list of criteria.

Pari opened the door at the first ring of the bell. Her subject couldn't hide his surprise at such a swift response. He looked like a performer caught red-handed practising his lines just as the curtain goes up. That was a good opportunity for Pari's forensic evaluation. He was already off balance; good, it left him more vulnerable.

His height was the first item to be ticked on her list. He wasn't as tall as Malous's uncles but he was tall enough for a man. She'd never have the worry of anybody calling him a shorty. His thick black hair was well-groomed. Pari liked that in a man. His face was embellished by a flattering moustache that highlighted a plump lower lip as red as pomegranate. His nose was well-formed for a male. Surprisingly pale brown eyes hinted at an inner peace beyond his years. His shoulders were broad enough but there wasn't much meat on his bones. He hadn't gone out of his way to dress formally but his attempt to appear presentable was pleasing to her.

Pari took the box of pastries he held balanced on an outstretched arm and greeted him. The living room had already been arranged to welcome a guest. A bowl overflowing with oranges, apples, grapes and plums adorned the centre of the coffee table with smaller bowls of mixed nuts and dry pastries scattered around it.

Malous was first to greet him in the living room. Zeeba caught his attention even before he sat down. Her appearance matched his expectations. Fresh-faced with a tightness around the mouth, not beautiful but neither was she ugly; *almost handsome* was how he'd describe her in a poem. She was impeccably dressed. The cut of her dress reminded him of Malous. Smart, sensual without revealing anything. Rahim and Foti joined them then Pari appeared carrying a tray laden with small glasses of tea and sugar cubes piled up in a tiny bowl.

"Did it take you long to get here?" Zeeba wanted to find out where he lived.

"About an hour. I had to take two buses."

"An hour? Which direction did you come from?"

"From the east side." Zeeba raised her eyebrows in acknowledgement. She wasn't impressed.

"I take it your parents bought their house in that area long ago and settled there."

"We live in the army complex. My father's been in the army all his life."

Rahim cut in. Zeeba's expression told him she was about to

deliver her judgment on the east side of the city. "I had a friend in the army here in Tehran. He's an army doctor. He was transferred to the Caspian Sea area."

"What does your father do in the army?" Zeeba managed to sound like she was genuinely interested.

"He's a lecturer at the academy."

Zeeba nodded. There was an audible collective sigh. Lecturer would do. Lecturers were acceptable to Zeeba. "I don't know if Malous has told you but I'm a teacher too. It's a very satisfying profession."

"Yes it is. I started a teaching job myself recently," Sina said, with some pride. "I teach fifth-graders at a private school. It's a nice feeling to be among children who give their full attention to every word that comes out of your mouth. It makes me feel worthy."

"You must be successful at what you do. Not every primary-school teacher experiences what you have," Rahim said with a huge nod that signified everything was going to be fine. Zeeba wouldn't throw a tantrum today.

"It's a pity that on the pay side teaching leaves a lot to be desired. I mean it's not an easy job. It takes a lot of energy and dedication. And for some unknown reason, people ascribe a low financial value to that. Wouldn't you say?" Zeeba was fishing. She wanted some assurance that the man sitting in front of her, the man that might ask for her daughter's hand one day, possessed an acceptable level of ambition. His father was a lecturer. That was good enough. He was a teacher. That was good enough for a friend but not for a husband.

"I guess." Sina threw a peanut into his mouth. If he was aware that Zeeba was testing him for marriage he certainly wasn't showing it. She might as well have asked him if he preferred beef or fish. It just wasn't good enough. Rahim hung his head a little in expectation. Zeeba simply couldn't help herself. Of course, it was too much to expect that Zeeba would be accepting of someone, anyone.

"Well, the low-paid aspect of the teaching job is a fact."

Sina chomped on a mouthful of nuts and looked at her blankly. Malous wondered if he was even listening to her. She consoled herself with the thought that Sina was above it all; he was probably writing Zeeba into a verse as she spoke.

"There's no need to mull over it."

Good, at least she thought he was listening, that would be enough to get through the ordeal.

"Look around you. Have you ever seen any well-off teachers? Take your father, for example."

Sina's eyes widened at this and the suggestion of a smile passed across his face. He grabbed a handful of nuts and pressed them into his mouth, leaving his hand covering it, but his eyes betrayed his amusement. Zeeba was, of course, oblivious, she had no inkling of what might be going on in the heads of others, and she wouldn't have cared anyway. "If he'd worked for a private company, a business, for the number of years he's worked as a teacher, he would have probably owned two houses by now." She sounded irritated. As if she were angry at Sina's father for not following some imaginary advice she had dished out in a previous discussion.

Sina went on chomping. He looked around the room at the embarrassed faces; except for the woman who had served tea, she seemed as amused as he was, and more interested in having a cup of tea than listening to this woman. It was obvious that this was not a singular occurrence. This was his hostess's hobby, her pastime, her character. She was a tyrant. Sina felt sorry for poor Malous. She was so far forward in her seat she looked like she might slide off any second. Sina licked and smacked his lips a couple of times. "I guess my father's career is something you should discuss with him. I'm sure he'd appreciate the input." He couldn't resist tacking on a little sarcasm. She certainly deserved it. He grabbed a handful of raisins and sat back.

Rahim had seen it all before. He braced himself for the storm. It was apparent to him that Sina had marred her hope of interviewing a suitable candidate for her daughter. Sina had already lost the shine that might have kept her at bay. Rahim had seen it all before, and he wasn't about to watch her pick him to death. He jumped up, picked up a tray of pastries and offered it to the guest. He knew it probably wouldn't keep his wife quiet but it was worth a try.

Sina's visit to his classmate's house cast a mist of doubt over any possible intimate involvement with Malous. It wasn't that he'd seen any resemblance in character between the mother and daughter, it was the difference between the two that gave him a fright. How was it possible to be brought up by a person and yet be so unlike her? Was he in for a nasty surprise one day? Was Malous her mother or would she become her mother one day? The old men had always said *Want to find out who she is? Look at the mother.* But Sina had hardly listened to them, until now. Was this the same person standing in front of him exposing her callous personality only with better looks? Or could it be that her father had a decent nature and he'd passed it on to her?

He had no answers to these questions and yet he wasn't sure if he deemed them serious enough to stay away from the same delicate creature who had stroked his emotions, his intelligence, his sensuality, when she recited the story of her enchanted soul in sweet language in her writings. He surprised himself a little for even questioning such things.

Malous didn't mention his visit to him. She thought that keeping quiet about that whole episode might help obscure the memory. Besides, she had other things to worry about. Zeeba had been on her case to start earning a living. This was no surprise to Malous; no one lived under Zeeba's roof without chipping in. Everyone had to pay their way according to their circumstances. Zeeba hadn't put herself through all the trouble of getting her daughter into higher education so that Malous could sit on her bottom and fan herself. She was to get a job that suited a woman who would, in time, have a family and a career but which provided plenty of free time. Zeeba told her to get a job that offered security and a decent pension for her old age. With Rahim's connections it was easy to get Malous a teaching position in a well-known private school. And so she went to work in a job that satisfied all of her mother's conditions and, thankfully, all of her own wishes.

She liked her job. If she was to graduate with a good degree in a year's time, teaching experience was necessary. She liked working with children. She felt safe in their imaginary worlds; places where no one could be hurt. She relished their little voices and the way they expressed themselves. She was a good teacher, and she derived enormous satisfaction at the results she got. She employed no formal teaching methods; she seemed to just 'know' how to do it. Working with children touched her deeply; for the first time in her life she could easily see herself as a mother.

She started contributing towards the family expenses. Having been brought up in a family careful with money, it came naturally to her to put away almost every spare penny. She broke her fierce saving habits only once: before Norouz she bought some fabric for Pari; an act that filled Pari's eyes with enough tears to get Malous thinking about her own value.

Zeeba demanded a little extra money from time to time, to fund her rummy sessions. She never called it a loan. But that didn't last long, she'd come to the conclusion that Malous had jinxed her money. Every time she played with her daughter's money she lost. There was no point mixing grudged money to taint the rest of her stake and put her on a losing streak. She would just have to use Malous's extra money for something else; something that didn't require any luck.

CHAPTER
31

Haady was a competent lawyer. He never had any problem finding clients but his financial situation had no obvious correlation to his turnover of court cases. His practice had never threatened to make him wealthy but now it was in serious decline. He'd already asked his sister, Zeeba, for a loan.

The arrival of his second child, now a playful two-year-old girl, hadn't made things any easier for his wife either. Hoori managed to run the household on the money he brought in, but only just. When she left her first husband for Haady, it simply hadn't occurred to her that her lifestyle might one day suffer.

And he was drinking, heavily. He had taken to stomping about the living room retelling, in full, his courtroom victories. He even imagined a judge and jury to hear his long-gone cases. He acted like he was choking to death on his own self-pity; a lost soul latching on to alcohol in the hope of reliving past glories.

When he went back to Zeeba to ask for more money his breath stank of strong liquor and tobacco. His drunken bravura did little to hide his desperation.

"What do you want the money for this time?" Zeeba waited for a single word out of his mouth; like a wolf waiting for a move from her prey.

"To cover some expenses. Nothing unusual."

"What happened to your own money? Have you become unemployed without any of us noticing?"

"No."

"So, what's wrong with spending your own money?"

"Obviously, I'm short. Otherwise, I wouldn't be asking you for a loan. Right?" Haady couldn't be bothered with the Q&A session.

"I don't understand. You've got enough clients to earn a comfortable living." She genuinely could not understand why he had no money.

Haady's lack of response lingered enough to set her on fire. "Who do you think I am? Some banker's daughter who prints money? God, you've got some cheek calling it a loan. In case you haven't heard, a loan is something you pay back."

"Ach, just forget it!" Haady stubbed his cigarette hard into the ashtray and got up to leave.

"I can't forget it. Your shameful reputation has everyone talking. And, as I'm your sister, it affects me too. I have a right to know what's going on."

"What shameful reputation? What are you blabbering about?"

"I'm talking about your alcohol consumption. You were so drunk one night that instead of heading to your own bedroom, you went to the guest bedroom and lay in bed fondling your mother-in-law instead of your wife. The poor woman almost died of shock."

"Who the hell told you that?" Haady shouted, almost soberly.

"Never you mind. Just so you know everything's out in the open."

"You want to have everything in the open? Well, let's do that. You want to know what's going on? What's going on is because of you." He jabbed his finger at her. She folded her arms, calmly. "You're the problem. Ever since I got married I haven't had a quiet day in my life. You and your informer have to poke your nose into every nook and cranny. God, why didn't you get a job with the tax office?" At this he started playing the part; he pretended to scribble on his hand in tiny writing. "The detailed, itemized reports you come up with are better than the ones anybody could hope to get from a paid private investigator. You spy on my wife every hour of the day. Hell, you even know when she goes to the bathroom. Your informer has a precise count of her underwear. I can't look at anybody without noticing a funny smirk on their face. Thanks to you everyone thinks my wife's at it with someone else behind my back. And I'm not even sure myself any more. There! Your propaganda has even affected me. Whenever she talks with a man I can't help suspecting she's after an affair. Look what you've done to me. Hoori is unhappy. The love she once had for me is turning into contempt. My marriage is falling apart."

Haady picked up his half-smoked, partly-crushed, cigarette and lit up. He looked crazed, like a man just finished stabbing his nagging wife a hundred times. He drew deeply on the broken cigarette. Sparks dropped onto his hand. "And what's your game with my children? You pretend you're happy to babysit for them and all you do is feed them nonsense instead. What's with brain-washing them that Neema's like us, our side of the family and his sister's just like Hoori with all the stigma attached? You're trying to drive a wedge between them from this age? Would it kill you to keep your favouritism to yourself? You want to know why I drink? That's why. You and your ill-intentioned piety."

"Don't blame your dreadful marriage on me. I've always gone out of my way to help you. But this is your way. Anything that goes wrong in your life is someone else's fault. You've never taken any responsibility for your actions. It's been Mother's fault for years and I guess now it's my turn to be blamed."

Haady stared into the heavens with the air of a mental patient about to take his pills. He'd heard the same tune from Zeeba so many times before. He'd developed a peculiar resistance against it; instead of the words all he could hear was the sharp resonance of her voice warbling about as if she were trying to sing a song.

"After all the ranting, you still haven't answered my question. How come you're in need of a hand-out?" Zeeba was determined to drag the information out of him.

He stared into space, his eyes out of focus, as if he were spying something just behind her with his peripheral vision.

Zeeba realized it was time to put a lid on her urge to batter him with contempt. It wasn't working, and as much as she wanted to thump him hard, she didn't want to lose her brother forever. "Look, I'm on your side. I want to help. Just tell me how it all went wrong."

Haady exhaled. He was entirely exhausted. He sat down and lit an already lit cigarette. He'd been here many times and he was not convinced that his sister could resist the urge to attack him. But at least he could have a rest. He smoked in silence for a minute then he started talking.

"I don't know. I guess you establish a certain lifestyle for yourself and that becomes the way you live; the way you spend your money; to keep up with the requirements of your lifestyle. You don't even think about it consciously." He looked at her sheepishly. She tried to look concerned. She *was* concerned but had never cultivated a concerned look that might tell the world of her concern; her facial muscles simply were not up to it. Haady wondered for a moment if she were in pain then he, as always, crumpled in front of her; deep inside him he wanted her to listen to him, to comfort him, to tell him everything was going to be fine.

"One of my clients forwarded a case to me. We shook hands on the fee. I spent a lot of time and a good amount of money on the case. I had to pass on some incentives to governmental employees to cooperate and advance my case. I won the case then I was told I had to be patient with my payment. The client had encountered a grave financial situation and couldn't recover my expenses right away." He jammed the cigarette butt into the ashtray and extinguished it with his thumb. He pressed hard on the tiny red ember, showing no sign of pain. "So, I called in a few favours. I asked a few clients for a bridging loan; just enough to see me through." He said it almost pleadingly, as if she were a judge and he were simply pointing out how reasonable it was to be in such a pickle. "After a while they wanted their money back. To pay my debt I accepted a couple of cases in lieu of the debt. So, I was working without bringing in any income. My time was allocated to cases that didn't pay. And before I know it I'm trapped. On the slippery slope. A downwards spiral."

"What about your savings?"

"Before I accepted the case, I lent money to a friend. A lot of money. He was in a dire situation. He was a friend."

"You don't have any friends. You *don't* have any friends. You've got a bunch of bloodsuckers who would bleed you dry. And apparently they have."

"What're you talking about? What do you know about my friends?"

"I know you're a sucker for praise. I know you'd do anything for their admiration. Did you get your money back?"

"Not yet. But I'm sure I'll receive it."

"Mmm. Your judgment of people has been accurate so far, hasn't it? That's why you're in such a rosy situation. God forbid you'd open your eyes."

"You mean I should do what you tell me?"

"If you listened to me, you wouldn't stumble as much as you do."

Haady was too tired to fight. He hung his head and rubbed the back of his neck.

"Anyway, I don't have any devices to print money here. I have to be careful about my finances. I can give you half the money you're after."

She waited for his reply. Haady nodded then he dug his fingers hard into his neck. It was difficult to tell if he was massaging a knot or trying to hurt himself. His sister had helped. She had extracted a price but she had helped. Though it was hardly any help at all. Half the money might have been no money. He needed what he needed.

"Come back tomorrow. It'll be ready." She said it in a soft tone, to calm the rage that had beset both of them.

Witnessing his gradual downfall was too difficult.

32

Zeeba's customers had an easy way of finding out about her family and their business; most of them had already met Malous. Some of them took part in Zeeba's rummy sessions, others arrived every week for a fitting and an opportunity to check the temperature of Malous's attitude. All of them had sons or brothers or nephews in need of a wife and they were always on the lookout for the right match. Malous was an independent girl; they knew that because Zeeba never tired of offering speeches that somehow praised and damned her daughter at the same time. Her profile was perfect; educated: from a reasonable family, pretty but not pretty enough to cause trouble; she was prime material.

Pari had already been assaulted with the resounding praise one of Zeeba's clients had heaped upon her own son. He was about to become an engineer, he was stout and strong, he had a good character and he loved his mother. The woman had decided that Malous had the correct physical measurements to offset any future embarrassments and all of the other boxes were either properly ticked or deemed less than deal breakers. Like all Iranian mothers it hadn't occurred to her for a second that a girl might not want to marry her son. After all, was he not the greatest, most handsome, intelligent, kind and generous man who ever lived?

Zeeba did not like the woman but she was realistic enough to know that waiting for the perfect family was unrealistic. She had a long list of questions to be answered before she agreed to an introductory meeting between Malous and this woman's son. She had to be sure, above all, that this boy was headed for a bright financial future and she had to believe that he would not embarrass himself, Malous and, most importantly, Zeeba herself.

It wasn't easy to break the news to Malous. She loathed the whole idea of being set up with someone she'd never met, or, even worse, had no intentions to meet. It made her feel cheap and low, as if she were a bargain item to be haggled over. Zeeba knew what to expect. She was aware of Pari's influence on her daughter and she wasn't above enlisting Pari's help if it meant getting her in front of a good prospect. Pari had no problem at all with the idea. She wanted a good match for Malous and Zeeba made a strong case. Zeeba told Pari to wait until the day of meeting to spring the news on Malous; less time to think, less room to wriggle out.

Pari expected some resistance but she knew that ultimately it was simply a game that had to be played with Malous proclaiming her modern attitudes but finally giving in as a favour to Pari. When Pari told Malous that her mother had a boy in mind for a meeting, that very day, she almost went purple.

"Calm down, *aziz-jan*. What's so terrible about it? You want to get married one day. Well, you get to meet someone. It's not the end of the world. What difference does it make if you meet someone here with the approval of your family or you bump into someone by chance? Do you know how unlikely it is that you could meet a proper match on your own? Marriage can be dangerous, my dear, even when your family is involved you never really know what you're going to get."

"It's belittling. It's humiliating. I'm supposed to serve tea to people who're there to measure me, test me to see if I'm ready, see if I'm ripe." She grabbed her buttock. Pari managed not to laugh. "They want to see me? To see if I'm suitable for some boy I've never even met? I won't do it."

"Don't make a big thing out of it. It's not like you have to carry on socializing with them. Just go through the motions. For all you know you might find their son pleasant. He might be handsome. You might like him." Pari could see that the possibility that the boy might be attractive had no impact at all so she changed tack. "Who knows? He might not find *you* agreeable."

Malous pondered this possibility for a moment, then she grabbed her head like it had caught fire. "That's it! If he finds me strange or disagreeable, I'll be off the hook. I need a plan. Something to scare the family and to make Zeeba think twice before trying to sell me to the highest bidder. Help me. You'll help me, won't you?"

Pari couldn't believe Malous wanted to turn her joke into a plot to wreck the introductory session and scuttle that family out of the game for good. It reminded Pari of herself when she was a girl. It rekindled the urge to forge mischief, to act like a careless child who knew she was doing wrong but had no fear of the consequences. It had been so long since she'd felt innocent mischief in her heart. She'd met the young Pari again and she wanted her to stay around for a short while; just for old time's sake. "You're serious about this, aren't you?"

"You have to help me. You always have a trick up your sleeve."

Pari knew what to do right away. She could hardly contain herself. She bustled around the kitchen taking out equipment and ingredients she needed for her mischievous plan. "Let's cook a nice lunch for you."

She poured a good amount of beans and chick peas in a pot of water and chopped cabbage, onions and some herbs to add later.

"I promise it will taste good and serve your purpose at the same time." Pari flashed a broad smile that made her look like a teenager.

The family arrived on time in the late afternoon. They'd done everything by the book to ensure a positive first impression. The engineer-to-be was carrying a colourful bunch of flowers, his hair was combed, his trousers had a crease in them to cut steel. His short, stocky figure made it almost impossible to tell whether he was wearing an expensive suit or a cheap one. He had broad shoulders but there was no tapering to a waist. He was shaped like a barrel. Big, brown expectant eyes and chubby cheeks scrubbed red gave his face a familiar, friendly sheen. A line of three people, his parents and his sister, followed his trail to the living room. He walked with the flowers out in front like he was carrying the Olympic flame. His mother, close behind, dabbed a handkerchief on red eyes that had shed proud tears all morning.

Malous arrived with a tray of tea after a short while to informally introduce herself and welcome them. She kept her false smile on while offering tea to all seven people sitting in the room. The woman's family grabbed the chance, as Malous poured tea, to have a thorough examination, head to toe, of their candidate before she sat down. Then there was a non-stop conference between them.

Malous looked at them as they talked about her. Their heads

seemed to meet at a single point where eavesdroppers could not penetrate but, quiet as they were, it seemed wholly rude to Malous that she be discussed in her presence as if she were a prize camel up for sale. Steadfast in her decision not to meet this family again, she nevertheless set out to give the boy a chance, to separate him from the cattle call in which he was the main protagonist. She didn't find him attractive in the least. He hadn't passed the height test to start with. Moreover, he was beefy with no neck; two insurmountable charges against him before he even opened his mouth. He was eager to impress and not bashful in the least. He was confident and articulate. As she listened to him talk, she became impressed with the range of his knowledge. So coloured were her preconceptions she had expected to meet either a dolt or a droning puppet tagging along with his mother in search of *her* ideal daughter-in-law. He had a wide repertoire of subjects at his command and Malous was impressed. He was up-to-date with politics. He was well-read and enjoyed traditional Persian music which became apparent as he boasted about the latest concert he had attended. It was plain from his delivery that he'd also detected the hostility in Malous when they arrived but he stared straight into her eyes as he spoke, challenging her to warm to him.

And warm to him she did. Always one for mind over matter she could easily see herself beside this man at her family's social gatherings. She felt guilty, as if they could actually see her intent in all this. She couldn't help herself; her plan flew out of the window. She started talking to him to show her human side, she felt the need to impress *him*. She painted a great smile upon her face, she sat up bolt straight and she even gave his mother a raised eyebrow to acknowledge her success in raising such an eloquent and educated son. She completely reversed her position, to the excitement of the young man who grew even bolder at her new enthusiasm.

She was about to interject when a pronounced grumble broadcast from her midriff. The room, alive with conversation a second earlier, turned into a yawning cavern through which the sound reverberated into an angry growl fit for a hungry beast. Malous blurted an apology. The growl abated. She gave a twittering laugh then covered her mouth. Her face beamed. After a few elongated moments the prospect that it was over entered her mind. Her audience simply gaped. The silence was again filled with a sound of even greater proportions.

She darted out of the room mumbling an apology. She stood in the corridor until she was sure her stomach was beyond any further betrayal. When she came back all she could think of was the next growl out of her belly, as if concentrating on it would somehow keep it at bay.

She sat, gingerly, as if excessive movement might be the problem. It might have been a great brown bear trapped in her innards and it was not yet passed its anger. A rumble of even greater proportions threatened to shake her very sanity. Her audience, slack-jawed at her capacity to produce this seemingly endless intestinal symphony, remained frozen, hypnotized. Then it roared. The young man turned to his mother in dismay. Malous ran. She ran up to her room and threw herself onto her bed in tears. Perhaps the beast inside her had seen enough for when she stopped sobbing her stomach stopped percolating. She checked her panda eyes in the mirror and cleared her mind of what the people downstairs must have thought. After cleaning herself up, and giving herself a precious few more minutes to guarantee the bear would not return, she went downstairs. When she got there the guests were already on their way out of the living room. They made polite goodbyes with expressions that said they would not be returning. The young man shook her hand and bowed deeply, avoiding eye contact he spun around and almost broke into a canter.

Malous wanted to do it all again. The remorse at such a poor performance was tangible. Where minutes before there had been creaking noises fit for one of the horror movies she'd watched surreptitiously, now there was a void. Her ego was seriously dented. Although she certainly hadn't wanted to take part in this excruciating custom, once it started she couldn't help but try to rise to the challenge; to have the man want her, desire her. She craved approval. She wanted him to want her and she wanted his mother to want her even more. She couldn't figure out why she wanted the approval of complete strangers but she did, and it was too late now. Pari's magic soup had done the trick.

Pari didn't have long to wait to hear about the success of her plan. The tone and volume of Zeeba's voice spoke for itself.

"What was wrong with you, girl?"

"My stomach wouldn't stop grumbling. It wasn't my fault."

"If you were hungry you should have eaten something. There were fruit and pastries lined up on the table. Didn't you have lunch before they came?"

"I had soup."

"What kind of soup did you have?"

"Chick pea and beans." She dropped Pari right in it without a second thought.

Zeeba went after Pari without missing a beat. Pari cleared the table in silence as Zeeba ranted.

"What were you thinking feeding her peas and beans? You're no spring chicken. You know better. Did you do it to scare them away? Do you want to keep her here next to you for the rest of your life?"

"I suppose I wasn't thinking." Pari spoke quietly, almost to herself.

"Don't you take me for a fool. Lucky for you I wasn't keen on that family."

"I didn't particularly like them either." Malous jumped in to calm the situation. "As a matter of fact, I don't like the whole idea of having people around for marriage purposes."

"Oh, really? Are you going to stay here and grow old with me? Maybe I can put you in a frame and hang you on the wall?"

"Bringing people in here to gauge my bust line isn't the only route to marriage. And for your information, I certainly do not intend to grow old with you."

"Ah, I forgot. There's always a poor boy with no future out there to settle for."

"If you're referring to Sina, first of all he's working part-time now and that's not his big ambition for the rest of his working life. Secondly, you have to be attracted to the person you're thinking of sharing your life with. You can't just rule out your likes and dislikes just because of someone's bank account. How long do you think that kind of marriage would last? Gosh, you married my father apparently for love and it still fell apart after a short time, never mind if there isn't any chemistry involved."

"There are so many people who got married through introduction and have lived for many years together. And yes, of course, one of the many aspects they considered was the financial one. You think it's easy to start a married life with nothing? I didn't raise my daughter to be a pauper."

"So, I take it these people are all happy and prosperous?"

"They've something to fall back on and they can hold their heads up with no shame."

"Shame of what?"

"All I'm saying is that you deserve more. I don't see why you should compromise like you're a leftover item on the shelf."

Malous couldn't be bothered any more. It wasn't getting anywhere. Besides, she needed to lie down; her stomach was indicating it wasn't quite done with her.

As Malous walked off Zeeba turned to Pari. "God forbid she should settle for a proper life. I just hope I don't end up with an old maid on my hands."

Pari piled up the dirty dishes on a tray and shuffled towards the kitchen in silence.

CHAPTER

33

Malous's graduation was getting closer. She'd already amassed a year-and-a-half of teaching experience and was ready to move up the ladder in her profession with her bachelor's degree. She was working in a field she enjoyed and could happily see herself as a teacher for the rest of her life, but she hadn't forgotten about her writing. She still wrote essays and composed the odd short piece on issues she felt strongly about and she shared her writing with the mind she valued the most: Sina's.

There was no doubting her feelings towards Sina. It wasn't a deep, passionate love. She wasn't even sure if she was capable of such feelings. But she was attracted to him physically, and intellectually. It wasn't passionate, but she believed it was better than that anyway. Passion fades.

He was a perfect match. She was sure that he felt the same way about her but whenever the subject of marriage came up he was non-committal, he displayed no opinion whatever. Where else would she find someone so in tune with his ambitions, his sensibilities? It was time to bring him out of his trance, to give him a nudge. It was time to make him realize that he should make a move and grab his chance before destiny changed its course and wrecked his smooth path to an ideal marriage. She could not wait forever.

Sina could feel the growing tension between them. Over the next few weeks she broached the subject often but always he turned to stone until the marriage talk passed. She became angry at his inaction. She had less patience when things didn't go her way. She snapped more often if he said the wrong thing. Her moods swung like a woman approaching menopause. She even availed him of stories of the number of introductory sessions her mother had lined up for her. She did not tell him that she had scared the first, and only, candidate out of the door, but perhaps the thought of another man spiriting her away might do the trick?

And it did. He proposed to her as if he were asking if she wanted sugar with her tea. It was matter-of-fact, expected, familiar. It was clear to her now that he had been considering the issue all along. Perhaps it was the thought that he might lose her that finally brought him out of his slumber? Malous didn't care. He had put the question, made up his mind. And that was all that mattered now.

He asked for only one condition: that this would be a marriage of their own making, there would be no interference, no carping from her mother over dowries and the like. On this he was adamant. He would share his life with his equal, they would share a single soul, a single purpose. They would face life and conquer it together. They would, of course, take part in a khastegari, the arranged meeting of two families with a view to marriage, but only to fulfil what Sina called "an archaic cultural imperative". Prenuptial agreements were for people without faith. Khastegaris were for people without love. He loved her enough to ask her to share his life, his whole life, with him. There would be no messy divorce for them. They were above the cattle market, which he believed destroyed so many marriages before they had even begun. Demanding money for a wife was entirely distasteful to Sina. His wife would have his whole world, and that was enough, that must be enough. They would go through the motions of the khastegari purely for show. Their families could believe a deal had been struck. After all, there was no possibility of a marriage without an agreement that provided for the wife, in the event of the marriage breaking down.

The dowry would be, at Malous and Sina's insistence, modest; enough to appease Zeeba's expectations of a respectable prenuptial agreement but not so much as to induce terror in Sina's parents. After all, Sina's parents were the ones who would be liable to pay the dowry, should the marriage meet a swift demise.

Malous had won. She had put an end to the lingering, the hesitancy that almost every woman she'd known had told her was the defining characteristic of the male side of the universe. She had made him take a stand and push his life forward.

She broke the news of the proposal to her family. Not that she expected applause, but deep inside she had hoped for some kind of positive reaction. Foti wasn't impressed, or at least she pretended not to be impressed. She acted as if she'd heard the news of the change of address of the nearby grocery shop. There it was; another girl getting married, forming her own family while she brewed more and more bitter. What difference did her happiness make to Foti? She'd piled up too much virulence to conjure any joy in her spirit.

Zeeba's silent rebuke was as predictable as hot weather in the Persian Gulf. She folded her arms and raised an eyebrow. No congratulations, no comment at all. She had made her position as plain as day many times and Malous knew she believed Sina was not a great catch. But at least there were no fights, no interminable lectures on the unsuitability of her life choice. In truth, her mother caught her a little off-guard; she had expected perhaps a little resistance and she'd even hoped, impossibly, for a blessing. Rahim was happy for his stepdaughter but had no intention of taking sides.

Pari gave Malous her blessing. She reminded her of what she herself had gone through, the parental rebukes, and how she had taken matters into her own hands and set off on her new life with a runaway wedding. Malous was encouraged that after all the difficulties Pari had encountered sharing her life with Yousef, she never regretted standing up for her choice of husband. She fell for the person a woman with her nature and characteristics would fall for. She knew if they gave her a second chance to be nineteen again, with no memory of the events that would unfold, she would do exactly the same thing.

Pari took her Holy Book, her Quran. She held it tenderly in both hands, closed her eyes, cleared her mind, then she said a silent prayer. She paused then she opened her eyes and opened the book. She let it fall open, it was important that the book open itself and not be forced. Her mother had always consulted the Holy Book on important matters. The holy men took the book literally. They feared God so they preached the word of the book. But there were women, holy women Pari would say, who consulted the book to see a little of the future. No one had ever written it down, this skill, this act of divination, but all over the land there were women who, with right spirit and pure heart, had something of the future revealed to them. Mostly they were older women but it was more to do with character than age. She consulted the Holy Book the way her mother used to,

257

the way her mother had taught her, with humility and devotion. Malous was to be married and Pari had to know if it was going to be a good marriage. The verse that offered itself wasn't the one she'd hoped for but it was satisfactory enough to predict a long married life for her. There was nothing to suggest happiness but the main thing was that there was no hint of tragedy, no deep sadness lying in wait, no bad omens to fret over.

The khastegari was a formality. Sina's parents came to Zeeba's house. They ate pastries and exchanged pleasantries; then they discussed the dowry. Zeeba simply nodded and smiled when Sina's father suggested a sum. Malous had been careful to suggest to Sina how many gold coins her mother might deem appropriate. Gold coins were a requirement but the addition of a few precious gems would surely keep her happy.

Sina, for his part, had previously assured his father that all was in order and that he should suggest this sum without question. His father took him at his word but he accepted in the knowledge that should Sina fail to accrue such a sum, and should Sina and Malous not find the happiness of which his son was so certain, then he would, somehow, meet the debt.

When the time came to discuss their living arrangements, Zeeba suggested that Sina's parents help the couple to buy a home. In the pause that followed, Sina interjected, declaring that they planned to rent a small apartment in a modest neighbourhood until such times as they could afford to purchase their own property.

This was the point where Sina expected resistance.

But, again, Zeeba simply nodded and smiled.

All the rituals had been observed. Or so it seemed.

"Let's you and I have tea," Zeeba said to Malous the moment the door had closed behind Sina and his family. "Goodness, your boy hardly allowed me to ask the question. Had he tutored his father so well?" Zeeba took a sip of tea. "I had no wish to embarrass his parents but you deserve to start married life in your own home." She waited for her daughter to answer.

Malous was all but in a trance. She was to be married to her own choice. It had happened just the way Sina said it would. "Mmm?"

"Don't sell yourself short. You're no less than any of my friends' daughters. You are a pretty, educated girl, who has already started a good career."

Zeeba gave a little sniff as she placed her glass on the table in front of her. Malous inhaled deeply, as if waking from a long sleep.

"I will give you the money. I'm not rich but I will give you the money."

Malous felt a familiar feeling welling up inside her. Was this why her mother hadn't objected? Of course her mother would interfere. How could she not? "Maman, were you not ten minutes ago listening? Sina and I have already decided. You heard him. We will take care of ourselves."

"Ah, yes. You'll take care of yourselves. And there will be gold and jewels if not."

"Maman!"

Zeeba pressed her finger gently on Malous's lips to hush her. "I will speak and you will listen, and you will listen well. For if you do not listen well then life will make you listen."

Zeeba took Malous's hand and seemed, for a moment, lost in memory. Malous looked at her suspiciously.

"You think I'm a harsh mother?" Malous lowered her eyes. "Well, I am harsh. But I made you and it's time for you to know that you were made well. You have chosen a husband but you cannot allow him to choose your life. Malous, this is not an issue I will force. You will accept my offer or you will not. What you will not do is blame me for any future misfortune, nor will you blame your husband for forcing your hand. If I have hurt you I ask that you wash away the past. But I cannot ask forgiveness for doing what was right.

"You think you have found your soul mate. And perhaps you have. You believe that nothing can come between you? Well, look around. Broken dreams are sad but homelessness is worse. I want you to have a house in your name for my piece of mind. What difference does it make to Sina if he's willing to pay rent to a stranger? It is time for you to enter the world. You thought I was torturing you when I sent you to your father? No, you were a child and I had to show you the pain of rash decisions. You are so much like me." At this, Malous raised an eyebrow. "You'll see."

Malous started to let her guard down, to actually hear her mother's words. It was good to hear compliments, with no agenda, no barb attached. And it was both comforting, and a little startling, to hear her mother acknowledge her own uncompromising parenting style.

The suggestion that she was the same as her mother struck a chord buried inside her. The woman she had spent her life fighting against, the woman whose approbation she had craved throughout her life, wasn't just making peace, she was revealing herself.

Malous avoided her mother's awaiting eyes. "I'm not so sure about this," she said with a voice bereft of determination.

Zeeba knew she had hit her mark.

With a few months to go before the wedding, Sina's request for a full-time position at his school was accepted. He would teach high-school literature after his graduation. As far as he was concerned he and Malous were set to move out of their parents' houses and start their new life together.

The time left to their wedding hadn't done Malous any favours. She was not irrational nor was she stupid. She knew how much their combined earnings would be. They couldn't afford a house in a presentable area. She couldn't close the door on the idea of entering her own home, in her own name. She knew if she kept silent, at some point, the load she was carrying would come back crashing on her. She needed to find the right time, the right way to couch her words. She needed him to somehow suggest it. But finally, when she could put it off no longer, she simply blurted it out. "You know, despite what we agreed on, your father could still help us buy our own place." She sounded like a person who had thought her words through beforehand.

Sina eyed her suspiciously. "We don't need my father's help. We'll save up for a few years and we'll manage on our own. What brought this on?"

"He's your father. It's not like you're going to ask the next-door neighbour for money."

"My father needs his savings for his old age."

"The way your father likes you, I'm sure he would gladly help out."

"That's not the point, is it? And anyway, what about your family?" He said it assuming the question would end the bickering.

This was her chance. "Actually, my mother *has* made a generous offer. She'll help us with the purchase."

Sina was flabbergasted. He had the look of a man betrayed. "Has she now? And when did her 'generous offer' take place?"

"Just a while ago..." She looked down to avoid his glare.

"There is something missing in this equation which brings me to this question: What's the catch?"

"There is no catch. Why should there be a catch?"

"So, she is simply going to help us buy a place and there is no other issue involved?"

She bit her lip. "Well, she wants the house in my name."

"Of course she does. She wants to plant an umbilical cord into us. She wants to own us."

"No, you've got it wrong. Really, this time you're wrong. She just needs to know I'm safe."

"Safe?" Sina took his rage and pushed it deep down inside him. This was what her mother wanted. He would not be manipulated. "It is not going to happen," he said calmly. "It will never happen."

"Everybody else walks into their own home when they get married. Why should we be different?" Malous could hear herself. She sounded weak, unsure.

Sina tried to sound measured but he was plainly hurt. "What you mean to say is 'why should *you* be different?' *You* don't *have* to be different. Perhaps you should settle with someone who can provide a home from day one? Your parents, especially your mother, think I'm useless anyway. By marrying someone well-off you can make everyone happy, including yourself. That way, you wouldn't have to feel embarrassed by your circumstances."

Sina waited for a sign, a word, anything encouraging. Malous was expressionless. It was as if even she was baffled with this conversation, with the hidden doubts that had been brewing unconsciously. Here she was, standing in front of the man she'd fought to get, and she'd just belittled him the way her own mother might have. The thought that her mother had driven her opinion into her so deeply gave her a moment to forgive herself; perhaps she was regurgitating Zeeba's words? But it was her, her will, her own words that she spoke; she meant it. Now that the reality of a marriage was upon her with nothing to fight for or against she realized that she wanted more.

Sina wore an expression that seemed to her as if he could see her thoughts. For a moment she thought she detected mirth, as if a smile might break across his face. A rush of emotion ran through her. She felt his warmth plunging into a deep well of regret.

"This conversation is at an end. It seems you still have a decision to make. I suggest you do not take too long." Sina walked away without another word. No anger, no backlash, he simply walked away.

Had she inflicted irreparable damage? This couldn't be undone, it couldn't be unsaid.

Now there was the possibility that the whole wedding plan would fall apart. It was obvious to Pari that something was amiss. Over the following days Malous became more and more withdrawn. The household became an altogether more peaceful place as Malous spent most of her waking day lost in thought, as if trying to unravel some great Gordian knot in her mind. Zeeba knew exactly what was going on. Her daughter had seen the light. She wanted her own home. The desire for true love had been shaken by the more pragmatic desire for true security. But Zeeba would not interfere, she would be neither an obstacle nor a scapegoat in these matters.

Pari cared too much about Malous not to break her silence. She'd seen it many times before, bewildered people who never found out what they really wanted from life, confused people who had never experienced true delight, real satisfaction. If she made a mistake now she might have to endure a harsh sentence; wandering through life, perplexed, trying to find a way to recapture what she'd lost years before. If Malous buried her feelings; ignored them as if they never existed, it would surely inflict a grave emotional scar, a deep wound that would eat into her and disfigure her spirit like leprosy invading human flesh.

Pari had witnessed the pain that lingering confusion can inflict.

It was time to dig up the dirt. "It's been a week since the last time you talked to him. Do you still want to be his wife?" she asked Malous, after making sure the coast was clear.

Her question opened the floodgates. "I don't know any more what's going to happen. I told him about Zeeba offering help to buy our own place. I told him that I agreed with her suggestion. He reacted like a holy man to blasphemy." She shrugged her shoulders like a child in a bad mood. "He could have contacted me. Couldn't he?"

"He didn't have any problems with the wedding plan. You did."

"I didn't ask for much. Why should he react like this?"

"You agreed to this marriage knowing the conditions and circumstances attached to it. Now you're taking a step back. Anybody in his shoes would be discouraged. You've broken his trust."

Pari could see two people in Malous's face. She could see a hard woman, powerful, assured, superimposed on a frightened little girl. Pari wondered why people lose their goodness, why they have to become like stone. Strength didn't need a black heart. But then she remembered her own lot. She had tried to be good, to help her fellows when she could and now she was a servant to her own family and the girl that she had once believed was her spiritual daughter was proving, again, that blood mattered more. She could see traces of regret forming under her skin. She could see how Malous's features were being sculpted by her behaviour. It was surely an old wives' tale that character is revealed upon the face, but it often was. The innocence, the sheen of youthful righteousness had gone from Malous and in its place lines were forming, almost imperceptibly. Around the eyes the skin was looser, not sagging but not entirely alive either. But underneath the skin there was a tautness that pulled at her eyes to make them colder. Her lips seemed thinner, her mouth cut across her face horizontally, geometrically, the little upwards curl at the corners of her mouth that had been so endearing, was missing. Maybe, for now, it was simply in hiding from the moods to which Malous consigned herself but Pari knew that soon enough it would vanish forever. Malous would look back at photographs of herself in a few years and wonder where her youth went, and Pari knew that she would never understand, or want to understand, that she had sold a little piece of her soul. Fear of the future would be her final excuse but perhaps these things are written at birth, perhaps she never really had a choice? Pari didn't know why these things happened but happen they did. Nevertheless, she could not stop loving Malous. Perhaps she would always see the little girl she wanted to hug every minute of the day, but she would not deny the woman Malous either; she had a right to exist as much as the girl that Pari wanted to cling to.

"Look, *aziz-jan*, it's obvious why he hasn't contacted you. He needs assurance that you're aware of the harm, of the hurt you've caused. He needs to make sure that you're not going to change your tune every time someone sings a new song to you. He has to know what he's offering you is what you want. No one gets into a marriage thinking it's only for a few years. We're talking about the rest of his life, the rest of your life. So, the question is really very simple. Do you still want the wedding to go ahead or not? If you do, you're the one who's got to come forward."

Malous didn't answer but Pari knew her words could get through to her. "We all make mistakes in our life but not all of us get a chance to undo them. Imagine yourself in a few years' time wondering what he's doing, whether he's married, if he still lives here. How would it affect you? Would it make you sad that you're not with him any more? Would you ever stop thinking about him? If you feel a load on your chest, on your mind, torturing you with no break, that's your true self telling you to sort out this mess before it gets out of hand."

Pari hoped that Malous's arrogance would give in to her intelligence. There was nothing more she could do. It was up to her.

Malous spent the following week fighting with herself. She knew she was right to demand some security in her life; she knew she was right. But in her ponderings over a way to make Sina change, the pain of separation trumped her problems and she would end up desperate to see him. By the end of that week her righteousness had crumbled. All she could think about was Sina. She had believed their relationship was more a meeting of minds than a passion but now she just wanted to be near him, whatever the cost, whatever the consequences. The thought that she might lose him, that she might see him, in the future, with another became almost manifest in her mind's eye. She had to act. It was time to fix things once and for all. She asked him over for a talk.

She started slowly; some tea, some pastries, the slightest smile. He knew what was coming and he knew she still hadn't managed to think about his feelings. It was all about her. It was all about what she wanted from life.

First, she explained how she had made a mistake, no apology but at least an explanation; she was confused, overwhelmed, worried about the future, it had all happened so fast, she even cited her mother. Sina raised an eyebrow at this but she didn't notice.

She wasn't sure what had come over her but now she was rejecting her doubts. She trusted him. Sina met her offer with a wry smile. He was getting another demonstration of her character, always honest, always believing herself and in herself but liable to enormous swings, from black to white with no shades in-between.

He didn't torture her; that was not in his nature. It had flashed into his mind but more as a vignette from a future short story than something he would actually consider himself. He pictured his own character fawning over her, playing the man with a second chance, then, when the oblivion had fully enveloped her, he'd walk away, without a word or look. She would be crushed. Sina smiled; lost in his story. He looked at her and wondered whether she might be his muse. He wondered if he could withstand the criticism she would surely offer when she felt he had to make more of himself, when she decided that he wasn't making enough money. But she managed to make it all sound so reasonable, so utterly forgivable. She was so innocent, so lost in her unique view of things that he couldn't help but want her. She had blustered her way into his affections and, even though he knew these leaps from cold to hot and back again would be a constant feature of their relationship, he found her simply irresistible, so full of certainty. Whatever she believed at that time was what she knew she was destined to believe for all time. Nothing could shake her on this. She was like the prototypical religious zealot.

He let her finish her speech; no need to interrupt such heartfelt outpourings.

He went to her. She stopped talking. In the silence, he took her hand and placed a kiss upon it.

266

34

The ceremony took place according to plan. To save money Zeeba had decreed that her daughter's wedding be held at her place. Pari was assigned the duty of catering the affair. She'd cooked for crowds before and even if her cousin hadn't dumped the task on her back, she would have offered. Malous's wedding dress was, without doubt, one of her mother's very best efforts; it was a work of art. Nobody could deny her vision when it came to designing and sewing garments. Her art was the ability to make it look as if she had moulded the human body to fit the dress and not the other way around.

Sina was not impressed by Malous's father. Dressed in his old army uniform, he pontificated endlessly on subjects he seemed to know nothing of, and when he talked he looked like one of those paintings from old black and white films where someone has cut out the eyes and is spying from behind the painting. He simply could not keep his eyes from rolling about in his head. It was obvious to Sina that the man was terrified of his ex-wife. His mannerisms were those of a small mammal in the vicinity of a predator. Army uniform or not, he was a man ready to bolt from anything that looked remotely like his ex-wife. He hid away from Zeeba during the whole ceremony. Zeeba played her part by throwing disdainful looks at the very mention of his name. It was turning out to be a normal wedding after all; feuding parents, sending their offspring off to their fate with a taste of how it might all end.

Another strong indication that the wedding was going well was the sight of Haady, completely legless, offering garbled closing speeches while trying to dance with himself. In the past Malous might have felt ashamed but poor Haady had become a caricature of himself, someone that people would cite as a warning of the dangers of alcohol. Haady was surely gone, his life as a busy litigator probably finished. Malous would never give up on her uncle but there was plenty of time to try to save Haady; today was her day, she was the bride of a wonderful man, her soul mate; nothing could spoil this day.

That night, two young people felt the touch of another for the first time. Sina was in the moment but also outside, watching, recording. Her skin, smoother than silk, warm, yielding, her lips, her firm breasts, her sweet smell. He ran the back of his hand over her body, knowing that these feelings were unique, there would never be another first time. He wrote the experience in his head as he lived it. Malous lay, eyes closed; the drama leading up to the wedding had deflected her attention from this moment and now she felt the warm body of another beside her, she could hear the hunger in his breathing. She could feel that he was holding back, determined to drink in every sensation. When she had wondered about her wedding night she had always imagined this but feared it might fall short. If all there ever was in her life was this man, touching her in this way, then she would be content.

That night, in a bed a little too small for two people, in a rented apartment just big enough for two people, Sina and his wife shared their first sexual experience and Sina left a part of himself in his woman's womb.

The news of her pregnancy cast seeds of joy among Malous's family. Even Foti looked forward to the arrival of a new life, a new change, a new tale to deflect from the banality of her own life.

The child would set foot in the world in the season of rejuvenation; Spring. Malous was infatuated with the concept of motherhood. She had pondered many times on how she would do things differently from her own mother; she would certainly do better and this was her chance to bring her theory into practice.

Zeeba suggested sending Pari to live with the new family. Malous welcomed the idea almost too enthusiastically. Pari had often dreamed about, and prayed for, a divine intervention that would rescue her from her cousin's unpleasant reign.

The deal was done. Pari would live with Sina and Malous. She would share a room with the baby. She could hardly wait to be awoken by the innocent cries of a life that could absorb the love she knew was still within her. Spring would bring many changes. There was no one on this earth Malous would rather have care for her child.

There was an old saying that Pari's mother used to use. She would tell Pari that the arrival of a baby smoothes the parents' way to a better life; that it enhances the quality of their life. Outside of the joy and the hope that a child brings she believed that a new life carried with it a tangible power, an ordinary magic beyond feelings or perception, like a kind of warmth; she believed, as did her daughter Pari, that children literally brought a small part of heaven with them into this world. And that it was up to the parents either to embrace this power, this goodness, or to let it fade and wither.

Sina had not let events interfere with his true vocation: his poetry. He'd finished two new collections of poems and received praise from respected, published poets. His social skills, his charm, had embellished his art and forged quite a few useful contacts. The end result was his introduction to a publishing house through a friend of a friend and a publishing deal three months ahead of the birth of his child. He'd finally managed to get a foot in the door; all he had to do now was to keep the creative work coming.

With their combined income and the prospect of a little extra generated by Sina's poetry they managed to buy a modest place close to her mother's. That Sina had managed to get a publishing deal was both beyond belief and somehow expected. He had dreamed for so long of being properly published that it hadn't occurred to him that any publisher would actually furnish an advance for a collection of poetry, much less provide a decent royalty, which, his editor assured him, would surely kick in when the advance was earned out. In the meantime, as a published poet he could approach literary magazines who were happy to pay for the work of someone for whom a great future was being foretold by those *in-the-know*.

Their daughter was born on a brisk May morning at the Mehr hospital maternity ward just before the call to morning prayer. Malous, exhausted by the prolonged labour, held her delicate little daughter in her arms and whispered the name *Hannah* into her ear. She'd never forgotten the gleeful anticipation on her uncle Mehdi's face when he'd placed a beautiful Russian doll in her arms and introduced it to her as Hannah. She'd also retained the melancholy memory of losing Hannah, and now this child would heal that particular wound.

She pressed her cheek against Hannah's tiny face. No matter what happened in the future, she was hers and no one and nothing could separate her Hannah from her. She promised the little newcomer that she would always take care of her and be on her side.

Sina, elated by the birth of his daughter, left his new family with Zeeba to fetch Pari, who was waiting anxiously at home for some news. As soon as she arrived Malous put the newborn in Pari's arms. "This is Pari," she said.

Pari was bewitched. The baby had cast a spell on her. She'd stolen her soul. Pari loved children, especially small children. It may have been inevitable that she would fall in love with Hannah but Pari hadn't experienced this depth of feeling with anyone else, not even with Aban, her stepdaughter. Hannah had enslaved her; Pari would have given her life for her. Perhaps it was her love for Malous magnified through this baby? Maybe she saw a pure, flawless version of Malous in her? Maybe she was going to be the one Pari could rely on without worry or doubt, with no conditions attached?

Pari's relationship with the little girl was completely different from the way she had cared for her stepdaughter. This was not an occasional job. It was not a temporary kind of fostering with the knowledge that the child would be returned to her mother by the end of the day. Pari did everything for Hannah. She took up every mother's task from changing her soiled clothes to sitting up for hours every night rocking Hannah to sleep. Pari's duties with Hannah did not exempt her from the more mundane chores generated by any household. She was expected to do all the cooking and cleaning, all the washing and ironing; she was expected to do everything. To Malous, motherhood was a beautiful thing, not to be confused with the menial tasks of rearing a child.

Pari had no objections to her hefty workload. She loved Hannah and cared about Malous too much to even entertain the concept of fatigue. For her, this was heaven. She got to do what she deemed right at the time she chose and the way she saw suitable. There was nobody barking at her. She was in charge of handling affairs with no ifs or buts attached. Besides, Malous valued her work and her social life too much to squander any time on housework.

Malous's life became much more the life Zeeba had hoped for her daughter. She forged a wide circle of friends, people she met through work and those she got to know through her husband. She used her free time to throw parties that helped to culture a solid social position for herself and Sina. The colourful parties suited Zeeba well. She was always on the lookout for more, and better quality, acquaintances.

Everyone seemed to have everything they wanted. Pari was happier than she had ever been. Malous was finding herself. And Zeeba could take the credit. "I gave you Pari, don't you ever forget that," she would say to Malous. And when she said it Malous would comfort herself with the fact that Pari seemed genuinely happy with the arrangements, but she never managed to quell the queasy feeling in the pit of her stomach that accompanied her pasted smile, nor could she stop herself from checking to make sure Pari had not been within earshot.

For three years Pari cared for the child. She was there for Hannah's first steps, her first words. She was there to give comfort. She was the constant in Hannah's life. They were bound together, an aging woman, and the little angel in her care.

Then came another child. Hannah's mother grew big then disappeared, off to a strange place, then back again with a tiny baby in her arms. A brother, Arash, a little playmate for Hannah; she was beside herself with joy.

Pari loved the new arrival just the same as she loved her precious Hannah. Hannah was jealous, her Pari spent less time with her now, though Pari knew Hannah's perceptions would soon change and all would be well. But the increase in her workload had brought more expectation than appreciation with it. Her pure dedication, which had seemed to *fit* the family perfectly, was no longer enough to care for a small child, a newborn, and all of the chores for a household now five strong. Her duties seemed to have lost a holy spark and become backbreaking. Now she was always behind, never quite enough time to enjoy her charges the way she used to enjoy Hannah. Nevertheless, in the tradition of her mother, Malous expected every ritual, every detail to be accomplished at an exact time, exact place and exact manner or it would become a matter for complaint.

It was clear to Pari that history was repeating itself as it had throughout her life. Joy followed by sorrow followed by work followed by humiliation. Despite the grief of re-experiencing the ragged corners of the human soul, she still felt blessed. For the first time in her life she had unlimited liberty to love two infants without hiding her true feelings, without establishing a borderline of crude temporary care. This time she could be a real mother. They were dependent on her and she cherished that.

Pari had seen an upsurge of thwarted egotism in people before. She had the notion that given the right conditions, the right circumstances, right time and place, the emotional fungi sprout and shroud the heart in no time. Apparently, it's hard to fend off the temptation of lording it over people when there's no penalty. She had fallen into the trap herself on more than one occasion during her mastership in her village. It was difficult to ward off the allure of taking advantage of a superior position. Fighting the lust of power wasn't for the weak and needy. She knew that. She knew that we adamantly choose to imagine the best in some people. It was all about our beliefs, our demands, our perceptions, our compulsion to define others as either good or bad. And when reality knocks at the door of our most treasured fantasies we feel betrayed, let down by the inability of others to live up to a picture that exists only inside our heads.

She'd seen it all. That was life. Malous snapping or raising her voice wasn't the worst thing she'd experienced. She could cope with it. This time she had the luxury of washing her sorrow and disappointment away in a flow of unconditional love from two little fountains of happiness.

It was lucky for Pari that the first-born child turned out to be a girl. Regardless of age, she could always rely on the awakening of the motherly instinct in a female. The four-year-old Hannah took pride in looking after her brother from time to time. Pari made her feel important as she assigned her the supervision of little Arash. Pari didn't make a habit of it but there were times when she was buried under such a huge workload that even a little help from a little person went a long way. Besides, Hannah had proven herself to be responsible and vigilant with Arash; there was a brightness in her eyes that spoke of deep intelligence, even wisdom.

But all was not always so simple. Intelligent, vigilant, responsible she was, but she was only four years old, and sometimes her carefree spirit overcame her prodigious talents as a carer. On a fateful midsummer day, Hannah and a little friend vanished. Pari had become immersed in preparing lunch for the guests. Malous had taken Arash and left Hannah and the little guest, a six-year-old girl, in Hannah's room to play. Come lunchtime, they were nowhere to be found. Everyone in the house searched frantically. Sina tried outside in the hope that they were with neighbours but he could see no trace of them.

After forty-five minutes of fruitless searching tempers were frayed, Malous was ready to blow, Pari was praying so hard her eyes were on the edge of bleeding.

Malous jumped at Pari; she was closest to her and therefore responsible in the eyes of a frantic mother. "How could you let this happen? Where were you?"

"I was up to my neck in the kitchen. I thought you were looking after them." Pari tried to answer without interrupting her silent prayer. Then she lifted herself from her self-induced trance. "What am I? Do I have four hands?" She could hardly believe Malous's accusation while at the same time she knew, of course, it had to be her fault. That she loved the child more than her own life didn't matter when there was blame to appoint.

"You're supposed to watch out for her. What am I to do if anything terrible has happened to her or her little friend? Her mother is coming to pick her up after lunch."

Pari tried to keep her head. Malous was beside herself with panic; it was understandable. But she couldn't help wondering why it wasn't possible for Malous to treat her like the surrogate mother she had been to Malous and her daughter.

"How can we live with ourselves?" Malous shouted at her.

Pari looked at her and knew that she meant "How can *you* live with *yourself*?" Even with her precious little girl in possible peril she could apportion culpability to the one woman who would certainly give her life for Hannah.

Malous had succeeded in planting doubt in Pari's mind. It *was* Pari's fault. She knew this family. They were who they were. For Pari to blame anyone but herself would be to deny her own character as well as theirs. She should not have let this happen and now that it had she wondered why it hadn't happened before.

Guilt rushed through the open doors of her conscience. It was true. She had let Hannah down. She had let herself down. She was not to be trusted. It was her mistake to assume that Hannah would be safe and attended to when her parents were present. She should not have relied on them. Even Hannah, a four-year-old, knew better than to count on them. Pari was her source of comfort, her solace, her protector. Pari was the one she sought after a bad dream. When she felt ill it was her Grandma Pari she ran to. When she was happy she shared her happiness with Pari and when she was sad it was Pari who made it better. She woke up at dawn with Pari. Pari performed morning prayers with Hannah beside her, following her movements. She woke up with her Grandma Pari at dawn and it was Pari's voice that sung her to sleep.

The doorbell rang twice. Pari ran to open the door.

Zeeba must have practised in front of a mirror because the expression moulded into her face hit Pari like a physical force, then as a deathly, sickly warmth spread out from Pari's midriff a little face, smiling, appeared from behind Zeeba's skirts. It was Hannah, giggling. The child's voice shattered the mounting horror. Pari grabbed the wall to support herself. The relief was so tangible she felt like she might float away. The other girl, Hannah's partner in crime, jumped out from behind Hannah and they both laughed as if they had perpetrated the funniest joke of all time. Zeeba stared into Pari's eyes as if she thought she could actually cut her with a look. The girls ran past Pari and into the house.

"You'd better thank your lucky stars that nothing happened to them," Zeeba said.

Inside, the rest of the household surrounded the two children. Malous thanked her mother as if she had rescued the children from the mouth of a lion.

"We walked all the way to Maman Zeeba's house. I knew the way all by myself. I didn't need anybody's help." Hannah was very proud of her navigational skills. She kept looking at Pari for approval of her adventure.

There was no limit to Hannah's sense of pride. She had led the other girl, who was at least two years her senior, on what must have seemed like a great journey to her grandmother's house and now that she was back home everyone seemed overjoyed at her achievements.

There would be no punishment of any kind for the girls. The relief of finding them safe was like a piece of heaven itself had descended into the house. Nobody could stay angry. Even Zeeba almost cracked a smile at Pari when she saw her eyes well with tears, but she stopped herself in time.

But more than ever the incident confirmed Pari's position. All the love she had showered upon Malous was long forgotten. Working like a scullery maid she was expected to perform all of the housework and take care of a child as if she were her own. She was so tired. If only she could just spend her remaining time in this world caring for Hannah that would be enough. But now she was guilty of neglect as well. Both women, the mother and the daughter, had combined into a single household tyrant. Pari indeed felt guilty that the child might have come to harm, but it was a guilt that these women should have dispelled. Instead they lied together.

Pari had a place to live and children to offer some joy but scant time or energy to embrace that joy. She dreamed that Malous might one day come to her and say, "Here, *azizam*, put your feet up, take some tea with me. You've worked enough in this life." She dreamed that Sina might take pity, that he might see her plight and come to her aid. He was a sensitive man, she caught him watching her sometimes but then he was a writer, he was probably stealing something from her to put in a book. She wasn't a person to him, perhaps a subject, at best, Sina lived in the house like a guest in a pension. He was a stranger to Pari and a sometimes absent father. He had climbed the social ladder fast and he was a fast learner. The sensitive boy who seemed to care about everything only cared about himself now.

There was never any thanks. Not any more. Malous used to talk to her for hours and still sometimes they would reminisce but invariably Malous would retreat from the conversation lest she remember that this woman was her primary source of love for most of her adolescence and into womanhood.

But still Pari had little Hannah and until Hannah was old enough to know better, Pari was her whole world. The love of a child sustained her.

Despite her premature sense of independence, Hannah wasn't a difficult child to handle. She was sociable. She enjoyed being among children from different ages and backgrounds, and finding friends to invite over was one of her specialities. Hannah was not only intelligent and self-aware, her over-developed confidence left her with little patience for other children who could not match up to her expectations; she felt most other children were rather slow. Pari once caught her striking a boy, four years her senior, for being "stupid".

Another boy, her age, who had attempted to steal a kiss by pushing her against a wall, found her no pushover. Pari had to pull her off the boy after she had bloodied his nose. Her vivid imagination was a constant source of entertainment for her Grandma Pari.

But at night her ability to create imaginary characters and plunge them, and herself, into great adventures became a source of horror. There was always a monster under her bed, always a creature in the closet waiting to pounce as soon as Grandma Pari left the room. It became Pari's habit to wait outside her room for a few minutes and then rush in to challenge the monsters. Pari would cast a spell to drive away the monsters and for little Hannah that was enough; the incantation always did the trick. Something, in later years, Hannah would never shake off was the feeling that Pari had more than wisdom. It was undeniable that Pari possessed true wisdom. Even all her years imitating a slave for her family did not diminish her natural weight, her pride, her clarity of mind, but Hannah knew she possessed more. Others would say that her playful incantations were absorbed by Hannah the little girl, a simple quirk of play burned as magic into the heart of a child. Pari would never have suggested she possessed a power beyond the natural. After all, if she had such a power would she not have used it to conjure a better life for herself? Such things were against the laws of nature and God himself. But, while she knew she had no power over her own destiny, she knew that in destiny she played a part.

But Hannah's monsters, banished by the sorcery of a servant woman, a former woman master, would one night come to stay forever. By happenstance Sina was passing Hannah's bedroom. He heard strange voices, some high-pitched, another rumbling deep. He barged into the room to find his daughter half-asleep and Pari, arms wringing above her head, talking gibberish.

He never gave her a chance to explain, a chance to laugh at the innocence of a tiny child that needed nothing but belief to see her through any fears. He didn't give her a chance to tell him it was all a joke. But Pari couldn't have known that Sina, who once wore his soul open to the world, could feel Pari's power. Perhaps he had strayed too far from himself? Perhaps the window to his own soul had become muddied enough that tarring the woman with imagined sins would save his soul, retrieve it from the world of commerce in which it had become entangled? The tragedy was that Sina could indeed perceive something more than a simple woman. He had never taken to her for this very reason. He wanted his own vision to remain clear, he needed no witches in his life. Witches could not exist. He would imagine them and write about them but he could never let anyone know that he believed in them, that everything he wrote came from another place, that a window had been opened to him as a child and still was open. But the images were becoming more and more obscure and every year he would substitute a little more craft for knowledge.

Sina put an end to bedtime shenanigans. He forbade Pari to sit by his daughter until she fell asleep. Neither Hannah nor Pari would ever forget her first night alone with her imagination. Hannah sat in the corridor outside her bedroom, in the dark, for hours, waiting for Grandma Pari to come and fight the monsters in her room. Pari's heart was shredded by the guilt of leaving Hannah on her own. She had no say in it. Hannah couldn't understand the apparent significance of a sudden separation but she never blamed her Grandma Pari. She never thought less of her for not violating the rules. She was alert enough to fathom that Pari's power was quite limited. She had seen her taking orders before. And she could realize that leaving her on her own at nights was an order Pari had to obey. Hannah sympathized with her. She was sure of Pari's feelings for her and Arash. Pari melted when the little girl explained to her that she knew her night-time absence was not of Pari's doing.

Hannah grew up enjoying her knack for making friends, being an attentive sister to Arash, taking pleasure in the make-believe events in her imaginary world and developing a slow but firm path to building up a mind of her own.

Pari's bedtime absence could not quell the child's imagination. If anything, her introduction to demons deepened her ability to lose herself in her own mind. As she grew she immersed herself in Grandma Pari's tales from the days of her reign over her precious Varamin village. Pari loved to tell the stories again and again, adding a wrinkle here, a missed reminiscence there, to keep them fresh and true. She loved the way Hannah seemed almost to put herself back in time and space, in the village. There were even times when it seemed to Pari that Hannah knew things that Pari had not related to her. Hannah didn't simply listen to the stories, she engaged with them, bonding with characters from another time.

Hannah took great pride in her Grandma Pari's ability to run a whole community on her own. She wasn't sure what specific characteristics were required to be a Zan-Arbab but she was certain that her Grandma Pari was the most patient person in the world and that nobody could offer solace like she could. To be in her presence was to feel comfort.

Hannah took Pari's love and in turn tried to pass it to her brother. Arash's hunger for attention and approval was insatiable. Sina tried to discourage Arash's "weakness". He believed Pari and Hannah encouraged his son to be dependent. Sina's plan for Arash was to work him like a man. He would do all the handy work around the house and his grandparents' house as well. As his son, he was not to take anything in life for granted.

Hannah was not an early bloomer. She envied her full-figured classmates and she had all but given up on the hope of inheriting her mother's ample breasts. She resented the increasing possibility that she had the physical make-up of her father's family. Flat-chested but at least the derriere had a little shape to it. She knew she'd be fine in that department but her breasts were sure to let her down. An Iranian girl who looked like a boy could never get a man.

By the time she was eighteen it was settled for good. Indeed, there was no late swelling but what developed was complementary to the topography of her body. She had imagined herself a sad little washboard but now classmates who had developed too soon were sagging where she brandished sleek curves. She liked her body. Her figure would qualify her as attractive, and that was sufficient. She would never be one to bemoan a flabby belly or sparse eyebrows, now that good fortune had surpassed her own minimum requirements. She ended up as she started: with her mother's lips, her father's intelligent eyes, and with her own intelligence flickering behind them. Men felt the need to challenge her.

Another quality, forged in childhood and brought forth into womanhood, was her sense of her own power. Were she a man she would have had leadership qualities for all to see. Even Sina was impressed with the way she handled people. Her brash attitude to men was a source of entertainment for Pari. It reminded her of the way she established her authority, her place among the dominating gender. Having come from an educated background, naturally Hannah had high hopes to pursue higher education and build a career for herself. She had made it clear to all that getting involved in a married life was the last thing on her mind. She could see no contest for her single life at her parents' with Grandma Pari. Being a wife and mother did not attract her.

Hannah's parents were proud of her ambitions for a higher education and a career. Times had changed. There were more women occupying university classrooms and filling good positions; especially in government organizations. Sina felt lucky that his daughter had naturally chosen the path of intellect and independence. Not that he would have stopped her opting for a premature married life. It was just that her flamboyant choice was a token, a seal of approval of the way he had brought her up.

Zeeba's craving for throwing parties was a useful source of finding a husband for the kind of granddaughter who intended to get settled early in life. Hannah had heard about a few approaches to her grandmother. There was a handful of people who found her desirable and worthy of wedding their sons.

She had neither curiosity about nor patience with any of them. She had made it known to Zeeba that she wasn't interested in their banal schemes; that she was not so much as to even speak of them.

One of Zeeba's distant relatives who'd attended her parties, infrequently, had become a headache with her persistence to introduce her son to Hannah. Her son was intensely interested in Hannah and his mother wanted a fair chance for him to accomplish his desire: to ask for Hannah's hand.

Zeeba had resisted for as long as she could. In truth, she believed them to be at least a rung below her own social rank and she wanted to use them to send a signal to anyone else who might want a crack at her family. Marrying off Hannah into this family wasn't something she would collude in. Her granddaughter had much better prospects. There was no need to settle for less.

Sure that Hannah's attitude towards marriage at an early age would leave them in a state of embarrassment, Zeeba went about coercing her granddaughter into agreeing to meet the stubborn relatives. After the nuisance they'd caused her, she had no hesitation in subjecting them to a formal refusal and the stigma attached to such a refusal. In fact, the more she thought about it the more she looked forward to it.

As livid as she was for having to give in to her grandmother's cajolery, Hannah strove to hide her aggravation and behave herself. She had no intention of offending guests or causing embarrassment. She served tea and pastries; pretending to herself that they were there only for an innocent afternoon visit. But it was difficult to ignore the enquiring eyes of the woman who'd pestered her Maman Zeeba for months. The look on the woman's face was descriptive of the scenario that was rolling through her mind. She could see the qualities that had entrapped her son. She could see the desirability and attraction. She could see a calm, unambiguous sweetness, a pleasant aura attractive to either sex.

Hannah had met the young man before. She'd never taken much

notice of him beyond the usual exchange of greetings. She'd never embarked on a real conversation with him. Somehow he simply didn't pique her interest. What she recalled was a well-mannered boy, a bit on the skinny side, and very tall. The young man enthusiastically ogling her in the sitting room was a taut, clean-cut student with a well-groomed moustache. Kiyarash, or Kiya for short, was close to graduating in pharmacy and he was clearly infatuated with Hannah. There was no doubt in anybody's mind as to his choice for a wife. He'd seen Hannah a couple of years back. There was no formal introduction, no engaging conversation, not even an exchange of smiles. What he'd seen a few short metres away from him was enough to engrave an unlikely mixture of lust and admiration into his mind. He had desires in almost equal parts to ravish her and engage her in conversation. It was love at first sight, it was animal attraction, she set fire to his blood and challenged his intellect. He knew she was The One: the other half, the complementary being that would complete him, make him whole. She was the only female for him; he felt it in every fibre of his being.

He tried to be reticent sitting next to Hannah, doing his best not to look greedy. He could feel the contraction in his back muscles, the uneasiness of his jaws almost locked together, held shut by a conscious effort to do the least possible damage. He knew enough to know that females seldom fell for the first man offered, but the chance that she might, meant he had to make sure he was the first. He wanted to grab her, to declare his undying love. He wanted to touch her tenderly, to show her how gentle he would be as her husband. He also wanted to lie naked with her. The only thing to do now was to be sensible; like approaching a wild animal, he had to make sure not to startle her while managing to make a positive impression. So far the different forces tugging at his behaviour had ensured he kept his mouth firmly shut. If he said anything out of place he might embarrass her. He might only get a single shot at this. Nevertheless, he had to speak. He steeled himself for a moment then, "Have you thought about what you'd like to pursue at university?" He gulped his saliva like he was swallowing a whole plum, then his mouth dried instantly, as if a desert wind had blown through him.

"I'm keen on law. I have to see if I can pass the matriculation."

Hannah tried to sound friendly. She had no idea what might be going on in the mind of a young man who had apparently decided that he wanted to spend the rest of his life with her, even though he did not know her at all.

"Good choice. Which branch of law are you thinking of specializing in?" Kiya was proud to have managed two sentences without fainting.

"I'm inclined towards family law but to be honest I'm not sure if I could withstand the messy aspect of married couples breaking up. Maybe I should keep my head down and go after tax law." His strained facial muscles needed respite. For a moment he kept the smile plastered to his face then, frantic that his face was vibrating, he let go.

She seemed not to notice. "You're about to graduate with a pharmacy degree, right?"

Kiya nodded. "I was lucky to follow what I enjoy. I've always enjoyed the mysteries in chemistry. Luckily, I've been accepted to work with the research team of a chemical company near Tehran."

He did it. He put together a coherent sentence. One he'd rehearsed many times. Now she knew he was successful.

"Sounds like you're surrounded by luck," Hannah giggled.

Kiya didn't know what to make of her comment. Was she sneering? Never mind. He kept silent. Maybe he'd tried too hard to let her know he had prospects, but what else was he supposed to do?

Hannah remained more or less silent for the rest of the evening, flashing pale smiles at her admirer to impart a truce. She had no intention of taking pleasure in rejecting his proposal. She just wanted him and his family out of her hair.

Zeeba faced a big job explaining her granddaughter's thoughts to Kiya's mother the next day. The woman sounded bewildered. What was there not to like about her son? Who could refuse the opportunity of wedding a dashing man about to graduate with a respectable degree and ready to work for a respectable company? Her son could have chosen anyone and yet he opted for her. Rejection was not what he deserved. She was more hurt than sorry. She was offended enough to avoid any conversation about Hannah for as long as she lived. She had no business with silly spoiled girls who lived lavishly above their station at the expense of other people's humiliation.

Kiya knew the limits to his mother's tolerance. There was no way of persuading her to try for another social gathering with Hannah's family. No matter how dearly she loved her son, she would never give them a second chance to belittle her. As far as Kiya's parents were concerned, that was the end of Hannah as their bride-to-be.

Kiya was torn. He loved her as passionately as he hated her. He'd hardly been given a fighting chance. A statue sitting nervously among people that expected him to behave in a certain way; the way a young, educated man of his type would behave. How could she just dismiss him? How could she be certain he wasn't for her? He knew they were supposed to be together. If only she were aware of his deep feelings. If only she could fathom how difficult it was to meet someone who would worship her the way he did. This was no simple infatuation, his feelings for her would never fade, his longing was impregnable. He could never see himself devoted to another woman and he could never bear to see her with another man. He would be the man to take her virginity. He would be the one who shared every minute of his life with her. She belonged to him, to his world, to his life, to his bed. He had to make her see that. He had to make her realize how valuable she was to his existence. He had to make her understand how precious and pure his love was for her. He had to make it happen.

He decided on meeting Hannah again on his own. There was no room to let his parents into his plan and have them drill their opinion into his skull. He was determined to persuade her, to lure her into liking him.

He had no memory of the people he saw or the streets he passed by before he reached Hannah's place. The sight of the doorbell brought him out of his convoluted thoughts. He rang it with no expectation of Hannah's parents opening the door. It was a working day. They must have left a few hours before he got there. He'd hoped that Hannah had stayed home that day. Her face sticking out of a half-open door sent a current of relief through his tense body.

"Oh…It's you…Hi…" She opened the door.

"Sorry to bother you. May I come in?" Kiya asked with a charming timidity.

"Of course. Please come in." Hannah ushered him to the living room. "Is everything all right? If you're here to talk to my parents, I'm afraid they're not home."

"Ah no, as a matter of fact I wanted to talk to you."

Hannah was curious. "I'll go and get you a cup of tea. Have a seat, please."

She wrestled with her emotions as she poured his tea in the kitchen. She guessed he was here to find out why she had rebuffed him. He had caught her off guard. She started to feel nervous and a little angry. He had disturbed her. To talk or not to talk about her reasons was her prerogative. He had no business intruding like this. She became irritated but was determined not to lose her temper.

Kiya stood up and took the tray from her hand with a little bow to demonstrate his gratitude.

"You should try my Grandma Pari's tea cake. If she was here she would have made sure that I offered you some."

Kiya took a bite of his cake, prolonging the uncomfortable silence hovering over the living room.

"I wanted us to meet again so that you get to know me better. I shouldn't say 'better' seeing as you didn't find out anything at all important about me the day we met."

Hannah wasn't sure how to react. She didn't want to be rude but she had no interest in finding out anything about this man. Her silence pushed him into expressing his intentions further. "I want you to know about my feelings, my thoughts on life, my way of thinking, my likes and dislikes, my…"

Hannah interrupted him, rather nervously. "I realize what you're getting at. It's just that right now the last thing I need to think about is getting married. To be honest, I only agreed to meet you out of respect for your mother's persistence."

"But how can you plan a future so dry? How do you know we're not a match made in heaven and you're passing up the best opportunity in your life because of your black and white way of thinking?"

"The way I think and plan for my future is my business, don't you agree?" Hannah had quickly become impatient.

"Yes, it's your business by all means. But there's no shame in making you realize that you're on the wrong path."

Hannah snapped. "Well, if I'm on the wrong path, it's my wrong path and my prerogative. I know what's best for me. There is no possibility of a marriage."

"Why? Aren't you even a bit attracted to me? Can't you ever see yourself living under the same roof with me?"

"It's a long way from attraction to living under the same roof." This was becoming more uncomfortable but she had no clue how to end it, outside of throwing him out; something she was not far from doing.

"If there's any attraction at all then that's the foundation."

"I don't want to get involved in this ridiculous squabble."

"But why don't you keep an open mind?"

"Why don't you stop harassing me?"

"I love you so much," Kiya pleaded. "I want you with all my existence." He dropped one knee to the floor, as if to make a romantic proposal. "I can't think of anything but you. And I promise you that no matter how many years we live together, my love for you would never, ever fade. Can't you see how precious that is? Can't you see how difficult it is to meet someone who would give his life without a second thought for you? How could you dismiss what fate has offered? Why wouldn't you give us a second chance? You want me to wait? I'll wait. As long as I know you're committed to me, I'll wait for your hand."

Hannah felt nauseous. This man was insane and she had let him into the house with nobody around. She swore to herself she would never take part in another khastegari. It was an ancient relic, a thing from another time; young girls would agree to please their mothers and because a few managed to actually find husbands the tradition survived but it would not survive in this house for another second. She had to get him out, or at least calm him down.

"No. You're making me feel so apprehensive." Hannah clutched her body. She hung her head and walked briskly to the door. She was shivering. She couldn't look at his face. For the first time in her life she felt trapped. She opened the door and held onto the door knob to tell Kiya that she wished him to leave.

Kiya's face was deep red, his eyes bloodshot and staring. This couldn't be happening. She couldn't be turning him down so flatly. It simply wasn't possible. He grabbed her hair. He did not pull violently but he did achieve his intent of making her look at him. Her confusion turned to real fear. He stood face to face with her, almost close enough to rub cheeks.

"Don't you see that I would give anything to have you? Don't you see that I can never see you in another man's arms?"

She couldn't speak. She prayed someone would come and save her. Kiya tried to press his lips onto hers. She turned her face away. He kissed her cheek, her forehead, her nose, her chin. He pulled at her hair to try to position her mouth against his.

"Get off me! Get off me!"

Kiya was oblivious. He clutched her hair violently. He whispered, but not to her, not even to himself. "She can't be somebody else's. She can't be somebody else's."

Kiya brought her down like a predator calmly pulling its weakened prey to the feast. He ran his hand under her dress and pawed her bosoms. He touched her belly for a moment, to get the proper bearings, then he yanked her pants down with a single action. His victim was paralysed with shock. He jostled his manhood into her. Hannah wailed as he entered her. He burst open the top of her dress and buried his head into her cold breasts. He rubbed his head against her neck, sniffing and licking at it. He was overwhelmed with passion. He had taken the virginity of the woman he loved. It felt right. He jammed himself hard into her. She made a distant squeaking sound. He held her arm behind her back and shifted his weight to one side. He could see the whole length of her body now. He ran his hand from her breast down to her thigh then he grabbed a handful of skin and thrust himself slowly into her. He tried, again, to possess her lips. She twisted her head to the side. He licked her cheek like it was an ice cream. He could taste her. He had never tasted a woman before. She was salty, hot; the pleasure overcame him, he released his passion into her. He jammed himself against her. His body jolted. He grunted then went limp, his full weight upon her.

Kiya rolled over and away from her. He lay, looking at her paleness, her beauty. Her eyes were shut tight. He leant towards her. He slid his hand under her back and lifted her hips a few inches off the floor then he pulled up her pants. He folded her dress around her then buttoned it tenderly. He stroked her hair, kissed her forehead and whispered: "Now you're mine. You're a woman now. You're my woman."

He closed the door behind him. She heard him leave, she knew he was gone. She closed her eyes more tightly, her muscles taut in a fight against movement; against change. She knew when she moved, when she opened her eyes it would be in a different world. She lay, motionless as her previous life slipped into oblivion. It might have been a week or a day or an hour before she emerged from the uneasy cocoon her mind had spun around her grief and pain. Just a moment longer, in the warmth, before the birth into this cruel new world. Everything in her previous life now she knew suddenly had been perfect, had been wonderful. She had died and now she was born again. She knew who she was and where she had been and where she thought she was headed but now her existence was a simple oneness defined by her experience. It was as if all knowledge had been at once revealed to her when all she had craved was freedom. Now she had no choices, everything had been chosen for her.

She felt a coldness between her legs. She instinctively pressed her palm against herself. It was wet. She held her hand in front of her. She opened her eyes quickly, boldly. Red, dripping, the blood was thick, crimson, almost black, it streamed down her arm. She sat bolt upright. There was blood on her thighs, her belly, it was on the floor but not as much as she had feared. She looked at her hand again and the blood seemed paler, there was hardly any; mostly it looked like no more than a fresh henna stain. She got up and walked briskly to the bathroom like one about to vomit but determined not to have the timing thrust upon her. She turned on the water and stepped into the shower. The water was cold then tepid then hot. Hot was good; she wanted her skin to melt so that a new one might grow in its place. She stood in the steam; skin blanched, she thrust her face towards the cleansing water, how good it felt. She pressed the soap into herself, between her legs and she remembered a sweet boy who might have become a friend or more, in time, and then she saw the man, the man that had settled her future forever. She had pretended to herself, like many modern Persian women, that she didn't need a man and she might never need a man, but it had really been a game; she had known that she would marry after she had proved herself to herself. And now there would be no man. She was damaged goods. Nobody would want her now. The boy seemed so sweet, as if he were actually in love with her. How could this be? How could this have happened?

A change of clothes then a drink of fresh water. She sat in the dark and cried enough tears to wash her inside. She didn't think of anything at all. Her heart was drenched in sadness. It must have been hours before she came to; until deep depression cleared a window for her to observe her life, her situation. Her heart was crushed, but she could see herself now. Without pain she could analyse her position. Would she tell anyone? She had no scars, no visible evidence of any violence. Had she fought back every instant? Right until the end was she eager to scrape an eye from his head or did she simply lie there and allow a man to take her? The victim is always sentenced to a life of shame. The only proud victim was one who perhaps took her own life or was mercifully murdered by the rapist. The thought of Pari flooded her mind; she would never have endured such a life. She would probably have killed the man, or she would have taken her own life; the old way, proof of innocence, she would have given her life to clear her good name.

The door swung open. Pari marched in and dumped her bag down before drawing the curtains. She sat down, opened her bag and took out a pair of shoes. She changed her shoes, watching Hannah but not saying anything. There was something very wrong indeed. The girl was ashen, she had the complexion of a corpse, she had the swollen eyes of a mourner.

"Why are you sitting here in the dark?" She watched Hannah, trying to gauge the extent of the problem. She could feel it was worse, much worse than anything she had seen before. A shard of sunlight lit up her face, but she made no answer, no sign that she had even heard the question.

"Why have you been crying? Tell me, child."

Hannah erupted into silent tears. These were the tears that children shed when they wanted their loved ones returned; pain twisting their little faces, they'd try to talk but could not. Pari knew instinctively that nobody had died but the pain etched into the girl's face was starting to reveal its story. Pari prayed to herself for peace for the girl. Hannah opened her eyes and her arms, and tried to speak. Pari sat next to her.

"Tell me what's wrong, *aziz-jan*."

Hannah stared deeply into a corner of the room. She spoke in a bland monotone like someone with perfect memory accessing a far-off event. Pari sat, motionless, without expression. It was like being plunged into the past, the past for which she reminisced most. The village days when she was a young wife in love and when everyone she knew would deliver their problems to her. Then all she had craved was the victim's respect, that they believed she had somehow helped them, though listening now to Hannah, her precious child, made her realize that she had understood nothing of their plight, their pain was not transferable, she knew now she had felt nothing, for now her chest was being ripped open and her heart crushed. Hannah retold the events and Pari listened. Pari would not allow the girl to relive the details; she held her hand up and waved it gently as if waving away the event itself. Pari knew the exposure would simply give strength to the pain, prolong it. Talking of dreadful times creates dread. Pari wondered for a second whether Hannah herself was aware of the inevitable outcome of this penetrative act. There was no time here to cry monster. No point praying for justice. There were but two paths from this event. One to the grave and one to marriage. This youngster had violated her precious child.

"I have to marry him, don't I?"

Pari nodded. There would be no argument here. She would marry this boy for they could turn this into violence and ruin two lives, or she could go on. "You can let this destroy you. You can report him and destroy both of your lives. You can try to go on as if nothing happened but then you'll be his victim forever, never sure of what he might do."

Pari took her hands in hers. "Marry this boy. Give him a year. He can't hurt you again. Now you're ready for him. I'm serious. After a year you've won, child. You can divorce and live your life as you see fit without a trace of shame." Pari knew this was the only course of action. "Imagine you're him, for a moment. Imagine there is something, someone that you want so badly you live a life in pain."

Hannah made to speak and Pari hushed her.

"You have to survive, my dear. You understand why he did this?" Pari said softly.

"So that I couldn't get married to anyone else."

Pari was glad Hannah was facing the situation squarely. "You could be pregnant, *aziz-jan*."

Hannah's submissive silence signalled awareness. Pari looked into her swollen eyes: "You have no choice, dear. You have to marry him."

"You won't tell anyone, will you? They'll never know if we don't tell them. No one needs to know."

"I won't tell if that's what you want. But you have to move fast in case you're pregnant. You have to make them believe that you've thought it through, changed your mind and want to arrange for the wedding."

Hannah nodded in surrender. She could see her future sinking in a swamp of sorrow and submission. Her dreams of independence were gone, ripped from her. How could her life fall into an abyss in the turn of a day? She dismissed a boy and now he had imprinted himself upon her forever. But she would not be owned by this man. The only way to win was Pari's way. She would marry him. She would use his obsession against him. He knew what he was doing. He was a dog pissing against a tree. But she would not be owned by him.

37

Hannah's U-turn on marriage was a shock to everybody. Zeeba was not thrilled with her granddaughter's choice of a man she felt was somewhat below Hannah's social rank but she refrained from criticism. Her parents, Malous and Sina, were more dogged in their pursuit of the truth. Hannah had told them of her new-found yearning to be a mother and that Kiya was the man for her. Neither of them believed her but they accepted her decision. They would not stand in her way.

The wedding was arranged in four weeks; no fuss, no flamboyance; a manageable number of friends and family, just the way the man and wife to be wanted it. Zeeba took charge of making the bride's dress, as she had done for her own daughter. Pari and Foti were to handle the banquet.

On the big day, Pari sought Hannah out. She sneaked into her room in hopes of at least a few seconds to check that the girl would keep her head. Pari worried that Hannah might do something drastic on her wedding night.

"How're you holding up?"

"As well as I can, under the circumstances."

Pari took both the girl's hands in her own, and spoke to her as her own. "It's terrible that you had to get married by force. But anyone can see that he loves you madly." Disgust flashed across Hannah's face. Pari would as soon see this boy in prison for his actions but Hannah had to believe the possibility of a life existed for her. "As terrifying as the start of this marriage was, it could still end up to be happy. Don't rule it out."

"I'm six days late. Looks like I'm going to have his baby."

Pari wasn't surprised. She was almost sure that he had left her with a memento. He'd gone out of his way to obtain what he wanted for his life. Pari had met him. He didn't seem dim-witted or self-obsessed by any means. He was surely aware that his ghastly way of declaring possession over the woman he worshipped was at the expense of alienating her forever. Pari could only hope that he knew a way of gluing back the pieces together. She hoped that he truly did love Hannah; that he hadn't left their house with his trophy solely to quench some eerie lust. She hoped that his desire for Hannah had a deep-rooted quest for her happiness at its core.

"A baby is a blessing. This is your baby too. It's your flesh and blood. You're always going to be its mother, whether you wanted it or not. Nothing can change that."

Pari didn't expect her words to sink in. She'd lived enough to know that words were useless. She didn't expect a recovery in Hannah. That was something Hannah and only Hannah could summon.

At the wedding ceremony Hannah sat on the stool positioned next to Kiya's in front of a white sheet on the floor of their living room. There were flowers, baskets of sugar rocks as a sign of sweetness in life, a long loaf of bread as a sign of prosperity, the Holy Book, two candlesticks and a mirror as a sign of light and happiness for the married couple. She avoided her future husband's gaze for the whole ceremony. Her almost inaudible "yes, I do" was cheered jovially by the garland of women surrounding the bride and groom. A stream of kisses covered her emotionless face as the women congratulated her. She returned a faint smile every time a gift, a gold coin or gold jewellery, was placed on her lap. That was it. What was done was done. There was no going back. No moaning and grieving, no complaints, no room for pity.

The night she had feared finally came. Hannah and Kiya were left alone in the bedroom of their small apartment. Hannah sat on one side of the mattress clutching her legs, with her back to her new husband. Her reluctance to share space, to embrace Kiya, to take part in conjugal closeness was unequivocal. She was ready to sit there till the next morning if that would keep her safe from harassment. Kiya waited for a few minutes in the hope of a truce then he took his pillow and headed for the living room. She was too precious, too fragile to be shaken.

Hannah was surprised that the same man who forced a living prize into her body left her in peace. She looked around the room in despair. This was the eternal darkness she had to walk through with no hope of finding the light. She wanted Pari. She yearned for the comfort and security Pari had granted her all of her life. How easily it all disappeared in a twist of a moment. How abruptly her life had been cut off from its smooth path. How brutally she was snatched away from her cosy world.

It was some few hours before fatigue overcame her unsettled mind. She woke up the next day around noon with a headache. There was no sign of Kiya. She wondered if her rejection the night before had pushed him away. The flat was neat and clean. A handful of white jasmine on a crystal plate filled the place with a pleasant fragrance. The low volume of the radio in the kitchen broadcasting a popular song told her Kiya was still here. She opened a kitchen cabinet for an aimless browse. Boxes of cutlery and crockery that her parents had bought for the new couple were on the floor. She opened one of the boxes. She'd always liked her mother's taste. Startled at the voice behind her, she dropped a fork.

"I went to get some fresh bread. I've already made tea. Shall I pour you a cup?" Kiya took two cups out of the box with no intention of waiting for an answer. "Why don't you take a seat? I'll set the table for breakfast." He was the picture of normality. A new husband doing his best to impress his new wife.

Hannah didn't utter a word. Kiya told a pointless story about one of the customers at the bakery. She gulped down her tea. She couldn't keep her eyes off him. This was the man? Her new husband? The man who raped her?

"Shall I pour you another cup?" he asked with the air of an adult talking to a young child.

"I think I'm pregnant." Hannah turned her face away.

His hesitance made her nervous. Could he really disapprove? Anything in this world seemed possible to her as she waited nervously for confirmation from her rapist, her husband, the man who'd just made tea for her. He could disapprove? What did he expect to happen? It wasn't like she was having a baby with the next-door neighbour. It wasn't like she'd asked for it.

"It's wonderful. This is wonderful news." He said it almost in a whisper. His voice broke. A tear burst from his eye and ran down his face. He hung his head. He pressed his fingers deep into his eye sockets. He was clearly torn. He wasn't a monster, Pari had been right. This was shame. He was ashamed.

"Did you mean to get me pregnant when you forced yourself on me?" There was no antidote that could subdue the venom in her tone. She almost hissed the words. It was as if his tears had exploded in her mind. She could hold back no longer. She had done her part. She had married him. She had simplified life for them both. And now he was crying for the unborn child that he planted with violence. How could he have done this thing?

"I never meant to hurt you." It was as if he was reading her mind. It made her hate him even more. Why could he not have shown himself before? Why did he have to claim her like some caveman? "I just couldn't lose you to anyone else. I couldn't bear the thought of living my life without you. Do you think you could ever find room in your heart for me?"

Hannah had a good hard look at him. She saw the same calm and respectable face she'd seen on the day of his first visit to her parents' house. Except this time his face was heavy with remorse, his eyes desperate for mercy. There was no trace of savagery, no despair, nothing nasty, no obvious psychoses that should have been painted onto the face of a rapist, a defiler. He looked more like an old dog who'd eaten lunch and now regretted it.

She wanted him to suffer. She wanted him to pay. She wanted him to beg forgiveness every day of his life. If he was true to his word, if she was all he yearned for, then she was in control. She could stick the pin wherever and whenever she deemed right.

Without speaking she got up and went to the bedroom, as a gesture to be left alone. Kiya waited, confused, then after a few minutes he followed her.

"Shall we head for the Caspian Sea in an hour? My uncle offered his villa for our honeymoon. He thinks we're both over the moon about his offer. I never told him I didn't tell you about it."

Again she was caught between incredulity and faint compassion. It was as if he really believed everything was normal. That they were a happy pair of newly-weds just getting to know each other.

"I don't feel like going anywhere with you."

"You don't think your refusal to honeymoon might arouse suspicion?"

She thought for a moment about what he said. Was it possible that anyone would interpret a spat between them as being caused by the bride being forced to marry her abuser? Would his uncle wonder if his precious nephew had torn the clothes from her body to win her?

Nevertheless, his statement made sense. People were always looking for hot gossip. A marriage so instantly in trouble would bring enquiries, questions she'd have to lie about. She didn't want to let anyone into her secret. Her plight becoming common knowledge would be a complete and utter defeat. She cringed at the thought of their pity, their despondency and contempt, and ultimately she would be shunned. There would be no acknowledgement as such but that's what would happen. Everyone talking around her; damaged goods.

A nod confirmed her intention to leave for the north.

She had taken the route to the Caspian Sea before. The woods, the mountains, the sweet sandy smell of the sea. It had always seemed so comforting when she came here with her parents. But there was no sense of anticipation now, no joy. The clean, familiar air gusting around windy roads that had once been ripe with expectation now offered only memories. She felt old.

Throughout the stay Kiya slept every night on a mattress spread on the living room floor. He spent the daytime playing the bumbling new husband. Each day he'd announce the day's adventures to her as if she were an audience, a family, someone who actually might care. He drove his woman and her silence right to the Soviet border. The bewitching beauty, he postulated, would breathe some warmth into the chill that was his new wife.

Each evening Kiya took her to the beach to see off the sunset. He'd stare dolefully at the dying sun and mumble about the future. Hannah thought he must have painted himself as a very caring man indeed. He talked about their child to be, a tear in his eye. He asked for her opinion often and enthusiastically. Hannah wondered what kind of lines incredulity would etch into her face. This fool already made it abundantly clear what lengths he would go to, to get his way. She didn't have to pretend to believe him or like him or listen to him. Their return from the honeymoon set off a chain of parties. Each night a different relative took turn to prepare a vast table in honour of the couple. Hannah's parents threw a dinner party for relatives from both sides.

Pari was sucking loosely from a wooden spoon, a hand cupped underneath to catch drips, when Hannah saw her. She went to Pari, grabbed her shoulders and placed a tender kiss on one cheek then the other, then she hugged her.

"How are you keeping?"

"I don't know." Hannah shrugged her shoulders.

"Was he hard on you in any way?"

"No."

"Did you tell him about the baby?"

"Yes."

"Has he forced himself on you?"

"No. He sleeps on the sofa."

"He does care about you."

"Please don't say such a thing."

"It's so easy for men to be nasty and uncaring, especially in your case. If he only wanted to conquer your body he would have forced himself on you every night and there isn't much you could have done about it. Believe me, I've heard of some monsters in my time."

"I should thank him for not being a monster? I owe him so much."

Pari brushed the back of her hand against Hannah's cheek.

"I know. Soon you have to let people know of your pregnancy. That will be a good subject to divert attention. You'll be rid of the nosy ones for a good while."

"And then all I have to do is pretend I'm overjoyed about my pregnancy."

"You'll love this baby more than anything in this life. You'll see." Pari looked at the pile of china trays to be filled with food then she looked at Hannah. "Come on, *aziz-jan*, give me a hand."

Pari's prediction came true. Although getting pregnant on the wedding night wasn't exactly what Hannah's parents envisaged for their daughter. For them the joy of having a grandchild outweighed the slight discomfort of its hasty announcement. Kiya's parents were ecstatic. Their son had all he wished for: a wife he adored and a child to make him a proud father. Hannah used the pregnancy to be whatever way she pleased. The hormones coursing through her body gave her the temporary right to be slightly mad. If she cried in public, if she sat at a dinner table, playing morosely with her food, if she lost her temper or lashed out, well, she was pregnant for goodness' sake. She was entitled to feel the way she wanted for nine months with no explanations attached.

Kiya hadn't backed an inch from his calm and tolerant behaviour towards her. It was no burden to him. He was no simpleton. He was aware that it would take more than sheer words to win any feelings from her. He had inflicted a deep wound; deep enough to demand months or even years of struggle. She was worth it and he had patience.

After two months under the same roof, but in different rooms, Kiya decided to test the water. He switched the bedroom light off, took his pillow, tip-toed to *his* side of the bed and slid under the blanket. Hannah curled herself into a tight ball and inched towards the edge of the bed, as far from her husband as possible. He moved towards her slowly, he didn't want to frighten her, until his leg brushed imperceptibly against her thigh. Her perch at the edge of the bed left no more room for manoeuvre. He could feel the warmth of her body. She didn't flinch. Almost in disbelief he glued his body to hers. He ran his hand from her shoulder to her knees. He leant over and kissed the back of her ear then he smelled her hair as if breathing mountain air for the first time. He craved to explore every inch of her. He wanted her to melt in his arms.

"I love you so much. I miss you every second of the day. Let me stay with you here. Let me in your life."

Hannah pushed his hand away then she sat at the bottom of the bed with her back towards him.

"Don't you ever think about giving us a chance? Giving it a try? Making it work?"

She didn't budge. She wanted her silence to shred his hope. Anyway, she was tired of it. She wanted to be left alone, to wallow in a quasi-hypnotic state where no one could bother her.

Kiya left the room in sorrow. Like an old dog shunned by its master. There was no trace of anger in him. Instead he was filled with a strange kind of calm. This was his life now. She would come around in time. That she was in the same house was enough to supply the hope his plan required. He had no option, no choice, he would win the war of attrition.

As the weeks passed Hannah's breasts bulged in preparation for the new life to be. She looked at herself and knew she was a woman now. The girl inside her was dead.

Kiya never disturbed the tranquillity of her bed again. He did all of the cooking. He took care of the shopping. He even sent her, for a spell, to the seaside to lift her spirits.

His eagerness to be a father, buying baby clothes, decorating a nursery, was deflated by Hannah's indifference. But he was aware that this had to be a part of his eternal punishment and he made himself accustomed to it. He had come to know his place. He had come to know the daily drudgery of a one-way marriage. He saw meaning in the slightest deviation from utter indifference on the part of his wife. A twitch of the cheek, a glance, might be Hannah betraying a stray smile.

Hannah's deliberate adaptation to her new life had left her with convoluted emotions. She'd become used to Kiya, like a prisoner giving into the four walls of her cell. Yet, there were times she remembered the joy she'd experienced during her comfortable, and protected, life with her family. How she missed teasing Pari until they would both explode with laughter. How she missed happiness. Her memories seemed to belong to a different dimension, a different life, a different person. She missed being alive. She loathed the cold statue she had become. She needed a dose of delight in her bloodstream. She needed to be human again but she didn't know how to make that happen.

It was in the late hours of a breezy September night when Hannah gathered every molecule of energy left in her, stared pain in the eye, and pushed out the being she'd joylessly carried for nine months. The oblivious scream of the baby filled the hospital room. They placed the wrapped newcomer in her arms. "It's a girl. Congratulations!"

She stared at the baby like they'd just introduced a stranger to her. Her stomach was churning. She threw up into a kidney dish then she shivered.

"It's quite natural. Don't be scared. This happens to all women after giving birth," she was told. The lethargy felt good; a substitute for pain, responsibility, and hard truth. It was a sedative, a drug manufactured from sixteen hours of pain. She soaked it up.

Kiya had already seen the baby on the way to her bedside. "Everybody's at the newborn ward to see our baby." He looked into her hollow eyes. "How are you feeling? You did so well." She stared deeply into the space in front of her. He kissed her forehead and stroked her hair.

"What do you want to call her?"

"I don't know."

"I thought we could call her Marjon."

Hannah said nothing.

"I'll go and tell everybody that you're ready to see them."

Pari moved in with Hannah and Kiya, for a month she said, to help with the baby. Kiya's mother had also promised to lend a hand after Pari was done. Apart from breastfeeding, Hannah's involvement during that month was mostly at arm's length. She was ready to quit the first time Marjon refused to latch onto her breast. Pari knew she needed time. She wanted to be there more for Hannah than the baby. She was Hannah's crutch, her guide to bring her to the path of motherhood.

The day Pari left, Hannah felt abandoned. She wasn't ready to take care of a baby. She would get up once during the night to feed her and ignore her crying thereafter until Kiya woke up to calm her down. Hannah's coldness towards her own baby meant Kiya had to change her, to bathe her and put her to bed. Kiya's love and patience with Marjon seemed limitless. Hannah could see he was a better mother than she was. His passion was dripping into Hannah's dry veins. She was caught between the desire to be a mother and the shame of failing to be one.

Kiya had already forged a crack in her wall of denial.

The person she had shared a roof with was gradually developing a face. A face she found herself glancing at with curiosity, with interest. The superfluous ghost hanging around the house was fading. His movements, his tone of voice, his facial expressions started to become familiar. Where previously she had not cared, now she hid her feelings. Watching him with the child, making mistakes that angered her and making jokes that made her laugh inside, she warmed to this man, the father of her child.

Marjon was not an easy baby. She cried endlessly, whether hungry or not. Kiya woke up many times every night to walk with her and put her back to sleep. Hannah's reluctance to take part in their family life became a trend. She took no part in Kiya's nightly rituals.

"Go to sleep darling, go to sleep," Kiya whispered for the hundredth time as he rocked her on his shoulder.

The performance usually didn't last more than thirty minutes or so but this night the baby was still screaming after two hours. Kiya's patience was endless but Hannah couldn't take it any more.

"What's wrong with her?" She yelled at Kiya.

"I don't know. Probably a sore tummy."

"Why didn't you give her some of that gripe-water my Grandma Pari kept in the cabinet?"

"There's none left. You think I would have let her cry for two hours without trying the gripe-water?"

Hannah racked her brain to try to think of a way to stop the noise. She looked around the living room hoping to see something that might help when she spotted Marjon's bottle. She marched to the kitchen and rummaged through the spice cabinet. She took out what looked like two translucent rocks and placed them on the counter. She took a mortar and pestle and ground the rocks down then she poured the crushed powder into Marjon's bottle. She boiled water then poured it on her mixture then she added some cold water.

"There. Let's try this. It won't harm her if it doesn't calm her."

"What is this? What's in the bottle?" Kiya asked suspiciously. It looked like it was filled with plain water.

"It's just a couple of melted sugar rocks. It works on adults with trapped wind, it might work on her. It's worth a try."

A few minutes after drinking her mother's concoction Marjon's crying subsided. It wasn't clear as to whether she gave in to sleep due to fatigue or whether her mother's solution worked some magic. Either way, the resulting quiet was bliss.

"Well done. Good thinking." Kiya felt elated that his wife, the mother of the tiny angel in his arms, had finally come around, had finally taken a step, an interest in the lives of the two people she was living with.

Kiya placed the baby in Hannah's arms.

Hannah held her for a few minutes. Felt her warmth, her little heart beating quickly. She smelled her head, eyes closed, to savour the scent of her little daughter. She whispered something to the baby then she laid her gently in the cot. Kiya was close to tears. He saw his wife, the person he'd loved since the first time he had laid eyes on her, falling in love with her child. He took her hand and planted a kiss upon it. He touched her shoulder, her neck, then he embraced her. Her body didn't react dismissively as it had done before. He led her to bed. There was no resistance. He pushed her to the middle of the bed with his body. He was hardly sure if this was a hallucination.

He grabbed her face with both hands, stared deeply into her sparkling eyes and kissed her first gently then heatedly on the lips. Hannah pressed her bosom against his chest. This was the first time in her life that she had been made love to. She welcomed his every move. She welcomed the unity of their bodies, the unspoken exchange of affection, the heady pleasure of being desired. She felt reborn. She belonged to this bed, to this union, to this harmony.

And it felt good. It felt good to be loved.

In the weeks that followed Hannah was a different person. She had become a woman. A woman who gave her virginity to tenderness, her previous experience lost in forgetfulness. She felt like a newly married girl. She demanded attention. She looked forward to bedtime. The same bed in which she'd spent so many nights in misery had become a haven for shared pleasure. This is what Kiya had dreamed about. She became insatiable for his touch. It was new to her but it felt right. It felt familiar.

Kiya had finally won his woman. Her anger evaporated, gone without a trace. There are those that might say she was worn down like a life prisoner, no choice but to accept the status quo. She preferred to believe that this man had truly loved her so deeply that he would not live without her. This was the truth revealed to her. Since the marriage he had been nothing but gentle and kind. Pari had been right. It had seemed impossible but she was right.

The memory of the ordeal itself changed so much that she no longer saw it as an ordeal. She could not remember him hurting her in any way. The present, more specifically, Kiya's actions over time, had changed, it seemed, history or reality itself. There was no objective experience outside of the current interpretation. She had become the man's wife, truly. He loved her deeply and she wallowed in his affections.

After the love came the friendship. Kiya believed all along that his actions were an expression of his love for Hannah. She would never have married him. He knew that. He also knew that she would love him, given the opportunity to actually see him.

Kiya was used to staying up most of the night with the baby and Hannah's new-found enthusiasm for motherhood and family meant they spent hours in conversation while she nursed or he changed the baby.

Hannah was so energized by her new life her dream of pursuing higher education resurfaced. Kiya was pleased his wife had found herself. He cared too much to stand in her way and allow her talents to atrophy. He suggested Pari might help by taking care of Marjon while Hannah studied.

Hannah decided to study accounting at Tehran University, enough of a challenge with a valuable degree at the end of it. During the next four years her relationship with Kiya deepened and she graduated. Kiya lent a hand to find a job at the pharmaceutical company where he worked and after working for just a year Hannah gave birth to their second daughter, Simin.

Three years later Kiya was offered a job at his company's headquarters in Montpellier in France. The idea of uprooting and travelling halfway across the world was both exciting and terrifying to Hannah. She had heard the South of France was a beautiful place but she would have to leave her friends, her family and, most especially, her dear Pari at a time when leaving would carry with it the risk that she would never see her again.

For Pari, the presence of Hannah and her family had been enough to deflect the aches and pains of old age. Simply being needed was enough for Pari. Hannah and her family had provided much joy. With Kiya working and Hannah studying there was plenty of child-minding to keep Pari occupied and she felt a little proud that they trusted her first with Marjon and then, for the first three years of her life, with little Simin. Obsolescence was Pari's one and only fear; to no longer be required was worse than death to Pari.

Hannah often consulted the old woman on matters regarding her household, her children, her husband, and now she would consult her on a move that might mean they would never see each other again in this world.

And then there was Kiya's family; his mother would be devastated at losing her grandchildren and her first-born son.

When Hannah told Pari the news the grief etched itself instantly onto her face. She was sorrow-stricken and while she would do nothing, say nothing, to change Hannah's mind she did not have the strength to hide the way she felt inside. It was like she was on the brink of an abyss and she had to fight not to beg Hannah to stay just a little longer; perhaps long enough to see her part from this world. But Pari had felt it coming. She knew something was about to happen and now she thanked God that it was something good for Hannah and her children. Secrets such as this are hard-kept and Pari knew something was afoot. But she knew that a selfish old woman should not, could not, stand in the way of a growing family.

"I promise to call you frequently. Once a week. I'll write to you too. You can be sure that I'll never forget about you. You're a part of my life. You're a part of me." Hannah felt almost as desperate as Pari looked.

"I know you won't forget. I know you. I know your nature," Pari uttered under her breath. She did not have it in her to pretend she was happy for Hannah. She wanted to be happy for her. She wanted to tell her that going off to an exciting new country would be a wonderful experience but really she just wanted her to stay; to stay until the end, to stay until *her* end. So many times it seemed she had loved only to have the object of her love disappear or die or crumble in front of her. She had indulged herself by never thinking about such a day as this. As always, little Marjon and Simin had become her own children, and now her precious girls were all to leave her. She wanted to hurl herself at Hannah and cry, "What am I to do without you?" But she did not. She sat with a straight back and she tried to be strong for Hannah. For as much as it hurt her to see her family go she knew that Hannah was hurting just as much and more and Pari would not plant a seed of guilt in she whom she most treasured. For a fleeting moment the idea that if Hannah had been her own blood she might not have left surfaced in her consciousness but she knew it was only her mind, in desperation, playing tricks, and she thought of the pain that Kiya's mother would feel, and she knew that love burned deeply in both blood and water.

Pari made all of her goodbyes long before the departure. People thought she was strong and perhaps she had been, once. But she had not the strength to watch her precious treasures leave her. The families would see them off and that would be enough. Pari would take the role of the ancient woman, close to the end, her time long past, and she would not let anyone know that the pain of losing a loved one did not diminish with age; it intensified. In the days before Hannah and the children left there were times when Pari thought she might faint from the mere idea of their loss, but always she did her best to hide her sorrow for it would only make it more difficult for Hannah and the children.

Kiya and his family found the adjustment to life in France quite natural and easy. Perhaps they had, in their minds, overestimated the difficulties they would face in a strange land? But he was content with his work and he learned the language quite easily.

Kiya had plans. A few years in Montpellier then he would move to Paris. He would rather stay with his firm but he was prepared to switch companies if he needed to. His plans were put into motion by the birth of their third daughter, Nahid, after four years in Montpellier.

*   *   *

Despite being the youngest, Haady was the first to go. Alcohol had administered to his liver a beating harsh enough to end him before his time. He never managed to bury his sorrows, his melancholy, his many personal and professional defeats. He drowned himself in an abyss of self-pity. His demise was lengthy and torturous. By the time his fragile body had given up, he had no one left around him, save Zeeba. With his children off to different parts of the globe and his estranged wife, Hoori, no longer willing to endure any more suffering, he died, lonely and almost alone, on a hospice bed.

Zeeba grew more and more bitter and intolerant after her brother's death. There was nothing she wouldn't use as an excuse to have a row with Rahim. It seemed that secretly (or maybe even unconsciously) she was angry at her husband for not trading places with Haady when the hand of death snatched him away.

Zeeba and her husband suffered a car accident while in the throes of a messy squabble of her instigation. She died on the scene and Rahim joined her after two days fighting for his life in hospital.

Pari took her cousin's death badly. They had known each other since they were small children. They had grown up together, Pari had stored too many memories, good and bad, not to mourn someone ripped so suddenly from life.

As for Foti, for some months after Zeeba's passing she led a life of freedom; no one to tell her what to do and when to do it. It was like being released from prison, she could add as much sourness to the food as she wanted. She could burn the breakfast bread, break glasses and not be shouted at. She could sew a dress for herself from morning till night without interruption. She had liberty and it felt good. It felt new, but only for a short time. The shine of her free life started to fade. Maybe she had become accustomed to her cell for too long to embrace a life of free will? She was afraid. She started to feel too deserted to appreciate her release. She had never imagined the day she would crave Zeeba's companionship. She never thought that loneliness would make her beg for the return of her prison warden.

Foti's health was failing. For some years she had suffered intermittent throat complaints but she had never visited a doctor. When she finally made the trip to see a physician to get it sorted the cancer in her throat was inoperable. She used the money her brother had left her to check herself into a hospice and there her life ended in weeks.

Pari had no fear of death. She believed too surely in God and his creations, heaven and hell, to be frightened of passing to the other world. Her only fear was of being abandoned; to die alone and without dignity.

Pari was afraid, without any children of her own, that nobody would take care of her. It was not that she doubted Hannah's good intentions but she was so far away, thousands of miles, on another continent.

Despite her deteriorating energy, Pari tried to stay "useful". But her failing health, high blood pressure, sight fading in her left eye, had no sense of forgiveness. Her once-robust body was wearing out.

Malous held a grudge against her children, for abandoning the invalid Pari and leaving her to pick up the pieces. She held a grudge against Pari for robbing time, precious time from a life that seemed to get shorter and more precarious every day. She resented the responsibility, the blame, the conundrum of wanting to break free but not wanting to be a heartless witch.

The consecutive loss of the people close to Malous had triggered a realization that it wouldn't be long before she would take her turn at the top of the elderly list. She missed the ones she'd lost but their demise had forged no emptiness in her being. Instead, she'd come to comprehend that, by all means, she should enjoy her old age. She decided to make her old age the opening of a new chapter in her life.

She started taking up activities she'd suppressed for years to suit her family's comfort and schedule. She planned trips to places she had always wanted to visit but never had the chance to.

So, she embarked on her new lifestyle.

With Malous and her husband frequently away to visit new places, Pari's time was spent re-running the memories of her life, some vivid and lively and some faint and distant.

She had no regrets, no hard feelings. She had her beliefs, her religion. She was content with God's will and the assurance that the children she brought up would always love her, would always remember her.

She was still rich compared to many other people. She had tasted the satisfaction of giving without the expectation of receiving something in return. She had been the source of comfort, the refuge, for the disturbed souls of people around her. She had tasted love, true love, the love that only children can bring. And if that was the outcome of all the mistakes she had made, all the hardship she had suffered in life, then it was worth it.

But there were only so many reminiscences, so many memories she could share with the photographs of loved ones in her room. It was sad to forget who she used to be. It was sad to forget what she was capable of. It was sad to recall her abilities as if they belonged to someone else, as if she were thinking about a different person called Pari.

How the walls around her were getting closer and closer. But still their familiarity staved off their stench of loneliness. She loved and hated her abode like a prisoner who would have to be dragged out of jail at the end of a long sentence. This was all she knew; her bonding with the stale smell of her room, her cosy bed with its scrunched up sheets and her sacred corner allocated to her daily prayers.

She had lived for too long. She believed that. And she resented it. It was certain that surviving every peer in her time could never bode well.

Malous and her husband had discussed, for years, the option of selling their house and moving into a smaller place. Now their children had gone away. There were no grandchildren around to harbour or entertain. Their house was now too big. Moreover, neither of them was in the right physical state to look after it.

She decided that the first step towards a simpler, more comfortable life for her and Sina was to get settled in a small flat. Something where the two of them could feel cosy.

The question of Pari's future bore only one answer.

Pari was to settle in an old people's home. A place she could receive proper care, as far as Malous was concerned. The attached stigma was a mere cliché; something to be righteous about, something to use for passing judgment on others and feel mighty about oneself. When it came down to the reality of life, Malous would do what it took to make living practical for everyone. There was no shame in that.

Hannah took it hard when she heard of Malous's dictates on the remaining days of her Grandma Pari's life. She contacted Malous to see what they might do to smooth Pari's exit from life. Hannah wanted to arrange for a personal nurse. She would find a suitable person and finance the expenses. That way Malous would be free. She wouldn't have to lift a finger to care for her Grandma Pari. That way her grandma would die in her own bed, the way she had always wanted it.

But Malous was adamant. She was the one who laid down the rules. Hannah's offer to pay for a private nurse was taken as an insult by Malous. She was serious about selling her property and moving on with her new life. Malous believed Hannah could care so much from afar because she was far away. She would put Pari in a home.

When Malous told Pari of her plans Pari simply nodded in acceptance. There would be no fight, no attempt to invoke a love that did not exist any more.

During their weekly telephone calls Hannah implored Pari to fight back, to utter any kind of defiance. It seemed that Pari was the only one left who could summon guilt or regret in Malous, to shake her determination. But she was of no use. She had fought all her life. She was tired of fighting. It was time to let go.

Pari handed over her existence to Malous to do with what she deemed right. Her time had come. Why make it more sour than it already was? Why turn it into a sullen judgment of Malous's humanity? Why alienate the sweet girl she once knew?

Pari was taken to a house and placed in a room with four other beds. In each bed an old soul, old women, each a mirror to the other. In the dead of night, each night, there was sobbing, and screaming, and fear and desperation.

Pari was disappearing. The shell that had been her answered when Hannah called on the telephone. But each time the nurse brought the phone she brought it to someone who was vanishing from this world. Now the old woman wished only for release from this life.

Hannah kept calling Pari, until she was told that Pari no longer wanted to answer.

*   *   *

Pari lay quite still now. The pain was still there but without the foreboding. The cruel anticipation was gone. Pain, in all of its forms, wasn't an effect, pain itself was alive. She had learned that in her life. But now, even pain was a distant enemy. It could assail her no longer. She watched her life. Banoo came to her, to remind her for the hundredth time that her cruelty would haunt her. *"Zan-Arbab, don't take that tone with me. Don't you tempt fate. You never know if my misfortune ever befalls you and one day you end up serving other people."* Was it a curse? But curses were nonsense. Being good or evil never made anyone suffer or prosper more than they would have otherwise.

She saw herself at her own wedding. She was a girl in a life of her making, she thought. A Woman Master indeed. All the children were grown now and her work was done. It was not for her to judge her own life. It was the life she was given and she did her duty; to live it to the best of her ability in the face of God.

Might she have had a better life? Dying in her own house under her own roof if she had married someone arranged for her by her father? But she had no regrets. Falling in love, running away and marrying the man she had chosen was the only path there ever could have been for her. There never could have been any alternative. She had cursed herself many times for marrying Yousef but never for taking the decision to marry whom she wished into her own hands. He did all he could do. He could only be the man he was and nothing more.

The old woman died alone, at night, in a room amid four strangers, immersed in their own sorrow; she finally slipped away, her will to live drained. No one held her hand or prayed as she slipped from consciousness to unconsciousness from life into death. Pari, Woman Master, Zan-Arbab was gone, her fight was finished.

Malous arranged the funeral. Hannah did not attend. She stayed in France. She could feel Pari's presence in her soul and that was enough. Witnessing her body going underground would only tarnish her memory. She needed Pari in her life whether she was alive or dead. She needed to remember her the way she had always been: resilient, strong, funny, fearless, a living book of tales. She had been one of the last of the Woman Masters, one of the last of a dying breed, brought to her knees in her youth by a feckless husband and treated like a slave by her nearest and dearest.

*   *   *

After retirement, Hannah's husband declared he wanted to return to Iran. Finally wearied of France and the French, of the West and Westerners, he wanted to seek asylum in the familiarity of his Eastern culture. He wanted to spend his remaining years in the place he was born. He wanted to revisit every street, find every house and neighbourhood he had known in his youth.

Hannah's return meant she could see her parents. After all, they were getting older and there was no way of telling how much time they had left before passing away to the land of immortality. An acquaintance, a widow with no children, had been staying at their house to care for them, in return for a small salary. Hannah's father, Sina, still wrote but no longer published. Some of his work was still in print and that was enough for him. Malous had contented herself with letters and phone calls from her daughter and granddaughters for so long, Hannah's presence, to Hannah, seemed to impinge upon her mother's routines. It was as if she needed to hear about Hannah, to discuss her daily trials and tribulations from afar; as if she really preferred a living memory of the girl who left over the woman herself.

The proximity to the cemetery where her Grandma Pari had been put to rest had made it even more difficult for Hannah to hide away from the guilt of not visiting Pari's grave for all of these intervening years. It was time to get out of her hiding place, face her fear and see Pari's final resting place for herself.

Finding her grave within the huge cemetery seemed like a daunting task. Following the directions her mother gave and help from people who must have been regulars, Hannah found Pari's tombstone; written on it was nothing but the sparse message: In loving memory of Tajel-Molouk Hatam.

How could this plain line be a summary of who she was, what she did, what she achieved? Memories of all her years spent with Pari flashed through her. She stood next to the grave almost in a trance for ten minutes before she burst into tears.

She knelt down next to the grave and stroked the cold stone. "Could I have done more? Did I give in too easily? Can you forgive me?"

Hannah sat near her grandma. She would come and visit more often. She would sit next to her and talk to her; like many women who came to this place. She would make Pari alive again.

Before long, she had become one of the regulars herself.

*   *   *

The laughter of the children next door woke Hannah. She had dozed off. It must have been three thirty; time for the children to come back home from a day at school. She felt drained and nauseous. She'd sat in the haunting loneliness of her room all morning. A bitter dryness in her mouth forced her into the kitchen. She took a few gulps of tap water but to no avail. The restlessness that invaded her body wasn't about to shy away with a little fluid in her system. She foraged in one of the cabinets to find her herbal remedy. A drink of borage mixed with a handful of sugar rocks had always helped take the edge off her apprehension. The familiar bittersweet taste of the concoction seemed to work its magic instantly. She gazed at the loaf of bread on the kitchen table but her stomach was too unsettled to host any solids.

She stared at the empty chair at the head of the table. That was Kiya's domain. He had sole ownership over that space. She remembered how he had become more and more enslaved to his habits with each passing year. And now he was gone. Her heart sank at the depth of her loneliness, at how much she missed him. She was not sure whether she was capable of going on without her soul mate.

She had cared for him day and night for a whole year while the claws of cancer dug deeper and deeper into his increasingly fragile body. There was nothing anyone could do. The invader had taken over his cells so ferociously he knew he had only a very short time to savour the company of his woman; her sweet smell, her energizing smile, her comforting face. And when the messenger of death came, she clung onto her husband and called out his name as if she might bring him back from death itself if only God knew how much she loved him.

Her three girls arrived from France a day later to say farewell to their father.

As her daughters rallied around her, and did their best to share the great pain their father's death had brought, she started to suffer from the same fear that Pari had carried with her throughout her twilight years: fear of feeling idle, fear of uselessness, the dreaded fear that nobody in this world really needed her any more.

*   *   *

On a sunny Tuesday, Hannah buried her husband. He was buried alongside the graves of his parents. Their three daughters stood at the edge of their father's resting place, crying silently, adding their tears to his grave. Hannah was too numb to cry; a comfortable easiness had possessed her body. It was as if she was watching a drama from a distance. *How did she get that awful short fringe?* She thought of her eldest daughter as she stared blankly at hair which was protruding from her headscarf.

The Mullah took his time finishing his last prayer. Hannah scooped a handful of dirt and spread it over Kiya's grave. "This will not separate me from you, my dear. You have a special place in my heart that no one can fill." She stood up and walked away from the grave clutching her daughter's arm.

It was nice to have the girls around, even for a short time, and even in such grave circumstances, and talk about the old days. Kiya's agonizing illness had deposited too much melancholy in her life to recall the joyful times when they were a family of five. The precious memories of her daughters' childhood had been obscured by the everyday sorrow of watching her soul mate wane away. It was as if Kiya and she had lost so much time, invaluable time. They were cheated. The evil disease had stolen away their priceless time.

Hannah wanted to remember and cherish all those memories and she felt remorse for not brightening Kiya's remaining days with them.

Her daughters returned to France within ten days after the funeral. They had their own lives to live and Hannah assured them she would be fine, she would survive.

And now Hannah was on her own.

Settling in her home, by herself, did not go as planned. The solitude quickly became crushing. She would wake up three, four, times a night and feel that Kiya was not in bed. Sometimes she would even search the house for him until she remembered the awful truth. She thought the dinner place she had set him would be a comfort but it was only a reminder. Memories of him were starting to cripple her.

She had become a source of uneasiness for her parents, every visit a prolonged memento of their son-in-law. At first, they tried to console her but her need to till her sorrow was endless. Her parents thought that unhealthy; she had to move on with her life. Hannah herself did not like the wailing widow she was becoming.

But Hannah was lucky. She did not have to bury her spirit within the walls of her home and pretend that she was too proud to bother anyone. It wasn't enough to relive her memories over and over. It wasn't right to suppress the urge to share those memories with the people she cared about. What was life for, after all? What was life good for if she didn't have her loved ones around her? So what if she got in their way from time to time? So what if she was a source of annoyance from time to time? Let them have one more thing in their daily life to wrestle with. They'd have their turn of old age themselves soon enough.

Hannah was lucky. She should appreciate her luck and not waste it. As her Grandma Pari used to say, 'human beings are not designed to be lonely.'

She arranged for her husband's "fortieth day" memorial ceremony, a gathering to remember the dead forty days after passing. She invited relatives to her house to pay their last respects.

Before the guests arrived, she visited the cemetery alone. She washed her husband's gravestone and sprinkled it with rosewater.

"I've made up my mind, darling. I know this is what you would have wanted for me too. You always wanted me to feel happy."

She watered the four geranium pots she'd placed next to his grave that represented her and her daughters. Then she kissed the headstone and left.

As the mellifluous tones of the Azan from the neighbourhood mosque started to invite believers to the evening prayer the phone rang. Hannah knew it was her eldest daughter.

"Maman! It's me. I called to see how you feel today."

"I feel fine, dear. I want you to do something for me."

"Of course. Anything."

"Find me an apartment in Paris. Make sure it's small and on the ground floor. I'm coming home."

"Home? To Paris?"

"Home to my family. I'm coming home and I'm going to write it down."

"Write what down?"

"All of it. You'll see."